LA DIVINA

Anne Edwards's numerous books include the best-selling novels *The Survivors*, *Shadow of a Lion*, *Haunted Summer*, and *Wallis*. Among her well-received biographies are the classic *Vivien Leigh: A Biography*, *Early Reagan: The Rise to Power*, *The Road to Tara: The Life of Margaret Mitchell*, and *The Grimaldis of Monaco: Centuries of Scandal – Years of Grace*. She divides her time between London and Connecticut.

Books by Anne Edwards

BIOGRAPHY

Sonya: The Life of Countess Tolstoy

Vivien Leigh: A Biography

Judy Garland: A Biography

Road to Tara: The Life of Margaret Mitchell

Matriarch: Queen Mary and the House of Windsor

A Remarkable Woman: A Biography of Katharine Hepburn

Early Reagan: The Rise to Power

Shirley Temple: American Princess

The DeMilles: An American Family

Royal Sisters: Queen Elizabeth and Princess Margaret

The Grimaldis of Monaco: Centuries of Scandal—Years of Grace

NOVELS

The Survivors

Shadow of a Lion

Haunted Summer

Miklos Alexandrovitch Is Missing

The Hesitant Heart

Child of Night

Wallis: The Novel

AUTOBIOGRAPHY

The Inn and Us (with Stephen Citron)

CHILDREN'S BOOKS

P. T. Barnum

The Great Houdini

A Child's Bible

LA DIVINA

ANNE EDWARDS

MACMILLAN

LONDON

First published 1994 by William Morrow and Company, Inc., New York

First published in Great Britain 1994 by Macmillan London Limited
a division of Pan Macmillan Publishers Limited
Cavaye Place London SW10 9PG
and Basingstoke

Associated companies throughout the world

ISBN 0–333–61407–0

1 3 5 7 9 8 6 4 2

A CIP catalogue record for this book is available from
the British Library

Printed by Mackays of Chatham PLC, Chatham, Kent

For Steve
Who gave me many treasures,
the gift of music being just
one cherished jewel among them.

Overture

SOMEWHERE IN THE DARKNESS, A RECORD SPUN BENEATH THE diamond tip of a phonograph needle. Athena held her breath in order to hear her own recorded voice, a barely audible, terrified *"Voglio vederlo"* in which Tosca, afraid that even such a small favor might be cruelly refused, begs Scarpia to let her see her tortured lover. Athena bit hard on her lower lip to keep it from quivering.

"Let me see him," she whispered. "Oh, God, let me see him just one more time." Her thick black hair fell in deep waves down her back; her full breasts overflowed the bodice of her red satin nightgown. Her commanding posture made her look taller than she actually was. To say that Athena Varos, perhaps the most famous diva of her day, was a beautiful woman did not do justice to the startling drama of her appearance: the huge, dark, expressive eyes, the chiseled grandeur of her Grecian profile, the wide jaw, generous mouth, and strong facial bone structure. Sometimes Athena was shocked when she caught sight of herself in a mirror or on a poster or in a magazine. She didn't feel like the dramatic woman the world saw; inside, she seemed condemned to be the overweight young girl who had never been able to please even her mother.

A pale morning light seeped in through one corner of the heavy crimson velvet curtains and cast a blurred streak across the carpet. She had survived the night. The day before her would not be easy.

9

By the end of it, Mano—*her* Mano, whom for eleven years she had loved more than herself or her music, for whom she would give her life—was to marry one of the most socially eminent women in the world: rich, beautiful, half his age (and ten years Athena's junior), with the international political connections that could help him achieve the power that was his driving ambition. And what could Athena do to stop him? Nothing, nothing at all. But if she could just see him for a few moments, look into his eyes, touch his hand, she would know—as only lovers who had meant as much to each other as they had could know—if he was truly in love with this American woman, the young widow of Clark Cameron ("Cam") McMaster and the sole heir to McMaster's multibillion-dollar real estate, oil, and shipping empire.

For three days Athena had locked herself in her bedroom, refusing to answer the telephone or to see anyone except Yanni, her maid. Outside her windows, Paris throbbed with life, yet Paris without Mano was so painful to Athena that she had kept the blinds down and the curtains drawn during the length of her self-imprisonment. Now she lay huddled under the covers in her cold room; the heat would not come on for another hour or so, at seven-thirty, and she had refused to let Yanni lay a fire the night before. She had to figure out what to do. The paparazzi no doubt remained encamped in the foyer of her building, cameras ready to capture a shot of her—the spurned mistress and aging diva, distraught, haggard from her sleepless siege—with the photograph slated to share front-page tabloid space with a glowing image of Mano's fresh-faced bride-to-be. Or even worse, one of the bridal couple together, setting off for their honeymoon on Mano's private island, Zephyrus, where her own passionate affair with him had begun.

Somehow Athena knew she must retain her dignity; if she didn't, she would never be able to face her public again.

"L'anima mi torturate!" she heard herself utter in a deep, sonorous voice.

"No! No! No!" Athena cried out. "It's all wrong!" She had played Tosca, not one of her favorite roles, many times, but had never sung it to her own satisfaction. It was a heavy part, yet the voice had to be kept light, limber like an athlete's body. She had failed completely in this recording, and the critics would notice. She couldn't tell them that the conductor was an insensitive oaf and that Beritino, her Scarpia, wasn't much better. She was Athena Varos, *la Divina*, and she was expected to be in top form at all times whatever the circumstances.

Athena pushed herself up on the pillows. The tempo was hopeless. She couldn't bear to listen any longer. She threw her legs over the side of the bed and, oblivious to the chill in the air, strode barefoot across the darkness of the familiar room to the phonograph, lifted the arm, and, almost in one motion, pulled up the record and hurled it into the dead fireplace. "It's all wrong! All wrong!" she shouted, a flame seeming suddenly to flare up in her head and sear through her entire body. "Wrong! Wrong! Wrong!" she cried. Her hands were trembling, her shoulders shaking. And then her legs gave way, and she crumpled to the floor with a horrifying shriek that brought an immediate hammering on the door.

"Madam! Madam!" Yanni shouted. "Are you all right?" There was a pause, then the hammering again. "Let me in, Madam! Let me in!" Yanni called through the locked door.

To Athena, all of this drama seemed to be happening to someone else. She felt herself transported out of her body, watching this offensive creature, which had to be her, screaming, pawing at the rug as though playing a role in a Greek tragedy. Then, abruptly, a sense of reality returned, and she was conscious of the cold air on her bare shoulders.

"Madam?" Yanni called again through the door.

Athena tried to stand but couldn't. She dragged herself over to the side of her bed and, clutching the footboard for support, pulled herself up on her feet. "Just a minute, Yanni, just a minute," she murmured, unaware that her voice was too soft to be heard outside

11

the room. The hammering started again. She grabbed for her negligee, stuffed her arms into its sleeves, and stumbled toward the
door. "Are you alone, Yanni?" she asked in a stronger voice.

"Yes, yes—I'm by myself."

Athena turned the key and cautiously opened the door. The sudden brightness of the lighted hallway made a blinding white blur of
Yanni's short, stocky figure. For a moment Athena stood there,
blocking the entrance, uncertain whether this was really her dear
old friend—for Yanni was as much her friend as her servant.

"Madam, look at you! You'll catch your death in the cold."

Yanni's fleshy arm came around her shoulders. Athena felt the
warm comfort of her ample body and let herself be led back inside
the room to the bed. Yanni helped her into it.

"Shall I open the curtains?" Yanni asked.

"No, not yet."

"I'll make a fire, then."

Athena allowed her head to fall back on her pillows and felt her
body go limp. She said nothing, watching mesmerized while Yanni
made the fire. The flames flickered into life.

"It's cook's day off, and Mademoiselle Caspari won't be here for
several hours. We're quite alone, so you mustn't worry about other
people," Yanni said gently. She was on her knees, her broad back to
Athena, brushing up the broken fragments of the record without
saying a word about them.

"Are the newspapermen still downstairs?"

"The concierge made them leave. When I last looked out the
sitting-room window there was still a gaggle of them waiting in the
park across the street. That was about an hour ago. You're not to
worry about them, either. Mademoiselle Caspari says that if you
want to go out you can go down to the basement. There's a door
to the next building, and you get past them that way." At that
moment the fire caught; the flames leaped up and shadows started
dancing wildly on the marble hearth. Yanni rose and came over to
the side of the bed.

"Madam, you'll get through this the way you have everything

else. I don't say you'll ever get over him. But you'll come to realize that there is more to life than what appears to be. There's a reason for all this—take my word for it. And in time you'll understand what it was all about."

Athena managed a faint smile and then shuddered slightly. Tears welled up in her large dark eyes. "What would I do without you, Yanni?" she said.

"Manage nicely, I suspect. Now, I've a breakfast tray prepared. I'll go fetch it if you think you'll be all right while I make the coffee and warm the milk."

"I'll be fine. But since we're alone in the apartment, you can leave the door open," she suggested.

Athena lay very still, listening to Yanni's heavy footsteps grow fainter as she marched down the hallway to the kitchen. When had her friend's hair turned so gray? Only recently, she thought, but she couldn't remember. Yanni had been with her for more than twenty-five years, since the day Athena had sung her first major role at the National Theater in Athens at the age of seventeen. Tosca, of course, a difficult role for such a young woman, and only given to her out of desperation because the diva had taken ill moments before curtain and there had been no other replacement. Athena hadn't done badly. She hadn't done brilliantly, either, but well enough for the performance to have launched her career.

The fire was glowing and she stared at it. Yanni was right. She had survived so many things—the war, her mother's ambition, her father's death, the nightmare years of her marriage to Roberto, her struggle for independence and fame. She sighed deeply. Her heart felt heavy in her chest. It seemed to have pushed aside her lungs and absorbed all the air. Now Mano's betrayal—must she survive that as well?

Although there was no record on it, the phonograph was still spinning and its whirr irritated her. She got up and turned it off. Outside, the gray had brightened into a soft lavender hue that seeped into the room beneath the closed curtains. The view of the Luxembourg Gardens, so beautiful through the changing seasons, was one of the reasons she loved this apartment. March was not a good month in Paris. But, nonetheless, the gardens were in delicate bud, and yesterday she had noted that the chestnut trees were about to bloom.

She made her way to the windows that faced the gardens and pulled hard on the cord to open the curtains. Then the fleeting veil of soft morning light was torn by a horrifying sight: a scruffily dressed young man, unkempt hair hanging to his shoulders, jumped forward from the corner of the balcony, where he must have been hiding, and pointed a camera at her. She screamed, and there was a blinding flash. The man was clothed in dazzling light; she couldn't make him out or see past him. She felt herself in danger of becoming part of that great white mass of light, and she screamed again. Terror froze her face; when the photographer reached out, intending to calm her fears somehow, her legs betrayed her once again and she collapsed onto the stone floor, crying out desperately, "Mano! Mano!" And then the stranger, the balcony's iron rail, and the treetops of the gardens fused into one image—Mano rushing toward her. Then even he was gone. That thought was too painful for her to accept. She forced herself to think back, to before—yes! that was it—to a time before Mano had become all there was to her life.

Prologue

The Bronx, New York, 1938

1. ATHENA WAS ONLY ELEVEN YEARS OLD WHEN HER MOTHER'S sister, Serafina, fell madly in love with Moisha Kadinsky—darkly handsome, fifteen years Serafina's junior, and the son of a neighborhood Jewish butcher. Moisha played the violin, quoted long passages of incomprehensible poetry, and talked about a time in the future when he would be a famous playwright. Although Serafina, who lived with Athena and her parents Kuri and Miklos Varosoupolos, was approaching her thirty-fifth birthday, she would have brought her sister's fury down on herself were she to be seen alone in Moisha's company. So, during the long, hot summer of 1938, Serafina conscripted Athena as her constant companion and coerced her into a conspiracy of silence by plying her chubby niece with sweets not permitted her by her mother.

Moisha and Serafina met almost every afternoon, when Kuri went to visit her Greek friends. The Varosoupoloses' railroad-style apartment, which was on the fifth and top floor of a converted brownstone in the Bronx, enjoyed exclusive access to the roof. Moisha would make his way to her over the tops of two adjacent buildings. If the door to the roof was unbolted, it meant that Kuri was gone. Since Serafina slept in the front bedroom just off the entryway, Athena's more private rear bedroom was chosen for the lovers' afternoon trysts. Athena's room also had the advantage of a window that looked onto a small fire escape, which was useful in case Kuri returned unexpectedly and Moisha had to make a quick exit.

On this sweltering August afternoon, the bed in Athena's bedroom was creaking and groaning. "Jesus! Jesus!" Serafina cried loudly enough to be heard through the closed door.

Her cotton dress sticking to her skin, her thick, plaited dark hair moist at the roots, Athena abandoned her listening post and went into the kitchen for a cold glass of milk. Having roof access gave the Varosoupolos family, and Kuri especially, a sense of power and advantage over the other occupants in the building. But being on the top floor also meant that the apartment froze in the winter and was suffocatingly hot in the summer.

"Did I leave my home in Greece for this sweatbox? Peasants, immigrant Jews, Italians, the Irish—maybe they can live like this!" her mother would shout, her olive eyes blazing, her voice vibrating with reproach, at her father. "But for me, Kuri Kakakis Varosoupolos, this is beyond belief! I never should have married you! Never! My father was a state senator, a respected man. I could have had my pick—rich men, educated men. And now what am I? A poor immigrant's wife. I told you we should never have left Athens. You wouldn't listen. You're a foolish dreamer who thinks only of yourself." Then she would sob so violently that Miklos, unable to comfort his wife, his lean, pale face quivering and his graceful hands trembling as he thrust them in his pockets, would leave the house and not return until late at night.

In 1926, Miklos Varosoupolos, then a young artist with great hopes, had emigrated with his wife and her sister to America. A year later, Athena was born. He had sold no paintings and his money was gone. To support his family he took a job designing decals for a printing company. When the Depression hit the country in 1930, he could only find work as a typesetter. With a resignation that Athena deeply resented, Miklos had put away his sketch book, canvases, and oils. Her father's artwork had filled her with pride and delight, and she had much enjoyed being his model.

"Why don't you draw me anymore, Papa?" she had asked him on

a cold Sunday afternoon one January, when Serafina and Kuri were helping to decorate the Church of St. Nicholas for the Day of Epiphany and she and her father were on their way to the Metropolitan Museum of Art by elevated train.

"It's over for me, Ati. No more dreams. Now I go to see the *real* artists."

"But you're a real artist, Papa," she quickly replied.

"No, Ati, I'm not. If that were so, even your mother couldn't have persuaded me to take a job in a print shop."

Athena loved to visit the Metropolitan Museum of Art with her father because he seemed happier on those afternoons than at any other time. He would stand in front of a painting for many minutes, explaining to her why it was a work of genius. Sometimes a small group of people would gather nearby to hear what he was saying, and when she glanced back she would notice that some of the onlookers had moved closer to the painting and were studying it with keenly interested eyes.

Whenever he had Saturday afternoons free, he took her to the public library to browse through the thick art books he could never afford to buy. The Central Library also had a lending department for gramophone records. In the rotunda one afternoon, Athena was drawn to a striking poster of a scene from the opera *Aïda* that advertised this fact. "Is that Aïda?" she asked her father as she stared at the imperious woman, arms outstretched, who was pictured on one side of the poster.

"No, that's Amneris, a princess who wants Radamés, the man Aïda loves—that's Aïda there, standing beside him." He went to look at the art books, leaving her in the music section to listen to the record. She remained there, replaying certain arias over again, until he came to collect her three hours later. She was so stunned by what she had just heard that she was silent for most of the journey home, holding the recording of *Aïda,* which she had been allowed to borrow, protectively to her chest.

"What is it, Ati?" he finally asked her.

She looked up at him with the eyes of someone who had just

19

found religion. "Oh, Papa," she said, "one day I'm going to sing like the women on this record."

Miklos laughed.

"I mean it," she insisted with biting determination.

"Well, first," he remonstrated, "you must learn a little more about music. Practice harder at the piano. Then we'll see."

"What will we see?"

"If you still feel the same way and if your papa can make enough money to pay for voice lessons, which will certainly be more costly than your piano lessons."

Athena's piano teacher, Signorina Agostina, occupied a small apartment on the ground floor of their building. Signorina said she had once been a performing artist on the concert circuit. However fanciful her claim, when sober she played with the passion that is the mark of a true musician. A woman in her late middle years, she had left a well-to-do home in Milan to follow her lover to New York. When he deserted her not long after, she had felt unable to humble herself by returning home.

Lessons with Signorina were fifty cents an hour, but Kuri felt it was important that a young girl grow up to be accomplished at the piano. Sacrifices were made and a small secondhand upright, purchased on the installment plan at the cost of even greater privations, had been hauled up the five flights of stairs by deliverymen and put in the place of honor in the living room, its top covered by a treasured, brightly embroidered shawl that Kuri had brought with her from Greece.

Aware of the burden her music lessons entailed, Athena never shirked her practicing. She had natural ability, but neither her parents nor her teacher—nor even Athena herself—considered it more than any young girl her age might have. She also had a good ear, sang on pitch, and liked to accompany herself, but she only sang the simple songs she had learned to play. Yet after hearing the recording of *Aïda*, her life seemed suddenly to change. She played the record over and over on the gramophone her father had given her mother as a present. When she knew most of the women's arias by heart, she had returned *Aïda* and borrowed a record of *La Bohème,* which was what she had been playing when Serafina switched off the machine before she and Moisha had retreated into Athena's room.

Athena sat down at the kitchen table, but the raucous laughter of her aunt and Moisha assailed her, so she got up and looked down the hallway. The door to Athena's bedroom was open; Serafina was standing in the doorway, her coarse black hair loose around her shoulders, her full body clearly defined beneath a crumpled silk slip, the only item of clothing she had on.

"Is this fair, Serafina?" Moisha said as he came up behind her and pulled her close to him. "You tell me I haven't got one more in me, but you don't give me a chance to prove that I do."

Serafina twisted loose. "It's late. My sister will be home soon," she said. Suddenly she caught sight of Athena. "Ati!" she exclaimed, "I thought you were down at Signorina's."

Athena went back into the kitchen, her eyes turned away from those of the furtive lovers as they followed her in. "Signorina has a headache. The lesson was canceled."

"You mean a hangover," Serafina scoffed. This was followed by some muffled exchanges between herself and Moisha.

"Moisha can go up on the roof," Athena called out. "I won't say anything."

She turned around. Moisha had his shirt in his hands, and his broad chest was bare, his shoelaces untied. As he passed Athena to take the narrow staircase to the roof, he patted her on the head. "Thanks, small fry. Do you a favor sometime," he said, grinning.

As soon as she heard Serafina close the door to her own bedroom, Athena raced from the kitchen into the living room, where she put *La Bohème* back on the gramophone. A short time later her aunt reappeared, fully dressed, her hair brushed back smoothly into the bun she most often wore. She walked directly to the machine and lifted its arm.

"Please, Ati," she said, her eyes pleading, "don't say anything to your mother."

"I won't. But, Serafina, if you ever do it again on my bed, I swear I'll tell on you," Athena replied. She turned back to the gramophone and restarted the record.

Neither of them heard the front door open and Miklos enter. He was standing in the archway that led to the front hall when Athena first realized he was there. Something in his attitude alarmed her. His face was flushed, his breaths coming in short gasps. It was three o'clock in the afternoon; he should still have been at work. She rushed to his side. "Papa! Are you sick?" she asked.

He took off his wire-rimmed glasses and rubbed his eyes. Then, with a deep sigh, he stepped into the room and lowered himself slowly into the nearest chair. Serafina and Athena exchanged worried glances over his graying head. "I don't know what Kuri will say," he murmured. He put his hands to his forehead and began to rock slightly.

"Oh, Jesus, you've been fired!" Serafina cried. "Turn off that music, Ati! How can anyone think with that noise going on?"

Athena immediately did as she was told.

There was the sound of the front door opening and closing. "Ati! come help me with these packages," her mother called.

"Yes, Mama," Athena replied, giving her father a desperate look. "What shall I do?" she asked him.

"Ati!" Kuri shouted impatiently. "My arms are dropping."

Athena rushed out of the room to the front hall, where her mother stood clutching several cumbersome grocery bags, and grabbed the one that looked to be in the greatest danger of slipping to the floor.

"Watch it! That one has the eggs," her mother warned, then followed Athena to the kitchen, talking all the while. "Five flights of stairs. What a life! Are there no windows open? The paint will peel, it's so hot in here."

"Mama," Athena whispered when they had put the groceries down on the kitchen table. "Papa's home."

"Papa? At this hour? Where? Is he sick?" With that she left Athena standing in the kitchen. "Miklos! Miklos?" she called.

Athena could hear her father reply, but not what he was saying.

Then her mother's excited voice: "Laid off? You mean fired! What did you do? You must have done something wrong. Maybe you should go back, apologize."

"It had nothing to do with me. Business is bad. There's no work."

"In the middle of the day they let you go, just like that?"

"No. There was a slip in the time box when I came in this morning. I've been walking around, not knowing—"

Her father stopped talking, unable to go on. Athena could hear him sobbing. She wanted to go to him, but she knew he wouldn't want her to see him cry. She began to unpack the groceries, and as she did so the thought came to her that if her father was unemployed her lessons with Signorina would have to stop. And just when they had discussed the possibility of her speaking to a voice teacher.

I'm a terrible girl to think only of myself at such a time! she thought. But she couldn't help it. For weeks she had been able to think of little else except the singing lessons she so desperately wanted to begin.

She glanced up and saw her father walk past the kitchen door. He was carrying his jacket and unrolling his shirt sleeves. He still looked strange, all red and perspiring as he strode down the hall, anger building in each deliberate step, and he slammed the door when he left the apartment. He would probably stay out until late at night again, as he usually did after he and her mother quarreled. Athena never understood what he did during all that time. Walk, she suspected, or stop for a drink or two with one of his friends on the block. Papa was not a heavy drinker. He had stomach troubles and alcohol made his condition worse. Serafina said he had a whore he went to, that most men had more than one woman. But Athena found that hard to believe.

In fact, Miklos did have another woman to go to in his times of desperate unhappiness. She had been painted by a great master and hung in the Italian room of the Metropolitan Museum of Art; it was there that Athena would have found him had she given in to her instinct and followed him when he left the building.

*   *   *

Kuri had named her daughter Athena for two reasons. The first was that Athens was not just her birthplace, it was part of the very core of her being. She would never have married Miklos and left Greece in 1926 had the coup d'état not thrown her father out of office and threatened her life and the simpleminded Serafina's. The second reason was that when her child was brought to her for the first time in the hospital she had thought, *Yes, Athena*—she'd name her after that most important of all Olympian deities, goddess of war and of peace, whose statue was said to protect the city that bore her name.

Kuri expected much of her daughter. By the time Athena was grown, she knew that her marriage had been a great mistake, that she and Miklos had little in common, and that he would never be successful. All of her ambitions were transferred to Athena, who, she dreamed, would one day marry a rich and powerful man and therefore be able to provide her mother the means to live a comfortable life.

But despite all of Kuri's efforts to nurture in her daughter a sense of elegance and upper-class gentility, Athena cared little for the way she dressed, could not be taught to walk gracefully, overate, and grew into a plump, awkward girl who had few friends. Kuri blamed her husband for their daughter's shortcomings. How could the girl ever aspire to be more than she was when she had a father like Miklos—a quitter, a failure—for an example? Now there was this obsession of hers to sing opera, which he encouraged. *Ridiculous,* Kuri thought every time she listened to Athena try to mimic the records she listened to constantly. Athena did not sing like a bird or sound like a bell; her voice was dark and throaty and not the least bit pleasing to Kuri's ears.

Miklos had not found work in many months, and during that time Kuri became more and more convinced that neither she nor Athena would have a good life if they remained in America. Her father was dead and the monarchy in Greece was now restored. She

24

was no longer in any political danger at home, and the thought of returning began to consume her. She, Athena, and Serafina would go to Athens. She had written to her father's brother, Spiros, and told him to prepare for their arrival. Her father had lost everything, but after his death and her grandmother's, Uncle Spiros had inherited the family house in Athens, where he now lived. Kuri felt that she and Serafina had as much claim to it as he did, and that had she remained in Athens they would have shared this legacy.

She confided nothing of her plan to anyone; she was waiting to hear from her uncle first, whom she had asked to send boat tickets. Every morning she would fly down the stairs and linger in the hall until the mail was delivered; when the reply finally arrived, she took the thick, blue, much-stamped envelope and, although it was a cold November day and she was wearing no more than a sweater over her dress, she ran down the front steps and into the small square across the street before she dared to open it. From the weight of the envelope she hoped that her uncle had sent her the longed-for tickets. Instead it contained, along with a one-page letter, some newspaper clippings about current conditions in Greece. Kuri's heart sank when she read the contents.

"Of course," her uncle had written in a flourishing hand, "you, your sister, and your daughter will be welcome in this house. But I beg you to reconsider. I have no means to assist you. As you can see from the enclosed, our homeland is in turmoil and there is talk of war with Germany in the air. Then, too, dear niece, remember your marriage vows. I cannot in good conscience encourage you to break them."

Kuri ripped the letter and its enclosures into small shreds and threw everything into a trash bin. Nothing would stop her from getting what was rightfully hers. After all, she had Athena to think about; whatever she did would be in her daughter's best interest. And what did she have in this country, where no one had any respect for ancestry, where Athena would always be looked upon as an immigrant's child? Such a loathsome word—*immigrant!* Everything was Miklos's fault.

She had managed to keep from being evicted by selling almost everything of worth that she owned. What kind of a man would let her do such a thing? Or would end up taking a job as a night janitor in a museum, returning home in the early hours of the morning, smelling of disinfectant? *He* could bury his pride, but she couldn't— nor would she allow Athena's chances for a better life to be snuffed out. Somehow she had to find the means for their passage to Greece.

A cold wind swept around her legs and she had to hold her skirt to keep it from flying up. The square, its trees stripped bare of leaves, was deserted except for a young boy running after a large black mongrel dog. The day was lead-gray, the run-down buildings on the street were streaked black with dirt and coal dust. She thought about the deep-blue Mediterranean sky, the warmth of the Greek sun, the lush greens of Athenian parks. She remembered the rich, fruity taste of the wine her family had every night at dinner. She could see herself as a young woman, handsome, sought-after. She should never have allowed herself to be cowed into marrying a man so far beneath her, a man she did not love and cared for even less now, after so many years of marriage.

Kuri wrapped her arms around herself and walked briskly back across the street. She was conscious that she had managed to keep her figure all these years, and that her dark hair with its striking silver touches enhanced rather than detracted from her natural good looks. It always puzzled her how she could have had a daughter of so little beauty. But she was more determined than ever to make the most she could of Athena, and returning to Greece seemed her only recourse.

She would sell what was left: the piano, her wedding ring, her gold cross. She would insist that Serafina turn over her savings from the small salary she earned working a few hours in the evening at a downtown flower shop. *Serafina*. Her sister was another burden she had to bear. Backward since childhood, she had always leaned on

Kuri for care and support. Serafina would never marry, nor be much help to Kuri around the house. But at least in Athens they would not be living in such close quarters, and Serafina, who was so fond of flowers, could keep herself busy in the garden of their family house near Kolonaki Square.

Recalling the olive trees in the large gardens of her former home, the great expanse of the rooms, the spacious salon, the kitchen with its two baking ovens, Kuri walked up the five flights to her apartment with uncharacteristic enthusiasm. As she entered the apartment, whose door she had left slightly ajar, she was greeted by silence. Miklos was still asleep, Athena in school, and Serafina visiting a friend. The thought came to her that this would be a good time to look through her sister's room to see how much money she might have, since she knew she kept her savings in an old biscuit tin on a shelf in her closet. To Kuri this seemed less an invasion of Serafina's privacy than a way to ascertain what help she could expect from her.

She went to the closet and took down the tin. She hoped her sister had been frugal, that there might be thirty or forty dollars in it—that would help a little. She sat down on the narrow bed, above which hung a picture of the Madonna in a gilt frame. It suddenly struck Kuri how small and bare the room was. *Poor Serafina*, she thought. She should have better, too.

Kuri opened the tin and dumped the contents onto the bed. For a few moments she sat there staring uncomprehendingly at the considerable pile of crumpled five- and ten-dollar bills that tumbled out. Then she smoothed, counted, and stacked them. To her astonishment, the total was $460. Since Serafina gave her ten dollars a week to help run the house and her sister's wages weren't much more than that, Kuri could not figure out how she had accrued such a large sum. It troubled her, but she quickly dismissed her apprehension that Serafina might have stolen the money. She stuffed about half of the bills into her skirt pockets, replaced the rest, and put the biscuit tin back on the closet shelf, assured that Serafina, who knew little about money, had no idea of how much she had.

Were she told that her sister had made the money by selling herself on the city streets it is doubtful that Kuri would have believed it. As it was, she left her sister's cubbyhole room much elated, knowing that her passage to Greece, and that of her daughter and sister, was now within reach.

Act One

Athens, 1939–1944

2. A WEEK BEFORE THEIR DEPARTURE, ATHENA CAME HOME
from school to find the piano and most of the furniture gone. "Your
father can't afford such a large apartment for the months we'll be
away," Kuri told her, having lied about the duration of their upcoming journey, and her decision to leave Miklos. "I put some of
our things in storage."

"But where will Papa stay?" Athena asked a short while later at
supper, glancing over at her father with troubled eyes.

"Closer to the museum. It will be easier for him that way."

"What happens when we return?" Athena pressed.

"There will be plenty of apartments better than this one to rent,"
her mother promised.

Kuri looked sharply at Miklos from across the chipped enamel
kitchen table, which along with the beds and a couple of old
chests was one of the only pieces remaining. In the future, that
moment—when Athena saw the distress and pain in her father's
eyes—would return to her over and over in its full weight of loss
and despair. Remembering her mother's voice coldly spelling out
his grim fate, and his anguished expression across the enamel surface of the table, she would wonder if they, too, had been conscious of the meaningfulness of the moment: that their daughter
knew they were both lying, knew that she might never again see

her father, the one person with whom she felt a true bond of love.

Athena sensed the finality in Kuri's attitude toward her father, the strange mechanical manner in which she framed her words and spoke. It was over between them. Her mother never intended to see her father or permit him to see his daughter again. It was to be his sentence for the crime of marrying a woman who didn't love him, and for failing to win even her slightest respect or affection.

Miklos glanced over at Athena. *She knows,* he thought. *Yes, of course she sees the truth.* Painful as their parting would be, maybe Kuri was right; perhaps opportunities could only come to Ati in Greece, although he didn't really believe that. Kuri had no concept of Ati's depth, her sensitivity, her exceptionality.

These tender and complex feelings about his daughter affected Miklos profoundly. He smiled reassuringly. *It will be all right,* he was trying to tell her in the mystic way they often communicated. But there was doubt and fear in the dark chambers of his heart, and at this moment they nearly overcame him. He got up from the table and went out of the room. Moments later, not saying another word, he left for work, slamming the door behind him.

If Athena had not already guessed that her trip to Greece was to be more than just a visit, her mother's thoroughness in packing or disposing of all of their possessions convinced her. Always somewhat of a loner, Athena had few friends she would feel sorry to leave. But she was fond of Signorina, who had given her a music pad and a beautifully illustrated copy of *The Wizard of Oz* as going-away presents, and she finally convinced Kuri to let her bring the gramophone downstairs to her former music teacher rather than sell it. The night before they were to embark, Athena, strong and tall as she was for her age, struggled to haul the heavy machine down the many flights of stairs; she had to stop to rest at each landing. There was no answer when she knocked on Signorina's door. She tried it and found it unlocked, and went inside. The curtains were drawn, the room was dark, and the acrid odor of stale alcohol cut at her nostrils. She left the record player on the table in the narrow entryway and left.

At 7:00 A.M. on the dark, bleak morning of March 22, 1939, a date Athena would never forget, Miklos accompanied his family to the Transatlantic Docks, from which their Italian ship, the *Europa,* was to sail. He felt like he was heading for the guillotine. Still, he kept a smile on his face for his Ati's sake, and even managed an enthusiastic travelogue about the marvelous sights she would see on the train journey from Naples, where the *Europa* would dock, to Athens. He insisted it would be better if he did not go on board the ship with them.

"Stand at the rail and wave to your Papa," he told Athena as he propelled her toward the gangplank amid a great jostling throng of excited passengers and well-wishers. Suddenly he pulled her back and hugged her tightly. "Ati, Ati," he cried, "remember always how much your Papa loves you, and that you are very, very special."

"Come with us, Papa. Please come with us!" she pleaded.

Kuri had been carried along by the crowd and for an instant lost sight of them. "Athena!" she shouted, her voice sharp and rasping.

"Go, Ati," her father said. "Wave to me from the rail." He broke away from her just as Kuri appeared and grabbed the girl's hand.

"Good-bye, Miklos," Kuri said. She didn't wait for an answer, but pulled Athena away from him and headed toward the gangplank, where Serafina was waving frantically.

Athena ran to the boat rail as soon as she boarded the ship, searching the crowds on the dock below for a sight of her father. At first she thought it was hopeless, that she could never find him among all those people. Then, suddenly, there he was, pressed against the low barricade and calling up to her, "Ati! Ati!" She couldn't actually hear what he was saying, but somehow she was certain it was her name. He took off his hat and waved it in the air, and she waved back at him. Then someone crowded in front of her, and when her view was clear again, he was gone. Nonetheless, she stood there until the ship's whistle blew and the *Europa* moved slowly through the early-morning haze amid the brooding, ghostly calls of foghorns.

*   *   *

A mood of fearful anticipation pervaded the ship on the crossing. Many of the passengers were returning home to Europe not knowing if war might break out in their country before they arrived. Despite the fact that the expense almost entirely depleted her funds, Kuri had bought cabin-class tickets for all three of them. They shared an outside stateroom on a lower deck, and although Kuri was irritated at the barriers that kept her from going into the first-class sections, she drew some satisfaction from being better off than the luckless passengers in what she called "the cow pens."

Athena was seasick and remained in the cabin for the first few days, but this didn't stop Kuri from enjoying the voyage. For weeks beforehand, she had diligently been altering her clothes to make them look presentable. She swept down the grand staircase to the dining room regally and sauntered around the decks with casual aplomb. Out of Serafina and Athena's earshot, she referred to her sister as her "loyal companion." By mid-voyage she was feeling quite exhilarated, which was ironic in view of the fact that the closer the *Europa* drew to its destination, the gloomier most of the other passengers became—especially when it was announced over the ship's radio that Germany had invaded Czechoslovakia.

Two weeks later, when the *Europa* docked in Naples and they boarded a train for the next leg of the journey, Athena was seized by a new fear. Her mother and her aunt had lived most of their lives in Greece and spoke the language. But she was an American girl, born in New York. Her parents had made a diligent effort to speak English in their home, and so she had only a cursory knowledge of Greek. How was she to attend school or make friends? After a young fellow passenger teased her about her New York accent, she recalled how cruel some of her schoolmates in the Bronx had been when an immigrant child was new to a class.

Almost no one spoke English in the crowded train that took them across Italy to the port where they were to board a ferry to the Adriatic coast. To add to Athena's anxiety, Kuri and Serafina fell back into old ways and spoke to each other in Greek.

"Don't go to sleep," her mother warned as soon as they were

settled in on the ferry. "No one can tell what might happen. These people . . ." They were sitting on a wooden bench. Passengers were stretched out on other benches around them, their coats draped over them, something else bunched up under their heads.

It was nearly midnight and they had been traveling all day. Athena tried to stay awake, but exhaustion overcame her. She awoke in the early-morning hours. Despite Kuri's warning, she and Serafina were asleep on either side of her. Athena carefully rose and wandered out onto the crowded deck, where passengers were keeping an eye on their baggage and families were huddled together. The ferry was nearing land. Pine-covered mountains lighted by a soft, violet-pink sky were visible in the distance. There was a chill in the air. The slapping sound of the water against the boat's hull, the birds flapping their wings overhead as if directing the ferry to shore, and the babble of strange languages made Athena feel that she had stumbled into something imagined, not quite real. She closed her eyes for just an instant and opened them again believing she would once again be back in the Bronx.

"Papa," she murmured, "Papa"—as if that was the magic word that would return her to reality. Then suddenly her mother appeared.

"Where did you go?" she asked, grabbing her hand and pulling her back inside. "We'll be docking in fifteen minutes. Come help your aunt and me with the baggage."

It was nearly noon by the time their passports were approved and they had boarded yet another train to their final destination. They were due to arrive late that evening.

"We are in Greece," Kuri kept repeating, tears in her eyes, staring out the compartment window at the vistas of her homeland. "See that sky? There's none bluer, I tell you!" Then she would turn to her sister and grab her hands. "We're home, Serafina. Home!"

But all Athena could think about were the empty rooms they had left behind in the Bronx. She tried desperately to imagine what her father's new apartment might be like, if there would be a kitchen where they could eat together and a room, however small, for her if they ever were to be reunited. All her efforts failed. She sat across from her mother, reading *The Wizard of Oz,* wishing that a cyclone might suddenly sweep her up and deposit her back in New York.

It was eleven o'clock when they arrived in Athens, and too dark for Athena to see much of the city after which she had been named. To her mother's grumbling disappointment, no one met them at the train station. "At least Uncle Spiros could have sent a car," she complained. But she had no problem getting a taxi.

Athena was crushed between the two women, baggage at her feet and piled high beside the driver, blocking the view. "Nothing has changed," her mother said.

"It's so dark, how can you tell?" Serafina asked.

"I can tell," Kuri assured her.

Serafina leaned back in her seat, dozing, but Kuri couldn't hold back her excitement. "Kolonaki Square," she announced as the taxi turned sharply into a block. "It's the street on the right. Number twenty-seven," she shouted at the driver in Greek. He skidded around the corner and pulled to a stop before an iron gate. "This is it!" she called out. "I'll go in first."

As Athena watched through the window of the cab, Kuri rang the bell. A few seconds later she rang again, and a light came on. An elderly man, plainly dressed, opened the gate. Athena thought it might be her uncle Spiros, but her mother's authoritative bearing toward him quickly changed her mind. The man—who, as Athena could now see, had pockmarked skin, thinning gray hair, and several missing teeth—came back with her to the car. "He's Spiros's servant," her mother explained, exasperated. "He's out for the evening but left instructions about which rooms we are to have."

Once inside the house Athena was reassured, although she noticed that her mother and even Serafina seemed disturbed. Times had been extremely difficult for Uncle Spiros, and he had been forced to sell nearly everything of value in the house. The once-overcrowded rooms were now sparsely furnished. The floors were bare in some rooms, the upholstered pieces were shabby, and the walls revealed discolored areas where paintings once had hung.

Still, what remained made the house cheerful. There were huge vases filled with fragrant flowers in the corners of some rooms. The table in the entryway was covered with an intriguing array of photographs taken of the family during better times: women in grand gowns, men in handsome uniforms, smiling and well-dressed children.

The servant, whose name was Taki, grinned encouragingly at her when he brought a tray into the salon and set it down on a small chest. There was fruit and sweet cakes and a pot of thick coffee, all served on a grand silver tray. "Well, at least the silver hasn't been sold," Kuri commented. After they had eaten, Taki showed them to their rooms.

Much of the house had been vacant for years. Uncle Spiros had a suite at the back that, Kuri explained, overlooked the gardens. Their rooms, rather smaller, had once, long, long ago, been the nursery. Kuri commandeered the center room, the largest. Athena chose the smallest, not out of deference to her aunt but because unlike the other room it did not connect with her mother's.

Several hours later, Athena was lying awake in her bed—an unusually narrow, high affair that she feared she might fall out of if she tossed restlessly in her sleep—when she heard someone singing down the corridor. The voice, pleasantly masculine, was loosened by alcohol. A door opened and then closed. *Uncle Spiros,* she concluded. She recalled the photographs of him in uniform that hung in the entryway and that her mother had pointed out to her. But he had been young when those had been taken; he would be quite an old man now—old enough to be her grandfather. She carefully turned over on her side and cradled her head in the crook of her arm. A jar of bright-yellow spring flowers rested on the windowsill, and she inhaled deeply to catch their full scent. Somehow, for the first time since she lost sight of her father from the railing of the *Europa,* she felt comforted.

Uncle Spiros glanced around the concert hall, his bright, humorous eyes scanning for some absurdity among the audience that he could amuse Athena with. Uncle Spiros turned everything into a joke. She had not expected him to be so jolly and distinguished a man. She knew now that he was not rich. But he was extremely handsome and looked surprisingly youthful for a man in his seventies; his hair and mustache were thick and silvery gray, his bearing military, his dark eyes sharp and laughing. He was a connoisseur of all the good things of life, an attentive host, always well-dressed although he didn't appear to have many suits, *soigné,* "a man of the world," according to Kuri, who never talked about his "secret life," although Uncle Spiros himself hinted at such intriguing things as a "good friendship" with a prima ballerina from the Russian Ballet and holidays spent many years before in the grand casino at Monte Carlo.

Every few months he sold something from the house. ("Just to tide myself over," he explained.)

"What do you like to be called?" he had asked Athena the very first time they met.

"My father calls me Ati," she replied.

"Ah! I shall call you A-*ti.* Life depends on where one places the accent. You see, A-*ti,* I would never sell the silver or the fine crystal your grandmother left me. Champagne must always be served in a silver bucket and sipped from long-stemmed glasses. And the artwork," he leaned in close to confide, "your grandmother had appalling taste in art. But when she took my counsel, that was a different matter entirely. Unfortunately, she did not listen as often as she should have. But if you look in the dining room you will see two extraordinary paintings, worth, perhaps, as much as the house itself. But I would never sell them."

He had taken her to the concert hall as a special treat for having learned from him how to judge a good wine. Three months had passed since her arrival in Athens, and during that time she had said nothing about her great love of music or her wish to one day become an opera singer; right now that dream seemed farther away than it had in New York. But when Uncle Spiros asked her what she would like for a reward, she had quickly replied, "To go inside one of the concert halls."

"Just inside?" he asked, puzzled.

"And to attend a concert," she added.

"I didn't know you liked music. Have you taken any lessons?"

"On the piano. But I really want to sing opera. I know all of Aïda's and Amneris's arias, and Mimi's in *La Bohème,* too."

"That's quite an accomplishment for a young woman of thirteen with no training. I must hear you," he insisted. The next day he brought home a recording of *Aïda.* He kept an old wind-up gramophone on his bedroom floor, but since Kuri refused to allow Athena to go inside there, he brought the machine into the dining room. He sat spellbound when the record ended and she had stopped singing. "A-*ti,*" he said in a serious voice. "You shall be an opera diva one day, I pledge an oath on that."

He spent a considerable time deciding just which concert they should attend, and finally chose an evening of Greek folk music and love songs in which the Greek soprano Illiana Minitos was to appear. "See that fat old pelican over there?" he whispered to Athena as they settled into their seats; Athena was dressed in her best frock,with a corsage pinned to its bodice. "He'll pop three buttons on his evening vest before the accompanist even comes on stage. Believe me, it's true. Just keep your eyes on his belly."

Athena had to cover her mouth to keep from laughing out loud when it happened. The lights dimmed in the auditorium. She pressed forward in her seat. There was a polite round of applause when the accompanist stepped out on stage. Athena found it difficult not to keep glancing at the old man in the audience whom her uncle had lampooned. But then Illiana Minitos, a massive woman in a glittering, jet-black gown, entered from the wings. From that moment Athena was so mesmerized by the diva's performance that she was unaware of anything else in the concert hall, including her uncle's astonishment at her enthralled concentration, which caused him to watch her rather than the performance.

"You must start your music studies right away," he said during the taxi ride home.

"Mama says we can't afford lessons now."

"Never mind what your mother says, A-*ti*. I will look for teachers first thing tomorrow morning." He glanced out the window. When he turned around a few seconds later he was smiling. "Yes, tomorrow your life will change dramatically. I promise you that."

He said no more, and she was too overwhelmed to ask questions. When the taxi pulled up to the gates of the house, he stepped out and, offering her his hand, lowered his head in a small, courtly bow. She giggled with embarrassment. "A-*ti*," he said with a seriousness that instantly sobered her, "if you are to become a diva, you must begin immediately to think of yourself as a diva. It will take many years, and you must never lose heart. If you believe you will succeed and you become in your head the woman you want to be, it will happen."

She was far too excited to sleep. Sometime in the early morning she was struck by the fear that even if Uncle Spiros performed a miracle and was able to afford voice lessons for her, she might not be accepted by a teacher. Then she remembered her uncle's words and repeated them over and over in her head: *It will happen.* By the time the sun rose on the new day, she had fallen asleep.

Very few Athenians in the early-summer months of 1940 realized how threatened they were by the approaching war. But war was feared by the men who held Greece's political and economic future in their hands. To Konstantine Sylvanus, the most powerful shipowner in Greece, war could mean the destruction of the empire he had struggled bitterly to build. There were ways to protect oneself that others, like Manolis Zakarias (whom he thought of as scum), had undertaken: Like them he could remove his fleet and register it in another country. But Sylvanus considered himself a patriot and felt contempt for any Greek who would abandon his country in this time of national crisis. He himself resolved to remain in Athens and allow the government to take over his fleet if there was a war. Meanwhile, he was grateful that his only child, his young daughter Nikki, was safe in the United States. He could be brave on his own behalf, but not where she was concerned.

It never occurred to him that she might be even in greater danger there—not from the guns of war, but from the man, Zakarias, he loathed so much.

3. WITHIN TWO DAYS OF MAKING HIS PROMISE, UNCLE SPIROS, amazingly enough, secured Athena an audition with Sofia Galitelli, a former star diva at La Scala and one of the foremost voice teachers at the Athens Conservatory. Kuri was pleased, despite her snide insinuation that Spiros and Signora Galitelli had once been lovers. This was untrue, but Spiros did not deny it—he very much enjoyed his Don Juan reputation.

The conservatory did not accept students under the age of sixteen. Citing Athena's height and maturity, Spiros dismissed this obstacle. Athena had not yet begun school in Athens, and the plan was that she was to tell the board at the conservatory that she was sixteen and already had an American diploma. After all, Uncle Spiros insisted, given that she had just celebrated her fourteenth birthday, it was only a small and unimportant lie. If she was accepted, her education would be well taken care of; she would have music and language at the conservatory and he could help her with all other subjects at home. The audition was set for a week later, and during the interim Athena could think of nothing else.

Great attention was paid to what she would sing. Spiros felt that her voice was still too undeveloped to attempt an operatic aria. The problem was that Athena had taught herself to sing by imitating divas on recordings. She had virtually no other music in her repertoire except for a few folk songs she had learned from Illiana Minitos's concert; there was no piano at the house. Finally it was decided that she would sing an aria from *Aïda,* which she could at least practice accompanied by the gramophone.

Equal consideration was given to what she would wear. She tried on all of her dresses and some of Serafina's. Her own clothes made her look too young, Serafina's too foolishly seductive; since she was shorter and slimmer than her daughter, Kuri's were difficult to alter. Serafina then disappeared into the attic and returned with one of her grandmother's folk costumes. Against Spiros's objections that the outfit might not be appropriate, Kuri made the necessary adjustment (Grandmother Kakakis had been a large woman), and as an added touch draped Athena's shoulders with the scarf that had once covered the piano in the Bronx apartment. Her thick black hair was pulled back from her face with Kuri's best tortoiseshell combs and allowed to fall in soft waves down her back. Despite these embellishments, Athena's chubby, adolescent figure was not masked, the slight awkwardness that came from being too large for her age was obvious when she walked, and her features were still too couched in baby fat to be well defined.

Kuri did not approve of Spiros taking control of her daughter's future, although she now saw Athena's musical talent in a hard-cast light. Her disappointment over the financial situation that she had met upon her return to Athens was keen. Spiros had accepted her into his home with good grace, and notwithstanding the improvement over the walk-up apartment in the Bronx (the house was impressive, located in a genteel neighborhood, and then there was a servant), hard times had stripped it of most of its luxury. She arrived with no funds, and Spiros could afford to pay for little more than their food. Out of his meager salary Miklos was only able to send her twenty dollars a month, and the money did not go very far. The idea that Athena might have a musical career that if successful could one day ease her mother's financial straits was a light, however flickering, at the end of a dark tunnel.

Kuri was pleased to be back in Athens, to stroll in the square with her head held high, aware that Kakakis, her family name, still meant something in her motherland, that Spiros Kakakis enjoyed, like her father and her grandparents, national esteem. She had shed the stigma of being a poor immigrant, and this went a long way toward diminishing her disappointment about the life to which she had returned.

Athena found her mother's semi-contentment a great blessing. Kuri did not complain and nag as she had in New York, although she did turn her sharp tongue on poor old Taki too often. She had gone along with the plans for the audition with surprising enthusiasm. Both Uncle Spiros and her mother escorted Athena to the conservatory. But over the nearly half an hour in which the three of them sat waiting in the small concert room for Signora Galitelli, Kuri grew more and more irritable.

"You must have written down the wrong time," she chided Spiros.

"Maybe she has changed her mind," Athena said. The fear that this might be true had made her hands sweat with nervousness; she pulled a handkerchief from her pocket and wiped them as inconspicuously as possible.

"Sofia will be here," Spiros insisted.

At that moment, Sofia Galitelli, a large, handsome woman in her sixties, her years as a diva evident in her natural command of the stage, paraded onto the dais from a side door. Behind her strode a balding, gaunt man with knobby hands that protruded awkwardly from the too-short sleeves of his jacket. He stopped and sat down at the piano to one side of the stage while Signora Galitelli walked to the center and said, in a deep, theatrical voice, "Spiros! I apologize! Have you been waiting long?"

Spiros jumped up from his seat and onto the platform. "Sofia!" he responded, taking her hand with its numerous jeweled rings and kissing it. "I grow older and you grow more beautiful," he said, looking down into her dark amused eyes.

"It's comforting to know that some things, like your charming lies, never change," the diva answered with a smile. She turned and looked over the edge of the platform to Athena. "This is the young woman, I assume?"

"A-*ti*, come up here and meet Signora Galitelli," Uncle Spiros ordered.

The piano scarf slipped from Athena's shoulders and caught between two seats as she rose and hurried clumsily up the few steps to where her granduncle stood.

After George Stantos, the accompanist, was introduced, and Kuri, still seated in the empty audience section, was acknowledged, Signora Galitelli asked Athena what she was going to sing.

" '*Ritorna vincitor*' from *Aïda*," she replied.

"You're certain this is what you want?" the startled teacher asked. "It's a most difficult aria."

"Yes," Athena said in a sure voice.

"Did you bring the music?"

Athena flushed red. "I'm afraid I didn't."

"George," Signora Galitelli said to the accompanist, "you might need to go to the library for the score."

"No," he replied, "I recently accompanied Irene Marquerios to that aria. I believe the piece is still in my music case." He rose to fetch it from the wings, where he had deposited it before coming on stage.

"Well, there you are," Signora Galitelli said to Athena. "Go over to the piano and Mr. Stantos will help you." She gave Athena a gentle nudge and then, linking her arm through Spiros's, led him down the steps to the seats, where they sat in the front row. Spiros signaled over his shoulder for Kuri to join them, but she remained where she was, watching her uncle and the former diva laugh over some shared memory of the past with the eyes of a sanctimonious witness to suspect behavior.

Athena approached the piano with great trepidation and smiled uneasily as George Stantos rifled through his worn black leather bag filled with music scores. Once he found what he was looking for, he spread the pages on the stand, sat down on the piano bench, and for a moment studied her with good-natured tolerance, certain that a misguided teacher had chosen the aria for her, and at the same time sorry that she was about to make quite a little fool of herself. The aria, one of the most dramatic in *Aïda*, was filled with bursts of fury and the anguish of a broken, tormented heart. It seemed a travesty that a young, untrained singer should attempt such an emotional solo piece. "There's still time to change your mind," he whispered to her.

"No, no, I'll sing '*Ritorna vincitor,*'" she insisted.

He shrugged. "I'll give you a small introduction and strike the A for you so that you can start off on the right note," he said. "The first few bars are unaccompanied and could be a problem for you. Nod your head when you are ready for me to begin." He smoothed out the music before him and rubbed his bony hands together, waiting for Athena's cue.

She stood there awkwardly. "Please don't play a note until after I start," she requested. With a pitying shake of his head, expecting the worse, he conveyed his agreement; to begin the aria on an A without accompaniment was difficult, and if she was off the entire aria might be pitched wrong. He had no way of knowing that she had studied and memorized the music, the Italian lyrics, the intonation, the rhythm, and the volume with which each line was sung from a recording—to alter any single element might confuse her as well as undermine her self-confidence. Stantos would have been even more skeptical had he known that she did not speak Italian. But from her father's telling of the story and from the hundreds of times she had replayed the record, Athena understood with surprising maturity that she would be expressing Aïda's great suffering and conflict about having to betray either her father or the man she passionately loved.

She stood up straight, her head held high, her right hand outstretched as though to grasp at something flying in the air, and, with a chilling stab of sound that silenced the three people in the audience and riveted their attention to her, she sang the opening words of Aïda's agonized plea for the victory of her lover's Egyptian army over that of the Ethiopians commanded by her father.

It was the first time she had sung the aria without the crutch of another singer. For a moment she was startled by the magnificent sound of her own voice, which had developed great strength and volume from competing to be heard above the soprano (the formidable Rosa Ponselle, as it happened) singing Aïda's part on Athena's much-played and cherished record.

George Stantos stared at her in disbelief, then began his accompaniment. She had absolutely perfect pitch. Her voice was raw, sometimes grating, and totally untrained, but it had such a forceful, emotional quality that the small audience was transfixed. As Athena sang, all her insecurities fell away. She felt herself become Aïda, experienced her pain, grasped the desperation of her besieged heart. When she reached the coda, *"Numi pietà!"*—in which Aïda prays for her own death—Signora Galitelli leaned forward in her seat, a look of great excitement on her expressive face.

No applause followed Athena's last, anguished notes, no sound at all. Her immediate reaction was that she had failed. Yet never before had she felt so fulfilled; to have sung with an accompanist on a stage had given her a sense of gratification she never before had experienced. This was a moment she knew she would always remember. But as she stood there, herself once again, she thought how ridiculous she must seem: dressed up in a Greek folk costume while trying to portray the torments of an Ethiopian princess forced to be an Egyptian slave. She was afraid to look down at Signora Galitelli or her uncle, and she cast her embarrassed eyes to the floor.

Signora Galitelli studied Athena and quickly decided that this awkward young woman had unique musical talent. The voice was not there yet; it would take several years to train. But this girl had the rare sense of drama a true diva must have—and then more. The voice also had incredible range for someone so young and untutored.

"You're not really sixteen?" she asked.

"Well, I . . ." Athena hedged nervously.

"Never mind. I don't care. Write on the application that you are sixteen; that will be enough." She turned to Spiros. "You will have to place the girl in my hands. It means long hours, much work. And the conservatory fees—can they be managed?"

"Yes, of course!" Spiros asserted.

Signora Galitelli got up, joined Athena on the stage, and took her hands in her own. "Athena Varosoupolos, from this moment you must pledge yourself to your music. It will be your religion, your god, and I will be the instrument to bring truth and glory to it." She kissed her lightly on the forehead and stepped back to look at her. "I'm sure the girl I see now will one day develop into a handsome woman. But you're not to think about the way you look, only about the way you sing and the emotions you feel. And your name—you shall be Athena Varos. It has a more musical sound to it." She turned to Spiros, who was standing below the platform. "You will bring Athena to me this coming Monday morning at ten. I may be late, but make sure she is not."

In her imagination Athena had played and replayed her first lesson with Signora Galitelli—and, each time, to a disastrous conclusion. She would be uncovered as a fraud with no musical talent at all, a parrot who imitated what she heard on a record. Twice during the stressful week of waiting she woke up in the middle of the night from a dream so real that she could still see the furious diva standing imperiously before her, pointing a jeweled, well-manicured finger at her, and shouting, "Impostor!"

At last Monday came. Kuri escorted her to the conservatory clutching an envelope in her hand that she presented to the olive-skinned young woman who greeted them pleasantly in the front office. "Uncle Spiros sold some silver to cover your fees, so you had better pay attention," Kuri told Athena. They were seated on a hard bench in the spartan anteroom, waiting for Signora Galitelli to appear.

That was what Athena had guessed Uncle Spiros had done, but having it confirmed made her very uneasy. To her uncle, the family silver was a symbol of a world that had long since vanished; each piece was something he could look at, hold in his hand, use to reaffirm the past. He had told her he could never part with any of it, and yet he had—for her. The realization brought tears to her eyes. As she listened for Madam Galitelli's approach, her great debt of gratitude dissolved into fragmented shards of guilt and responsibility.

What if Signora Galitelli decides she has made a mistake? she asked herself. Her hand flew to her throat as though she had just seen something terrifying. Small beads of sweat began to trickle down her forehead. She raised her hand and wiped them away with her fingers.

"What is the matter?" Kuri asked. "You're sweating like Taki when he's forgotten what you asked him to get!"

Mercifully Athena didn't have to answer, for at that moment the door facing them swung open and Signora Galitelli rushed toward them, her arms wide in a welcoming gesture, the full sleeves of her black dress making her look like a vulture in flight. Athena vaulted to her feet and smiled uneasily. "You are on time," the diva said, her raven eyes fastened on Athena's face. "Good! Punctuality is important. Control and regimen are two of the first lessons you are to master." She took Athena's hand and drew her toward a door that led to one of the studios.

She caught a glimpse of Kuri and her injured expression. "Oh, you are the mother, of course," she said, pausing before going in. "Your daughter is in my hands now. You can leave with an easy heart." She looked around the room. "Did you bring a suitcase? I thought it was clear—Athena will be staying at my house with three other students during the week."

"I had no idea," Kuri replied, startled.

"Apparently. Never mind. The office will send someone over to collect what is necessary. Kiss your mama good-bye, child," she told Athena.

Athena was unable to conceal her surprise and confusion. She looked from her mother to Signora Galitelli and back to Kuri again, trying to fathom from either woman's expression what her next move should be. The diva's unrelenting stare made Athena feel compelled to obey her. The thought of being away from her uncle's house was more upsetting to Athena than the prospect of being parted from Kuri, and the idea that she would be living in the home of this remarkable woman was both terrifying and wonderful. Signora Galitelli was not a young woman (Uncle Spiros had told Athena that her greatest miracle was making her debut at La Scala in 1897 at twenty-one, and fourteen years later appearing at the Paris Opera at the age of twenty-five). But Athena had listened to a concert recording she had made only five years before, and her voice seemed to her the most beautiful she had ever heard, much different from other divas. "Bel canto," Uncle Spiros called it.

Athena glanced sheepishly at her mother. "Good-bye, Mama," she said softly.

Kuri was visibly shaken. Her indignation almost consumed her, and she was about to grab Athena by the hand and pull her bodily away from Signora Galitelli—drag her screaming from the room, if necessary.

"Mama, I'll be fine," Athena assured her.

Signora Galitelli quickly opened the door and propelled her new student inside the studio, where George Stantos was seated at the piano. Then, with a smile and a wave of her hand, she bid Kuri, "*Ciao,*" and closed the door behind them.

The room was large and, except for a grand piano and several straight-backed chairs, bare. On one side its windows overlooked a dark green garden planted with several tall trees whose shadow further dimmed the light in the room. Upon the pale gray surface of the marble mantlepiece stood an hourglass. Signora Galitelli walked over and reversed it; the sand began to flow slowly through the narrow bottleneck.

"I don't like clocks," she said. "Their ticking intrudes on the music. We will work an hour—no more, no less. George has agreed to help us today because I want to make some notes. After this we shall be working alone. What I want to do in this first session is see what your voice can do. It is fortunate that you have had no lessons; we won't have to unlearn bad habits." She came over to Athena, who was trembling, and took her hand firmly in her own. "Child," she said, "you have a great natural talent. Opera audiences are filled with men and women with great natural talent who could never even attempt to become professionals. After a year at the conservatory, we will know if you belong on the stage. If I did not think you had the makings of a diva, I would not be in this room with you today. Unfortunately, I have been wrong before—but not often.

"You will be expected to work and study hard: voice, music reading and interpretation, acting, language; some fencing and dance to give you grace. The students here are older than you and very serious. Still, you will find friends, and you can go home to visit your mama and Spiros on weekends and holidays." She sat back and studied the plump young woman in front of her. "We must get you to stop sweating," she said. "It's most un–diva-like. Tell me—were you terrified when you sang for me last week?"

"Only before I started. Once I was singing I forgot you were there," Athena told her honestly.

Signora Galitelli laughed gently. "That's a very good start, very good indeed," she said. "Now, go over to the piano. We shall see how much work there is before us."

Athena studied at the conservatory all day, and after a light dinner walked with the diva herself the short distance to Signora Galitelli's house, which bordered the conservatory grounds. She was given a private room on the second floor, in the rear. Her suitcase was sitting on top of the bed when she arrived. The room contained a single bed, a small desk, a chair, and a wardrobe. There was no rug on the floor, but the bed cover and the curtains were of a bright, cheerful pattern. Though compact and modest, the room was not bleak, since the window had a splendid view. It was Signora's idea (Athena now knew that that was the proper way to address Galitelli) that because of her extreme youth Athena should have a room of her own. Signora did not want the three older girls, who shared a large attic room, to stir Athena's imagination with romantic stories and fantasies.

Athena liked her housemates very much, but quickly learned that Signora's students had little time to waste. They were expected to do vocal exercises before and after breakfast, and in the evening to memorize songs and scores to help build up their repertoires. For recreation, Signora would gather them in the living room, which had thick wine-colored velvet drapes and silver frames with signed pictures of costumed opera singers massed on every flat surface— tables, mantle, even the windowsills—and on her ebony piano play themes from operas, which they had to identify; they listened to recordings of great singers and were expected to discuss what they learned from them afterward. At exactly ten every evening, Signora put an end to whatever they were doing. "To your rooms," she would command, "and if you can't sleep, run an aria or two through your head, *andante con espressione!*"

Signora's four private students who were known as "Signora's songbirds," were considered to be privileged, and were viewed with a certain awe by the other pupils at the conservatory, where one and all worked from nine A.M. until six P.M. on a rigid schedule. Nonetheless, Athena felt bonds of companionship she had never experienced before. At school in the Bronx she had always been an outsider, unable to communicate with her classmates, whose interests she did not share and who, she felt (most probably correctly), thought her peculiar because she was so withdrawn. Until now she had only been comfortable in the company of Signorina Agostino or her father. Now she was surrounded by young people who shared her enthusiasms and were struggling to achieve similar goals.

During the first week, she sat in classes, listening as if hypnotized, drinking in what she was being taught like a parched person who has been given a pitcher of water. She could not hide her enchantment with Signora; when she sang, her voice was a magnet that drew Athena in, surrounding her with the clear, vibrant force of its sound. The blue of the sky seen through the trees outside the lesson-room windows, the sway of their branches, the blackbirds that cackled and flapped their wings—it was all like a theater backdrop, unreal, and Signora was the only performer on the stage.

Athena's nights were filled with unsettling dreams. At times she was alone on the stage and Signora's voice had become hers, or she was in a concert hall, listening to herself sing, when suddenly the audience rose up like blackbirds, flapping their wings, and flying over her head and past the performer, who was also herself, to vanish into an impenetrable mist. She had no idea what any of it meant, or if it had any meaning at all. But she did understand that she was now obsessed with the sound of her own voice as well as of Signora's, and that she would never turn away from that singing figure on the stage. She felt no fear even when the birds in her dream seemed threatening. And when she awoke, she was convinced that once she could sing like Signora she would be invincible.

4. ONCE AGAIN, UNCLE SPIROS PERFORMED A MIRACLE. THIS time it was the act of obtaining two tickets at the opera house to a gala performance of *Madama Butterfly*, in honor of the visiting son of Giacomo Puccini. King George II, his younger brother Prince Paul, Premier Ioannis Metaxas, and the shipping magnate Konstantine Sylvanus were to be present at the performance, which, in effect, signaled the opening of the Athens social season. The opera was to be performed on Sunday evening, October 27, and afterward there was to be a grand reception at the Italian legation, hosted by the aristocratic Italian ambassador, Count Emilio Grazzi. Uncle Spiros's miracle had not included an invitation to the party, but Athena cared little for such celebrations, however splendid. She had been studying at the conservatory for over a year, and, although it was a coveted dream, had never attended a performance at the grand opera house.

It had been raining relentlessly for days, and water was streaming through the streets of Athens. A taxi would be impossible to find on a night like this, but Spiros had thought of everything. Down from the attic had come the old chauffeur's uniform. Its former wearer had apparently been a large man; Kuri altered and shortened the suit so that it wouldn't look too baggy on Taki's spindly figure. The old retainer, whose eyesight was none too good and who hadn't sat behind the wheel of a car in ten years, was to drive them to and from the opera in a long black limousine with darkened windows that Spiros had managed to borrow for the night from the local undertaker. Its occupants received a good deal of attention when Taki pulled the car up to the opera house.

Their seats in the first balcony gave them a good view of the stage, the orchestra, and the royal box. Athena felt a rush of excitement as the great auditorium was dimmed and a spotlight was directed at the royal box. She stood proudly beside her uncle, amazed by the great resemblance between him and the king (he and his brother were standing on either side of the premier, with Konstantine Sylvanus behind them); it was, she decided, the pride in each man's bearing, the same slim, tall figure and handsomely graying hair. She was too far away to actually make out the king's features. It was only an impression, yet she turned to Spiros as soon as the figures in the royal box took their seats and whispered, "You could be the king."

"My dear," he whispered back, "that would be tragic, because then I could not be seated here next to you."

The conductor stepped into the pit and there was a burst of applause, which fell silent the moment he raised his baton. The overture began, and Athena leaned forward in her seat. From the time the curtain rose until the final scene two acts later—when Butterfly knows she must give their beloved small son to Lieutenant Pinkerton and his American wife, bids the child a tearful farewell, and then stabs herself—Athena was overcome by the music and the unfolding drama.

During the enthusiastic curtain calls, Uncle Spiros pressed his large white handkerchief into her hand. "Everyone cries during *Madama Butterfly*," he comforted her when the lights came on. "See? Sniffling noses and wet eyes everywhere. Sometimes I think people love this opera so much because it is such a cathartic experience."

Taki was waiting with the black limousine directly outside the entrance. The street was filled with vehicles that had come to collect

the other opera-goers, but the limousine commanded a certain respect and curiosity from nearby observers, who stood beneath umbrellas in the heavy downpour. Taki, with Athena and Spiros in the
rear seat, made his way slowly through the congested thoroughfare.

"Drive past the Italian embassy," Spiros told Taki. "Maybe we
can't go inside, but we can see a bit of what's happening," he said
to Athena. He then went on to tell her stories of earlier times, when
he had attended balls at that legation, and vividly described the
beauty of the crystal chandeliers, the majestic staircase that guests
descended down into the ballroom after being announced by a
liveried servant, the ravishing women with whom he had attended
these parties, the famous men and women whom he counted as his
friends.

"It's no good to live in the past, A-*ti*. I am a weak man to do so,"
he concluded with a sigh.

"Oh, no, Uncle Spiros! That's not true!" she retorted.

"I'm afraid it is. Nonetheless, memories can be their own pun-
ishment. There is no useful occupation for an out-of-work politi-
cian, especially one whose ideology and principles are no longer
fashionable. But then you arrived on your old uncle's doorstep and
gave him a new lease on life." He patted her hand and then turned
to look out the side window. Taki slowed the car down; they were
approaching a large porticoed building flying both the Greek and
Italian flags.

Rain streaked down the car windows, blurring the view, and so
Spiros partially opened the one on his side. Athena felt a spray of
water when she moved closer to the open window to get a better
look at the fine cars drawing up to the curb and the elegantly
dressed guests huddled under large umbrellas and hurrying up the
steps to the legation's covered front portico. The doors were wide
open, and servants were collecting the wet outer clothing of the
celebrants before they made their way into the brilliantly lighted
interior.

"I wanted you to see the façade of pomp," Spiros said, rolling up the window and sitting back in his seat. "True glory has nothing to do with what you see here. True glory is what you witnessed in the opera house—the music of Puccini, the voices of the singers, the magic that was created on that stage. Do you understand, A-*ti*?"

"Yes, I do," she said softly. Shivering from the chill inside the car, she linked her arm through his and rested her head on his shoulder.

She went to bed that night with images of Butterfly still vivid in her mind. And she fell asleep with Puccini's glorious music swirling in her head, pushing out all other thoughts and impressions.

Early the next morning, she was awakened by her mother's running into her room and shouting, "It's war! the Italians have attacked us! Oh my God!" Kuri threw herself on Athena as if the Italians were already at the door.

Athena struggled to sit up and to loosen her mother's hold on her shoulders. "Mama, what are you talking about? The Italians wouldn't attack Greece. They had a reception last night at the legation. The king and Prince Paul attended." She slipped out of her mother's grasp and swung her legs over the other side of the bed. "You must have had a bad dream, Mama."

Kuri straightened. Her face was ghostly pale, unrouged, with shadows under her dark, frightened eyes. "Those bastards! It's true! They attacked us only moments ago. It said so on the radio. Mussolini, that poisonous snake, sent an ultimatum . . . You know what an ultimatum is? Well, never mind. In the middle of the night he sent the premier a telegram demanding us to let their troops occupy Greece. Do you know what Metaxas said? *Ochi!* No! And now their army has crossed over the border from Albania and attacked us! Oh, my God! What is Greece to do? What are *we* to do?"

Kuri was rocking back and forth on the edge of the narrow bed, the short fingers of her strong, broad hands pulling at her uncombed black hair and making it look as if jolts of electricity had just passed through her body. Athena didn't know what to do. It seemed that her mother had lost her sanity. Athena could still envision the front of the Italian legation, so few hours before, with the

Greek and Italian flags flapping limply side-by-side in the wind. She recalled Uncle Spiros pointing out the Italian ambassador and the premier standing laughing together during the opera's intermission, and the glowing face of Puccini's son as he came up on stage to accept a bouquet of flowers with the cast and the conductor.

She walked around the bed and knelt down beside Kuri. "Mama," she said, "it's just a bad dream, I know it is."

"Soldiers will come!" Serafina cried as she entered the room barefoot and in her nightdress. "They'll rape us all!"

Athena attempted unsuccessfully to calm both her aunt and her mother, but they refused to be placated. It was not until Spiros, having been awakened by Taki with the same news, appeared in his bathrobe about ten minutes later that Kuri and Serafina finally quieted down. Athena wrapped a blanket around her aunt and made her put on a pair of slippers. Then they all went down to the sitting room and gathered around the radio. The same news was repeated. Greece and Italy were at war. But, the announcer insisted, Mussolini's troops were a very long way from Athens, and the Greek army was strong. It would push them back in a matter of days, maybe even hours.

"We must not panic," Uncle Spiros told them. "I'm sure the announcer is right. This is an act of madness on Mussolini's part. If our army doesn't stop him, Hitler will. Much as I hate that man, I'm convinced he had no part in this attack and will pull his fat partner out of Greece and maybe hang him by his toes as well! After all, Greece is neutral. Now, go about your day as always. I'll take A-*ti* to the conservatory." Then he left the room to get dressed.

Within a few weeks, Mussolini's ill-equipped troops were in headlong retreat, surrounded by the Greeks at the ports of Durazzo and Vlorë, their backs to the sea. But then the Italians reorganized and came charging back, razing whole villages as they swept through the mountainous interior and blocked all the supply routes. Many of the young male students at the conservatory had gone off to fight for their country. As word came back of deaths among them, Athena found herself being initiated into the solemn rites of war.

There was a severe shortage of food in Athens; grain, cooking oil, and fresh vegetables and fruit were almost nonexistent. Ration cards had been issued, but there wasn't much to be found at the markets, even with the combined coupons of everyone in the household.

Athena was now spending most of her time with Signora, and when she came home it was usually for Sunday only; she thus gave her teacher the major part of her ration book. She had shown incredible progress in the year they had been working together, and although Signora Galitelli was careful not to display any excitement for fear of filling Athena's head with confidence and impeding her development, she firmly believed that the young woman had a promising career before her. In fact, Athena had done so well at several school recitals that Signora was planning for her to make her debut at the Parnassus Concert Hall with some other young artists in May. Athena was to sing two arias from *Aïda* and a duet from *Tosca* with a professional tenor. Since she was not yet sixteen this was a tremendous challenge, and Athena was working every evening and Saturday, with Signora at the piano, to improve her intonation and interpretation.

Christmas was grim, but everyone had great hopes that the Italians would be pushed back again after the beginning of the year. Then, in that brutally cold January, Premier Metaxas died of cancer; within a few weeks, the man who replaced him committed suicide. "Do you believe that? I don't. Not for a moment. They were murdered. But who cares? They were pro-Nazi anyway!" Kuri exclaimed when she heard the news on the radio.

"Perhaps," Spiros agreed. "But Metaxas did keep the Germans from joining in on Mussolini's outrage against us."

"See! It's as I said! We'll be raped and killed before any of us see the spring!" Kuri wailed.

By February, Athens was cut off from any food shipments at all. The Italians were advancing, burning villages and leaving the few survivors to starve. When the weather permitted, Uncle Spiros and Taki took a bus to the edge of town and then walked several miles into the countryside to find anybody who had food and was willing to sell (for many farmers were hoarding what they had). Then they started on the long trek back to the bus stop. But neither man was very strong anymore, and when March came with its cruel winds, they were unable to make the walk.

After several meatless weeks and a constant stream of complaints from Kuri, Serafina appeared late one afternoon with two rabbits, and the family feasted for several days on the hearty stew they made. Serafina claimed that the rabbits had been a gift from a widower, a parishioner at the Church of St. Demetrios whose elderly mother she had been helping. No one questioned her, but Kuri dropped several hints that perhaps he was an admirer, that she might do well to encourage such a relationship.

"I told you, he's not my type," Serafina replied.

Anti-Italian sentiments grew so strong that Sofia Galitelli was forced to resign at the conservatory. Athena moved back in with her family, attending classes during the day but studying with Signora privately in the evening. Despite the privation and the obvious fear on people's faces, Athena found it difficult to grasp the reality of the war or that Signora was viewed as "the enemy." She still thought of herself as an American, and she never stopped wishing that she were back in the Bronx. The worst thing about the war was that she no longer received letters from her father. She wrote him every week, but the effort was futile: although the post office took the letters, there was no mail coming in or out of Athens now that Germany had begun to mass troops on the Greek borders.

With the Nazis now allied with Italy in the siege of Greece, a fatalistic conviction that the country might soon be occupied began to take hold; those foreigners who had not already left hurried to find any means to do so. Word had it that the last outgoing vessel, an Egyptian passenger ship headed for Alexandria and docked at Piraeus, was departing on the evening of April 20. That morning, a Sunday, Spiros gathered everyone around the kitchen table after the family had returned from church.

"Now, Kuri, you will listen to me," he ordered. "You three still have American passports and could board the Egyptian boat if there is any room. You must go; I'll not hear any arguments on the matter. I've already sold the rest of the silver, and that money should give you enough to manage in Alexandria until you hear from Miklos. Here are the addresses of some old family friends living there. They should be able to help you with whatever arrangements you'll need to make."

"We can't leave you here," Athena insisted. "Or take all your money."

"I'm the man of this household, A-*ti,* and you're to do as I say. Pack your bags right now. We're leaving this house in one hour's time. Possibly hundreds of prospective passengers will be waiting for a place on the ship, and only a certain amount will be able to get on. Take only what you'll absolutely need."

They bundled things together as best they could and started out for the harbor. There were no taxis and the bus schedule had been drastically cut. Gas coupons were only given to emergency vehicles like fire trucks, ambulances, and hearses. A hopeful spring sun was shining overhead as Spiros herded his family across the square and down the narrow side street to the house of his old friend Andreas Ionnais, the undertaker with the limousine. Andreas was about to transport a body to a cemetery across town in the hearse, the only vehicle he now possessed, and after much cajoling he gave Spiros the keys to the car. Taki was the driver; Kuri sat in the front seat beside him, while Spiros, Serafina, Athena, and the baggage rode in the back with the deceased.

They were supposed to deliver the coffin first, but once they were on their way Spiros ordered Taki to drive straight to Piraeus. "The corpse won't mind the delay, I'm sure," he said grimly.

Kuri refused to look back over her shoulder. Serafina held her crucifix on the coffin and prayed during the whole length of the journey. The ride was bumpy and the wooden casket kept rocking from side to side, threatening to slip its bonds. Athena sat hunched in a corner opposite her uncle, since the hearse's ceiling was extremely low.

The dock was absolute bedlam; half the city of Athens, it seemed, wanted to flee on the Egyptian ship. People were crowded together, pushing forward, screaming for attention, pressing against the barrier. "You all stay here with Taki and the hearse while I go see if I can buy tickets for you," Spiros said.

Athena watched him stride off, elbowing his way through with an arrogance that caught people off guard long enough to let him pass. Then suddenly he seemed to have disappeared, and a band of fear tightened around Athena's chest; she had lost her father in such a crowd. "Uncle Spiros!" she shouted, starting forward.

Taki grabbed her by the shoulders and pulled her back. "No! No! Stay here!" he bellowed. It was the first time that Athena had ever seen the old man assert himself, and it startled her so much that she did exactly as he said.

"I'm to be an immigrant again," Kuri sighed. She glanced down at the motley collection of bags they had packed, then at the swarming hordes of mostly ill-dressed people. "I can't believe this is happening."

"But we'll see Papa again," Athena said with a tear in her eye.

"Yes, yes. Your father. That will do us a lot of good." They had been standing around waiting for Spiros to return for nearly half an hour. "I'll get back into the front seat of this horrible vehicle and wait there," she said. Taki helped her up over the high running board.

A few moments later a uniformed guard appeared at the back of the hearse and looked inside. "Coffins are delivered to the cargo gate," he told Taki, and asked him for clearance papers. Taki was having a difficult time explaining that the deceased was not going to be placed on board ship when Spiros reappeared.

"It's an empty coffin," Spiros lied to the man. "We're delivering it after the ship sails." The guard was not satisfied, and Spiros took him over to one side. Athena saw some money pass from her uncle's hand to the man's, then Spiros came back to the vehicle to speak to Kuri. "We have to wait and see if there's room. Many people got here first with as much money as we."

"How long do you think it will be?" she asked.

"Well, the ship is to sail at nine P.M."

"But that's six hours away!"

"What are we to do about the dead man?" Serafina cried, looking as if she had just seen the corpse raise the lid of the coffin.

"It's a woman," Spiros informed her.

"Holy mother," Serafina began to intone.

Spiros disappeared several times during the early evening to see if he could get the purser to give him some hopeful information. At last he returned with a sour expression on his face. "There are no more tickets to be had," he announced. This was greeted by sighs of mixed exhaustion and disappointment from Serafina and Athena, but Kuri was almost exultant.

"Good," she said. "I'd rather be raped by the enemy than be an immigrant anyway!"

The city was blacked out at night, and so they made their way back with the dead woman through inky darkness. Taki could barely see where he was driving, and the area of the cemetery where they were to deliver the casket was unfamiliar to him. It was after ten when they reached the gates, only to find them locked.

"What do we do now?" Kuri asked.

"Bring the departed home with us," Spiros decided from the rear of the vehicle. "Taki and I will go back to the cemetery first thing in the morning."

Suddenly, Serafina began to laugh, and after a moment or so the others joined her. The situation was so bizarre that it seemed—yes—laughable. And, perhaps, it stopped them from thinking of the danger they might be facing. For despite their American passports, the women were as trapped in Athens as the body in the coffin that had been their companion for the day.

Manolis Zakarias read the war dispatches from Greece upon awakening every morning. America had not yet been drawn into the war in Europe, and its people had just emerged from a decade of depression; they wanted to enjoy the good times that seemed to have dawned. Zakarias was a sought-after man-about-town and greatly relished the new social esteem that had come with the money and power he now possessed. With Greek and British shipping fleets frozen by war, his own was in high demand. He was not without a conscience, and his heart wrenched with every word he read about the struggles in his homeland. But he had left Greece long before the war, and felt no guilt about the fact that his swiftly increasing fortune was due to the terrible times in his country.

He was aware that men like Konstantine Sylvanus considered him something of a traitor. But, hell, that old pirate would have done exactly the same thing had their roles been reversed. At least that was what Zakarias chose to believe.

This morning's news was most discouraging. Athens—beautiful Athens—was a besieged city. What did it matter what Sylvanus thought? Zakarias knew how deeply he cared about Greece and her suffering. He felt tears forming in his eyes. No one knew more about how war could tear people's lives apart.

He swung his sturdy legs over the side of the bed and sighed. Last night he had come home alone. He mustn't let that happen too often. He knew the demands of his appetites, and a beautiful, willing woman to share his bed was as important to him as insulin to a diabetic. Someday, maybe, he would marry, but fidelity—ah! what was that? A very un-Greek concept, he thought.

He got up and stretched. Today he would conclude a deal he had been working on for months. Tomorrow morning he would wake up a richer man, and beside him in the bed would be that smoky-eyed South American beauty he had not taken home with him last night.

The anticipation of what was soon to come greatly aroused him, and he hurried into the bathroom to turn on the cold water in the shower. No one could do business with a stiff prick.

5. ATHENA WAS HOPELESSLY UNHAPPY IN THE DAYS THAT FOL-
lowed the family's abortive exodus from Athens. Once Hitler joined
Mussolini and entered the war on April 7, with the mighty power
of his panzer and motorized divisions, Greece lost all hope. Two
weeks later, King George, Crown Prince Paul, and the government
escaped first to Crete and then to Egypt, and Greece braced itself
for the inevitability of occupation.

Athens looked deserted. Its streets were empty. Silence overtook
the city. Shops closed early, and entertainments were canceled.
Then, by Saturday, a curious phenomenon occurred. There was a
sudden burst of activity. People rushed around buying what little
was left in the markets and stores. They stopped by to see their
neighbors, friends, families. The beauty salons opened and women
went to have their hair washed and set.

"Women are crazy," Kuri announced when she returned to the
house from a shopping expedition that had not been very successful
but at least put a few more tins of sardines in the larder. "They sit
under driers, their hair in curlers, while the executioner is ready to
chop off their heads!"

Shortly after noon on Sunday, the family was gathered around the
kitchen table when the thundering sound of hundreds of men
marching through nearby Kolonaki Square rang out. Spiros forbad

anyone from leaving the house to see what was happening. Taki brought the radio into the kitchen, and everyone sat, waiting expectantly, while he pulled out the toaster plug to connect it. The Germans had occupied Athens, raised the swastika on the flagpole atop the Acropolis, and were displaying the strength of their and the Italian occupying forces throughout the city. Serafina, terror on her face, went to the window.

"No one is to open the shutters," Uncle Spiros commanded.

"I just wanted to see if they were outside," she cried, her entire body shaking.

Athena attempted to calm her. "It will be all right," she said, although she didn't believe that was true.

"How can it be?" her aunt managed through her sobs. "We have so little money. And the Germans eat women."

"Don't be an idiot," Kuri said. "Rape, maybe. *Eat?* Impossible! The problem is not what the Germans eat, but what *we* will be able to find to put on our table."

"It is not for women to worry about such things," Spiros pontificated. "I am the man of this family and I shall provide for you."

In the days that followed, this did not prove to be easy. Whatever food was available was commandeered by the occupying army. There was no grain, no bread, no oil. Kuri had managed to obtain a dozen or so tins of sardines packed in oil in the various shopping excursions she had made during the weeks before the occupation, and cleverly created several meals out of one can by using the fish for one meal, grinding the bones to flavor a soup for another, then draining off the oil and using it to fry the stale bread she had stored during the winter to make a dish called *paximadia*. Athena grew to loathe the smell of sardines after weeks of this diet, but Kuri's culinary inventions at least warded off hunger.

One moonlit night, Taki and Athena stripped the garden's two pear trees of their still-green fruit and the women made jam of them. A week later, they picked the unripe fruit from their one olive tree and pressed them for oil. Kuri then ground the skins into a paste that could be eaten on pieces of dried bread.

Classes continued at the conservatory. Athena went out of her way to avoid enemy soldiers on her walks to and from the school, crossing the street if they were approaching on the side she was walking, or turning into a building if any were passing. She still went to Signora's in the evening; often, since a ten o'clock nightly curfew had been imposed, she had to run all the way home in deadly fear of being arrested. The only positive aspect of this was her loss of weight; the meager rations greatly contributed to giving her a slimmer, much more attractive figure. But this also had its disadvantages—the enemy soldiers had begun to whistle and make advances toward her.

Since she was an Italian citizen, Sofia Galitelli had a larger food ration, but she also was under constant surveillance from the Germans and Italians because of her long residence in Greece; at the same time, many of her old Greek friends and associates shunned her. She remained a strong, determined figure, and still dressed in her unique manner. Because she was unable to hold master classes at the conservatory any longer and had lost all her other students, Athena's future had become all-important to her.

The concert at Parnassus Concert Hall, which had been canceled after the occupation, was now rescheduled for Sunday, July 20, at 5:00 P.M. (so that the curfew could be observed). Athena and Signora had been working diligently on her program. Despite Athena's protests, since the middle of May Signora had insisted that their lessons no longer take place at her house; she explained that her neighbors might think her student was conspiring with her, a foreign agent, and suffer because of it. Hostility toward the local Italian population had accelerated wildly once Greece began to fall to its invaders. "I am under suspicion," she had confided to Athena. "People I trust have told me this. In England they have killed little Dachshund dogs for being German. And the Greeks are far more emotional—which is, perhaps, the reason I have always been so happy among them."

The idea that anyone could believe that Sofia Galitelli, who had lived in Athens for nearly twenty years, was an enemy spy was utterly ridiculous to Athena; she knew how much Signora loved Greece, its folk music, and its people. Nor could she see how Signora might be thought guilty of the odium of collaborating when she had given so much of herself to the development of young Greek artists. But it was symptomatic of the madness that overtook the city while the populace waited fearfully to be conquered that such a woman would be thought suspect.

Asking the girl not to come to see her was a great sacrifice to Signora, but it had been a jolt to Athena. "You must see me, you must work with me. What will I do without your guidance? Oh, please, Signora," Athena pleaded when Signora called a halt to the lessons.

"I tell you, it could be dangerous," the diva replied flatly.

"I'm an American!" Athena countered. "No one would accuse an American of being a spy!"

Signora laughed but quickly turned serious again. At last they arranged to meet on Saturday afternoons only, and Athena came to look forward to each one of these sessions with extreme excitement. Every time she left, Signora would press a packet of tea or a tin of food into her hand; there would be tears in her large, black, sunken eyes. "I will pray you can return next Saturday," she would say, her voice cadenced with drama.

Over the next month and a half, Athena's rehearsals for the upcoming concert gave her a sense of normalcy compared to the unreality of her daily life. Uncle Spiros had tried to convince Kuri to get word to the American consul that Athena, a United States citizen, was trapped in Greece. But her mother was adamantly against such an action, even if a way could be figured to achieve it. "They could take her away from me to God knows where," she protested. That put an end to further discussion.

A hot July sun dazzled down on the day of the long-awaited concert. Athena was to be at the auditorium at three for a final run-through with the orchestra. Kuri had made her a bouffant summer dress out of some old hyacinth-patterned bedroom curtains she had found in the attic and a violet ribbon sash from a bow that had once graced an Easter bouquet. The purplish colors complemented her dark complexion, and Athena was quite pleased with her appearance. The young tenor with whom she was to sing the duet from *Tosca,* Stefanos Coundouris, lived nearby. He swung by to pick her up on his motor bike. The rest of the family was to follow by public transportation.

Athena tightly grasped Stefanos's slim body as they sped across town. The vehicle leaned to one side every time they raced around a corner, and the warm wind the sudden movement stirred blew Athena's hair across her face. Still holding Stefanos securely with one hand, she pushed back the loose strands to watch the road. It had taken her a long time to be caught by any of Athens's beauty: the spectacular view from one of the higher elevations, with the city spread out below, or looking southward beyond, where in the summer the sea stretched in a magnificent azure flow to the pale islands and the serene mountains in the distance. She had never felt happy to leave her father and her birthplace, and the war and what they were now suffering made her feel antagonistic toward the country in which she was literally imprisoned. If not for her Saturday lessons with Signora and her great love of music, which was becoming so much a part of herself, she would have been desolate.

She and Stefanos arrived at the concert hall without incident. To Athena's surprise, Signora was not there, nor did she appear in time for her first aria, nor could she locate her either in the wings or in the audience during the concert. Early in the performance she realized how very much she still had to learn. People were clearing their throats during her second solo number. She didn't have their full attention, and when she and Stefanos joined together for the duet, *"Amore sol per te"* from *Tosca,* she was conscious that his broad vocalism was destroying the piece's emotion and that she was incapable of compensating for the loss of drama. Nonetheless, to be standing onstage with an orchestra behind her and a full audience in front of her, to hear applause meant specifically for her, was a memorable experience.

After the concert, Athena sought out anyone Signora might have contacted to ask them why she had not appeared, but no one had heard a word from her. "I want to go to her house and see that she's all right," Athena told Spiros when he came backstage to collect her.

Spiros didn't hide his concern. "A-*ti*, if Sofia wasn't here for your debut, there must be a good reason. And perhaps—just *perhaps*—she might not wish for you to go to her house."

"I'm going anyway," Athena insisted.

Spiros studied the young woman standing so defiantly before him. She had eyes filled with pure emotion—eyes, he recalled, like his mother's. Athena's great-grandmother, Olympia, had been a woman of strength and purpose and immense feeling. He recalled how she had stood in the doorway of their house, barring the path of armed officers, when he and his brother, Stavros—Athena's grandfather—were about to be arrested during the civil war. Vanquished by the undaunted passion in her eyes, the officers had been unable to go against her will—just as he was about to acquiesce to the determination of Olympia's great-granddaughter.

He sent Kuri and Serafina home by public transport, and then he and Athena started off on foot to Sofia Galitelli's house. The sky had turned from the softest blue of a summer evening into the dark indigo of encroaching night. It was half past seven; the moon had not yet fully risen, and where the sky and the horizon met was a band of copper-helianthus. The Acropolis was outlined against this brilliant backdrop, its magnificent columns like the limbs of a mythical creature standing on top of the world and supporting the sky.

Very few people were out, perhaps because it was Sunday evening—or simply that there was nowhere to go in an occupied city at this hour, with the curfew close at hand and armed German patrols passing by every few minutes.

"I will never get used to this," Spiros muttered through tight lips as a patrol slowed down, followed them for half a block, and then continued on.

Signora's house was dark, but Athena and Spiros went up to the front door anyway and rang the bell several times. There was no reply. They were about to go around the rear to check the back door when they heard a rustle in the bushes that bordered the house. Spiros grabbed Athena and pushed her behind him. There was silence, then the rustle again.

"Signorina Varos," a woman called out in a thin whisper.

Athena stepped away from her uncle and began to move toward the bushes.

"It's Yanni. Signora's maid," Athena murmured over her shoulder. "I recognize her voice." She followed the sound of the woman's call to a more secluded spot along the side of the house. "Are you all right, Yanni?" Athena whispered. The terrified woman emerged, her dark hair thatched with leaves and small twigs. "Where's Signora?" Athena asked.

"She's been arrested. Only a few hours ago. She made me leave just before they came to the door." She was staring at Spiros with a mixture of suspicion and fear.

"This is my granduncle, Spiros Kakakis," Athena told her.

"I'm an old friend of Signora's," he added. "What is this about? I'll do what I can to help."

Yanni stepped closer and looked from Athena to Spiros. "I don't know what to do," she said. She grabbed Athena's hand and pulled her to an even more sequestered spot. Spiros followed close on Athena's heels.

"Signora has been helping the underground by hiding some British officers who were trapped in Athens when the Germans came," she told Athena. "That's why she wouldn't let you come here very often anymore." Yanni shook her head from side to side. "Oh, I don't know what to do," she moaned.

"There's nothing for you to do," Spiros said. "If your mistress told you to leave, that's what she wanted you to do. You will come back to my house with Athena and me."

"No, no! You don't understand," the woman—who Spiros could now see was not much older than Athena—continued. She took his hand and gripped it tightly. "The British officers are still inside, in a room in the attic that's concealed by a false wall. I saw the Germans lead Signora away. First a man came and gave her a message, and she told me to leave. But I didn't know where to go and so I hid in the bushes." She began to cry, and Athena placed her arms around her shoulders. "The Englishmen were not with the Germans and Signora when they left the house," Yanni continued. "And I didn't hear any gunshots. I've been hiding here all the time until you came, wanting to go in to see if the Englishmen are alive. But Signora warned me that the Germans often leave a bomb that will explode when you open a door or window."

"Where is this secret room, Yanni?" Spiros asked.

She looked as if she might not reply. Then she said, in a hoarse whisper, "Up the rear staircase to the room over the kitchen. There is a closet there. In the back, behind some old stored curtains and things, is a door. It leads to the room."

"You'll go back to my house with Athena as I said, Yanni. I'll take care of this. Now, both of you go, quickly." For a moment it seemed that Athena would defy his order, but then she took the distraught young woman, who was a good deal shorter than she, by the shoulder and started back toward the street, pausing only for a moment to brush the leaves and twigs from Yanni's hair to avoid suspicion.

Spiros stood watching until their dark figures had disappeared into the distance, then made his way around the rear of the house and let himself inside. The house was shuttered, and he stumbled through the darkness, searching for the staircase that would take him up to the attic room. As he stepped over a threshold to what seemed to be a pantry, he tripped over a large bundle—or at least that's what he thought it was. He lit a match and leaned down.

At his feet was a dead man, his throat slit. Only a few feet from him was the body of another killed in the same manner. That, Spiros realized, was why Yanni had heard no gunshots. Both men were wearing blood-spattered Nazi uniforms, and both were bareheaded. Spiros stood up, sickened and puzzled. His match had gone out, so he lit another and searched the area around the bodies. The staircase he was looking for was directly to the right of the first dead man; he slowly climbed the narrow steps and easily found the closet that Yanni had described. The door was open, and the small, box-like room empty.

It didn't take Spiros long to figure out that the men Yanni saw leaving the house with Sofia had been the British officers she was hiding. In all probability, they were wearing the German soldiers' caps—and possibly some other German outerwear that Sofia might have provided them with.

Spiros left the house as quickly as he could and hurried across town in order to be home before ten. As he walked, his hands deep in his pockets, he silently prayed that the men had reached shelter unharmed. For if they were safe, it seemed logical that Sofia was too—at least for the time being.

When winter set in, it was severe. The temperature dropped to lows not experienced in many decades, and there was no firewood to be had anywhere. Even the trees in the parks had been cut down. Worse, food supplies were almost nonexistent. Bakeries and markets were shuttered. Ration cards were worthless. Meat was only a memory. Pets were killed and cooked. But even such drastic efforts to ward off death failed. By Christmas, over 300,000 people in the city had died of illness or starvation. Added to that appalling figure were the thousands more who had been killed in mass executions after being accused of conspiracy, of helping the underground, of sabotage. No word had been heard of Sofia Galitelli. Lists of the executed were not released, and their relatives had to rummage through their effects to see if a loved one had been killed.

There was an active black market, but even a gold wedding band could buy little more than a scrawny squirrel to stew. Grave robbers stalked the cemeteries. The living could not afford to bury their dead, and left them out on the street at night. The corpses, which were picked up in the morning by a special detail sent around by the occupying forces, were dumped into mass graves in what had once been the palace gardens. At night the hills above the city were ringed with hungry, howling stray dogs that the Germans only held back from the city with nightly rounds of machine-gun fire.

Spiros and Taki had cut down, one by one, at night, all the trees in the garden. They hid the firewood beneath floorboards of several rooms. The family would be warm enough, and able to cook what food could be scavenged through the winter. But as they entered the grim new year, with little left in the larder except a few jars of pear jam, some barley for ersatz coffee, and a bottle of ouzo closely guarded by Spiros, the family—now enlarged by Yanni—was facing starvation.

The conservatory was closed, but Athena signed a contract with the Acropolis Theater—which had managed to remain open for the benefit of opera and classical-music fans in the occupying forces—to sing with its small company. Her salary was a pittance, but she was able to continue lessons with Floria Peredis, one of the directors of the company and a former teacher at the conservatory.

Life was hard. Athena's father, the Bronx, her simple life in America, now all seemed like a distant dream. She had been studying Italian and German at the conservatory and, along with Greek, these—and not her native English—were the languages she now spoke. Privately she cheered when America entered the war in December, 1941, which gave her some hope that her country and the Allies would soon rescue Greece from Hitler and Mussolini. But by the time a full year of occupation passed, even she began to lose hope, especially since conditions at home had seriously declined: the elderly Taki, to whom she was much attached, was ill and weak, needing food and medicine, and Uncle Spiros had seemed to age suddenly and dramatically before her eyes.

Yanni proved to be a godsend; she helped Kuri through the difficulties of running a house in which there was little food and no electricity or hot water. Secretly, Kuri now rued the day she had ever left America, but she kept up a front and—if her sharp tongue was any indication—maintained her spirit.

In June, the second summer of the occupation, Taki took a turn for the worse. The old servant was now little more than skin and bones and he couldn't raise himself up from his bed. Serafina was helping to nurse him.

"I won't let that old man die!" she told her sister one morning when it seemed Taki might not last the day. "What he needs is a good meal. That's all. Some real meat broth, a piece of soft bread."

"He'll die when God wants him to, and you'll have little to say about it," Kuri replied fatalistically.

Serafina left the house a short time later and did not return until just before curfew that night. "Where have you been?" Kuri asked. "You've had us all worried sick."

Serafina was grinning like a small child who has just been given a toy; she drew a bag from behind her and presented it to her sister.

"What's this?"

"Open it," Serafina said.

Kuri's eyes were wide with amazement as she pulled a dead rabbit from the crumpled paper sack. "Where did you get this?" she asked, shocked.

"Reach down farther," Serafina prodded with glee.

Kuri put the rabbit on the kitchen table and plunged her hand to the bottom of the sack. Serafina had somehow managed to obtain a jar of honey and a loaf of bread. "Serafina, you must tell me what you have done," Kuri pressed.

"I won't let the old man be carted away like garbage and dumped somewhere," Serafina replied. "And I won't tell you where I got it."

Serafina held to her word. Every few days she would disappear for several hours at a time and return with fresh bread, a tin of fish, another rabbit, some goat cheese—and Taki began to improve, although not enough to leave his bed. She also refused to answer any queries about how she came by such marvelous treasures. It was Spiros who finally discovered Serafina's secret through his friend, the undertaker, Andreas Ionnais.

"You mustn't think too harshly of your niece, or of me," Ionnais told him. "I have a right to survive, as we all do. No one bothers with funerals anymore, and I have a great big hearse just sitting in my garage. So the thought came to me: so many soldiers here, and so few women. As you know, the back of the hearse is big enough for the largest man to stretch out in with room to spare. Men are men. So I park the hearse just off the square, and any soldier can rent it for a short time while off-duty. Without their men, it is a way for some of our women to survive until the enemy is routed by the Allies. Serafina—she came to me of her own volition. She heard about it from one of the women, not from me. Don't judge her, Spiros. None of us can face judgment in such times as these."

Spiros was shaking with anger and disgust. "I shall never speak to you again!" he shouted at his old friend.

The man just shrugged and walked away.

Spiros stormed across the square; he could see the hearse parked nearby. He had intended to open the rear doors and pull Serafina out, for he guessed that that was where she was. But as he came up to the vehicle, he was unable to act; he found the idea of any Greek other than himself or Andreas knowing that a woman in the Kakakis family had slept with the enemy was simply too painful to bear.

Of course, Serafina was simple, really. A child in many ways; she didn't fully understand what she was doing. He loathed and pitied her at the same time. And she was saving Taki's life.

He turned back, crossed the square, and returned home. He seldom spoke to Serafina from that time on, and never again was able to look her in the eyes. He was the man of the house and he had failed his family. Whatever sin Serafina committed was his fault, and he took the blame for it. Still, he never knowingly ate a mouthful of the food that came from her shame and his.

6. Athena walked through the city streets under the moon, feeling lightheaded and infused with a new sense of freedom. The war had ended; that very day the British forces had landed in Piraeus after three and a half years of oppressive occupation. The streets were crowded with people singing and shouting, but they were so emaciated that they looked like ghostly specters. Stark reminders of the war abounded: the empty stores and deserted houses, the general dilapidation.

During the long, difficult years since she had come to Greece, Athena had learned to ignore what was happening around her and to concentrate on the music whirling in her head and on the day-to-day tasks of simply surviving. The music was *hers*—not even the loathsome Germans could take it away from her. The harder life became, the more her music fixed itself in her being.

She turned a corner and, buffeted by the October winds, brushed back the web of dark hair that clouded her vision. The moon was full, the street was a long, white, shimmering ribbon. People were dancing everywhere, casting wraithlike shadows. Others were shouting exultantly from windows. Still, she remained apart, confined in her own thoughts, listening to her own music.

She was free now to leave Athens and wanted to do so as soon as possible. She had spent so much time in lonely musings, in anguished memories, in bitter anger. Her mother had robbed her of her right of free choice, spirited her away from her father and her homeland, held her captive in a dream while denying Athena the chance to pursue her own. And yet, *and yet* . . . If not for that, would she have cocooned herself in her music? And Uncle Spiros— would she ever have come to know that remarkable, unconventional, dear man?

She pushed forward into the wind, pulling her shawl—her only protection against the chill of the autumn night—closer around her shoulders, conscious of her now-slender figure, proud of the woman she had become, mature enough to sing *Suor Angelica* and *Tosca* in the coming season, difficult roles for someone just turned eighteen. But she had learned that no matter how hard a part was, a voice must be kept light and limber like an athlete's body. She had absorbed so much in so short a time; the war had seen to that. Somewhere, a very long time ago, she had lost her youth. In exchange, she had reached a dedication, a concentration that she doubted she would have achieved under easier circumstances. But now she was free to lift her wings and fly away to where her future waited— which was not in Athens, she was certain of that. She needed a great teacher, an opera company with an international reputation, like the Metropolitan in New York. Of course, she was not yet ready for such a formidable company. Still, she would have a better chance of being accepted by them one day if she was in New York.

She yearned to go home, home to where Papa was, where, as Serafina was constantly reminding her sister, "the smell of death is not on the streets and there is hot water in the pipes to take a bath and food to fill your stomach." Her aunt and her mother would need papers if they were to be allowed to return to the United States, and that might not be easy. But she was an American citizen, and she didn't see how the authorities could deny her a travel permit.

No foreign mail had reached Athens since the early days of the war. Nearly four years had passed since she had heard from her father. Tonight she would write him to express her hope that they would soon be reunited; tomorrow she would find out whom she could speak to about returning to the United States. The idea that she might soon be on her way to New York, to her father, to a career as an American diva, filled her with an uplifting buoyancy and sense of exultation. As she turned away from the wind and crossed Kolonaki Square, having to elbow her way through the spirited revelers, she began to sing the "Star-Spangled Banner," startling some of the people she passed. She had spoken so little English in recent years that it sounded strange, even to her. But Athena's powerful rendition of the anthem, the exquisite, bell-like ringing of her voice that grew in volume as she moved through the crowds, caused them to part and cheer her as she disappeared down the short, narrow street to Uncle Spiros's house.

The street had changed considerably during the war. The rows of three-story houses that lined its sidewalks had mostly all been turned into multi-family homes and small apartments, since their owners had not been able to maintain them on their own. Beyond their tiled roofs rose Mount Lykabettos, a dark, jagged peak against a moon-washed sky, atop which stood the little white Church of St. George, lighted at night for the first time since the occupation.

The wrought-iron gate that distinguished Uncle Spiros's house from its neighbors was rusted and creaked loudly when she opened it. Taki was no longer able to do much physical labor, and there had been no oil to grease such a frivolous item as an ornamental gate. With Taki more of a burden than a help, Yanni's presence in the household had been much appreciated, but seldom did a day pass when Kuri didn't remind Athena of her selfishness in spending more time than she needed to, rehearsing at the theater. "And what do they pay you? A pittance! Not enough to buy a daily loaf of black-market bread!"

Her mother was waiting for her in the dim shadows of the living room; two stubby candles were burning on the mantlepiece.

"Where have you been?" Kuri demanded. "Do I have to worry myself sick about you, too? There are crazy people roaming the streets. Uncle Spiros was knocked down right on Vasilissi Sofias only a few feet from the American embassy—not even open yet and it's surrounded with riff-raff and traitors ready to run like rats if they can get a visa. Spiros could have been crushed to death. No one cared that an old man was on the ground. Thank God Mr. Papagos, thief of a baker that he is, happened to be nearby. He helped Spiros home. Poor man, he'll be bruised black and blue by morning. I gave him some tea and put him to bed. And Serafina—where can she be? I haven't seen her since noon. She can't be trusted out alone at such a mad time. You know how confused she can get, and Mrs. Alexandropolos from next door told me she saw her at St. Demetrios's, and the crowds there were almost as crazy as on Vasilissi Sofias."

"I'm sure Serafina is inside the church and in no danger, but if you want I'll go get her."

A look of terror crossed Kuri's face. "Are you crazy, too? You're not going anywhere. You're staying right here." She began to cry; she tried to talk between her sobs, but her words came out tossed like waves on a stormy sea. "Oh, why did I ever leave the United States? No one suffered there during the war. No one went hungry or died of the cold. No one had to bear the humiliation of living under the Germans, men without a grain of compassion for the people whose country they had occupied. All these years being watched by the eyes of a machine! I should have taken the boat to Egypt before they came. But who knew? I ask you, who could have known what monsters the Germans would be and how awful life in Athens would become?" She gave a loud, agonized cry and began striking her hands together in a kind of frenzy. She lost control and started to rock back and forth, sobbing, "We are poor, poor. Everything is gone and the house is falling apart. Oh my God! That the Kakakis family should come to this!"

The sight of her mother in such distress shook Athena. She realized that even during the worst days of the war Kuri had maintained tremendous self-restraint and had never once broken down before her. Suddenly she was filled with a strange pity for this woman, who had gotten what she wished for and now found it wasn't what she wanted at all. She went over and sat down next to her mother and placed her arms around her quaking shoulders. A flutter of wind came through a crack in the window next to the fireplace and one of the candles was snuffed out. A thin, acrid scarf of smoke twisted above it. Through the deepening shadows Athena could see the agony etched on her mother's face. "Don't worry, Mama, we won't be poor for long. I will be famous one day soon."

Kuri made a curious sound, half-laugh, half-cry. She pushed Athena away and stood up, squaring her shoulders, pulling her hair away from her face, and then wiping her tears with the back of her hand. "I shall feel better when Serafina is home," she said. "And when we once again have electricity, hot water, and full bellies," she added. "Now go see if your uncle needs anything."

Athena started out of the room.

"Athena," her mother called.

She turned and paused. Kuri was looking at her with narrowed eyes, struggling to see through the dim light in the room. "You have a good voice. Maybe a great one. I'm really no judge of that. But you are ambitious. That I recognize because we share that particular trait. I, however, had only ambition—and, once, youth and a family name. I squandered both. If I seem like a bitter old woman at times, it's because I know there's no way to get them back. Make sure that you don't sell yourself cheap to a company like the Acropolis—or to a man." She leaned back in her chair. "If you become famous, will you take care of your mama, eh?"

"Of course I will!"

"Of course you will." She laughed, and the sound was as creaky as the rusted front gate. "Go, go," she ordered, waving her hand.

"What's the matter, A-*ti*?" Spiros asked when she brought him a cup of tea later. "You seem distracted."

Athena sat down on the edge of his bed and studied his face in the candlelight. The flickering shadows emphasized its gauntness and darkened the lines beneath his eyes. But when he smiled at her, she knew he had not lost his spirits. "A-*ti*," he said. "Whatever you decide to do, let it be your decision. Listen to no one but your conscience." He leaned forward, flinching from a sudden pain, then laughing about it. "Imagine being almost trampled to death in front of the American Embassy! And you know why I was there? Don't laugh at this old man. I was to meet the baker's wife for a stroll along the avenue. Of course, when we made the arrangement neither of us had any idea that today would be the day the British would arrive and set Athens free. Or that her husband would insist she stay at home, and by curious fate walk by the exact spot where we were to rendezvous, and so be there to save my life. One never knows, A-*ti*, how things will turn out, but if I hadn't gone to meet her I would have always regretted not having done so."

Later that night Athena sat wrapped in a blanket by her bedroom window, watching the silver leaves of the one remaining olive tree in the moonlight, waiting for morning to come so she could go to the American embassy. She was more certain than ever that what she had to do was return to New York. Somehow she had to figure out how she could get the embassy to allow her mother and Serafina to accompany her. She had confided this to Uncle Spiros, who had agreed it was a good plan. She fell asleep leaning on the sill, and was awakened by an innocent morning sun that turned the olive leaves into glittering gold. A moment later her mother, fully dressed but with her long, thick hair loose and uncombed, burst into her room.

"Your aunt is still not home," she cried, her eyes wide with alarm; Kuri had awakened with a premonition of some impending tragedy. "She should not have left the house yesterday. Even to go to church. We must get dressed and go to St. Demetrios's. There is something wrong. I feel it in my body."

Twenty minutes later they were on their way. The bright sun turned the tile roofs to bronze. A flock of birds (*going or coming from where?* Athena wondered) flitted by under a promising sky of sun-touched gray. It was not yet seven A.M., a time of day when silence usually prevailed in the city. But although their street was deserted and most of the windows remained shuttered, the shouts and excited voices of crowds of people filtered through from somewhere close by.

"Those idiots can't still be celebrating," Kuri complained, her arm linked tightly through Athena's, and pulling her along at such a pace that Athena had to struggle to keep step with her. The air was crisp and cool, but the sun was like a soft hand of benediction on her head. As the voices grew closer, Kuri slipped her arm out of Athena's and began to run. Her black wool shawl blew back under her arms, and her loose gray hair swept like thick smoke around her frightened face. Kuri sensed danger and seemed drawn to it but afraid of it at the same time. Athena fell back slightly, not under-standing her mother's hysterical, irrational behavior. Athena was fully a hundred feet behind when Kuri turned the corner into the street where the Church of St. Demetrios was. Athena heard a piercing scream, and then Kuri reappeared, running toward her. When she reached her she grabbed Athena's hand.

"They're going to kill Serafina," she said in a terrified voice.

"Who?"

"The people! The crowds! The barbarians!" Kuri cried, dragging Athena forward with her. The two women were out of breath by the time they reached the corner.

Athena stood there horrified by what she was seeing. At least a hundred people crushed together on that narrow street, all of them screaming and shouting, "Collaborator! Collaborator!" A woman with a shaved head was raised above them, passed from one to another, spat upon and abused. "Oh, my God!" Athena whispered, almost unable to speak. "It's Serafina."

Without realizing the danger of what she was doing, she shoved herself forward, pushing and fighting her way through the crowd, unaware that Kuri was right behind her. She had almost reached the section of the mob where Serafina was being tossed about when there was a clamorous sound of church bells and St. Demetrios's bearded head priest, clad in black, flowing robes faced with strips of blue and black silk, appeared on the church's small balcony over-looking the street. Some members of the throng glanced up at the sound of the bells, and, seeing the priest with his arms raised and shouting (hopelessly, because of the clamor of the bells) for them to stop, fell back. Meanwhile, two priests came out of the church and fought their way to where Serafina, now lowered to the ground, was lying down, terrified, expecting to be beaten or crushed to death. Athena fell to her knees and covered her aunt with her own body while the priests pushed back the crowd. Finally, one of them helped Athena to her feet; the other picked Serafina up in his arms and started back into the church. Kuri brushed ahead of Athena, sobbing and holding her sister's limp hand.

As soon as they were safely inside the dark, cavelike interior, Serafina lapsed into unconsciousness and the doctor was sent for. After a cursory examination he decreed that her life was not in danger, although she had been badly bruised. She was taken by ambulance to the hospital, where Kuri and Athena traded shifts at her bedside. When, three days later, Serafina finally regained consciousness, she simply lay silently on the bed, eyes staring into space. No one was ever to know what was going through her mind; Serafina was never to utter a word again.

During the last years of the war, Yanni had become Athena's confidante—much to Kuri's irritation, for she was unable to dispense with class distinctions even in such desperate times. But Athena truly liked Yanni, who held her in open admiration and could sit silently for hours listening to her practicing or rehearsing, who would help her with the long speeches and lyrics she had to memorize, to whom Athena could always divulge her true feelings. Athena had little in common with other girls her age, and viewed sex, of which she had no personal experience, as something both humiliating and distasteful—a belief that Kuri nurtured and that Serafina's behavior had confirmed. She was cool with the few young men who worked with her at the Acropolis Theater, and either they found her unappealing or respected her distant attitude, for not one among them ever forced his attentions on her. The women at the theater all thought her overly ambitious, and she was reputed to view each and every one of them as a threat to her lofty position in the company. This was not far from the truth.

Athena's life was centered on a world of music, and all her post-war hopes were pinned on becoming a well-known diva with an international company. Hardly a day went by when she did not think about Signora Galitelli, wondering whether she was safe, wishing desperately that she could turn to her for advice. This drew her closer to Yanni, through whom she felt something of the great woman's presence. So many terrible things had happened during the war, but to Athena Signora's disappearance seemed to have been the worst. And now, just when the war's end had given her such optimism about the future, there was this atrocity perpetrated upon her aunt.

From the hospital, Serafina was sent to recuperate at a convent on the outskirts of Athens. Athena went to see her several times a week, but Serafina's large, dark eyes gave no indication that she recognized her. The horror that had befallen Serafina had touched each member of the household, and nothing could ever be the same again now. Uncle Spiros was up and about, but a deep sadness was clearly visible in his wistful smile, his slower step, his stooped shoulders. Taki hobbled about the house issuing great, trembling sighs.

Now able to get cigarettes, which had been denied her during the war, Kuri chain-smoked and was more short-tempered than ever. Her eyes were red a good deal of the time, and she could be heard muttering, "Sons of bitches!" between drawn lips. It was as though there was a devil inside her clawing to get out. She never made it clear who she was cursing—Serafina's attackers, the Germans, or the new staff at the American embassy, which had reissued a passport to Athena but was hedging on Kuri's visa and had refused outright to even consider one for Serafina.

Six weeks after the war's end, Athena received a letter from her father. She was surprised to note that the return address was their old building in the Bronx. He had written her many letters during the occupation, he told her, always hoping that she would receive them, but there had been no word from her. Now, thank God, he knew she was safe. He went on to tell her that he was living with

Maria Agostino in the same apartment where she had given Athena piano lessons. The letter went on:

You are perhaps old enough to understand about such things now. A man cannot be left alone for so long a time. It is against his nature. Maria has been very good to me and she is as anxious as I am to see you again. Although the apartment has only one bedroom, we are turning the dining room into a place for you. I am arranging your passage; the American embassy will notify you. Meanwhile, I have enclosed twenty dollars and will send you and your mother more next week.

Ati, I have thought about you every day since you have been gone. I always knew you had the gift of music. To me, you were music. Maria says to tell you that she will help you any way she can. She knows many people connected with the opera. I love you dearly, my darling Ati. May God be with you and deliver you safe, sound, and swiftly to me.

Yours—Papa

"Son of a bitch," Kuri spat when Athena had finished reading her the letter.

Athena handed her the twenty-dollar bill.

"I don't want his dirty money," her mother said, and then—changing her mind when Athena kept her hand extended—snatched it from her and stuffed it in her dress pocket. "Money has no master," she explained, "and all the merchants are thieves."

A week after this letter arrived, Athena was notified that she could leave Athens in four days. She was to take a British ship to Alexandria, transfer to another ship going to Lisbon, and then board a transatlantic ship for New York. It would be an arduous six-week trip, and the last leg of it through rough winter seas.

She considered delaying the journey until spring so that she could sing *Tosca* at the Acropolis. And the weather would be better, too.

"No. Since you have made your mind up, you must go," Uncle

Spiros insisted. "Things are bad in Athens now, but they will get worse. The communists are getting stronger. Look what happened in the town of Meligalas. Hundreds massacred, including women and children, and all of them left to rot. And now, with King George on his way back, there will be trouble."

"In that case, how can I leave you all here?" Athena asked.

"Because you must," he answered.

Kuri was quieter than usual the day before Athena's departure. She sat in the corner of the sitting room, smoking one cigarette after another, making only monosyllabic replies when spoken to. It was gray and dismal and bitterly cold the next morning. Athena had only one suitcase, which was filled mostly with music. Kuri was standing in the vestibule when the time came for Athena to leave.

"All my life has been for you, and now you are going to *him*," her mother said.

"Kuri, keep quiet," Spiros warned.

"I'm her mother. Why shouldn't I speak?"

"Because what you're saying is bad. It's evil. What is there for Athena here? She must go to the United States, and that is all there is to it. She is a citizen of that country."

"She is Greek!" Kuri shouted.

"She is a young woman with a promising future that could be destroyed if she stays here," Spiros countered. "There will be war again. Remember that you refused to go on the ship to Alexandria."

"Her place is here with her people," she replied, the lines in her face tightly drawn.

"You forget—Miklos is her father."

"Son of a bitch!" she cawed. Tears welled in her eyes and she shook her head to hold them back. Suddenly she looked a little like the old, prewar Kuri, shoulders squared, head high, arrogant, proud, and willful. She took a deep breath; after letting it out, she put her arms around Athena and hugged her. "Go then. You must go. Go. But you're not to stay in the same house with that whore."

"Mama . . ."

"Swear to me."

"I swear . . ."

"In the name of Jesus, Joseph, and Mary."

"Mama . . ."

Spiros intervened and grabbed Athena by the shoulders, propelling her to the door. "We shall miss the boat," he said. He let go of her to lift her suitcase. "What do you have in here? The Holy Cross?" he laughed.

"Music," she said.

Yanni was standing nearby, hat and coat on. She was going to accompany them, and leaned over quickly to take the suitcase from him.

"My weakness has always been strong women," he said, and smiled ruefully.

"Mama, maybe you'll change your mind and come with us to the boat?" Athena asked from the doorway.

Kuri just shook her head. She went to the front window as soon as the door was closed and watched the three of them get into the waiting taxi. "Tell that son of a bitch and his whore that he has a wife to support!" she shouted at them. But the taxi had already driven off down the street.

Intermezzo

New York,
1945–1947

7. "YOU ARE REALLY A HORNY BASTARD," YORGO PAPPAS laughed as his good friend Mano Zakarias emerged, nude and with a full erection, from the indoor swimming pool at his ostentatious house in Oyster Bay. Upstairs in Mano's bedroom, the beautiful Konstanika Sylvanus—Nikki—had not yet rung for breakfast. She was exhausted, no doubt, by a tour of Manhattan's nightclubs that had brought them all home near dawn, and by the athletic romp with Mano—which Yorgo would have had to have been stone deaf not to hear (his room was across the hall)—that had ended an hour before.

Nikki was only seventeen, the daughter of Konstantine Sylvanus and an English actress who had died when Nikki was five years old. At the outset of the war, Sylvanus sent her out of harm's way to stay with his sister, Olympia, in New York. He had not anticipated Nikki's current sexual appetite, or the ambition and ruthlessness of a man like Manolis Palamedes Zakarias, who would seduce her (without facing much resistance, it must be said) for his own greed and ambition.

Quite simply put, at this moment Mano needed Sylvanus's backing to increase the number of ships in his fleet, and what better way than to become his son-in-law? He was, of course, twenty years older than Nikki. But that, he knew, was part of his attraction to her. The rest had simply to do with sex. Aunt Olympia had kept Nikki in a convent school since her arrival from Greece. It was a lucky stroke, Mano believed, that he was the first man she had met upon her leaving St. Ignatius. It was also fortunate that Aunt Olympia had been called back to Greece at the war's end to spend some time with her ailing mother.

"Not only are you a horny bastard, you're a lucky bastard as well," Yorgo grinned. "What man wouldn't give a ransom to have Nikki whisper sweet nothings in his ear?"

"I don't want to hear sweet nothings. I want to hear sweet somethings—somethings I can use," Mano replied, slipping on his white terry-cloth robe and stepping into a pair of rubber-soled slippers. He was a short, bronzed, muscular man, with amazingly little hair on his chest but dark, thick patches of it beneath his arms and at his crotch. He had unusual navy-blue eyes and a lion's mane of hair that, unless slicked back with water or pomade, fell over his broad forehead and touched his dense eyebrows. His features were too large and irregular for him to be called good-looking. But he possessed a kinetic quality that gave him a vital presence, made his speaking voice compelling, and narrowed his keen eyes into what many women found to be a seductive gleam. His conquests were legendary in his circle, nearly all of them rich or with connections that he needed or simply wanted to make.

Mano was an artist in the game of using important people to further his career, add to his large and growing wealth, and bolster his power. Money, he felt, was only good for buying pleasure and power, and he spent it shamelessly on both. He had little conscience when it came to acquiring it. He was a man who would sacrifice the interests of others to his private ends, and he was extremely cavalier about his methods. Even Yorgo had accused him of not knowing the difference between right and wrong. "There is no right and wrong," Mano replied. "Only what is possible."

He had met the husky, rough-and-tumble Yorgo when they both had been young seamen on one of Konstantine Sylvanus's ships. Mano had signed on so that he could get to Argentina, where he knew a rich older woman whom he believed could help set him up in the cigarette business. He had limited knowledge about the tobacco industry, however, so when that enterprise collapsed he had left the bountiful lady's bed for a woman whose rich husband had run off with her niece. She sold several pieces of good jewelry to finance the purchase of his first ship, which he gallantly named *Ursula* in her honor. Then he packed his belongings. "You're a pirate," she told him when he departed, "but you made me laugh, and I hadn't been laughing much before we met. And at least I know now that my body can respond if properly stimulated."

Mano had been born in Smyrna, on the west coast of Turkey, in the city's Greek quarter—the section the Turks called *ghiaour Izmir*, "infidel Smyrna." His parents had started out as humble, working-class people, but Plato Zakarias passed his own gnawing ambition and need for power on to his son. By the time Mano was of school age, Plato owned two ships. He was on his way to becoming a rich shipping merchant when war broke out between the Greeks and the Turks and the former were driven from Smyrna. Plato Zakarias was murdered along with his wife by the Turks, and his only son, a mere nine years old at the time, escaped to Greece.

Orphaned and penniless, Mano had hustled then as he did now. He saw no other way to make what he wanted of his life. Survival was not enough, and security was a false illusion. Power and money were the only true safe-conducts. And since he was as adroit in bed as in a boardroom, he took advantage of his full talents. His capacity for work and his sexual energy seemed boundless, for to build his one ship into a shipping business meant laboring at it day and night, seven days a week, using money and information he had obtained from pillow-talk the way others use gasoline to keep their cars running. He bribed, played one shipping agent against the other, and went anywhere he found a lead—Paris, Rome, London, Athens, Buenos Aires, New York, always first class. He wore expensive, dark, hand-tailored suits, a fedora hat, rode in limousines, and kept his keen blue eyes hidden behind a pair of large sunglasses, which he lowered and removed, when face-to-face with a woman he wanted to impress, in a practiced gesture that never failed to excite interest.

He came to New York shortly before Pearl Harbor. He grew richer during the war and bought the house in Oyster Bay, with its two white grand pianos (which he couldn't play) in the living room, mirrors and gold trim abounding throughout. What he wanted was to be accepted by Manhattan's social set and the rich emigrés who had escaped the war in Europe. He liked to boast that he knew everyone worth knowing, and it was true: he sought out and managed to meet many of the city's rich, famous, and powerful. But he had no real friends among them. Most saw in him what polite circles often referred to as his "excessive Greek vivacity," which was irritating at the very least. He would snap his fingers or hiss like a snake to summon a waiter, or—as if it displayed slightly more respect—rap a glass with a piece of silverware to call the maître d'.

Yet there was something about Mano—perhaps his intense belief in himself, his flamboyant style, his open disregard for convention—that the very rich found intriguing. And he was almost clairvoyant in his ability to single out women who would be easy prey to his particular charms and at the same time further his business interests.

Although hardly more than a girl, Nikki Sylvanus was just such a woman. Having been separated from her father since she was a child and then cloistered in an all-female school, she was hungry for a man's attention and a father's love. Liberated for the first time from the strict convent life and the watchful eye of her aunt, she was able to fill both these voids with Mano, an ardent lover and a strong protector at the same time. And though he was old enough to be her father, at thirty-seven he was also young enough to be a romantic figure. They had known each other for ten weeks now, the last six of them as lovers, and Nikki had no doubt that Mano was the only man she would ever love. She was grateful that he had been with many different and glamorous women but had not married; she was equally happy that they shared a Greek heritage and that he was in the same business as her father, who under these circumstances could not, she was sure, withhold his permission for her to marry Mano. Of course, he hadn't yet proposed, but Nikki didn't doubt that he would, and her instincts were quite sound.

"I will be going into the city in thirty minutes. Meet me at the office at two P.M.," Mano told Yorgo, who had the title of Associate Manager of Mano's company, Helle Maritime, but whose function could more accurately be described as Mano's trusted right hand and flunky. The two stepped into the small, gilt elevator that took them up to the bedroom floor. "Be sure no one disturbs Nikki before you leave. I've disconnected the telephone in my room. She must get her rest. I'll be back by six. She has it stubbornly in her head that she wants to go to the opera tonight. I hate the opera. Maybe I have a tin ear. No matter how hard I concentrate, it always sounds like a bunch of Italian chefs screaming at each other."

Yorgo laughed while the door opened automatically onto the upstairs hallway. "I think she wants to wear that flashy diamond tiara you bought her. Where else but the opera would it be appropriate?" he said, stepping out of the elevator.

"See how a man traps himself when a woman gets under his skin," Mano sighed. He walked briskly down the corridor to the door of his bedroom suite, carefully opened it so as to make as little sound as possible, and disappeared inside.

The drapes were closed and the room in almost total darkness. Mano made his way cautiously across to his dressing room, leaving the door just slightly ajar before turning on a light.

"Mano?" Nikki called out.

He stepped back into the bedroom. She was sitting up; the small lamp beside her was lit. Her golden hair was tousled, her fair shoulders bare above the ivory satin sheet that she clutched just above her breasts and that outlined the slim curves of the body beneath it.

"You should be sleeping," he reprimanded.

"I need you to hold me in your arms. Then I'll go off just like a baby."

He came over to the side of the bed, still wearing his terry-cloth robe. When she rose to her knees, the sheet fell in a pool of satin around her body. She reached up to untie the belt.

"My," she smiled, "your soldier is already at attention."

"I have to leave here in exactly twenty-eight minutes," he said.

"I should be sound asleep by then," she replied and, leaning toward him, pressed her warm lips to his exposed member. Her hands caressed its base, brushed the short hair that surrounded it, and then inched up over his taut stomach and his chest.

He threw off his robe, swept the sheet aside, and pushed her gently back against the pillows. He stroked her cornsilk hair away from her smooth forehead, kissed the lids of her doelike, amber eyes, the corners of her wide, vulnerable mouth. He embraced each breast and ran his tongue down her body like a cat, then in turn held each of her small, slim feet and licked her carefully between the toes.

"Mano, Mano," she moaned, raising her body toward him. He poised above her and then gently, almost teasingly, entered her.

"Are other men like you?" she asked when they were lying side-by-side a few minutes later. The only light now came from the dressing room and cast a faint trail of gold across the steamy darkness.

"I plan for you never to find out," he said.

"Is that a proposal?"

"Do you want it to be?"

"Well, I don't think my father would think kindly of his daughter creating even a little scandal. But I would stay with you in sin even if you don't propose."

He rolled over on his side and looked hard at the finely carved, delicate face with its surprisingly full and sensual mouth. "I propose," he said.

"I accept," she replied, putting her arms around him and pulling him close to her, folding her body into his as though he was a giant teddy bear. Holding him that way, she fell asleep.

He very carefully removed her arms, slipped out of the bed, covered her up, and tip-toed into his dressing room. From there he went into the connecting bathroom to shower. Never had he felt so alive and full of energy. He had just collected a valuable prize. Of course, he loved Nikki—she was an extraordinary and beautiful young woman with a deliciously mischievous streak and a sensual nature. But he was not at all certain that he would have decided to marry her had she not had a strong commercial and social value, or had he been able to achieve his purpose some other way.

The United States Congress had just passed the Ship Sales Act. Liberty ships were available at the bargain price of half a million dollars, most of it payable over seven years at a ridiculously low interest rate. Mano wanted to buy ten of them, which would make his company, Helle Maritime, a major shipping power. He had raised the million dollars needed for his down payment. The catch was that the ships could only be sold to wartime Allied operators with the approval of their governments. Mano was a Greek citizen and could only buy the ships through the Union of Greek Ship-owners, which was the government's agent. But he had applied to the Union for the right to purchase the Liberties and had been refused. Helle Maritime had never had offices in Greece and its ships flew the Panamanian flag. The most powerful man in Greek shipping and the Union itself was Konstantine Sylvanus, who was buying eighteen Liberties for his company.

Turned down by the Union, Mano conceived a plan to induce Sylvanus to add Mano's ten ships to his own order. In return he would pay Sylvanus a generous bonus and assign him a small interest in Helle Maritime. He considered the proposal a good one and likely to be accepted by Sylvanus, who for over a year had been putting out feelers for a stake in Helle Maritime and its American base of operations. Sylvanus, however, had flatly refused. "I am a loyal Greek and you are a bandit!" he had shouted in his native language over the long-distance line. "These ships are being sold to us because ours were bombed by the Germans while you were making money from our suffering!"

Mano took this very much to heart. Being called a bandit was one thing, to be accused of not being a loyal Greek another. Two weeks later Mano had managed, through friends, to be introduced to Nikki. Four weeks later they became lovers.

A virgin eager to master the rites of womanhood, Nikki was not a difficult conquest. With Mano as teacher she had learned exceptionally fast. What he did not teach her was what he did not want her to know. And although she thought of him as her grand protector, in actual fact he made sure that she had no protection against becoming pregnant with his child. All this month he had counted the days, and now he was sure, even before she was, that Nikki had missed her period. His alternate plan was falling neatly into place.

His first meeting that day was with the president of the New York Bank and Trust, where he signed an agreement pledging two of his ships as collateral for the down payment on the Liberties and some working capital. One of Mano's cardinal rules was never to do business with underlings: It was the top men he needed, men with the power to make their own decisions. They would not turn to a board or a committee for approval. They were expected to know what collateral was worth and whether documents were legitimate. The ships Mano pledged were his oldest, both badly in need of repair and in fact about to be sold as scrap. The appraisal that he gave the bank president was actually made on two of his best ships. It had been a simple matter of switching names on the documents. Mano did not consider this crooked dealing, but rather the resourcefulness of a good businessman.

The documents signed and the check already deposited to his account, Mano went to his office in an office complex on lower Broadway, near the impressive Cunard building. In his suite he could hardly duplicate the luxurious interior of Great Britain's largest shipping and passenger company, with its vast domed hall and murals depicting the voyages of Leif Eriksson, Christopher Columbus, and Sir Francis Drake. But he hadn't stinted on its decoration, which made it bear a great similarity to the Hollywood sets created for Astaire and Rogers in their shipboard movie musicals—and with good reason. Mano had hired one of that studio's top decorators for the job.

His private office was a study in white—carpets, drapes, curved desk, leather couches and chairs, and the ubiquitous white piano (to give prospective clients or business associates the impression that he was a man of many and varied talents). Even the telephones (and he had several lines) were white. Sitting behind his desk, suntanned and wearing a dark suit, he was the immediate focal point of any one who entered, as he was when he moved across the room to make a drink at the mirrored bar. His secretary, a gray-haired, very well-dressed Englishwoman named Miss Dickens, sat at a scaled-down version of his desk directly outside his door. She added what he called "a touch of class to my pirate's den."

"Miss Dickens," he said as she followed him into his office, taking his fedora and his black overcoat with its persian lamb revers and putting them in the closet, "get me Mr. Sylvanus in Athens, and don't take no or tomorrow for an answer. Then call the travel agent and tell them I have to fly to Athens tomorrow and arrive no later than Thursday morning. I don't care how many transfers I have to make to do it. Also call Cartier and ask the manager, Mr. Goldstar, to send down a selection of diamond solitaires today. Nothing under five carats."

"We're getting married, are we?" Miss Dickens asked, her brows arched.

"I am—*your* private life shall, I hope, remain private," he said, smiling, as she left the room.

Five minutes later Sylvanus was on the line. "What is this emergency?" he asked in Greek.

"I have to speak to you about something in person," Mano replied in English.

"If it's about the Liberty ships, there's nothing more to say," Sylvanus answered, still speaking Greek.

"What I have to say to you isn't strictly about business," Mano said, refusing to speak in anything other than English.

"What else could you have to discuss with me?" *English now.*

"Your daughter, Nikki."

"What about my daughter?"

"It's private. You wouldn't want this to be overheard. I'll be in Athens on Thursday. We can talk then. I just want to make sure you'll be there. Otherwise, we can meet in London, Buenos Aires— wherever you'll be at that time."

"What about Nikki? *Scata!* You haven't been seeing her, you little bastard?"

Mano bristled. "So, we'll meet in Athens then. Lunch at the Grande Bretagne at one P.M. on Thursday."

"*Pousti gamimenoi!* If this is a trick of some kind I will kick your ass all the way across Europe and the Atlantic Ocean!" Sylvanus shouted, his voice echoing over the wires. The call was abruptly terminated when he slammed down the receiver, leaving Mano with only static at the other end.

"You're not to let Nikki out of your sight while I'm away," he told Yorgo when he arrived at the office at the appointed time. "Yorgo, I'm going to beat the shit out of Sylvanus. I'm at war with that son of a bitch!"

"It seems like a damned strange way to fight a war—to marry the enemy's daughter," Yorgo said dryly.

"Quite to the contrary. You must have forgotten your Greek education."

"Or you just recalled yours in Turkey," Yorgo responded.

They both laughed good-naturedly. Yorgo liked kidding Mano about his youth in Turkey—the country and the people that were a malediction to the Greeks.

"You know, sometimes I think only a crazy Turk could take the chances you take," Yorgo said, grinning, the gold showing in his large mouth and his enormous black mustache curling upward.

They were interrupted by the representative from Cartier.

The performance at the opera that night was Bellini's *Norma,* which was unfamiliar not only to Mano and Nikki but also to a large portion of the audience. Nonetheless, the Metropolitan Opera House was packed. After decades of near-bankruptcy, the fairly recent Saturday afternoon radio broadcasts from its stage had won it a popular audience. By the time Mano and Nikki drew up in the limousine before the warehouse-like yellow brick structure that occupied an entire block on Broadway between Thirty-ninth and Fortieth streets, most of those holding tickets for the balcony and family circle had already taken their seats in order to see the occupants of the two tiers of boxes, the "Diamond Horseshoe," which were owned by members of New York's highest society, arrive in all their bejeweled and begowned splendor.

Nikki walked by Mano's side, shoulders straight, head held high. "It's heavier than I thought," she whispered to him, pointing discreetly to her diamond tiara. "However does old Queen Mary do it? Hers must weigh a ton, and I hear she's been known to wear *two* at a time," she snickered.

Heads turned as they made their way into their box, a particularly well-placed one with the name "Morgan" on a dignified brass plate to identify its owner. Mano had had to donate a thousand dollars to the Metropolitan Opera Association to have it for the evening.

Nikki was wearing a magnificent green off-the-shoulder velvet gown cinched at the waist by an undergarment that also pushed up her ripe, golden breasts and formed a river of cleavage between them. The skirt swept out in stylish panels, and beneath it she wore silver sandals on the small, perfect feet that Mano so adored.

The emerald-cut solitaire he had chosen for her was in a Cartier box in the inside jacket pocket of his tuxedo, where it was sticking uncomfortably into his chest. Once they were seated he transferred the box to an outside pocket and decided he would give Nikki the jewel at the intermission, along with the champagne he had ordered to be served in the patron's lounge. He hadn't yet told her that he was leaving for Athens in the morning, but he assumed she would be pleased that he was going there to ask her father for her hand in marriage.

The giant crystal chandelier dimmed in the magnificent, spacious hall—which was always a surprise, considering the plainness of the building's exterior. Tiers swept around in great horizontal arcs from the proscenium. Vigorous carved decorations gave a certain rich-

ness to the generously proportioned and handsome auditorium.
Nikki was aware of the eyes looking down upon the glamorous
occupants of the two box-rows from the balcony and family circle,
and she turned impulsively, smiled up to them, and raised her hand
in a simulated royal gesture. Mano pulled gently on her arm and,
giggling, she spun around in her seat just as the lights went out and
the conductor appeared at the podium, a small glimmer of brightness on the music stand before him. There was applause, then
silence, and the overture began.

Ominous music, Mano thought, wondering why he had ever
agreed to bring Nikki here when they could have had a far more
festive evening at El Morocco. He was entirely unprepared for the
opera, which, when the curtain rose, opened on a scene depicting
Gaul in 50 B.C. A large soprano dressed in the robes of a high
priestess began to sing in a somewhat strident voice. A few moments later he dozed off.

When Athena heard that *Norma,* an opera she had never seen
performed, was to be one of the Metropolitan's productions that
season, she saved what little extra money she had so that she could
attend. After confiding this to her father, he surprised her by bringing home three tickets—for her, himself, and Maria Agostina—in
the expensive seats in the first row of the balcony. It was, he said,
to celebrate their being reunited.

Athena had broken her promise to Kuri not to live with her father
and Signorina, who insisted on being called Maria. At first she had
planned to remain with them only until she found a job and could
be self-sufficient. But shortly after her return she began to study
with Maritza Gabori, a former protégé of the celebrated soprano
Lilli Lehmann. A wobble in Madame Gabori's voice put an early
end to her operatic career, so she had turned to teaching. Athena
went to her studio in Carnegie Hall three times a week, and when
she wasn't practicing she helped Maria with some of her younger
students on the piano, which gave Maria a chance to take on more
advanced students for higher fees in their homes.

What Athena earned in this fashion barely covered the cost of Madame Gabori's lessons. But the former opera singer was so impressed with Athena that she lowered her usual fee. ("Never mind," she told Athena, "I'll charge my rich students more to compensate.") She also agreed to arrange a Metropolitan audition for her as soon as she felt she was ready. She gave Athena hope to believe that it would be in the autumn—a matter of less than six months.

Athena was surprised to find her father looking so much younger than the way she rememberd him. His step was lively, he smiled often, laughed a lot, and was a happy man. They had quickly fallen back into the intimacy they had shared before the war. He loved to hear her sing and his dark eyes would sparkle when, in the evenings, she did so just for him, with Maria on the piano. "My two ladies," he would say, beaming proudly.

There was little doubt that he and Maria were deeply in love. Athena now suspected that perhaps they had been lovers for years. Fragments of memories would come and go: Papa passing Maria on the stairs, pausing with some embarrassment before he continued on, she looking up until he had disappeared around the curve of the landing; the small details about their family life that Maria had seemed to know almost as they happened.

Athena refused to sit in judgment of her father. He was happy and not alone, that was all that mattered. Her mother would never have gone back to him even if she had returned to New York. Kuri had been very clear on that point when they were still hopeful of her getting a visa. Once she found out about Maria, she had torn up her application and now never mentioned the idea in her letters, which she sent care of Madame Gabori. Athena hadn't had the courage to tell her mother that she was living with her father and Maria, and instead had led her to believe that she was staying with her teacher.

There was never a question in Madame Gabori's mind about Athena's ability. She had an extraordinary talent. But she possessed a voice and a dramatic facility that were too prepossessing to allow her to be cast in a minor role. She had, in fact, never sung a supporting role. Considering her age this was astonishing, but not as much so as the heavy leading parts she had sung. She would have no difficulty in obtaining a Metropolitan audition for her. The test was whether—despite the fact that she was a prodigy—the company's selection committee would be able to put aside her obvious drawbacks. For the Metropolitan needed leads of international renown to support it. Madame suspected that the committee would suggest that Athena sign with a smaller company, perhaps Chicago or San Francisco, or in Europe, where opera houses were now reopening, to gain a reputation.

Madame Gabori felt this would be a good thing. But Athena was dead-set on an audition at the Metropolitan first, and now, sitting in the balcony and waiting for the curtain to rise on *Norma*, she could not help but fantasize what it might be like to be backstage right now, in one of the star dressing rooms, preparing to step out on that enormous stage in that enormous hall. She was distracted from her reverie when she happened to glance down at the boxes and see this beautiful young woman, a diamond tiara glittering even in the dim light, raise her hand in a majestic wave in her direction. For a moment she thought she might be someone she knew. But, of course, that was ridiculous. She had never made the acquaintance of anyone so obviously rich. She pondered a second on what that would be like—to have money to do whatever she wished, buy whatever she wanted. But then the girl turned, the hall fell into darkness, and the curtain rose.

Athena once again drifted into her dreams, and she was soon lost in the music that filled her head and swelled her heart.

Act Two

Italy, 1947–1955

8. ATHENA MADE HER WAY SLOWLY THROUGH THE GROTTO-like lobby bar at the Hotel Lucca, wondering now why she had ever come to Rome, and yet afraid that if she did not find a place in an opera company soon she would have to leave and return to Greece. It did not surprise her that the group of young Italian men at the bar—their dark hair swept high in the front and kept long in the back, the latest style, and dressed in thin-waisted short jackets and narrow trousers, their eyes predatorily appraising each new woman who passed by, ready for love or money—glanced passively at her. She had been at the Lucca for six weeks and they long ago had discovered she was not rich. She accepted their lack of interest; she was aware that the enormous amount of weight she had gained gave her body and legs a swollen, matronly look. She ate compulsively, out of nervousness, and since she couldn't afford meat or fish, she stuffed herself with bread and pasta.

The last year had been filled with bitter disappointment. Although she reached the final auditions for the Metropolitan, where she insisted on singing *"Casta diva"* from *Norma,* in the end she had been rejected. This came as an incredible shock: she had been so confident that she had done well and that the committee had liked her. Under Madame Gabori's aegis, she then went on to audition for the Chicago Opera Company, only to be rejected again for the same reasons: they were looking for *comprimarios*—secondary singers. Athena's voice was too powerful for these roles and she lacked the experience and name to be taken on as a lead soprano. Madame Gabori then suggested that she return to Europe, perhaps Italy, to make her reputation.

"Americans are insecure, you see," Madame Gabori told her. She went on to explain: "They need to know that what they listen to, whom they choose to see and hear, have already been approved of and are well-known. They want to tell their friends that they saw Lili Pons in *Lakmé* or Ezio Pinza as Don Giovanni. In Italy audiences attend the opera *because* of the opera. They cheer only those singers who meet the highest standards, and they hiss those who do not—whether they're novices or world-famous. Only once singers are celebrated *there,* are they courted by the best companies *here.* One day, when Americans are surer of themselves, that may change. Right now, that's how things stand."

So once again Athena said a tearful good-bye to her father, and with a loan from Maria she returned to Athens, which was still embroiled in a bloody civil war, and once again endured wartime hardships, this time along with her mother's caustic jibes. Kuri could not be mollified when she learned that Athena had stayed with Maria and Miklos in New York. Also, the house had been sold (for a pittance), Taki was dead, and no one seemed to know where Yanni was. This left the mute Serafina, Uncle Spiros, who was in ill health, and Kuri to share a small three-room apartment in a crowded and much less affluent section of Athens. The only good news was that the communists had moved their headquarters out of the city. Although this meant that villages and towns elsewhere in Greece were under fire, Athens was, at least, relatively calm.

Before coming to Rome, she had played part of a season with the Acropolis Theater, but it was so under-capitalized that the productions were embarrassing and she had quit in frustration.

Madame Gabori had sent her a letter of introduction to the great Italian conductor Gian Carlo Capuleti, who lived in Rome. Thus armed, and with her meager earnings from the Acropolis, she arrived in Italy only to learn that Capuleti was in America and would not be back for six weeks. She took a single room at the Lucca, which was near the site of the Theater of Pompey, where Julius Caesar was murdered on the ides of March in 44 B.C. The dust of history was all around, intermingling with the bustling cafés and market stalls that crowded the neighboring streets. Although the Lucca was a small, modest hotel, its picturesque location and ancient setting (the subterranean dining room was, in Caesar's time, part of the backstage of the Theater of Pompey) made it popular with the burgeoning Italian film and literary set and intrigued tourists looking for a bit of "local color."

"God! The way Italians drive!" a middle-aged Englishman, his receding hair ruffled, his full face flushed, said by way of greeting a waiting friend. Athena was walking past their table on her way back to her room.

The seated man jumped to his feet. "Athena Varosoupolos! Is that really you?" he exclaimed.

Athena stopped and stared at the man, who was grinning at her. His accent was American and he was good-looking—dark, well-built, with strong features and brown eyes that fixed a person directly in their gaze.

"Mark Kaden," he said, and then, with an even wider grin, "Kadinsky, Moisha Kadinsky—the Bronx." He grabbed her hand. "You haven't changed since I last saw you. Same big, sad brown eyes and solemn expression. Hell—that would have been before the war. You were hardly more than a kid. I heard your mother took you back to Greece. Must have been tough." His smile faded a little. "How's your Aunt Serafina?"

"Oh, fine . . . fine. Married to a very nice man. A banker," she lied, not at all sure why she said it.

"Yeah? Jeez, that's swell. And you? What are you doing here in Rome?"

"I'm an opera singer. I have a meeting with a conductor."

"An opera singer! Fancy that! Hell, I remember you playing those opera records over and over on your phonograph. Pretty disconcerting when—" He paused, embarrassed, but quickly recovered. "An opera singer! That's wonderful, really wonderful. Hey, sit down. Have a drink with us." He took a chair from an adjoining table, swung it around, and helped her into it. "This somewhat discombobulated gentleman here is John Saybrook, former wartime buddy of mine in Special Services. We made some raunchy film documentaries for the combined armies about the dangers of venereal disease—things of that sort. Now he's co-producer of a movie I'm writing. Variations on a theme, I guess you'd call it, being as more and more it's getting to be about the glorious and still raunchy path to venereal disease!" He laughed sarcastically and glanced sideways at his companion. "It's set in Rome. I'm trying to convince old Saybrook here that it should be shot on the spot." He leaned in close to her, smiling toothily. "Remember? I always said I'd be a writer." He straightened and looked scathingly at Saybrook. "I didn't know then that it would mean taking an express train straight to whoredom."

"For God's sake, Mark, making a few changes in a script doesn't make you a whore," the still-flustered Saybrook countered.

"You probably have things to discuss," Athena said, feeling uneasy with the two men despite (or perhaps because of) the inner excitement she felt at seeing Moisha Kadinsky. "I really have to be going." She stood, smiling unevenly.

"Sure, kid. Well, good to see you," Kaden said, rising to his feet. She turned, abruptly left the table, and continued, hurriedly now, on her way.

She was just about to start up the staircase when she realized that he had followed her. "Athena," he called. She turned. "Those bastard Germans give you a hard time?"

"We survived. But yes, a very hard time."

"Look kid, I don't know what it was about you that stayed with me all these years. Your eyes maybe. I always thought they saw more than most people's. I never felt guilty about Serafina. But I did about you. You were just a kid and she was your aunt." He paused for a moment and stepped a little closer. "She didn't marry a banker, did she?"

"No, the war and . . . what she suffered, it was too much for her," Athena admitted. "She can't speak anymore. She had a . . . terrible experience. She was in a convent for a while after the war, but she lives with my mother in Athens now."

His eyes misted momentarily and he cleared his throat to shake off any trace of emotion. "And you?" he asked.

"Oh, that was the truth. I'm an opera singer."

"Now that I really look at you I can believe it. You are perfect casting for an opera singer."

"Fat, you mean."

"That's me. Brassy Bronx Bozo. Always putting my foot into it. You were a chubby kid. Your size didn't surprise me or strike any bells. No, that isn't it. You damn well could be a diva. Medea, parts like that. You have a Greek aura about you. The ancient, mythical kind, something that makes a person aware of your presence. I felt it the moment I saw you in the bar, before I realized who you were. Hell, yes, you're overweight for a broad your age, but you're still a damned handsome woman, too much woman for those gigolos and *fegelahs* at the bar. You hold your head differently from most other dames, like it's a prized possession. I'm a writer and I see stories in people. Writers have to have a special antenna. We pick things up that others pass right by. You've got a big story in you, kid. Maybe just starting, but a really big one."

He took her hand and gazed into her eyes. Images flashed in and out of Athena's head. She was back in the apartment in the Bronx and she could hear the sounds of lovemaking coming from her room, where Serafina and Moisha, the butcher's son, were fornicating. She remembered sitting at the kitchen table drinking a glass of milk when he came out of the room, smelling heavily of sex, a musky odor intensified by the relentless summer heat. She recalled that he had looked her straight in the eyes then, and she had not been afraid to stare right back at him, but after he was gone she had felt an unfamiliar quaking in the pit of her stomach and a trembling that she couldn't control on the soft inside flesh of her thighs—the same sensations she was now experiencing.

"I think I was rude back there," she confessed.

"No. No, you weren't."

"I was just surprised to see you, that's all. And it brought back memories . . . Things I'd rather not have remembered. Especially now that Serafina is—*ill*."

"I understand."

"Do you?"

"Yes, I do."

He stepped closer to her. He was wearing a spicy aftershave, and his hand moving up her arm was warm and insistent. She removed it with a sudden gesture. "Don't touch me," she said in a firm voice.

"Yes, ma'am!" He saluted in a military fashion, then drew back and flashed a dazzling smile. "Good luck, kid. Any time you want to ring me up, I'll refund your nickel." It was said glibly, a way to ease the tension between them.

She turned and continued up the stairs. He didn't follow, and when she reached the landing and looked down, he was gone. Once in her room she locked the door and then latched it with the security chain. It was not an attempt to lock the newly christened Mark Kaden out, for she knew he wouldn't press his attentions further, but a symbolic gesture at locking herself in.

She would never sell herself cheaply, as Serafina had done. But the encounter with her aunt's onetime seducer (or, perhaps, it had been the other way around) had deeply affected her. Mark Kaden was the first man who had so keenly aroused her sexual interest. Like most girls and young women, she had fantasized sexual encounters and played the flirt. Still, until that moment in the bar when Kaden's and her own gaze had locked, she had not felt herself vulnerable to seduction.

When it came to such matters, she was not a prude. It was just that she had seen young women at the Acropolis, talented singers, fall that way. Their ambition and dedication vanished as soon as they allowed a man—not their music—to be their master. She had vowed she would never permit that to happen to herself. Kaden's brief hold on her had been a frightening experience, hinting at the possibility that, after all, she was susceptible to a man's advances.

The apprehension remained with her all that evening and throughout the night. She awoke with a start several times, imagining that Kaden had broken into her room. In her half-dazed state, she thought she saw him gliding, as if in a dance, toward her. As soon as she turned on the bedside light and reassured herself that the door-chain was securely in place, she realized that what she thought had been a figure of a man was merely the shadow play of the curtains blowing into the room, twitching back and forth on the night breeze.

She fell back asleep and awoke, what seemed mere moments later, to a rapping at her door. She sat up, certain that the sound belonged to whatever she had been dreaming, and she was trying to recall what that had been when the rapping came again.

"*Signorina. Telefono.*"

A strong morning light streaked across the room. She glanced at her bedside clock. It was a few minutes after ten. "*Un minuto!*" she called out. She stuffed her feet into her slippers and pushed her arms into her robe, tying the belt as she shuffled to the door, then lifted the chain and opened the door to a narrow crack. An elderly porter stood just outside, a bored look on his gaunt face. She had a telephone call, he explained, and the caller, a woman, insisted it was *urgente*. He had told her that Signorina Varos had no telephone in her room, so the woman insisted he go and fetch her. And here he was. No, he didn't get the person's name, but it was an international call—the United States.

She smoothed her hair with her hand as she followed him down the staircase to a telephone at the back of the lobby.

"Athena! It's Madame Gabori," the familiar voice wavered and echoed into her ear.

"Is something the matter?" Athena asked. "It must be the middle of the night in New York."

"It's four in the morning and I set the alarm so that I would get you as soon as possible. I saw Maestro Capuleti last night. He leaves for Rome this morning. I told him about you and he said he would see you two days after he arrives. That's next Monday. Three P.M., at his studio. You have the address?"

"Yes, yes!"

"Athena, you must rehearse well before the appointment. I have a former student, Vesta Caspari. She lives in Rome. She doesn't sing anymore, but she knows how to find everything. She will locate a place for you to practice. Her telephone number is six-five-five-nine-zero-five. Have you got that?"

"Yes," she said, writing the number onto a page of a telephone directory close by with a pencil she had pulled from the pocket of her robe. She then tore the page out. "But what shall I tell her?"

"That you have spoken to me, and that I told you to contact her because you need a place to rehearse for an audition with Maestro Capuleti."

"I'll call this morning."

"Is everything all right, Athena?"

"It will be soon," she replied optimistically.

"I hope so. I think you are the most promising student I've ever had. I would feel—yes—redeemed if you should be given the proper opportunity. Oh, and Athena, please don't sing *'Casta diva.'* It's really a most difficult aria for an audition, not only because a fine legato is essential for it, but because you're so vocally exposed that should you begin wrong it will be hard to get back. Perhaps *'Ritorna vincitor.'* Not much easier, but you've sung it so often that you're comfortable with it."

"Perhaps," Athena replied with a half-smile.

As soon as they had said good-bye and hung up, she dialed Vesta Caspari. The woman's speaking voice was brooding and heavy, a contralto—strange for Madame to have taken a pupil of that range. Caspari suggested Athena come right over to her apartment.

"You can work here," she said. "I have a piano, and no one in this building cares much about noise."

*   *   *

Vesta Caspari lived on the top floor of a building in a narrow side street not far from the Piazza Navona, one of the city's liveliest squares. Athena was breathless after climbing the four flights of stone stairs past numerous children playing in the hallway. A drunken man stumbling in the opposite direction almost knocked her down, and when she reached the third floor, two small, yapping dogs threatened to bar her way until a woman appeared from an apartment, scooped them up in her arms, and disappeared back inside.

The door to Vesta Caspari's apartment was open. Inside was a huge, cluttered room, a piano to one side, books stacked high on all the tables and on the floor. Sun streamed into the room through floor-to-ceiling windows. Athena rang the bell and a moment or so later a tall, dark figure loomed into view, blocking the light and filling the doorway. "Athena Varos?" she asked in a distinctive, throaty voice.

"Yes. Signorina Caspari?"

"Vesta. Come in." She stood back as Athena entered, appraising her from behind the half-shuttered lids of her heavily mascaraed dark eyes. "The stairs are a bit much and the occupants a rowdy bunch, but once you do make it—you *are* all right?" she interrupted herself. "I won't have to call an ambulance?"

"I'm fine. Just a bit out of breath."

"A dangerous condition for a singer."

She spoke with an accent, but it wasn't Italian. Hungarian, Athena guessed correctly. She was in her mid-to-late thirties and looked striking: sleekly bobbed hair almost the color of purple plums, sharp cheekbones, and a distinctive nose with a high bridge and elongated nostrils. She was dressed in a black pinstriped man's suit and a tailored white shirt with a richly patterned paisley ascot at the neck. She was not a slim woman, but her height and her amazingly arrow-straight posture made her seem statuesque. Although Athena had not met many lesbians, at least not knowingly, she had no doubts about the sexual preference of the woman standing in front of her.

"There are three nice things about this apartment," Vesta was saying. "One—through that door is a little rooftop garden squashed between the surrounding buildings, but it's a nice garden and it has a magnificent view. Two—no one gives a shit who goes in and out of these apartments. And three—no one cares how much noise is made during the day; there's such a racket in the building anyway." She walked over to the piano, dramatically took hold of the colorful Spanish shawl that covered it, and pulled it off in a sweeping gesture. "*Voilà!* The piano. I'm going out and so I'll leave you to it."

"This is very kind of you," Athena said.

"Anything for Gabori! I'm afraid I caused her a good deal of unhappiness. She put me up *and* put up with me during the war. I shouldn't have left but love—you know about love?"

"Not firsthand."

"That's the only way one *can* know about love. It—she—was Italian. So here I am. Where my love is I cannot tell you because I don't know. Gone. That's all." She smiled broadly. "Don't worry. I'm not sad. She turned out to be a most tiresome creature. No poetry. No sense of humor. Well, if the telephone should ring, don't bother to answer. If someone should come to the door, tell them to go away. If you get hungry there's wine and cheese in the kitchen, which is behind that curtain over there. I'll be back before evening. Stay until then if you like. If not, lock the door when you leave and write me a note as to when you think you'll be back." She had picked up a pocketbook and a manuscript case that were lying on a chair. "I'm currently reading pornographic novels for a publisher. What the hell! It's a living and they're usually quite amusing." She opened the door. "*Addio,*" she said, and left.

The following day, one of bright spring sun and warm breeze, Vesta sat in the roof garden reading a manuscript while Athena practiced. When Athena paused, Vesta came back inside and, staring at her in frank admiration, said, "I would have given my life for a voice like yours." From that time she seemed reluctant to leave the apartment while Athena was there, although she managed to remain as unobtrusive as she could, staying out in the garden or in the bedroom with the door to the living room opened only a crack.

"Should the maestro not wish to help you," Vesta told her on the day of her appointment with Capuleti, "you must not lose faith. Someday people will boastfully say, 'I heard Varos sing.'" She kissed Athena lightly on the cheek.

The great conductor lived in a graceful house, once the rectory of a long-ago demolished church, at the end of a cobblestoned cul-de-sac lined with cypresses and umbrella pines off the *via* XX Settembre, and just a few streets from the smart *via* Veneto. A gray-haired, heavyset housekeeper let her in.

"Signorina Varos?" A young, studious-looking man, wearing horn-rimmed glasses and a loose-fitting tweed jacket, appeared directly behind the housekeeper.

"Yes."

"I am Arnoldo Giobaldi, Maestro Capuleti's secretary. Follow me, please."

He turned and led her across the large, tiled, dark entry hall through a much brighter sitting room to a door at the rear of the house, which opened to reveal a high-ceilinged studio containing two pianos and shelves filled with music scores. Large windows looked out onto a beautiful garden, well-tended and burgeoning with colorful spring blossoms, where even now a gardener was bent over a row of bushes, pruning away the dead branches.

When she first entered, Athena thought the room was empty. But then the secretary cleared his throat and a man appeared from behind a handsome lacquered screen that, she was later to discover, concealed the maestro's desk from the rest of the room ("So that Lucía, my housekeeper, won't complain about the untidy way in which I work, papers all over the desktop and the floor around me," he would confess to Athena).

He was nearly completely bald, short and thin, a man who appeared youthful for his seventy years. He was dressed informally in a pair of dark-gray pants and a cardigan sweater with deep, bulging pockets from which, as the afternoon progressed, she would be increasingly fascinated to see what emerged—pencils, erasers, bits of paper with notes on them, a packet of tobacco, matches, lozenges that he would pop into his mouth every so often, a magnifying glass to help him read small print, and at one point an envelope of fish food that he emptied into an aquarium on a table in front of one of the windows ("The fish quiet my nerves," he was to tell her).

The most striking thing about him was the intensity of his eyes; deep, deep blue, like the sea when a storm is rising, with the brows above them great, bushy thatches of gray, as if compensating for the nakedness of his skull. "Sit down, Signorina Varos. Sit down," he said in a voice that suggested both a habit of giving orders and impatience. "Perhaps you would like a cup of tea?" he asked once she was seated on a stiff leather chair. He was standing near one of the pianos.

"No, thank you."

He nodded to his secretary, who immediately left the room.

"Ah—now we are alone and we can talk. I understand you have come here to have me hear you sing so that if I like what I hear I can help you find a place in an Italian opera company. Let me say right now that Italy is the mother of opera and she has many splendid children singing her music. I am not being pessimistic. But I want you to know even before you step to the piano—you have brought your music?" he interrupted himself to inquire.

"Yes, I have."

"No matter, there are few arias I don't know."

He smiled, smugly she thought, and then realized with somewhat of a shock that the maestro himself would accompany her.

"As I was saying," he continued, "I do not want you to ask yourself afterward, if it turns out that I cannot help you, 'So why did I sing for him?' Remember—always you sing for yourself. Now, let me see what you have brought me."

She stood up, opened the worn leather music case that Uncle Spiros had given her when she left for New York nearly three years before, and, walking over to him, handed him the music.

He glanced down at the pages and then up at her, since she was taller than he was. " '*Casta diva,*' " he said, with a curious shake of his head. "Not the usual choice."

She couldn't tell if it had pleased or displeased him; a masklike expression spread over his face once he sat down at the piano. "Forget me. Forget this room," he counseled. "Remember only that you are Norma and you are singing for yourself, *as* yourself, and that in this aria Norma is dominating the savage, ferocious people she serves as priestess. They are crying out for battle against the Romans occupying their land, and she is struggling against them. Why? Aha! She has broken her vows as priestess, taken a Roman lover, and borne him two children."

He struck a chord on the piano to help her set her pitch, then raised his hand to signal her to begin.

As Athena's voice began to soar and fill the room, Capuleti's expression grew more intense, but she was not aware of him or of the great excitement that seemed to electrify his body while he listened to and watched what he quickly realized was a phenomenon. She had followed his advice and immersed herself in Norma's dilemma, and the drama and emotion she wrung from the aria was almost overwhelming. *This young woman is as good an actress as she is a singer,* the maestro thought to himself. By the end of the aria, he knew that Athena Varos would one day—soon—become a great diva.

He sat in his studio at the piano with her for several hours, testing her range, amazed at its breadth. When Lucía entered the room with a tea tray, complaining about how dark it was and that she was certain to trip and fall, it was with some surprise that they realized the sun had already gone down.

"I will be conducting *La Gioconda* in Verona in August. It will only be four performances, and the pay is very small," he said when she finally got up to leave. "Meanwhile, when I have time, we can work together on the title role. And if you do well in Verona—well, we will take things one at a time."

Athena was so light-headed walking to the *via* Veneto to take a bus back to the Lucca that she nearly stepped directly into the path of an oncoming car. Not until she had returned to her small, cramped room did she realize that she would somehow have to support herself until August, which was several months away. She could no longer afford to remain even in the modest Lucca. After an hour or so of torturing herself with the fear that her lack of money might compel her to return to Athens (and the news from Greece lately had been terribly grim), she went downstairs to the lobby. With some reluctance and trepidation she telephoned Vesta.

"Of course," Vesta replied quickly when she heard Athena's request. "Of course you can stay here with me."

9. Roberto Vallobroso was the senior partner in Verona's leading law firm, which had been founded by his grandfather, but his life revolved around the opera. Not only was he on the board of directors of the Verona Opera Association, but he was generally considered the official host to all visiting artists. A fifty-two-year-old bachelor, he lived with his spinster sister, Grazia, who was four years his junior, in the palatial home that had been in their family for three generations.

"I have invited her to stay here as a courtesy to Maestro Capuleti," he said sharply to Grazia during breakfast on their terrace one warm morning in late July. "It's only for one week, and he would like Signorina Varos to be as comfortable as possible."

"It breaks a precedent," Grazia replied primly.

In their small, dark, slightly almond-shaped eyes and their thin-lipped mouths, sister and brother shared a strong family resemblance. They were also both sparsely built, but whereas his leanness gave Roberto an aura of elegance, especially since he never appeared anywhere, even breakfast, without being impeccably groomed, Grazia's gaunt figure, her flat breasts and narrow hips—and the buttoned-up, unfeminine way she dressed—made a sterile impression. But Roberto's interests had turned him into a far more outgoing person, who, despite what might be described as a set

123

expression of wryness on his face, was known to everyone as a man possessing considerable charm. A clever businessman, a sharp adversary, and a witty observer of people and their foibles, he was a much-welcomed guest, especially when an extra man was in order (and since the war, the demand was great in this category). Grazia, on the other hand, seldom left the cloistered luxury of their home.

They lived together in an atmosphere of chilled harmony. Circumstances, not choice, had made them companions in life. Their parents had died within a year of each other before Grazia celebrated her twentieth birthday, and in their society an unmarried young woman simply did not live alone. Had there been an elderly aunt or a cousin to take care of Grazia, Roberto would have been much relieved; even when they were children he had not got on well with his quarrelsome and boringly provincial younger sister. But at the time there had been no one he could call upon. On Grazia's part, she felt bitter about her reliance on her brother, who had been left the house and the business interests while all she had was a small annuity.

"What precedent are you talking about? Didn't we open our home to the maestro himself last year? And to Francesco Culpi the year before, when he appeared in *Il Trovatore*?" A self-satisfied smile slowly curled the corners of his mouth. "I shall never forget how he held a D-flat for eight beats, three beats after Gasatti ended her own bell-like accompaniment!"

"He was an imperious, conceited man!" she sneered.

"Well, yes—you're right. There's a peculiar form of arrogance that comes only with being an exceptionally handsome man or a tenor who can sing astonishing high notes clearly and strongly. Culpi is both." He was about to refill his coffee cup from a silver pot, but he changed his mind and set it down. "You're being irrational about Signorina Varos. There's no precedent."

"We have never had a young woman here as our guest. Especially one who is unaccompanied," she replied.

"That's a weak argument, Grazia." His chair scraped on the patio bricks as he pushed it back and stood up. "And it's settled anyway. I've agreed with Maestro Capuleti that Signorina Varos can stay here during the final rehearsals and her appearance in Verona. So it shall be. I am a man of my word." He crossed over to the French doors that led out from the dining room. "I've informed Carmelina that our guest will have the room overlooking the garden and that flowers should be placed on the bureau. I'll be meeting her at the train myself. And Grazia, I expect that you will be a most welcoming hostess to our visitor."

He hurried across the dining room, his heels clicking against the tile floor. *Why,* he thought, *was Grazia always so tiresome?* She could not be so absurd as to be jealous of a young woman she had never met. No, it was a matter of possessiveness. As he recalled, she had been in no better humor when their guests had been men. And it was, he decided, about time he did something about the situation.

He paused in the front entry, took out his gold pocket watch, and glanced at it. He was early for his first appointment at his offices and so he told the chauffeur waiting by the door that he would walk. Then he added: "But collect me at five P.M. We are to meet the five-twenty train from Modena, unless there is word that Signorina Varos did not make her connection from Rome."

He stepped out into the brilliantly sunlit July day and set out for his office at a brisk pace. He was much affected by the vagaries of the weather. A Verona drained of sun weighed heavily on him, since he couldn't bear to see its magnificent Venetian-Gothic architecture and piazzas, so dazzling in the bright light, cloaked in gray.

He loved Verona and never ceased to marvel at its beauty. As far as he was concerned, it was as great a city as Rome or Florence or Venice, which, of course, had dominated it politically for many centuries. Due to its strategic position close to the Austrian border, Verona had suffered heavy Allied bombing during the war; there had been even worse desecrations when the Germans withdrew in 1945. Only three years had passed since then, and although the rubble had long been cleared, there were still gaps in the streets where a building or a church had been destroyed, and many buildings had not yet been restored. Yet, miraculously, much of Verona's beauty had survived completely intact.

Verona, of course, had once been home to Romeo and Juliet (and it always surprised him that English tourists seemed to think the story had been completely invented by William Shakespeare). Thankfully, the houses of both the Montagues and the Capulets and Juliet's tomb remained in good shape. And then there was the Arena, big and solid in the enormous Piazza Bra, which could hold 25,000 people if an opera was sold out. Sales were brisk with *La Gioconda,* but nothing like what a performance of *Aïda* could produce. No other opera could compete for massive, exotic decor, for eye-boggling pageantry, a whole province's worth of extras to wave peacock plumes from the vergitinous heights of Egyptian walls. *Aïda* was the ultimate crowd-pleaser. Still, it seemed best to let a few years go by between each production.

He hoped that Signorina Varos had a voice strong enough to satisfy every ticket holder in the Arena; for him, it took both a great voice and great artistry to claim *his* attention. As a young man he had traveled to New York to hear Caruso, to Paris for Galli-Curci, and to London for Chaliapin in a performance of *Boris Godunov.* And now he was in a position to bring some of the great artists to Verona. But since the Arena's budget was not very large, in order to have one celebrated singer per season, the other operas had to be cast with lesser-known and less costly artists.

He took a circuitous route to his offices through winding alleys where once-grand Venetian and Renaissance houses had long since decayed and been split into small working-class apartments. He was in no hurry to reach his destination. Lately he had come to realize how much he disliked his work, how intensely he wished he could retire. *Perhaps in a few years,* he thought. *Time to train a young lawyer to take my place.* He sighed. He had come out on a main thoroughfare only a few streets from his offices. Several church spires punctured the fair, blue summer sky. Verona was overchurched, in his opinion; the steeples and crosses were diligent moral overseers to their enslaved flocks. *Guilt, and fear of the afterlife,* he thought, *have proven to be stronger weapons than those any enemy ever raised.* But his concern was *now,* while he was still capable of living the good life.

"No appointments after four-fifteen, Bernardo," Roberto told his secretary, a young man in his late twenties. Bernardo had been on the telephone when Roberto passed his desk upon his arrival.

Bernardo nodded and then covered the mouthpiece with his hand. "Your sister. She wants to know if you'll be dining in tonight."

"I'll call her later," he said. "No, wait a moment. Tell her I have reservations at Zeno's. When she's off the phone, call and make them. Four or five people. I'm not sure." He disappeared behind the beautifully carved Venetian door that led to his inner office, a large, paneled room with signed photographs of opera singers covering the walls.

Athena had been inclined from early on to believe in premonitions. Her mother could possibly have been responsible for this respect of the occult in her, but Kuri tended to entertain predictions of a tragic or cataclysmic nature that, when they proved wrong, she would claim had only been averted by the hand of God. Athena seldom felt forewarned of failures or disasters, which was why she was so devastated by them when they occurred. In her case it was change for the better, good fortune, that she sensed. When good things didn't happen, *that* was God's hand punishing her. But for what? She was never sure.

The train service in Italy left much to be desired in terms of comfort. Athena's journey from Rome to Verona, a distance of approximately three hundred miles, required three connections, since there was no direct line. She had boarded the first train at half past six that morning, not a decent hour to travel. She was now on the last leg of the journey, from Modena to Verona. Though she had been in transit for over ten hours and should have felt exhausted, she was experiencing an amazing sense of exhilaration. The nearer she came to her destination, the greater the surge of excitement. Something marvelous was about to happen. And she felt ready to accept it, to carry it with her.

She pressed her face against the window. The train was crossing a bridge over the Po River, and it was as if the great, snorting, snakelike vehicle were moving through the air. She tilted her head to see as far down below the train as she could. There had been heavy rain that spring, and even now, in early summer, the river was high and the land around it rich with green and thriving farmland. It seemed incredible that so little time had passed since the war, when the same expanse must have been strewn with debris and the bodies of young men, all brave, all too young to die, whatever side they fought for.

She sighed and turned away, refusing to contemplate such dispiriting thoughts when she was in so happy a frame of mind. In the three months she had been working under the maestro's guidance, she had accomplished more than in all the years since the disappearance of Signora Galitelli. What she had learned from that man! He had taught her the *depth* of music, and she had absorbed as much of it as she could from him. Just a few days earlier, before he had left for Venice (from where he was driving to Verona this morning), he had told her, "Remember, the voice is the first instrument in the orchestra. 'Prima donna' means just that: 'first woman,' the focus of the performance. Now, when you need to find a gesture or how to move onstage, all you have to do is look for it in the score; the composer has already put it in the music. Never move your hand unless you follow it with your mind. And when a colleague sings to you, make it seem as though you are hearing the words for the first time."

It seemed strange, after all her bad luck in America, to feel so good, so right, about the performances she was about to give in Verona. The maestro would be conducting, and that gave her a sense of complete confidence, but she was thankful that she was traveling to Verona alone—she needed the time to herself. What was she to do if *Gioconda* turned out a success, as she was certain it would? She had no money to support herself while waiting for another role. And she had no intention of returning to the living-room sofa in Vesta's apartment.

She had moved in with trepidation, fearful that Vesta might make unwanted advances at her. Vesta quickly put that anxiety to rest. "Fat women don't appeal to me sexually," Vesta told her outright the first night they were alone in the apartment. "It's your voice I'm slave to." But her very obsession at times became so intrusive that it nearly drove Athena mad. "Don't go out in the rain . . . Capuleti is driving you too hard . . . my poor exhausted girl, I'll rub your neck, your back, your legs for you . . . You mustn't eat before you sing . . ." Constant concern, advice, and smothering. And Vesta had begun to insist on knowing when Athena would be home so that she could be there to take care of her.

"If I needed a mother, I would have sent for my own," Athena snapped at her one evening. In point of fact, Kuri had never coddled her, or even made an attempt to do so. But Athena had to say that to Vesta; she needed to be free, to not have someone over her shoulder telling her what to do or how to take care of herself every moment.

She would have preferred to have been given a room at a hotel in Verona rather than in the home of a Veronese attorney and his sister, however rich they might be. But the maestro had made the arrangements, and she would agree to them. She leaned back and closed her eyes. She had been up since dawn but, given her exhilaration, until this moment hadn't realized how tired she was. In a few minutes, influenced by the even clacking of the train and the soft rocking motion of the car, she was lulled to sleep.

She awoke with a start an hour later.

"Verona! Verona!" the conductor was calling through the train.

Athena jumped to her feet, pulled down her suitcase from the rack above her seat, and dragged it to the door. When the train pulled out of the station five minutes later, she was still standing on the platform with her suitcase. She had thought someone was meant to meet her, but perhaps she had misheard. She went to signal a porter to find her a taxi when she realized she didn't know the attorney's address. While she was pondering what to do, a short, balding, rather elegantly dressed man approached her.

"Signorina Varos?" he asked in an accent that she was soon to learn was particular to the region.

"Yes."

"Ah! I apologize. I wasn't sure, I . . . Forgive me." He took her hand, kissed it, and bowed slightly. "Roberto Vallobroso. It will be my pleasure and that of my sister to have you as a guest in our house while you are in Verona." He snapped his fingers and a porter instantly appeared to take her suitcase.

Actually, Roberto had been on the platform looking for "the young opera singer from Rome" from the time the train had pulled in. Considering himself a man with good instincts, he had felt sure that this somewhat unkempt and heavy woman, her hair in disarray, her shoes flat, scuffed, and unattractive (Athena had worn them for comfort on the journey), could not be Athena Varos. He now slipped his hand beneath her elbow and guided her toward his car, his mind preoccupied with how Grazia would react to their guest.

"It's been a long day," Athena was saying. "I was up at dawn. I'm afraid I fell asleep and almost missed Verona completely."

"Well, we would have brought you back," he said in a kindly way. "After all, what is *La Gioconda* without *la gioconda?*"

She laughed nervously. They had reached his car. A chauffeur was holding the door open, and she slid into the finely upholstered interior. Roberto followed. She was suddenly conscious of her mussed hair, and, looking down at her feet, she realized she had not changed back into her dress shoes. "I'm afraid I look a mess," she said.

"Train rides are tedious. Everyone understands that."

He smiled at her and she felt easier.

"I reserved for dinner in a restaurant, but if you think you will be too tired . . ." he began.

"No, no! I think I would like that very much."

"Good. Now, while you are in Verona, you are to think only about *La Gioconda*. I will take care of everything else."

Somehow, she knew he would.

Grazia smiled politely when she greeted Athena. After showing her to her room, she returned to the grand salon, with its painted ceiling and concert piano, where Roberto was pouring himself a drink from a crystal decanter on a silver tray. "I think it might be better to eat at home," she scoffed.

"Not at all. Maestro and Signora Capuleti are to join us. It has been arranged."

"I will remain here, then. I have very little to say to music people."

"Do as you wish. But I reserved a table for five. Nine P.M." He took his drink and the evening paper, which was folded nearby, and left the room.

When Athena reappeared later, she was dressed in a fresh cotton blouse and a full skirt. Her dark hair was brushed neatly into a double bun behind her head. She lacked style—*moda,* something Roberto very much admired in a woman—and she was greatly overweight. But then, of course, so were many of the divas who sang at the Arena. Yet there was an aura about her that could not be ignored. She had the head of a lioness, proud, almost fierce. And then there were her eyes; he thought he had never seen any so dark and piercing. She was Greek, and that might have had something to do with the drama of her face.

Although he usually only attended the final dress rehearsal, he thought he might stop by the next afternoon, when the maestro and the director were to hold a first run-through. He was curious about Athena Varos, anxious to hear her sing, confident that if Maestro Capuleti had chosen her to sing *Gioconda* she had to be very good.

In the end Grazia joined them for dinner. After several glasses of champagne that she drank at Roberto's insistence, she managed to smile now and then. At one point in the evening, when the champagne had gone to her head, she was even so startled by the loud *pop* of a bottle being uncorked that she slipped off her chair, giggling like a young girl. Her brother, who seemed more amused than disturbed by the incident, helped her up from the floor. In fact, Grazia's unprecedented tipsiness delighted her brother, who had never seen her act so unguardedly, and his own mood became one of extreme gaiety.

Athena could not help but notice how relaxed the maestro and his wife were in Roberto's company. He possessed a great talent for playing the host, of amusing people and making them feel that he was sincerely interested in them. Athena had never been to a restaurant quite like Zeno's before, with its luxurious decor, fawning service, and bountiful food. After much deliberation, since there were so many choices, she settled on *bistecca alla fiorentina,* which Roberto informed her came from the special breed of beef found only in the valley of the Chiana, near Florence. When he caught her looking greedily at his pepper-scented dish of *peposa,* a beef stew that he insisted no one could prepare better than the chef at Zeno's, he unobtrusively instructed the waiter to serve her some on a side plate. She had not been in the least embarrassed. The long, lean years in Athens during the war and the diet of pasta that her pocketbook had dictated since coming to Italy, made her hunger for meat.

Athena was impressed with the way Roberto played the part of host. When he discussed music and the opera with the maestro, his knowledge was astonishing. He very adroitly brought Signora Capuleti—a normally retiring woman—and Athena into their conversation, even managing to include his sister from time to time.

Signora Capuleti, an attractive older woman, had shimmering silver hair, pleasant blue eyes, and a generous smile. Despite the fact that Athena had been to the maestro's house so many times, she had only twice met his wife. Signora Capuleti did not like to intrude upon her husband's business or career, and even upon this social occasion chose to smile and nod her head to whatever was being said rather than to voice her own opinion. But as the evening progressed, Athena was taken aback to note that there was something in her glance toward their host—a note of dislike or, perhaps, censure—when he refilled her husband's wine glass yet another time.

"You must forgive me," she broke in, "but I am terribly, terribly tired. The car trip from Venice and settling in to the hotel, I suppose."

"Yes, of course, my dear," Capuleti said, looking at her with sudden concern. "I have been a thoughtless husband. And, of course, Athena and I both have to be at rehearsal at ten in the morning." He stood up and helped his wife to her feet.

"I'll see you both to my car," Roberto offered dutifully, rising as well. "The driver can take you to your hotel and then return for us." He glanced down at his sister. "Well, Grazia, I shall leave you to look after our guest for a few moments."

Farewells were exchanged, and then Athena was sitting alone at the table with Grazia, whose tipsiness had worn off and left her in a state of nervous agitation. "Well, you can see who wears the trousers in that marriage," she commented drily.

"You are mistaken," Athena replied. Grazia was silent but her mouth stretched into a grimace of disapproval. Athena knew she had said it wrong, but she hadn't been able to help herself. She owed a lot to the maestro and, she now suspected, Signora Capuleti as well, and she felt defensive about them. "Great artists often need someone to protect them," she added. She waited a moment, expecting a harsh comment from Grazia, who was gazing off, glassy-eyed, toward the front door, anxiously drumming her fingers on the table while watching for Roberto's return.

The warm, lighthearted mood of the evening had suddenly chilled and darkened. At that moment Roberto reappeared, his step lively, the familiar droll smile on his face as he approached the table. "My, what fascinating conversation have I interrupted?" he inquired. When neither woman answered, he motioned the waiter for coffee, which Grazia refused. "Are you Greek or American?" he asked Athena while the two of them sipped the dark brew in their demitasse cups.

"Sometimes I'm not sure. Both, I guess. I was born in New York, and when I returned there from Athens after the war, I thought I wanted to be American almost as much as I wanted to sing. But now I don't know. I felt a stranger there. A foreigner." She sighed. "I feel I'm a foreigner everywhere I go."

"Poor Signorina Varos," he consoled. "Well, here in Verona, and in the house of Roberto and Grazia Vallobroso, you will be made to feel at home. Right, Grazia?"

Silence.

"Grazia," he chided, frowning, "it troubles my heart that you are being rude to Signorina Varos."

"I humbly apologize." The atmosphere crackled with antagonism.

"My sister has had too much champagne for one not used to alcohol," he said, all charm. Grazia shrugged her shoulders and smiled blandly. But he seemed unaware of anything except Athena's beautiful, smoldering dark eyes, which were studying him with disarming admiration from across the table. He foresaw—as she did the very same minute—that in the near future they would look back on this dinner as the beginning of an important relationship.

Athena awoke the next morning to a light tapping at her door. She raised herself up in the bed and was about to reach for her kimono when a maid entered with a breakfast tray.

"Buon giorno, signorina," she said, placing the tray on the bed beside Athena.

The shutters were closed and the only light in the room came from the hallway, but even so Athena could see that the maid was not a young woman. She was built very squarely; broad shoulders, wide hips, almost no waistline to define the two parts of her body, and short legs. Yet there didn't seem an ounce of spare flesh on her.

"Come si chiama?" Athena asked.

"Carmelina," she replied, and crossed to the windows. She turned a handle beside one to open the shutters. Blinding sunlight splashed into the room, and Athena covered her eyes with her hands. "Oh! *Mi scusi! Mi scusi!*" Carmelina apologized, giving the handle another twist and dimming the bright light.

"Grazie," Athena said. She glanced at the clock on the mantle-piece. It was half past eight; she had to be at the Arena for rehearsals at ten. As soon as Carmelina left, she got up and went into the adjoining bathroom. Never had she known such luxury. The bath-room was half again as large as the bedroom, and covered in black-and-white tiling from ceiling to floor. There was a huge bathtub with a massive white towel folded beside it. While running the water for her bath, she returned to the oversized bed to drink the steaming coffee and hot milk and eat the piece of sweet warm bread, nestled in a starched white napkin to hold its warmth.

She examined the room while she ate. It was pervaded by an air of old-world stability, a feeling that the room now was much the same as it had been a century before. Nothing was new. Indeed, everything appeared ages-old. The wooden furniture, heavy and dark, was burnished from years of buffing. The rugs were worn but woven in glorious designs. A huge pottery bowl with a network of fine cracks held a magnificent bouquet of full white roses, their petals opened wide to reveal their red-splashed hearts.

When she finished her breakfast, she soaked leisurely in the warm tub. She couldn't help but think about her mother, who would, she knew, have been much impressed by the luxury of the Vallobroso house. *No,* she decided, shaking her head. *Mama would have found something wrong. She's the kind of person who wants the windows shut if they're open and open if they're shut.*

She was suddenly sorry that she had recalled Kuri; it made her feel guilty. The news from Athens was not good. It seemed that the bloody civil wars would never end. Food remained scarce and there wasn't much in the markets. Every letter that Athena received from her mother was filled with horror stories about this new ugly con-flict and the terrible struggle it continued to be just to survive. There was always a plea for something—money, cigarettes, a pair of shoes—and complaints that her father no longer lived up to his obligations now that he was with "that whore."

Her blissful mood thus destroyed, she got out of the tub and briskly dried herself. When she turned and looked into the tall, gilt-edged mirror that hung on the wall opposite the wash basin, she was genuinely shocked. She was fat—Vesta had been right about that—and not in the least attractive. She dressed quickly, as though the bloated flesh would no longer exist once it was hidden from view. But suddenly she *felt* fat, and she wondered if Roberto would, like Vesta, find her body in its present state unappealing.

This was a disturbing thought. After all, Signor Vallobroso was just being kind to her. It was madness of her to ascribe any serious meaning to his behavior. And then, he was a few years older than her father, thirty years older than herself. He was balding and not the sort of man a young woman might normally desire. Actually, Athena didn't desire him. She hadn't experienced the flesh-crawling feeling she had when Moisha Kadinsky had touched her arm. Quite the opposite. When Roberto took her elbow and helped her in and out of his beautiful car, she felt she was being guarded, protected in a way she had not previously known. She had been somehow re-lieved that—on her part, at least—there was nothing sexual in his touch.

He was already in the front hall when she came downstairs. "We must hurry if you are to be at rehearsal on time," he said. The car was waiting outside the front door, and he bustled her into it and then got in himself. "The Arena, Mario," he told the chauffeur.

"Are you going to be at rehearsals?" she asked, with some sur-prise.

"I thought I might—for a short time. Would you mind?"

"No, no. Of course, not," she assured him. "I'm never aware of who might be watching."

But, in fact, when the rehearsal began she was conscious of his presence, even though he was seated a good distance from the stage.

10. It grew late, and the sidewalk cafés on the enormous Piazza Bra were crowded with women in formal gowns and summer shawls and middle-aged, paunchy, respectable gentlemen in tuxedos; in a short time, they would begin entering through the main gate of the Arena for the evening performance of *La Gioconda*. While they were filing in from the front, the side entrances would jam with the less-elegantly dressed occupants of the seats in the upper rings.

Athena arrived backstage before sunset, while technicians were giving a final check to the speakers spaced throughout the huge amphitheater. She paced up and down her dressing room, pausing from time to time to glance at the beautiful basket of white and red roses sent to her by Roberto. The day had been scorchingly hot, and the intense heat had made her feel immensely fatigued. By coming early, she thought, she might rest for a bit on her dressing-room cot before the performance. Unnerved by the sight of the vast Arena and the frantic nature of the final preparations for the evening's performance, she was unable to relax or even to remain calm.

The dress rehearsal—the performance critics traditionally review in Italy—had not gone as well as she had hoped. Although inexperienced, the dynamic young director, Ugo Gianni, was in full control and had some wonderful ideas about interpretation. The orchestra under the maestro's baton was excellent. The problem lay in the casting of the tenor and baritone. The two men were not up to the vocal sparring needed to bring Athena's own character dramatically to life, and the critics had made note of it. Roberto had tried to keep the morning newspapers away from her, yet she had insisted on seeing them. Failure terrified her—but to fail because of the deficiency of others was frustrating and infuriating.

In fact the reviewers had not said she had failed, only that the production had not succeeded. *La Gioconda,* they all agreed, demanded a quintet of powerful principals and full-blooded singing from the two lead male roles. This Gioconda was forced to carry the opera solo. One critic ventured that, despite this obvious drawback, "Varos kept the drama alive by the concentration of her singing." He added that, "Her voice is beautiful in tone." Another critic was awed by "the dark and vicious animalistic emotion Varos can command when she dominates a scene, the cutting scorn her voice can evoke, the high drama when she brings her low voice into active play."

Such praise seemed trivial to her in light of their unanimous dislike of the overall production—"except for the excellence of the orchestra under the sure baton of Maestro Capuleti." The critics having had their say, it was now up to the first-night audience for the final verdict, and the pressure and doubts this raised in Athena had turned her into a bundle of nerves. In Italy a hostile audience can destroy a singer's career more effectively than any number of dissenting reviews.

By the time the dresser—a slight, thin woman with small, intense eyes and a tendency to move quickly—came to help her into her first-act costume, Athena was in a frenzy. She accused the woman of deliberately pricking her with a pin, of pulling the waist too tight ("How can I sing if I can't breathe?" she shouted). She railed against the tenor, Vincenzo Boschi, when he came by to wish her well ("We will be hooted and jeered and *you* mouth platitudes!" she cried, pushing the portly singer in his fifteenth-century Venetian nobleman's costume from the room, his indignant curses trailing behind him as he stomped down the corridor). Finally, when Ugo Gianni, forewarned, knocked at her door, she refused to open it.

"Athena, if you do not let me in I will announce to the audience that an understudy will sing your role," he shouted back at her.

This prospect apparently was even more frightful to her than failure, for she threw open the door and propelled herself into Gianni's arms, her face creased with anguish. He stiffened with surprise. "No! No! Ugo! Ugo! I will sing!" she insisted, leaning her head against his barrel chest. A moment later she straightened and, eyes gleaming, grabbed his hand, pulled him into the dressing room with her, and closed the door. "Please don't tell the maestro I've been so *ugly*," she begged.

"Bad behavior has a way of getting around," he said flatly, his voice calm but his gaze searing. "No matter what you may think, Athena, a prima donna does not have license to disrupt the rest of the company. If you had any serious doubts about the production, you've had a week to express them. Such things are counterproductive and could be disastrous so close to a performance. I tell you this because I know at heart you're a true professional. You'll serve yourself better by serving your co-workers well. Whatever you may feel privately about Vincenzo, remember that his character, Enzo, is the object of Gioconda's obsessive love, and in that magical moment in the first act when she sings, 'Enzo adorato,' the audience must feel this passion and hold it in its grasp through the acts that follow."

"He looks at me with the eyes of a dead fish," she moaned. "How could any woman feel passion for something that will end up in a frying pan?"

"You must make the audience believe otherwise. I grant you, neither Vincenzo nor our baritone are vocally or physically what Ponchielli had in mind when he composed the opera, nor are they the singers I would have chosen for the roles if I could have cast it ideally. But the budget was a potent consideration. If you're as

clever as I think you are, you'll try to make the rest of the performers look as good as possible. It will only reflect your own effective-
ness. You understand what I'm telling you?"

"Yes, yes. Of course," she agreed. "But Vincenzo is a glassy-eyed
fish. My God! He even smells like a fish. But I'll look at him and in
my mind he'll be Lauritz Melchior."

A smile stole slowly across his broad face, and he pulled at his
dark, neatly trimmed goatee. "You shall be wonderful!" he told her.
"I've never heard a better Gioconda."

"You mean that?"

"Sincerely." He kissed her on the cheek, patted her on the shoulders, and left. A moment later the dresser reappeared in her room.

"Shall I loosen the waist?" the woman, pale and nervous, asked
timidly.

"No, no. It's fine. I'm used to it now." She thought for a moment.
"What's your name?" she asked.

"Berthe."

"You're not Italian?"

"Austrian."

"Are you married to an Italian?" she asked, having noted the
woman's gold wedding ring.

"I was. I am a widow."

"The war?" The woman nodded her head. Athena instantly suffered a wave of guilt for her earlier, snappish behavior.

Sensing Athena's nervousness, and having dressed many similarly
afflicted prima donnas over the several decades she had worked in
opera, Berthe was quickly forgiving. "You remind me of the great
Selma Kurz, whom I dressed when I worked at the Vienna Opera
when I was a young girl," she said. "Frau Kurz left orders to see no
one but myself for fifteen minutes before curtain. Most people—
even directors—don't understand the terrible tension before a performance." Her voice, soft and rhythmic, was somehow soothing.
"Of course, you have even a more glorious voice than Frau Kurz,"
she added with a sincere smile.

Athena leaned back in her chair and Berthe, without being asked, began to massage the back of her neck and shoulders. "You will bring the audience as one to its feet," she avowed. "You will see."

Since the dress rehearsal had been performed late in the afternoon the previous day, when the sun had not yet set and the audience had been scant, nothing had prepared Athena for her entrance onto the stage of that vast amphitheater, the rows and rows of occupied seats seeming to rise into the starlit August sky. She had never sung before such a large audience, and for a brief moment fear gripped her heart; she didn't think she would be able to utter a sound. She glanced down at the maestro, and when he looked up at her she felt a sudden infusion of life, as if through his gaze the music was being transmitted from his head to her throat.

Halfway through the first act, she had the exhilarating sensation that the audience was entirely with her; her self-assurance took hold, and she was able to fully become Gioconda. She had no idea of how electrifying the audience found her high-voltage performance. The range of her voice, from the high reaches of the dramatic soprano to the seemingly bottomless sound of contralto richness, stunned them. But it was the powerful quality of her acting that was the greatest surprise. The rest of the cast was perhaps only slightly better than at the dress rehearsal, yet her performance was so riveting and believable that the production suddenly came alive. Several of her arias received standing ovations. In her final scene, when Gioconda thrusts a knife into her heart and sings *"Volesti il mio corpo, demon maledetto,"* her voice lunged thrillingly to an A-flat on the last syllable before she fell dead in a heap, the footlights so close to her that the heat they exuded almost overcame her.

As she lay motionless on the floor of the enormous stage, the throb of her heart felt like a drumbeat in her ears. Beyond the footlights, in the vast space of the Arena, the moon and stars momentarily dimmed by shifting night clouds, there was a terrifying and confusing silence. Athena feared the worst. They had not liked her last aria. The drumbeat filled her entire head; despite the warmth of the air that entombed her, a sudden deathlike chill pervaded her body.

The footlights were turned off, and in the darkness Athena rose. Then, after a breath, the audience, almost as one (as Berthe had promised), jumped to its feet with screams of *"Brava! Brava,"* and the shouts and applause and continuing *brava*s went on for nearly ten minutes.

Athena took numerous curtain calls, but the note of hysteria in the wildly enthusiastic clapping and cheering unsettled her at first. Then she began to absorb what it meant.

Verona had passed its judgment. From this one performance, she had become a *prima donna assoluta*.

Sitting in her dressing room only moments after her last curtain, while Berthe hovered about her, Athena experienced a tidal wave of ecstasy that crested over her head, then thundered down and almost drowned her in waves of euphoria. Feeling suddenly quite dizzy, she leaned forward and held her head in her hands. "I didn't dream it, did I Berthe?" she whispered, her voice seeming to have deserted her. "They truly liked my Gioconda?"

"Loved it, Signorina. You were a great success."

"My knees were shaking when I died. I thought I truly was dying. Did you see the audience? How did they look?"

"Signor Gianni likes to keep the wing area clear. I only managed a glimpse. You were already collapsed on the stage and there was a hush over the audience. *Silenzio.* I think they believed you were really dead!"

Athena laughed, a kind of soft giggle. From the corridor outside, the sound of approaching footsteps and the excited voices of a large group of people could be heard. Athena paled.

"Well-wishers," Berthe assured her. "Shall I tell them to wait?"

There was a knock at the door. "Athena? Are you ready to receive?" It was Gianni.

She was seated at her dressing table, still in costume. She leaned forward, mopped the perspiration off her forehead with a handkerchief, and then nodded at Berthe to open the door.

"Mia cara! You were sublime!" Gianni placed his hands solidly on

her shoulders and looked at her reflection in the mirror. "And you saved my ass," he murmured sotto voce.

A crush of people, mostly young men, was pressing in the doorway. "*Brava!* Varos!" someone called out. "*Brava!*" Others joined in. Athena didn't recognize the faces.

"Fans," Gianni whispered in her ear. "Stag fags."

Athena was not sure what to do, but at that moment Roberto shouldered his way through the group and, once inside the dressing room, turned around and announced in an authoritative voice, "Signorina Varos will be out shortly." He then shut the door in their faces and came over to Athena. "You were dazzling," he said. "Brilliant. Never have I heard *La Gioconda* sung that way. I know now. Ponchielli meant for her to be a lioness, fierce in her battle for those she loves." He took her hand and kissed it.

"I feel like I've drunk a magnum of champagne!" Athena declared.

"Ah! Champagne! Exactly what we'll need. Shall we go to the Tre Corone?" Roberto turned to Gianni. "The entire cast is welcome, of course as my guests."

"Perhaps Athena should rest tonight," Gianni advised.

"Yes, yes! You are right," Roberto agreed. "But one or two toasts will help her sleep, don't you think?"

"What about what I think?" Athena broke in.

"Yes, certainly," they both said in chorus.

"What would you like to do?" Roberto asked.

"Have some champagne here, backstage, if that's possible."

"A splendid idea," Gianni concurred. "We'll let you change, then we'll meet in fifteen minutes backstage." He took Roberto by the arm and started toward the door.

"I would like to ask the fans who came to my dressing room door to join us," she added.

"They won't expect that. You can greet them and sign a few autographs if you like. Nothing more is necessary—or customary," Gianni said.

A self-satisfied smile slinked across Athena's face. "Perhaps. But I would like to hear the sound of their *bravas* one more time."

When she came out of her dressing room she was surprised to find about twenty young men waiting for her. They shouted their *bravas* and pressed close around her, carrying her along with them down a long corridor and up a flight of stairs to the rear of the enormous stage, where Gianni, the cast, crew, Maestro and Signora Capuleti, and Roberto had already gathered. The moment she reached them she slipped aside and took Vincenzo Boschi's arm, then reached up and kissed him on the cheek.

"Ah, Vincenzo!" she sighed dramatically. "It's you I have to thank. You made Gioconda come alive for me. Your Enzo tore the heart right out of me."

The stout tenor turned red and then smiled. "You will be a great diva one day," he promised.

Roberto leaned in close and whispered to her, "You are a great diva right now." He looked at her closely and saw that her face was brightly flushed and her entire body quivering with life and feeling. He also realized that she was on the verge of happy tears but would shed none. Instead she smiled at him, then raised up her hands to smooth back her already smooth hair, a touch of her earlier nervousness in the gesture. "I want to talk to you tomorrow about your future," he said.

"My future?"

He grabbed two glasses of champagne that had just been poured and handed her one. "Yes," he began, an engaging lilt in his voice. "I believe it will need to be managed carefully."

At that moment someone raised a glass in a toast, and one of the young men who had escorted her from her dressing room took Athena's arm and gently wheeled her over to meet some of his friends. From where Roberto stood, Athena was in full view; he watched her through narrowed, appraising eyes.

"Varos has great charisma," said Gianni, who had just moved up to him. "Don't you agree?"

"It's in those soulful eyes, the lioness's head, the aura of drama that seems to envelop her," he replied, as if thinking aloud. "Every once in a while singers come along whose audiences talk for the rest of their lives about having seen them, if only once. Caruso was one, Chaliapin another. And now Athena Varos. What she has in common with these others, besides an extraordinary voice, is a kind of magic, an ability to possess the stage as if it belongs only to her."

"Do I detect envy in your words?" Gianni asked.

"Admiration," Roberto shot back.

"Ah, Roberto! I know you better than that! Somehow you see your own fantasy future reflected in her glory. And I cannot help wondering, my friend, how you will make it come true." He was considerably taller than Roberto and glanced down at him with a bemused smile. "Poor Athena," he cooed. "She doesn't know the avarice fame inspires. One day she will, perhaps, but not until its jaws have consumed some flesh, eh, my good friend?"

Roberto didn't reply. Moving briskly, he started across the room to where Athena was laughing with her admiring flock.

Athena awoke the next morning with Ponchielli's music still ringing in her head and with no idea what time it was. The shutters were closed. She rose sleepy-eyed from the bed and crossed to the windows and let in the light. The sun was high and she realized, even before she stumbled back to the mantlepiece to look at the clock, that it had to be nearly noon.

Indeed, it was five past. She couldn't recall ever sleeping so late before. But she had been exhausted from the emotion and the excitement of the previous evening, and the champagne must have knocked her out. For the moment, she couldn't recall undressing for bed, or even returning to the house.

There was a light tap on the door and she belted her kimono. "*Buon giorno!*" Carmelina chirped as she entered from the hallway with a tray.

"*Buon pomeriggio!*" Athena replied with a laugh. She stepped aside while Carmelina placed the tray on the bedside table and then, bowing slightly, left her alone.

Along with her breakfast, there was a note under a vase that held a single white rose. *Could we have tea this afternoon?* it read. *Mario will be at your service until then. He will drive you to my offices. I am still glowing from the dazzling light of your performance last night. Roberto.*

Now she recalled the wonder of the previous evening. It had been a successful debut and she knew it. Of course, there had been her seasons at the Acropolis, but they couldn't compare to an appearance at the Verona Arena in an opera under the baton of a great conductor like Capuleti and before an audience of over twenty thousand people. It was curious, she thought, that Grazia hadn't been with Roberto for the opening night—his sister was making no secret of the fact that she disliked his opera friends. Athena could only speculate why, and to her it seemed to be a simple case of possessiveness. Brother and sister lived together in a kind of hostile familiarity that reminded Athena of the atmosphere her parents had once lived in. Remembering her encounter with Grazia at Zeno's, she wondered about Roberto's obviously deep sense of loyalty and devotion toward her.

When she was dressed she went downstairs to find Grazia. She was going to tell her that she had some errands to run, but was relieved to learn that her hostess had left for noon mass and hadn't yet returned. Athena would have loved to have gone shopping in the chic shops along the *via* Mazzina, but she had very little money and would not be paid for her performances until the end of the week. Instead she had Mario drive her over for some coffee and less expensive souvenir-hunting in the market square, the Piazza Erbe, where she bought some postcards and settled herself down under the sun at an outdoor café, watching prams, proud mothers, and the few tourists (mostly French and Italians, but some Germans as well) go by, and to admire the waiters' adroit manipulation of self and trays through the narrow spaces between tables. In the square, beyond the colorful café umbrellas and shop awnings, were market stalls filled with foods, flowers, postcards, toy gondolas, and religious keepsakes.

She sipped at a cup of thick coffee and shifted her glance to the blank back of a postcard depicting the very square in which she was sitting. She was poised, pen in hand, to write a few words to her mother and Uncle Spiros, but she was unable to think of what she wanted to say. Well, that wasn't exactly the truth. There was much she could tell them about—her success last night, Verona, the luxury of Roberto's home, her hopes for her career. But it all seemed inconsequential when she remembered what hardships her family was bearing in Athens.

Just before leaving Rome for Verona, she had received a long letter from Uncle Spiros, the first news from him in several months. Written in a cramped hand, the thin blue paper had been covered with what at first glance looked like chicken scratches. Athena had made several unsuccessful attempts to make sense of it, and now she took it out of her pocketbook, where she had slipped it before leaving Roberto's, to read it through once again. She moved the coffee cup aside and spread the paper smooth before her. Shading her eyes from the sun, she began to read.

Uncle Spiros wrote that the situation was still grim and that the war did not look as if it would end soon. Most of the fighting was in the mountains and villages, where the guerrillas and government forces were locked in battle. Even in Athens, there were few families that had not lost some close relative. Uncle Spiros went on:

So many Greek men, women and children have died that our country has been mortally wounded. When peace finally does come, I cannot see how we can ever be the same. Still, dear Ati, there are things that never change. One is my love for you. That is why I write to tell you never to come back here, even when the guns are stilled and people can live normal lives again. I am too old to protect you and your mother would devour you whole. The years of hard times have only made her more bitter. She blames your father for everything and will never be content until that poor man is dead. She will try to make you responsible for what she sees (through in-looking eyes) as the wrongs that have been done to her.

I was so proud to learn that you are studying with the great Capuleti. Ah, I would give the rest of the days of my life to be with you the night you open in Verona. I have managed to find a re-

cording of La Gioconda *and play it over and over on the phonograph, which I recall with misted eyes seeing you seated before, lost in the beauty of the music to which you were listening.*

There has been no change in Serafina's condition, but she seems happy living in her own private world. (So, perhaps, are we all.) There has been a rumor that Sofia Galitelli is dead. How or when, no one seems to know. Still no word from Yanni. But why am I writing you all these sad things? This must be a happy time for you. It is all I wish each day upon awaking.

Tears filled her eyes while she carefully refolded the letter and replaced it inside her purse. To distract herself she got up and wandered through the stalls. She bought a *panna montata*, whose creamy richness satisfied some inner need of hers, and she ate it greedily. She bought a second and took it back to where Roberto's car was waiting for her. It was too early for her appointment, so she asked Mario to drive her down by the river. And there they remained inside the car for nearly an hour while she looked at the water, with its unusual, swift currents, and at the towers of the fourteenth-century castle on the other side, and gave her mind over to more immediate thoughts than the struggle her family was having in Athens.

She had only three more performances of *La Gioconda,* and so only three more days in Verona. The question was—then what? The money she would receive would last a very short time, especially if she did not go back to Vesta's apartment. Roberto's note had said they would discuss her "future." What, she wondered, could that mean? Perhaps he was going to see if he could get her a contract with the Arena. That would certainly help, but only as a stopgap. And since the Verona Opera depended on visiting artists to draw audiences, she might well be asked to play small roles. She was aware that Capuleti was the star attraction in this production. (UNDER THE BATON OF MAESTRO CAPULETI was written above the title and the cast on all the advertising.) She decided she would decline such an offer of assistance from her host.

What if it is a personal proposal? she asked herself, and then quickly dismissed such a foolish idea. After all, she had met Roberto Vallobroso less than a week before and knew very little about him. He was middle-aged and still unmarried. It seemed there had to be a story there. Perhaps a mistress, a married woman. Maybe a great love he had lost in the war. And then there was Grazia. Surely he must feel responsible for his unmarried sister.

"Time we should go, Signorina," Mario said over his shoulder.

"Yes, of course. It's fine. We can leave," she acquiesced. She would soon know whatever it was he planned to tell her. What she had to remember was not to act like a foolish girl or an artist without any business sense, for once again her psychic powers had been awakened. The something good she had thought was coming her way when she was en route to Verona, she now believed, was not the *Gioconda* performances, but her meeting with Roberto Vallobroso.

He had set up an elegant tea on the balcony directly outside his private office, which in itself was most impressive, with its many shelves of leatherbound books, the awe-inspiring collection of signed photographs, and the massive desk with papers so neatly stacked upon it. "This is the perfect time of day for August," he assured her as he led her through the French doors and drew a chair back so that she could sit down. "The sun still high, but a soft evening wind beginning to rise. Sit down. There! Are you comfortable?"

"Fine."

"Warm enough?"

"Yes, quite."

"Not too warm?"

She couldn't help but laugh. "No. Fine. *Really*. And the view! Verona is a beautiful city."

He sighed and sat down across from her. "Ah, yes! And always a poor sister to Venice."

"I've never been to Venice, so I couldn't be a judge."

"Never been to Venice?" he said, startled. "Well, we will have to rectify that, won't we?" He poured her a cup of tea and offered her a pastry from a selection on a china plate. It took her a moment or so to decide on which she would have. He waited patiently. "You eat and I'll tell you something about myself," he said.

She suddenly became self-conscious, lowered her fork to her plate, and sipped her tea.

"I am fifty-two years old, not exactly an old man, but at an age where new opportunities don't often present themselves. I am also a bachelor by choice. My heart has been pledged since youth to the opera. Circumstances have prevented me from leaving Verona. There was my family business, my sister, then the war, for which I was considered too old to serve. Instead, I helped in the defense of my city."

Her attention to him was complete. He was fascinated by the way she sat slightly forward on the edge of her seat, eyes riveted on his face, her lips parted narrowly as though she was sipping the air. He reached out and placed his hand on hers. She did not pull away. He strained to keep his emotions in control, to appear concerned but businesslike, while all the time there was a gripping anxiety in his chest and he was thinking, *Oh my God, I must not say this wrong. How I need you! If ever I am to have the life I know I was meant to lead—I must get you to believe in me!*

He smiled at her. Above her head, the sun was blazing so pitilessly in his eyes that he had to blink. He glanced down for a moment and grasped her hand tighter. She still did not draw away.

"For years now," he continued, shifting his position to avoid the glare of the sun, "I've done my duty, what has been expected of me as a son, a brother, and a loyal Italian. Until you entered my world less than a week ago, I thought the *real* Roberto Vallobroso, the man who secretly has music in his very heart, was condemned to vicarious pleasures and to a career of bloodless briefs and legal documents, to a life that made little difference to anyone and brought no beauty to mankind."

He released his hold on her and stood up, then paced back and forth just once before turning back to her. "Athena," he said, his voice intense and strong, "I have decided that I will—if you agree—commit myself to you and your glorious voice. You do know that you possess a gift of the gods?" She reddened and was about to utter a denial when he rushed on. "Yes! A gift of such magnitude that it must be carefully, tenderly, and astutely nurtured. You are young. How old are you?"

"Twenty-three."

"That gives you perhaps fifteen years before your voice develops a wobble or you suffer a throat affliction. Once a soprano enters mid-life, she becomes a member of an endangered species. This means you must dedicate the next ten or fifteen years to spreading the word of your gift, to putting it on record"—he stepped in closer—"to making you, Athena Varos, world-famous. To do that you must have someone behind you who knows how it can be done."

He sat down and took her hand in his again. He was holding it so tightly that Athena had to control an involuntary wince of pain. Yet she didn't attempt to loosen his grasp. She was caught up in the fervor of his words, unsure what it was he was trying to tell her, what he might be proposing, and terrified that any wrong move of hers, anything that might break his train of thought, could cause him to change his mind before she even learned what he wanted.

"I helped negotiate this silly contract you signed to sing in Verona. Did you have an agent or a lawyer look at it for you?" he asked.

"No. The maestro said . . ."

"The maestro!" he released her hand and stood up again. "Everyone must look after his or her own interests. I respect Capuleti. But for him to have his name over the title and the largest share of the pie, he had to be the only recognizable name in the production."

"I can't believe that," she protested.

"You had better begin to see things in their true light. What I'm suggesting—and please understand, I've been up all night considering this, whether it was right for me or fair to you. I propose that I become your agent and manager. You, of course, could argue that

I've never done anything like this before, I've never represented an opera singer. I would agree. Still, I know a great deal more about opera than most agents, and even more about contracts—after all, they have to hire lawyers to interpret the legal terms."

"I don't think I know what to say," Athena began. "Am I to understand that you want to take me on as a client?"

"No, Athena. As my life's work. If you say yes, I'll leave my firm and handle you and your career exclusively. This isn't altruism. I will be part of a world I've always wanted to enter—and at its top, for you are going to be one of the greatest stars the opera has ever known. I promise you that. And, dear girl . . ." He sat down again, this time taking both her hands, but more gently, into his; he raised them to his lips and kissed the opened palm of each. "You shall have all that is your heart's desire."

Her breath caught; at that instant she was certain he was about to propose marriage. A confusion of thoughts whirled through her head. The deeply sensual feelings she had experienced with Mark Kaden were absent here, a fact that eased rather than compounded her emotional chaos. *If he asks me, I'll say yes,* she thought, and leaned toward him with eager attention.

"I would like to draw up a paper between us that puts me legally in charge of your career," he said. He looked into her pale, uncomprehending face, not understanding either what she expected him to propose or her disappointment when he did not. "Don't say anything yet," he begged. "Think about it. Think hard about it. Consider the advantages of a manager who is astute at contract law and who will have no divided loyalties, no other clients, who is prepared to be your torch, your protector, and your truest confidant. We would be working as a team, and my only commitment would be to you and your career. You see, I'll turn over the firm to my junior partners and leave Verona to travel the world with you, if that is what is required to make you the supreme among all divas—*la Divina.*"

Athena was so startled by what Roberto had just said that for a moment she sat as though in a trance. Her eyes widened and her lips trembled; she wanted to speak—she had so much to ask—but found herself incapable of uttering any sound at all.

"It will be all right, Athena. Please believe me," he insisted. He smiled, stood up, and began to pace again, pausing before her from time to time to make a point as he spoke. "First we will decide where your next engagement should be and then we will pursue it. Whatever time it takes, you needn't worry. I'll advance what it will cost for you to live comfortably. I also want you to start thinking about your appearance. You are a very beautiful woman. But you don't capitalize on it. You must have new clothes. A hair with style. Would you agree to let me go forward with such plans?"

"I don't see how I could say no," she managed to say.

"Then, that much at least is agreed. Yes?"

"Yes."

He took her by the hand and walked with her to the balcony railing. The setting sun was shining on the city's rooftops and turning its many church spires into glowing columns of light. "Verona is where I was born," he said, as though to himself. "But why choose only Verona when one can have the world?" He sighed and then turned to her, smiling broadly. "And why settle for less when you can have more—oh, so much more?"

Why, indeed? she thought.

11. Roberto was greatly disturbed at the sight of Ugo's profile on the pillow beside him. It was a young, handsome face, sharply drawn, striking in the strength of its features, its broad cheekbones, the immaculate trim of the goatee that framed his finely curved mouth. But it was Ugo's tense expression that drew Roberto's attention. Ugo had been his lover long enough for Roberto to recognize when his highly intelligent mind was straying onto dangerous ground. He did not like the look in his lover's eyes as they stared up at the bedroom ceiling in Ugo's apartment on the Piazza Sant'Anastasia, near the river. For many months they had been meeting here late at night.

Roberto had been homosexual all his life, but because of his great charm and attraction to women, and the burden of having an unmarried younger sister, most of Verona did not suspect his secret. He had never been foolish about the men in his life. Male prostitutes disgusted him, and sexually he never ventured out of the circle of men whom he knew could not—like himself—afford to have the dark side of their lives exposed. This had always meant spending a great deal of time and effort in keeping his affairs covert, making sure they were well-cloaked and free from suspicion, and building his image as a self-sacrificing bachelor, devoted to his sister.

In earlier days his sexual relationships had been limited to when

154

he was traveling to distant cities and foreign shores, but the war made it necessary for him to become celibate if he didn't want to risk exposure, arrest, or worse. Since then, his involvement with the world of the opera had provided him with both a safe subterfuge and access to men who shared his interests, often needed his help, and also valued their privacy. No better arrangement seemed possible.

Only once in his life, years before, had an affair touched his heart. Like most of the others he had been in, his relationship with Ugo was mainly based on sexual compatibility. Roberto considered the act of sex an art. He was extremely proud of the length of time he could hold an erection, and always demanded he be the dominant one. This seemed to excite the partners he chose. Ugo was no exception, but for the last few weeks Roberto had sensed an apathy on his part. Now, as they lay nude, side-by-side after orgasm, Roberto detected something cool, almost hostile, in Ugo's attitude.

"What's wrong?" he asked. "Not satisfied?"

Ugo continued gazing into the smoky darkness through which the dim lights from the adjoining room cast faint shadows. "No, but not because your technique is slipping."

"What is that supposed to mean?"

"Just that I'm beginning to yearn for more than textbook sex. Also, that your interest in Athena Varos unsettles me."

"Jealous of a twenty-three-year-old girl? You disappoint me, Ugo."

"Heaven forbid! But you fawn over her as though wooing her is part of some grand scheme you have. What's behind it, Robbie?"

"You've no right to ask me that."

"You won't give me an answer?"

"I don't think I have to," Roberto grumbled.

Ugo reached over and clicked on the bedside lamp. He drew a cigarette from a pack on the table, lit it, and then pushed his large body up into a sitting position. "As you know," he said, his eyes watching the smoke he had just exhaled snake its way toward the ceiling, "I am the last man on earth to question the ethics of someone else's actions. I found out long ago that however tormented a man is, he has only to take action and he'll find peace. You've been agitated both times we've met this week. Tonight you made sex by rote, but the agitation was gone. It seemed fair to assume that you had come to a decision."

"Perhaps," Roberto said impassively.

"I hope you don't plan to seduce Athena. Innocents are not fair game to men like us—especially when the motivation is self-serving and not what it pretends to be."

Roberto got out of bed with a suddenness that caused it to shake. He disappeared into the adjoining bathroom without a word, but he left the door ajar.

"I was a walking time bomb until my first homosexual relationship," Ugo continued, his voice raised to make itself heard over the sound of running water in the bathroom sink. " 'So that's it, Ugo, my boy,' I told myself. 'You're a fucking queer and could be sent to a concentration camp along with the Jews if someone rats on you!' That was during the war, of course. You haven't forgotten how it was for us queers during the war, have you, Robbie?" He laughed grimly. "My war was over when it ended. Yours, on the other hand, is still raging." He sat wrapped in thought for a moment, drawing on his cigarette, watching the smoke fog the air around him. The water had been turned off, and he shifted his gaze to the bathroom door, where he caught a glimpse of Roberto.

"Underneath that veneer of charm is a frightened foot soldier, Robbie," he declared.

It didn't seem to matter to Ugo that Roberto wasn't responding. His gaze grew keener as he stared across the distance from the bed to the bathroom. He was unraveling thoughts that had been tangled in his head for a long while, and now he was experiencing a sense of release while he spoke. "Whatever you've told Athena about your intentions, it damn well hasn't been the truth, and you know it," he continued.

Roberto stood in the doorway, a white towel wrapped around his well-bronzed naked body. The towel ended at his knees to reveal the shapely, muscular calves that he was extremely proud of and exercised daily to maintain. He eyed Ugo with unconcealed fury. "My interest in Athena Varos is pure and sincere," he asserted between drawn, white lips. "She's a great artist, and I can help to bring her to the attention of the world."

"Bullshit, Roberto! You plan to bugger her just like you buggered me! No rear entry? Bullshit!"

Roberto stormed back into the bathroom, slamming the door behind him.

Ugo crushed out his cigarette in the overfilled ashtray. He got out of bed and, the naked flesh on his large body shaking, strode over to the closed door and pushed it open.

"Get the hell out of here!" Roberto shouted, pulling up his trousers.

" 'I don't do that kind of sex,' you told me the first time. Like hell you don't. But only when you're on top. What have you told Athena? That is, other than that you can make her a world-renowned diva?"

"I've been one hundred percent truthful with her," Roberto replied indignantly. He took his shirt off a hook on the wall and put it on.

"She knows you're a fag?"

"I find that term offensive. But, no, I did not discuss my sex life with her. Ours is strictly a business relationship."

"Do you really believe Athena isn't nurturing a notion that you're in love with her?"

"Of course not."

"You can lie to yourself, Robbie, but you can't dupe me. You've used all your smooth older-man-can-teach-you-much-and-help-you-much charm to woo her, just as you did me. In my case, you gave more than you took. I had lost any romantic notions I might have had long before I met you. So I got a contract at the Arena and some good sex. But Athena? What you plan to do is to ride her star and steal whatever you can from her."

Roberto gave him a hard look. He tried to move past him, but

Ugo blocked the doorway. "She thinks you're going to marry her," he said.

"She thinks nothing of the kind," Roberto snapped. "Now move aside."

After a moment's consideration, Ugo did so. Then he watched Roberto sit down on the edge of the bed and methodically put on his stockings, braces, and shoes, a ritual Ugo had often watched over the last several months. Roberto always left his apartment shortly after they'd had sex.

"Doesn't it even slightly weigh on your conscience that you'll probably destroy her?" Ugo finally asked. "And you'll do so to satisfy your own hunger, not, sure as hell, to make her dreams come true."

"Put some clothes on or go back to bed," Roberto said curtly. "You never look your best with a limp prick."

"I asked you a question."

His laces tied, Roberto stood up, tucked in his shirt, and crossed to the chair where his jacket and tie were draped. "You have no right to ask, but I'll tell you anyway. I have no intention of proposing marriage to Athena Varos. If she believes that in her youth and innocence, she'll quickly learn otherwise."

"Maybe, but the contract between you has already been signed. Athena is now completely dependent on you to advance her career."

"That, of course, is true." Roberto walked over to the door and started down the corridor that led from the bedroom to the living room. Ugo grabbed a robe from the foot of the bed, slipped it on, and followed him. When they reached the front door, Roberto turned back and the two men exchanged a cold, knowing look. This was the end of a relationship and, perhaps, the start of an enmity that would cost both of them dearly.

"You're too arrogant, Robbie," Ugo said. "You think you have the right to make all the decisions for the people in your life. But eventually Athena will make her own, just as I have tonight. This thing between you won't work out. She'll want sex and love in the bargain, and she'll realize soon enough that what you have to give her is simulated. You're an aging man dying of hunger and thirst for what you haven't got, and you think Athena will get it for you. What she doesn't know yet is that there are hundreds of Roberto Vallobrosos but only one Athena Varos. She's not self-confident yet. But when she is, I hope to hell she has the courage to save herself."

"You know, your problem, Ugo, is that you've seen too many operas," Roberto sneered. He lifted the latch, opened the door, and immediately became another man—suspicious, somewhat nervous, almost timid. He stepped out into the darkness of the communal hallway and, keeping to the shadows along the stair wall, made his way noiselessly down the rough tiled steps to the entry guided only by the light coming from the opened door of Ugo's apartment several flights up.

Ugo stood looking over the iron railing on his landing, a perceptive and sad smile on his intelligent face, and watched Roberto cautiously leave the building. Perhaps Ugo had not been able to rescue Athena; he had, on the other hand, ended a relationship that had become most tedious.

It was past midnight by the time Roberto made his way up the Piazza Sant'Anastasia, keeping close to the buildings so that he could feign going into one should someone approach. It was his habit to walk over to the Piazza Erbe, which was still filled with people at this hour, and take a taxi home from there. That way, if Grazia was awake when he returned, he could always say he had been having coffee with a friend and hadn't realized how late it had grown. But these subterfuges and excuses deeply irritated him, and he no longer had any patience for Grazia. Not only did his work bore him, but Verona was becoming a prison and his sister was his warder.

A young couple, laughing and singing, turned the corner onto the street he was walking along. He ducked his head down. *What right,* he thought as he picked up his pace and cut diagonally across the road to avoid them, *does Ugo have to be my conscience?* None. There had been no commitment, and he had more than recompensed Ugo for his company. Ugo, of course, was a vastly clever young man, and eventually he would have made it on his own. There was little doubt that he would soon outgrow Verona and go on to become a celebrated stage director. But Roberto had helped accelerate the process by recommending him to the board at the Arena last season when Ugo had only some minor provincial productions to his credit. Well, that affair was over—so be it.

Of course, his relationship with Ugo had not been without its rewards. Ugo was extremely intelligent, maybe too much so for his own good. He was also a fine musician with a shrewd insight into the librettos he directed. His association with Ugo had brought Roberto closer to understanding opera from the inside than he ever had as a fan. Oh yes, he had learned much from Ugo in the course of their affair, and now he could put that knowledge to good use. It seemed to him that everything that had happened to him in his life had led up to this, his next move. He had to leave Verona with Athena. Grazia, of course, was a serious problem, but at first he would say he was simply going away for a month or two on business. There was their widowed cousin in Modena, Maria Rosa Lambertini, whom he helped out financially from time to time. He would invite her to come stay with Grazia.

By the time he reached the Piazza Erbe, his step was sure and his confidence fully returned. His spirits were so high that he decided to stop for a coffee. The young man who served him was especially pleasant and moved away from him with a lilting stride that emphasized the neat curve of his ass. Roberto laughed lightly to himself. A surprising thought had just come into his head. A way to have his cake and to eat it, too. He left the waiter a few extra coins, hurried to the gate at one end of the piazza, and flagged down a taxi. He was anxious to get home; the next morning, the first day of his new life would begin.

*　　*　　*

Athena was still having difficulties accepting the amazing sequence of events that had taken place since the successful close of *La Gioconda*. Roberto had insisted she go to a spa on Lake Constance in Switzerland for several weeks to rest and lose some weight while he set her career in forward motion. At the end of her stay, she returned to Rome, robust and ten pounds slimmer, to a small but charming hotel suite in the elegant Cavalieri Palace. Roberto had a room on another floor.

When she voiced her concern over the amount of money he was spending on her, he laughed it off and said, "But, my dear, precious songbird—you will very soon be able to repay me many times over." Less than a fortnight later, with the maestro's enthusiastic backing, she had been cast in the Florence production of *Norma*, replacing Regina Tetta, a singer who was well-known for the role but was said to be suffering from a prolonged throat problem.

For the next five weeks, Athena labored day and night with Capuleti, an accompanist, and the director. They worked at the maestro's home, then at a rehearsal hall with the whole cast. The technical demands were enormous. Norma was on stage for nearly three fourths of the opera, whose unique power, as the maestro kept repeating, lay in the way each aria contributed to the development of the story and in the recitatives that blended and embellished the arias. In a very short time Athena had to master the breath control and stamina required by the role, the sustained high notes, trills, scales, and the difficult bel-canto ornamentation. Throughout, flights of lyricism segued, often without a pause, into dramatic outbursts. And so she would detain the pianist long after the rest of the cast had gone home for the day, while Roberto would linger around to escort her back to the Cavalieri Palace late at night.

She was so obsessed with the role and preparing for it that Capuleti feared she might fall victim to exhaustion—or, worse, to an affliction similar to her predecessor's. "No, no!" she insisted whenever he suggested she take time off to rest her voice. "It will never be as good as in my mind, but I must try to make it so."

During this intense period of study and rehearsal, Roberto remained at her side when she needed him but never pressed for her companionship otherwise. He ordered meals to be served in her room and made sure they were filling yet not too fattening. A masseuse appeared in her suite every evening after her rehearsals to help her to relax her taut muscles. She looked upon Roberto as one might a rescuer. Her faith in him strengthened as her reliance upon him grew.

Dear Uncle Spiros, she had written to her one confidant, *I am madly in love with Roberto Vallobroso, who is older than Papa. Can this be wrong? I know that he loves me and that he's as confused about our relationship as I am. Mama, of course, would only be interested in the fact that he is rich. Her approval won't solve my dilemma. Yours could.*

Spiros replied that she had little to lose by waiting, at least until her career was more secure. He added that men—particularly Mediterranean men—did not like to be pressed.

Now, as she rested in bed in her hotel suite in Florence, with its windows overlooking the Ponte Vecchio, the city's oldest bridge and the only one not destroyed by the Germans during their retreat four years before, she pondered her present situation. She sat propped up on several pillows. The door clicked shut behind the maid, who had just removed her breakfast tray. Spread out before her on the satin coverlet were the reviews of her performance in Bellini's *Norma* at the Teatro Comunale the previous evening—all praising her skill and concurring that her effect upon the soul of the spectator had been hypnotic.

She had longed and longed to play *Norma*; now that she had, it seemed both fated that she do so and yet a miracle that it had actually happened. Roberto had been persistent in his efforts to convince the maestro and the Teatro Comunale that she could carry such an important role, but she had been certain that she wouldn't be offered the part, especially not so soon—only four months—after *La Gioconda*. And *Norma* was a major production, under the baton of the maestro and with a supporting cast made up of singers far better known than she was.

She dressed leisurely and carefully. Roberto had promised to take her out for lunch. She still had seen very little of Florence, but she liked the few people she had met at the Teatro Comunale; none of them was her age, but they were all friendly and talkative. It being a cold, bleak November day, the Arno beneath the Ponte Vecchio was dark and surly, and the statues and lampposts along its banks were cloaked in a gray mist. Even Brunelleschi's great red Duomo, which could usually be seen above the city's rooftops, was shrouded in a dismal fog. She could only imagine the great beauty of Florence aglow under the sun. But she couldn't keep her mind off her own excitement—about tonight's performance, which she wanted to make even more powerful than last night's, about the marvelous luxury she was now enjoying, about the almost dizzy sensation of realizing that she was a recognized singer, about the wonder of having a man as worldly and intelligent as Roberto taking care of her.

It was impossible for her to believe that he wasn't in love with her. Despite her uncle's advice, she was determined to force an admission from him. Although she knew she could not just come out and ask him to declare himself, playing the coquette was not her style. And what did she really expect of Roberto?

This last question gave her great pause. It suddenly occurred to her that though she considered herself madly and deeply in love with Roberto, she had no real sexual urge to have him make love to her. What she felt for him was of a more romantic and—*yes*—comforting nature. She was terrified of the kind of impulses that someone like Mark Kaden aroused in her, or the uneasiness she had experienced with Vesta hovering nearby. Roberto made her feel more, not less, herself; his every thought seemed directed toward making her the person—the performer, the singer—she had dreamed of becoming since her childhood.

Their relationship was far different from the one between her mother and father; it more closely resembled what she sensed was the driving force behind the Capuletis' marriage, although in their case it was *she* who was devoted to *his* success. Athena was unsure why she felt romantic rather than sexual passion toward Roberto, but she was convinced that the latter would grow out of the former once they were married.

And that was almost a fait accompli as far as she was concerned. Now she had to convince Roberto of the rightness of it. Subtly, of course—*very* subtly.

To Athena's disappointment, they had lunch in the hotel dining room, which was cavernous, with its arched ceiling and frescoed walls, and close to empty. "Can't we try one of the jolly-looking restaurants we pass on the way to the Teatro?" she asked as they were standing in the entryway waiting for the maître d' to appear.

"That had been my intention, but there's a cutting wind outside and it looks like rain, perhaps even sleet. I'm not letting you take any chances on coming down with the flu. Maybe tomorrow?" He turned to her, a fond smile on his lips. "We'll have many tomorrows, *mia cara*." When they were seated and he had ordered an aperitif, he leaned across the table toward her. "You read the reviews I sent to your room?"

"Yes, they were flattering, but I prefer it when you send me roses," she said, surprising even herself with her sudden courage.

"You make fun of me," he laughed. "I like that."

"I didn't mean it that way," she said, coloring.

"Athena, perhaps it's time I said something I've given much thought to." She lowered her eyes in embarrassment, and he placed his hand under her chin, raised it, and looked deep into her eyes. "*Mia cara,* how I love you, and how I should like to tell the world about it. Every morning I wake up and I think—this will be the day. I will ask Athena to marry me."

His sudden avowal so startled her that she went pale.

"Yesterday I thought, 'I shall give her my mother's diamond necklace and emerald ring as a token of my intentions.' But then last evening I stood in the wings as you sang and looked out at the audience. They all seemed to be reaching for pieces of you, and I knew then that this was not yet the time, that I must hold my passion however my heart aches with the strain."

The waiter approached with their drinks and he fell silent until the man had withdrawn.

"Your career is not yet solid enough and you don't understand its full importance. You're young. You want roses and *bravas*. You're in a hurry for everything. But we have much to do to establish you internationally. Both of us must concentrate on accomplishing this aim. Then, *mia cara*, we can talk about what I believe is in both our hearts."

Athena was staring at him, slightly frowning, a forced smile on her lips. "You're right, of course," she admitted with chagrin. "But Roberto—"

"Yes?"

"Since I know now that you love me and you seem to be aware that I love you, couldn't I wear your mother's emerald ring, even in private?"

Roberto exploded with laughter.

"Is it that funny?" she asked, an injured expression on her face.

He instantly collected himself and reached across the table for her fair white hand—which, as he went to cover it with his own, he realized was larger than his. "I will talk to Grazia first and then you will have the ring." He straightened up and withdrew his hand. "Now, good news for you. Capuleti has agreed that you will sing Brunnhilde in *La Walkiria* in Venice with him next season. It was not easy to convince him; it is a role perhaps even more difficult than Norma, and he wasn't aware that you had ever sung Wagner. I told him about Athens, the Acropolis Theatre, and the demand of the occupying army for Wagner and other German composers. But, of course, since it will be sung in Italian you won't have a language problem.

"You'll work together as you did on *Norma*," he continued. "He'll help you prepare for the role. It's a major engagement, Athena, with much publicity. From there we can go to Milan, Paris, New

York." His eyes gleamed, and for once the wry set of his face was replaced by a genuine look of pleasure.

Athena was as instinctively thrilled about what he was telling her as she had been when she heard him say the words, *I love you.*

"We'll see the world, *mia cara,* from the stages of the greatest opera houses," he concluded.

She smiled with affection and delight, for she was experiencing both, but at the same time there was a flutter in her chest, no more than the wings of a butterfly pausing to rest on a leaf. A thought had come to her mind: he had never kissed her, and at this moment she felt a desperate need to make physical contact with him. She reached out, grasped his hand, and pressed her lips passionately to his palm. He drew back with surprise.

Oh God! she thought, *I'm no better than Serafina!*

He made no comment but signaled the waiter for the menu and then, all experienced charm once more, made a great fuss about what to order for lunch. The conversation turned to Wagnerian singers, the genius of Wagner, and the regime—*work, practice, work, and more practice*—that stretched before her.

The maestro and his wife, Editta, were relaxing in their home in Rome one evening a few weeks after returning from Florence. The maestro had spent the entire day in his studio with Athena and an accompanist, and Editta had done her best to entertain Roberto Vallobroso. "Gian Carlo," she began, her wide hazel eyes thoughtfully scrunched up. She rested the sewing she had been doing on her lap. "What do you honestly think about Roberto Vallobroso?"

"He's a shrewd businessman."

"I mean, what do you think he really wants from Athena?"

"Editta, who can tell about people? Are we always sure what to expect from those close to us?"

"Do you trust him?"

"In that he will honor, without question, whatever contract he signs on her behalf, yes."

"Am I hearing a note of suspicion?"

"I think she's going to marry him."

"So?"

"He's queer."

"And you don't think she knows that?"

Capuleti looked up over the top of his wire-frame glasses. "In the back of her head somewhere, yes. But she's young and still vulnerable and he's mature, hungry for great wealth, and ambitious."

"I thought he was rich," she commented with surprise.

"By Veronese standards, which I don't believe are his. I think he wants to make sure the goose is really golden before he marries her." He got up from the deep armchair in which he had been sitting and stirred the dying fire with a poker. "See how the flames flare up and then die down if the draft is wrong or the logs are damp? So many things can go wrong before a fire catches, even when the first flames are truly intense. Vallobroso knows that."

"And Athena?" his wife asked.

"Ah, Athena. I think I shall never see another young singer as gifted as she, or as determined. How a girl from a musically unsophisticated family, and raised in an atmosphere devoid of operatic tradition, could have the instinct for such incisive musical interpretation is a mystery. Less of a mystery is her tremendous need for fame and approval. And she deeply believes that Vallobroso can win these for her."

He sat down again and stared into the fire for a few moments. "I don't think she has ever read her contract with him, or she wouldn't have signed it. I made him show it to me so that I could be sure he had the authority to make decisions for her. He has complete power over her money as well as her career. A crafty man."

Editta trembled. "Well, I don't trust him. He's far too slick and charming. Somehow I wish Athena had never met him." She sighed. "I very much like that young woman and she seems—oh, I don't know—*bruised*. For all her ambition and determination, she seems like a victim to me. Easy prey for a man like Vallobroso. He has eyes like a cobra."

"What do you know about snakes?" her husband asked, laughing.

"Enough to get out of the way when one is about to strike," she replied.

Suddenly the fire sputtered, and Capuleti got up again to stir it.

12. During the same weeks that Athena was to sing eight performances of *La Walkiria* at Venice's La Fenice theater, Capuleti was also preparing Bellini's *I Puritani* to run for the same length immediately afterward. The two companies arrived eight days early so that they could rehearse on the spot. The maestro had worked Athena hard in Rome (although, perhaps, no harder than she had worked herself), and she was looking forward to spending some time with Roberto and seeing a bit of the much-vaunted wonders of Venice, a city he knew well. She was also eager to sit in on a few of the rehearsals for *I Puritani*.

The opera was rarely performed, even in Italy, because so few singers could cope with the vocal demands of the role. This production was to star the great coloratura soprano, Gina Macarso, in the leading role of Elvira. Although Athena knew several of the arias, she had never seen a production or heard a full recording of *I Puritani*, and so she was pleased to have this opportunity. Two days before her own debut in *La Walkiria*, she and Roberto sat in the back of the theater during Macarso's first full rehearsal.

The coloratura was a surprisingly frail woman with auburn hair, dark, wood-sprite eyes, and pale white arms and hands that moved in a flutter at times, as though she might somehow have wandered in from a production of *Swan Lake*. She was famous for her trills and the bell-like sound of her voice. To Athena, who was listening intently to Macarso's opening aria, it seemed that the coloratura was holding back, something she didn't approve of in a first rehearsal, because unless you sang full-voice, neither you nor the rest of the singers in the cast got a clear view of the problems to overcome or the potential that could be achieved.

During the moving aria, *"Che la voce,"* Macarso appeared more dazed moving across the stage than the libretto required of her. Athena straightened in her seat, sensing that something was wrong, and watched with growing concern as the ethereal singer, dressed in a loose, flowing chemise, stumbled, regained her footing, took two tentative steps forward, and then collapsed unconscious in a heap on the stage. The billowing fabric of her chemise settling down on her seemed as though it was devouring her.

Mass confusion followed, and no one was able to assess how seriously ill she might be. Athena started toward the stage, but Roberto held her back. A doctor was called, but before he arrived Macarso regained consciousness and asked to be helped to her dressing room. At this point, the rehearsal having been suspended, Athena and Roberto left the theater.

The incident unsettled Athena and fueled her own mounting fears of a possible catastrophe that could keep her from appearing in *La Walkiria*. Of course, she was healthy and strong and the possibility of such a calamity seemed farfetched. Still, she could not help harboring such thoughts. Even simple ailments like laryngitis, an earache, or a nosebleed could force a singer out of a production, and this engagement was vital to her career.

As she was dressing for dinner in her hotel room that evening, there was a knock on the door. She tied the sash of her kimono, went to open it, and was surprised to see Editta Capuleti. Although Editta had accompanied her husband to Venice, where they had rooms in the same hotel as Athena, she had never sought her out before.

"I'm so sorry to intrude," Editta apologized as soon as she entered. She wore a soft gray tweed suit that almost matched her eyes and hair, and the lilac scent of her perfume seemed suddenly to fill the room. "Gian Carlo wondered if you would be able to meet him at the theater as soon as possible. I'll take you there myself."

"But I have to go to dinner," Athena stammered.

"Yes, I know. You mentioned it earlier. But Roberto will understand, and this is very important," Editta persisted.

"The maestro isn't ill?" Athena asked, suddenly concerned.

"Oh, no. It's Gina Macarso, poor woman. They think she's had a minor stroke. They've taken her to the hospital."

"How terrible! But what can I do?"

"Well, of course, *I Puritani* is in danger of being canceled, and there is nothing to replace it. Please come—Gian Carlo will explain."

Athena suspected that she would be asked to extend her performances of *La Walkiria,* and she would rather have discussed it with Roberto before seeing the maestro. But you didn't say no to the maestro, and in any case she didn't know where Roberto was at the moment, so she threw on some warm clothes while Editta Capuleti waited downstairs. Before going, Athena left a message for Roberto, who was still not in his room, telling him where she was.

The two women walked at a brisk pace, mostly in silence, across the open piazza where the hotel stood and along the narrow path to the theater, only a matter of two streets. It was mid-January and there was a cold chill in the air; Athena pulled up the collar of her coat to protect her throat. Night was approaching, and the water in the canals looked dank and dismal. *Why,* Athena thought, *am I constantly in cities that lose all their magic in the bleakest months of the year?* Roberto had told her so much about Venice that she had been eagerly looking forward to seeing this city of magnificent churches and palaces floating on water, blazing with color and light, and filled with art treasures. But since they had arrived there had only been rain and cold winds, and a decadent gray light washed over everything.

As they approached the partially darkened theater, she had the sudden thought that *La Walkiria* might also be in danger of cancellation. She felt immediately distressed by the idea, but by the time she and Editta had gone around back and entered by the stage door, she dismissed it as irrational. All the dressing rooms were empty; the rest of the company had obviously left for the evening.

Capuleti and the accompanist he had hired for rehearsals, Luigi Ramacco, were waiting for her in the lighted orchestra pit. "Athena," the maestro said, "I remember once hearing you sing *'Che la voce.'* Could you sing it now with Luigi?"

"But I only used it to vocalize. I don't think it would please you much," she replied, surprised at the request.

"Let me decide that," he said.

She was confused: He had asked her to hurry over to the theater to sing an aria from *I Puritani* that she hardly knew. But why? It fleetingly crossed her mind that he might have her in mind as Elvira, but since the role was not only difficult but in another range than her own, she rejected the thought.

The maestro was impatiently waiting for her to do as he asked, so she removed her coat, threw it over the back of a chair, and went over to Luigi at the piano. He was an especially personable young man, very close to her in age, with a thick mane of red hair and a smile that revealed a small cleft in his chin. He gave her the music and played a few bars to help her warm up.

"You can begin," the maestro commanded after a few minutes.

And she did. She had not actually studied the aria, and it was not an easy piece to sing. The voice had to be part oboe, part clarinet. Elvira, the character singing it, had to seem aware that she was in danger, and the aria had to be sung with a lavish amount of vocal color; it had to be authoritative as well as touching and delicate. Not a simple matter. She recalled what Ugo and Sofia Galitelli and the maestro had all told her about paying attention to the phrasing required by any score. Luigi followed her voice well, his backing instantly intuitive to her pauses and accents.

When she finished, Capuleti came over to her and placed his arm around her shoulder. "Look, Athena, I know this is a great deal to expect of you, but you are going to sing both *I Puritani* and *La Walkiria*."

"I can't," she managed, taken aback, and began to recount all the reasons—and more—why she had so quickly removed the idea from the realm of possibility. "It's ridiculous—my voice is too heavy to sing Elvira, Maestro," she said, her tone pleading for clemency. She was filled with a sudden fear that to attempt something as ambitious as singing two such entirely disparate roles in succession would end up in disaster. "No, no. I just can't," she repeated, her eyes revealing her inner conflict.

"I guarantee that you can," he insisted.

"But I only have six days to learn the part, and at the same time I have Brunnhilde on my hands."

He drew her aside, sat her down, and pulled a chair up close to hers. "Athena," he began in an intimate and yet commanding voice. "I grant you, there are probably no less similar two roles. Elvira is one of the highest coloratura roles in opera and Brunnhilde one of the most dramatic. I can't think of a singer beside the great Lilli Lehmann who has ever sung both roles, and that was in the last century. Never having heard her, I can't say how well she managed it. But from the first time I heard you, I was astonished by your range. You are able to reach and sustain the high notes of Elvira's arias as well as the deep, dramatic sounds demanded of Brunnhilde. Right now, your top notes are not always beautiful. But they can be, I know it."

He drew closer to her, lowering his voice so that only she could hear. "Luigi will help you. You are well prepared for *La Walkiria*, so you will concentrate most of your efforts on *I Puritani*. If in rehearsals I see that Brunnhilde is suffering because of Elvira, we will cancel *I Puritani*. All right?"

She knew it was a gamble, and that losing it could cost her dearly. If she failed, if she was poorly reviewed in both operas, her momentum would be lost, and she didn't know what it would take to regain it. Of course, if she succeeded . . .

She sat nervously looking over the orchestra pit's rail into the obscurity of the auditorium, whose tiered rows of plush red seats, etched in gold gilt and encircled with jewel-like lights, seemed almost unreal, a vision of a golden past.

She was confused, not knowing what to do, and wishing the maestro would give her more time to decide. But she understood that he had to make an immediate decision, that there was no other singer he could call upon on such short notice to sing Elvira, and that a season with only one opera, *La Walkiria,* was not what Venetians expected of the maestro. "I'll do my best," she finally replied. Without realizing it, she placed her hand over her heart, which was beating so hard that the sound filled her ears.

"Good!" Capuleti cried. He grabbed her hand and kissed it.

At that moment Roberto climbed onto the stage in front of the huge oval hall and shouted down to the orchestra pit, "Maestro! What is this about?"

"You go back to the hotel with Editta," Capuleti whispered to Athena. "I'll deal with Roberto." He patted her on the shoulder and stood up. "Luigi will be ready to work with you at nine tomorrow morning, so don't stay up too late. You're very precious to this company—and to me."

She looked back over her shoulder as she and Editta were leaving the theater by way of the hall itself. The maestro had come up on stage, and the two men were talking. She couldn't help but note the anger in Roberto's voice. "Why wasn't I informed first?" he thundered.

She hesitated before continuing, worried that he would be angry at her. But she had left a note telling him where she had gone, and she had no way of knowing what was to transpire once she reached the theater. She went directly to her room at the hotel. When Roberto joined her later, eyes dark and an expression of displeasure on his face, he castigated her for not telling the maestro that she had to speak to him before anything could be discussed.

174

"He hoped to play on your sympathies, and he did," he said as she nervously toyed with the string of pearls, a recent gift from him, around her neck. "Well," he added, beginning to smile, "I have managed to work it to our advantage. You are to receive the same salary as Macarso for *both* operas, and the star billing. You are also to be transferred to a larger suite for your comfort while you are in Venice."

"I'm truly comfortable here," she protested, still unnerved by his initial disapproval.

"It's less than the accommodation given Macarso. I refused to hear of it," he told her with a touch of arrogant pride. "You're a star, Athena, and you must begin to live and act like a star."

She worked long, exhausting hours with Luigi to learn and interpret the score, but doing that left her unable to work with the director on the libretto and action as intensely as she would have wished. In dress rehearsal she was still not sure of her blocking, and simply prayed that she wouldn't move in the wrong direction onstage. The news that she was to play both Elvira and Brunnhilde had been leaked to the press several days before their debut by Roberto, who was hopeful that the gamble would work and bring Athena wider attention. When she succeeded brilliantly in both roles, the unique accomplishment was hailed in newspapers throughout Italy, and word of it quickly reached the other opera centers of the world.

It was the turning point of Athena's life. She was not only internationally famous but courted by every major opera house. Roberto was working on a tour and a lucrative record contract. Not being things she took much interest in, she left all such business matters to him.

He was now so occupied with contractual arrangements that he couldn't assist her with the less pressing details of everyday life. And so they decided she needed someone to help her shop for a wardrobe that would enhance her public image, and to deal with the many letters, invitations, and requests for interviews she was now receiving. Athena was nervous about hiring a stranger and so suggested Vesta Caspari, who not only had style and a fine education but was "of the music world." Roberto agreed, as he did again when Athena asked that Luigi be brought to Rome as her private accompanist. She was now a star with a personal entourage.

The only thing left to make her life complete was Roberto's agreement to get married soon. Sure now that Athena's career was under way, he set the date for June 16, still several months off. He needed time to settle things for Grazia, to finalize the contracts he was negotiating, and to buy and furnish an apartment in Rome as their home base.

It's finally happening! she wrote to Uncle Spiros. *I am to be married to Roberto!*

But it was Kuri who replied, telling her Spiros was very ill and that the doctor did not think he had long to live. Being Kuri, she added: "Now that I have a rich daughter, perhaps my life can be made a little easier."

Roberto agreed that Athena should go to Athens to see her family. Despite the week of sadness since she heard about Uncle Spiros's serious illness, she was visibly cheered when she boarded the train for Athens. On her finger she was wearing the emerald ring that had belonged to Roberto's mother.

Athena held on tightly to Uncle Spiros's arm while helping him into the one comfortable chair in the living room of the apartment he, Kuri, and Serafina shared in Athens. He had been allowed to sit in the living room while Serafina was putting fresh linens on his bed. An acrid wind carrying street smells—car exhaust and food being hawked by vendors—came through the opened windows along with the sounds of car horns and voices engaged in vigorous conversation. The chair in which he sat looked out upon a busy road, but he seemed not to notice or care what was happening outside.

Uncle Spiros's appearance was a shock to Athena. Chest caved in, shoulders hunched, and his thick silver hair thinned to sparseness, he seemed to have shrunk into a much smaller man. Her disturbance at finding him so aged and ill (she understood it was a form of leukemia) was reflected on her face. Once he was seated, he smiled and took her hand.

"Sometimes, A-*ti*," he said wistfully, "when I pass a mirror I see, out of the corner of my eye, a shadow I can still imagine as young and straight and with a lion's head of hair. But what can I do? I am obligated to live with myself."

By way of answer, Athena reached over and kissed him on the cheek.

"Oh my darling A-*ti*," he sighed. "I do love you! You'll soon see all that I have missed—you'll see it for me. I'm trapped, you see? Trapped in this old body, in this apartment, in Athens." He stared into space for a moment, his mind elsewhere. When he came to there was a quizzical expression on his gaunt but still handsome face. "Did I say I was old?" he rambled. "I lied to you. I'm tired, not old. Halfway through an important sequence of thoughts, quite suddenly I ask, as I am now—what was it I wanted to say to dear A-*ti*?"

She pulled up a stool and sat at his feet. As she glanced around the room, she was very much aware of its shabbiness. There were few reminders of the past. The silver and paintings had long since disappeared, but her uncle's familiar leather-bound books lined some shelves, and a china set she still remembered was arranged on the old buffet table. Tears misted her eyes when she realized how difficult times must have been since she left Greece. "What did you want to say, Uncle Spiros?" she asked, forcing a smile.

"Last night your mother sat by my bedside and told me to my face that my whole illness lay in my mind," he continued. "Was that last night? Or when we first moved here? The house isn't there anymore, you know. Nothing is the same in Athens anymore. They tear down and rebuild with such a vengeance that soon nothing will be left of the past."

He looked up at her. "Why, A-*ti*! That's wonderful news!" he exclaimed abruptly. "My damned memory is suddenly improving. You plan to get married, you say?"

"In June—next month."

"Where?"

"Verona."

That seemed to signal something in his mind; he glanced up to the ceiling and began to recite, in a lyrical cadence, " 'His words are bonds, his oaths are oracles, his love sincere, his thoughts immaculate, his tears poor messengers sent from his heart, his heart as far from fraud as heaven from earth.' "

"Who is that, Uncle Spiros?" she asked, caught up in the smooth lilt of his voice and the earnestness of his expression.

"One of Shakespeare's gentlemen of Verona." He tugged at her arm and she moved closer to him. "You know, A-*ti*," he confided, "I think you have inherited a quirk of genius from my dear mother, your great-grandmother. She couldn't sing—well, not like you do— but she could write. It was amazing. No one knew where the words or the ideas came from. She had a simple education; women in this country rarely get much more. But she wrote as though Shakespeare inhabited her soul. She never published anything because her husband forbade it, and when she died she asked that her notebooks be burned. Your grandfather—my brother—obliged."

"That's terrible, Uncle Spiros," Athena empathized.

"Your great-grandmother was a gentle woman who possessed real beauty. Your mother—her granddaughter—bears no resemblance to her. When Kuri fastens onto an idea, she's a barnacle, she won't let go, you can't talk reason with her because she doesn't understand reason. Talking to Kuri is like hammering a nail into stone. Her mind is numb and she isn't even aware of it. If anything actually does penetrate, she becomes hysterical at once. I've managed to live with her because she could never control me no matter how loud her cries. When I die she will be a loathsome burden on you if you let her. Don't, A-*ti*. Leave her in Athens."

He glanced over his shoulder and saw that Kuri was coming in from the bedroom where she had been supervising Serafina's work. "Do barnacles have ears?" he asked.

"Time to get back to bed, Spiros," Kuri said. She came over to the chair and pulled him to his feet. "He doesn't know what he's saying half the time," she called over his head to Athena. "Don't let it upset you."

"I was telling A-*ti* about my mother," he said.

"Your mother! Always played favorites. My father was brushed aside while you received all her attention. And her money," Kuri complained.

Athena stood in the narrow hallway leading to the bedroom and watched her mother and Serafina put Spiros back to bed. He was so thin that the women had no trouble lifting his body and placing it under the covers. He immediately closed his eyes, apparently having fallen straight off to sleep. Athena went back into the living room, where Serafina and Kuri soon joined her. Serafina seemed like a child, an angelic one at that. She smiled at Athena, her face hauntingly innocent, and stroked the new gold cross around her neck that Athena had brought her from Rome. Serafina was, she realized, no longer a part of this world; mercifully, she had blocked out the horror of the war.

"All the people that old man has helped through the years," Kuri said, "and no one comes to see him."

"Has it been very bad, Mama?" Athena asked.

"Your uncle is as silent in his way as Serafina," she replied. "So I don't know what he feels. I'm the one who suffers for them both. The war robbed us of everything. Then these madmen make war again on their own people. They still kill and rape up in the mountain villages. These communist guerrillas are animals. But soon the nationalist forces will end this insanity and we'll finally have peace. Everyone expects the civil war to end in a matter of months, perhaps weeks, and for the communists to be outlawed. The royal family will return. But for me it is worse than my most terrifying nightmare!"

Kuri was living in circumstances that made her life with Miklos in New York seem grand by comparison. When they had moved from the house to the one-bedroom apartment, she and Serafina had occupied the bedroom while Spiros slept in a cot in the sitting room. When he fell ill, the arrangement was reversed, with Serafina sleeping on pillows in the kitchen and Kuri on the living-room sofa. There was no bed for Athena (who was thankful for it), so she took a room at the Grande Bretagne hotel.

"You see the pimps and the whores outside your hotel?" Kuri asked. They were leaving the house a short time later to do some shopping. "That's what Athens has come to."

"Why don't you return to New York after . . . well, later?" Athena asked, unable to even verbalize the idea that Spiros was dying.

"And what am I to do about Serafina? Leave her to the pimps?" They had reached an open market square, and Kuri examined each egg before the vendor put the six she had purchased in her shopping bag. Then, when he handed it back to her, she opened it and counted them to make sure all six were truly inside. "The man is a swindler. All the merchants are. Thieves!"

Athena reached into her purse and gave her mother two hundred drachmas. "Let's buy some fruit," she suggested. "And some cheese. And a bottle of good wine."

"That's very nice, of course," Kuri said. "My rich daughter stays at the Grande Bretagne and buys cheese and wine for her poor family."

"Mama, I'm not yet rich. Maybe after I marry Roberto and I make some important tours. But I'll help, I promise."

"Handouts! That's what it has come to. And your father and his whore? What do you hear from them?"

"Why do you ask? You don't care, do you?"

"Of course I care. That whore is living on what should be mine."

"Well, why don't you go back and reclaim Papa then?"

Kuri spat on the dusty earth beneath her feet. "Who would want him?"

"You were the one who left him, Mama."

"And do you think you could have become the famous Athena Varos if I hadn't?"

As there was no logic or answer to that question, Athena changed the subject and invited Kuri to come back to the hotel with her for tea.

"I'm not dressed properly," Kuri replied.

Her mother was wearing clean but worn clothes. Athena realized now that she had aged considerably; her former dark attractiveness was fading. Despite their differences and their incompatibility, a great sadness for Kuri overcame Athena. She put her arms around her mother and hugged her (a gesture that Kuri did not rebuff) and then took some more money out of her purse and handed it to her. "Please, Mama, buy a new dress for yourself," she said. She started to walk away and then turned for a brief moment to call to her. "I'll be back at your apartment at six, and I'll bring something special for dinner."

She rushed up the street and only jumped into a taxi when her mother was out of sight. She was so distracted by the time she returned to the hotel that she forgot to inquire if there were any messages. A short time later a telegram from Roberto was slipped beneath her door.

MIA CARA I HAVE SIGNED FOR YOU TO EMBARK ON A TOUR OF SOUTH AMERICA SIX WEEKS HENCE STOP NORMA STOP I PURITANI STOP TOSCA AND AIDA STOP TERMS EXCELLENT STOP WE WILL BE MARRIED BEFORE YOU DEPART STOP I PRAY FOR YOUR UNCLE STOP YOUR LOVING ROBERTO

She was ecstatic and almost unable to contain her joy. Everything, she thought, would be so perfect if it weren't for dear Uncle Spiros. Well, of course, there were always her mother's jibes. That hadn't changed, and she was certain it never would. The point was that she and Roberto were at last to be married. Then something in the cablegram began to disturb her. "I have signed for *you* to embark . . ." Surely that was an error. Roberto must have meant "we."

She ordered a bottle of red naoussa from the hotel wine steward and had several servings of *keftedes* (the spicy meatballs in grape leaves that had always been one of her uncle's favorite dishes) placed in a casserole to bring for dinner. After freshening up she went downstairs to get a taxi. Her mother had been quite right. Most of the taxis lined up near the entry were already occupied with heavily rouged women; every time a man left the hotel they would roll down their windows and shout, "Mister! Where you go?" She turned to the doorman for help in getting her a free cab.

The moment she opened the door of the apartment she knew something was terribly wrong. The living room was empty, but in the bedroom beyond it she could see Serafina on her knees before her Uncle's bed and hear Kuri's sobs rising and falling like tidal swells. She put down her parcel and rushed into the bedroom. At first glance Uncle Spiros appeared to be exactly as she had left him earlier in the day: his gaunt, almost skeletal head resting against the pillows that Serafina had plumped for him, the covers tucked under his arms neatly, and his eyes closed in sleep. She hesitantly approached the side of the bed.

"Uncle Spiros?" she said, leaning over him and placing her hand on his forehead. His body was cold. She looked across the bed to her mother, who was still sobbing loudly.

I should be crying, too, Athena thought, but the tears would not come. She felt strangely empty, as though all the emotion and recent high spirits had been drained from her body. She walked slowly from the room and sank down in the chair, which still held the imprint of her uncle's body. She spotted the old phonograph on a shelf across from where she was sitting. There was a record on it, and she got up to see what it was. *Madama Butterfly.* She placed the needle on the disk and then sat down again to listen. Tears rolled down her cheeks. In her memory she was fourteen years old and Uncle Spiros had taken her to this, her first opera, the same night that war had been declared. She had been trapped in a life that she never had felt belonged to her, that she would never have survived had there not always been—*always*—the great love of Uncle Spiros to sustain her.

The funeral was held in an ancient church on the top of Mount Lykabettos. When the taxi Athena was riding in with her mother and Serafina let them off in front of the chapel, a man selling candles emerged, glanced about him mechanically, then shuffled back inside. Serafina stretched her hand out; Athena gave her some change and she hurried after the man.

It was late afternoon, the wind brisk and cooling. A low white wall surrounded the graveyard attached to the church; an open grave was waiting to receive Spiros's remains. Kuri and Athena stood outside the chapel until they saw the hearse come into sight around a turn in the road. Spiros had not been a devout man, and had asked to be buried without a eulogy or a full service. But a notice of his death had appeared in the newspapers, and Kuri looked surprised to see so many veiled women seated in the soft yellow light that flickered from the candles inside the chapel. "That old man got around," she whispered to Athena.

The interior of the church was so dark and the women so heavily veiled that Athena found it difficult to identify more than a few of the men present, all former cronies of her uncle's from their old neighborhood. After a short prayer was said for the dearly departed, the mourners filed out and made a procession to the grave, with Kuri, Athena, and Serafina directly behind the coffin. Beyond the wall of the graveyard, the Acropolis gleamed in the last rays of the sun; further on was the sea—still bright blue and crested with white—and, a scrim in the far distance, the blue mountains of the Peloponnesus rimming the horizon.

Kuri was weeping noisily beside her and great tears were washing down Serafina's cheeks, but Athena found it hard to equate Uncle Spiros with the black box now being covered with earth; as far as she was concerned, nothing was ever made that could contain his spirit. Although she tried hard, she could not concentrate on the words of the priest's final blessing. Her mind kept flying back to the past, remembering the day she and Uncle Spiros and Kuri and Serafina had traveled to the dock and back in a hearse with a body they were supposed to have delivered to a cemetery. A smile slipped across her face, and she was grateful that her black veil hid it from the others gathered around the grave.

When the short service was over and she had turned to go, a woman took hold of her arm. "It is me—Yanni," the woman said. For a moment, Athena stared at her, then, with a start, recognized her.

"Yes! Yes! Yanni! Oh, my God! Yanni, Yanni!" she cried, grabbing hold of her and hugging her close. "Mama, Serafina! It's Yanni!"

They all clung together for a moment, and then Athena and Yanni walked together out of the graveyard toward the waiting taxi. "I can't believe this!" Athena said. "Uncle Spiros was so certain something terrible had happened to you. He thought that since you hadn't contacted him you had to be dead." She insisted that Yanni come back to the apartment with them.

"I couldn't let anyone know where I was," Yanni explained later, when they were seated around the kitchen table. "When the civil war started I received a message from Signora Galitelli. She asked me to meet her that night in a secret place outside Athens. I wasn't to tell anyone. I had to go off without saying anything to your uncle. I wasn't sure if I would return that night, but I truly believed I would be back. It was freezing cold. I hid in a burned-out barn, where I was shielded from the wind but could still see the remains of a bombed-out truck about fifty yards away. That was where I was to meet Signora."

She swayed slightly in her chair, and after a long pause took a deep breath and continued. "It was nearly midnight when I saw the figure of a tall woman emerge from the bushes. Because of the dark and her cloak, I wasn't sure right away that it was Signora, and she had told me to be very cautious. So I waited, very still, for a few moments until she drew closer. That's probably what saved my life, for just then a sudden semicircle of light flicked on behind her and there was the flash and burst of submachine guns. With all the noise they made, I couldn't hear if she screamed. Then there were more gunshots, but coming from another direction. I slipped down onto the burned earth beneath me and pressed myself as close to it as possible."

"Was it Sofia Galitelli?" Kuri interrupted.

"Shush, Mama. Can't you see this is disturbing to Yanni? Let her continue at her own pace," Athena said.

"Yes, yes, it was Signora, but I still didn't know that. I waited until the sound of the guns stopped. And still I waited, afraid that someone with a gun was still out there. Finally I got up and looked around. There was only silence and darkness. There was no cover between the burned-out barn and the spot where I was to meet Signora. I decided to drag myself along the ground slowly so that I might look like an animal if someone was still out there.

"When I finally made it across, I was horrified to see several bodies strewn on the ground nearby. I crawled closer. There were several more bodies, one piled on top of the other. I heard a soft cry and pushed the top ones off. There, in a pool of blood, was Signora. She was badly injured, so I took off my underskirt and tied it around her leg, which seemed to be bleeding the most.

" 'Oh, my poor Yanni,' Signora cried, 'I almost led you into an ambush.'

" 'It's all right. You mustn't talk,' I said.

"Her voice was so low that I could barely hear her, but she insisted on explaining that she was helping survivors from some of the pillaged villages, hiding those she could from the guerrillas, just as she had done during the war with the resistance. She had asked me to meet her because she wanted me to get some money she had buried under her old house.

" 'The house is gone,' I told her. 'They tore it down. There is a new building there now.'

"I couldn't leave her in such a condition, but she refused to let me go for help. So, very slowly, the two of us made our way back through the bush. Two armed men had been guarding her when she came out into the clearing to meet me. It was then that the guerrillas appeared and the shooting started. Apparently the ones who survived ran away and left her for dead."

Serafina could not bear to hear more; she got up and left the room.

"It took us several days to get back to the group with which she was affiliated. They had taken over a small, deserted church. Signora was sick for a very long time. Then she couldn't walk, and so I remained to take care of her."

"And now—where is she?" Athena asked.

"She died two weeks ago, and so I returned to Athens. I went back to your house, which was no longer there. Then I saw in the paper the announcement of Signore's death and where he was to be buried."

Another silence. Both Kuri and Athena were trying to take in everything that Yanni had told them. Kuri wore a particularly puzzled expression. "This is the truth? You swear?" she asked.

"Mama! How could you!" Athena yelled at her.

Kuri smiled faintly but said nothing.

"Where are you staying?" Athena asked.

"Last night I slept in the Church of St. Nicholas. They didn't know I was there, of course."

"Tonight you'll stay with me at the hotel. We'll talk about what you'll do next; maybe you can return to Rome with me."

Athena then recounted almost everything that had happened to her since they had last seen each other. Kuri sat silently throughout, not commenting, taking special notice of what her daughter said. Athena did not miss the disapproval in her mother's expression. Once again she had done it all wrong; she had confided in Yanni, a former servant, instead of her own mother, and this so offended Kuri that she was unable to rejoice with her daughter over what she was saying—that she had succeeded in being recognized as a major diva and that she was very much in love and about to be married.

Why can't she be happy for me? Athena asked herself. She could find no answer and was certain she never would. Not that it mattered anymore: Now there was Roberto, whose every thought was always for her.

13. Grazia was standing in the center of the grand salon of the house in Verona, her eyes flashing with mixed hurt and anger; Roberto had just told her that he and Athena were to be married. "You think you will possess her but it will be the other way around," she said, offering the words sharply through drawn lips.

"Do you imagine I don't know about possession? I could write a book about being possessed and needing to possess," he countered, facing her. "And I also recognize that marrying Athena is more about the latter than the former."

"She'll make you miserable. You're too old to marry an ambitious girl. What will people here in Verona say? They'll laugh behind your back."

"Verona, my dear Grazia, is not the world."

"It is the only world you have known. It is *our* world."

"Yours, perhaps. Not mine."

She gave Roberto a quick look, which irritated him. Everything about Grazia irritated him recently, her arch expressions, the scent of boiled starch from her stiff-fronted dresses, the silence she imposed as a penalty for any gaiety he might be feeling. He was above all irritated by the guilt she created in him because at the age of fifty-three he had decided to leave her side and live his own life.

His voice hardened. "Grazia, Athena and I are to be married in

188

three weeks. We have chosen to have the ceremony here in Verona at the Church of Santa Maria, Saturday morning, the eleventh of June. There will be about fifty guests, and I will expect you to have a fine lunch prepared when we return here from the service. My bride and myself will leave for a short honeymoon later that afternoon and return to Rome a few days later. Now, if you refuse to be accommodating, or you are even entertaining the notion that you can stop this marriage from going forward, reconsider. For I am not prepared to be lenient."

Grazia acknowledged his mandate with an intake of breath and an insulting droop of her eyelids that indicated her exasperation at his "bad behavior," but her attitude only increased his displeasure with her. "As of this moment I'm offering you the house for the rest of your life; I will support both you and our cousin Maria Rosa comfortably," he continued. "But at the first sign of any interference on your part to either break up or set back my marriage, I'll sell this house and you can go live with Maria Rosa in her apartment in Modena, which you always say isn't fit for a dog."

"This marriage—this woman—means *so* much to you, Roberto, that you would deny your sister—your very *blood*—for lust of her?" Grazia rasped, her face so red and her gaze so fixed upon him that she appeared to be in imminent danger of a stroke or heart attack.

"What I feel for Athena is not your business. What I ask you to do is your duty. And if you fail in that, I refuse to be made to feel responsible." All patience had left him. He surveyed her keenly and as he did his expression darkened. It was no more than a twitch of a cheek-muscle, but it revealed a cold implacability.

"She has made you a devil," Grazia said, her voice shrill, the color draining from her face. When she saw how his eyes burned with fury, her tone instantly became placating. "You needn't look at me with such loathing. You know I've always loved you more than anyone else on this earth. There's nothing I wouldn't or won't do for you. Who has cared for you all these years? Who saw that you were safe and fed during the war? You think I don't know the truth? That you have desires not normal to men or accepted by the

Church? I have eyes, and my deep love for you gives me a profound understanding of your *real* self. I would betray my faith before I would turn from you. We belong together, Roberto. You and I. Blood ties us. I will shield you; she will leave you open to attack."

"You don't know what you're saying. I've had enough." He started toward the high archway that separated the room from the front entry. "Don't forget that I warned you," he said, turning tentatively back to her.

Grazia paled. Fear gripped her. She knew Roberto well enough to sense the finality in his voice. She recalled the time shortly after their parents' deaths (which had been separated by only six months) when he had refused to take her to London and Paris with him and sent her to the convent school, where she remained until his return. Her brother could be cold-hearted when it came to having his own way. She quickly decided that if she were to sway him at all, she must change her approach. "You know I'll do anything you say," she cried. "Don't leave this house, *please,* I beg you. I'll have nothing to live for if you go away."

He gave no reply and again started from the room.

"You'll have my blood on your hands!" she shouted.

Slowly, he turned back to her. "Grazia, don't ever threaten me in such a way again," he replied.

To his astonishment, she flung herself across the room toward him and fell to the ground at his feet. There were tears, sobs, hysterics. He helped her to rise. He tried to calm her. He took her in his arms and stroked her back as he once had done when she was a young orphaned girl and he was her protective older brother. Memories flooded his head of how she had entertained an SS officer during the war with stories of her brother's many love affairs with Verona's most beautiful married women (extravagant lies, of course) when he was being investigated for associating with a known homosexual. His coldness quickly began to thaw.

"Grazia, let's put this ugly scene behind us," he said. "There's much to be done before the wedding. I'm sure I can count on you."

"Oh, yes, Roberto," she conceded, placing her arms around his

neck, inclining her head against his shoulder. Then came the re-
pentance, the apologies, the promises that she would welcome his
bride into their home, that she would prepare a feast for their
wedding luncheon that would have pleased King Victor Emmanuel
in the days when Italy was at the height of its glory.

Finally her tears and entreaties subsided and he was able to dis-
entangle himself from her. "I shouldn't have spoken as I did, Grazia," he said. "But you must understand how important this
marriage is to me. I'm not an artist. I've never conjured music out
of nothing, out of the air, so that it breathed with life and sang to
people and was discussed and revered. I'm now an artist's manager,
there to guide Athena's career, to propel it forward. For that I do
possess talent—my ability to negotiate good contracts, my educated
sense for and my appreciation of opera. I see it as my mission and
my salvation. You do understand that, Grazia? Opera is the world,
the only world I have ever wanted to be a part of. If you truly care
for me as you say, you'll try to help me achieve my goal."

Grazia began to cry again.

"You don't really love her?" she asked between caught breaths.

"I'm not sure," he replied honestly. Then he left the room and
managed to get out of the house before she had a chance to start the
confrontation anew.

As he walked up his street and turned in the direction of the river,
the soft spring breeze carrying the scent of new greenery and fresh
spring flowers, his tensions began to dissolve. Had the exhausting
exchange served any real purpose, he wondered? But, he decided,
the situation with Grazia would resolve itself. His sister did not figure into his plans for his future, and he was foolish to have wasted
so much energy on her emotional outburst. Grazia was an unhappy
and unfulfilled woman, a spinster with only a brother upon whom
to concentrate her attention. She wouldn't change with age, but
there was a hope she would mellow. Once he was married, he
could afford to be generous with her. She could travel with Maria
Rosa if she wished, begin to have more of a life of her own.

He quickened his pace. Somehow he felt soothed, almost cheerful when he contemplated the new path of his own life. He was pleased with his stylish apartment in Rome, really two adjoining apartments that would afford privacy for both him and Athena. Shopping for the furniture, a combination of antiques and modern pieces, had delighted him—at last he would be living in a place free of the must of his ancestors.

He would have to pay careful attention to how he told Athena he would not be going with her on the six-week tour to South America. She would have to understand that he had to talk to the directors of the major opera companies—the Metropolitan, Covent Garden, La Scala—and that this was the best time for him to do it, when she was generating so much excitement on her successful tour (which he was certain it would be). And, of course, she would be well taken care of. Vesta Caspari would go with her, and Luigi, and this new maid, Yanni, if she wished. And everywhere she went there would be representatives of the opera houses, directors and conductors, to see that she was kept busy and happy.

He paused suddenly in the Piazza Sant'Anastasia; he had come here purely by instinct without realizing where he was headed. He and Ugo had not been in contact since the night of their fight. Someone had told him that Ugo was leaving Verona to direct a film, a fanciful notion that he was certain Ugo would entertain. Well, Ugo was an artist, a man driven to experiment with new forms. That was one of his great attractions.

No more thought about Ugo, that's over, done with! he told himself. He was about to turn back and retrace his steps when he heard the sound of angry voices. A tall, slim, fair-haired youth came sprinting out of an alleyway about a hundred feet away; blood was oozing down the side of his head and he looked terrified. Suddenly, a group of five or six rough-looking young men wearing black leather jackets appeared from the same narrow alley, hands flailing, cursing in raised voices.

"Buco! Buco!" they shouted. *"Frocio!"*

A stone whizzed through the air about ten feet from Roberto. The bleeding youth dodged it and kept running, nearly knocking

Roberto down as he passed by. Roberto pulled back into a doorway, and the attackers skidded to a halt near him. He held his breath. This was no time to chance a confrontation with a group of queer-bashers. He stood silently, staring hard at them, trying to assume the role of the well-dressed businessman exasperated at being inconvenienced by rowdiness. The young hooligans poked one another. One moved toward him, but his friends pulled him back. Then they laughed ugly, raucous laughter, linked their arms, and went off down the street.

Roberto had remained frozen on the spot until the noise of the attackers died away. Fear still gripped him as he walked briskly in the opposite direction, glancing over his shoulder from time to time, although he knew his dread was no longer warranted.

Long-awaited moments are always a disappointment, Athena thought. She was standing in the vestry of the Church of Santa Maria. In a few moments she was to enter the sanctuary and exchange marriage vows with Roberto. The room was damp and cold and the lavender organza frock she had chosen as a wedding dress was too thin to ward off the chill. The morning should have been brighter than any she had ever known. But it had been raining for three days, an interminable deluge, and though the downpour had finally stopped, the sun was hidden behind ominous dark clouds that threatened more rain. One chose a June wedding in the hopes that a brilliant early-summer sun would shine over the proceedings. Athena felt let down, cheated of what was her due.

She peered through the crack in the vestry door. About fifty people, only a very few of them familiar to her, were seated quietly in anticipation of the ceremony. White lilies decorated the altar, where a profusion of sweet-scented, lighted candles were flickering like funeral tapers.

Why am I feeling so glum? she thought. This was the promised day she had so desperately been praying for. Soon she would become Signora Roberto Vallobroso. No longer having to put up with her mother's conniving and complaints, no longer having to worry that she would be left on the shelf to molder, for the first time able to shout her name with pride. Not that she didn't love her father—but "Varos" was a manufactured name, with no history, roots, or identity. No one who shared it bore any connection to her.

Perhaps, it was the mere fact of being in this small, ancient church that depressed her; it brought Uncle Spiros's recent death and funeral back to her. Despite her pleasure at having the maestro take his place, she would so have loved to walk down the aisle on Uncle Spiros's arm. Then, too, she had put off the decision to bring her mother to Verona until only a few days earlier, and now she was feeling shameful about it. The dilemma had not been caused by her desire to exclude Kuri, but by a genuine concern as to what to do about Serafina. There was no one to leave her with in Athens, and Athena had been apprehensive of how her aunt would react to the journey, and at the service and the reception that were to follow.

"Are you ready?" Vesta whispered in her ear. "As soon as I say 'now,' step forward through the door. The maestro will be waiting for you. Go down the aisle right foot forward." The first chord of the wedding march from *Lohengrin* was struck on the church organ. "Now!" Vesta said and gave her a small shove.

The maestro smiled reassuringly as she entered through the sanctuary. He took her hand and placed it on his arm. But when they started down the aisle with Vesta—the maid of honor—directly behind them, Athena recalled the horror that, in Wagner's opera, follows the wedding march; Lohengrin leaves his bride, who collapses and dies when she sees his boat vanish in the distance. Suddenly the choice of music—*her* choice—seemed like a bad omen, and she wanted desperately to shout to the organist to stop playing. But as she looked up, she saw Roberto standing at the altar waiting for her, with Verona's mayor, his best man, by his side, and she knew she had to control her anxiety and think only of happy things.

Thoughts of Roberto filled her mind. He, and he alone, could make her life complete. She still wasn't sure if what she felt for him was love, but she had no experience with which to compare it. She wanted him to be hers, intensely and enduringly hers, and she knew she would give him whatever he demanded in exchange.

As soon as she reached him, her spirits lifted. He touched her hand with a secret gesture concealed from all onlookers and a tingle suffused her entire body. She should have been concentrating on the words being spoken by the priest, but when she glanced surreptitiously at Roberto, dressed so handsomely in a striped morning suit, she was struck by the elegance of his profile. She recalled seeing a similar one—Caesar, perhaps, or maybe Alexander—on ancient coins in museums.

She was filled with pride and drew herself up, becoming several inches taller than he. He must have felt her eyes on him, since he smiled cautiously at her, which so reassured her that she let out a small sigh. The priest briefly glanced up at her. Roberto touched her hand again, and her happiness overwhelmed her. Her head felt light as the priest pronounced the benediction.

"I do," she said in a clear voice when he asked her to reply to the marriage vows.

When his turn came, Roberto spoke up with the same assurance. There was no kiss after they were pronounced duly wed, but Roberto grasped his wife's hand and they exchanged a long, lingering look. *I am, at last, Signora Vallobroso,* Athena thought.

A smile touched the corners of Roberto's mouth. He was now in absolute control of Athena, her money, her career. No one could take away his ticket to a new but long dreamed-about life.

Waiting for the wedding guests, Grazia glanced with satisfaction at the luncheon table. She could not be blamed for the dreary grayness of the skies darkening the house or for the eerie wheeze of the wind blowing past the dining-room windows; what she could take credit for was the large table, extended by putting several together, covered in sparkling white damask and set with glistening crystal, gleaming silver, and vases filled with white roses and orchids.

Lunch was served by waiters borrowed from Zeno's for the occasion. And if not spectacular (although the pasta was sauced with cream and wild mushrooms, the veal seasoned piquantly, and the wedding cake a tiered white-cream tower of perfection) or equal to anything set before King Victor Emmanuel, it was a meal that pleased Roberto, a meal of which Grazia could be proud. Indeed, she sat in the straight-backed chair to Roberto's left (with Athena at his right), dressed for this special occasion in a gown of sheer, rose-colored silk-velvet, with her mother's five strands of pearls encircling her long neck, looking as arrogant as Victor Emmanuel's consort, Queen Helena.

Grazia was following her brother's dictates to the letter. However surprised they may have been, all the guests were convinced that Grazia approved of her new sister-in-law. She had devoted much care and attention to the luncheon, and even when asked about her unexpectedly, Grazia was warm and flattering toward Athena, praising her choice of wedding dress, complimenting her on her new, slimmer figure, her composure in church. And whenever Athena's performances were mentioned, Grazia quickly said how proud she was to have such a brilliantly talented family member.

Observing all of this, Athena felt a warm kinship with her new sister-in-law. When she returned to her bedroom to change into her going-away outfit, she was therefore caught by surprise to find that Grazia had followed her silently up the staircase, closed the door, turned the lock, and was now standing and staring at her with a look that could only be interpreted as sheer anguish.

"What is it?" Athena asked.

"There is something you must know," Grazia said. "Something I have debated all week about telling you."

The apprehension Athena had felt earlier now returned. There was something about Grazia's voice, its cold, deliberate tone, the hard set of her jaw, and the taut lines about her mouth, that signaled an alarm. She was prepared for expressions of bitterness on Grazia's part; she was even ready to deal with tears and self-pity. Athena was too knowledgeable about close family relations and the ugly passions they could engender not to expect that Grazia would deeply resent her taking from her a brother who was the ruling fixation of her life. But there was something far more frightening about Grazia's appearance, and the locked door.

"Can't it wait until later?" Athena asked, hoping to put off, at least for this happy time, what she knew was going to be a disagreeable encounter.

"No. I want you to know that I begged my brother not to marry you. He wouldn't listen. Roberto is a determined man and not easy to influence even if he is headed toward disaster. Which I think this marriage is going to be."

"Roberto and I would be the best and only judges of that, Grazia."

"You! What do you know? You are a silly young woman with stars in your eyes. Having a voice that brings you attention doesn't give you good sense."

"I have to ask you to leave this room, Grazia. I don't want to say anything that I'll regret, and I'm sure I don't want to hear what it is you feel you must tell me." Athena turned away and reached into the wardrobe to get out her travel dress.

But Grazia was not to be deterred. "Do you know it is a crime in Italy to be a practicing homosexual?" she said.

Athena spun back. "I can't see why that should matter to me." Completely unaware of the deviousness behind it, she was puzzled as to why Grazia even brought up such a curious subject.

Grazia had kept her promise not to play her hand before her brother's wedding; she was now, however, set on wrecking the marriage in such a way that Roberto would never suspect her complicity. Her one purpose now was to turn Athena from him so that she, Grazia, would once more be the only woman in his life.

The wind suddenly rose again. Rain slashed against the windows of the room. Athena felt a chill and rubbed her arms.

"Since I was sixteen years old, which is when I lost both my parents, I have been closer to my brother than many women are to their husbands," Grazia said, breathing hard. "I learned the truth about him and *still* love him." Her hand pulled at the pearls around her neck; Athena watched with mounting fear and fascination, certain that she was in the presence of a madwoman.

"I have spent my entire adult life protecting Roberto," Grazia continued, allowing no pause for Athena to interrupt even if she had not been too stunned to do so. "I have kept him from harm and helped him conceal his terrible secret from the people in Verona, the army, the police. There were interested men in my life, good men, rich men. But I never married, because then Roberto would not have had to be responsible for me. He would have been alone and expected to marry, to have children. And I feared he would be exposed for what he is—a homosexual."

She moved away from the door, closer to Athena. Her dark eyes were glazed; she continued to tug at the pearls at her throat as though they were choking her. "The Nazis sent such people to concentration camps. Even now they are in danger. There are groups that seek out and beat and kill men they call—*buchi*," she said with abhorrence. "Roberto is a *buco*!"

A cold paralysis took hold of Athena. She wanted to push Grazia aside and bolt from the room, but she simply could not move. She refused to believe that what Grazia was saying was anything but the spiteful lie of a deranged woman. Pity assaulted her, then disgust.

"This is your brother you're slandering," she said.

"I'm telling you the truth. It doesn't matter what you think now. You were married by a priest in a Catholic church. There is no divorce for you. You will be Signora Roberto Vallobroso until you die. You cannot run to a lawyer like a hysterical girl if you find he has been with a lover," she warned. "If you know what's best for you, concentrate on your career and leave Roberto in the hands that have protected him all his life—*mine*."

Grazia unlocked the door and left the room; Athena stood frozen, staring first at the closed door and then at the window. Rain washed over the glass in swirling waves that blurred everything outside.

She wanted to believe that Grazia was indeed mad, jealous—anything that would make a lie of her words. But instinctively she knew that Roberto's sister had spoken the truth. Perhaps she had suspected all along that he was a homosexual—that would explain her lack of sexual passion for him, or his for her. She experienced anger and then confusion. Why hadn't he been honest with her?

The answer came to her in a simple flash: Roberto loved her so much that he was trying to overcome his very nature. It seemed to be the only possible explanation and the one she was most willing to accept. Dear, dear Roberto. He would not need to conceal such a dark and ugly secret again. What she must do is help him to overcome his problem, forget his past, and make a new start with her. The idea pleased her. She would be the first and only *real* woman in his life.

She hurriedly removed her wedding gown and put on the expensive blue dress with its matching hat and shoes, which she had bought in Rome under Vesta's supervision. Then she rejoined Roberto, who had also changed into more suitable attire for a train journey. To Grazia's startled surprise, she kissed her sister-in-law warmly as they prepared to leave. "Thank you, dear Grazia," she whispered in her ear.

Mario drove them to the railroad station, where they boarded a train for Venice; Roberto had insisted she see that extraordinary city in the sunlight. *Well,* she thought, as they settled themselves in a first-class private compartment, *it can't matter if it rains on one's honeymoon, even in Venice.* The idea caused her to giggle.

"What's so funny?" Roberto asked.

"Life," she replied.

The train ride between Verona and Venice was comparatively short. The newlyweds would even arrive in time to enjoy a festive dinner. If gasoline weren't still being rationed, they might well have driven. But Athena was grateful for the comfort of the overstuffed seats, however dreary and dilapidated the cars themselves were, the Italian railroads not having been refurbished since the war. Heavy rains dulled her enjoyment of the landscape and the car was so drafty that Athena's feet felt like blocks of ice in her flimsy high-heeled shoes. Despite these discomforts, she was certain she had never been on a happier journey.

As she sat across from Roberto, who was dozing, eyes closed, his head resting on his chest, she experienced a completely new feeling of well-being. It was not until they had boarded the train that Grazia's revelations sank in. Although Athena was not foolish enough to dismiss the possibility of problems to come, she still felt confident that Roberto's past would bring them even closer together. It was this sense that was giving her such pleasure as the train rocked and whistled through the rain-obscured countryside: secrets bind people more tightly together than, perhaps, even love. To have both love and a secret seemed to her an unfailing combination for happiness.

Signora Vallobroso. She said the words over and over in her mind. They had music, a lilting cadence. *Signora Vallobroso, Signora Vallobroso.* Almost Pucciniesque. She turned away from Roberto to look at the closed, glass-windowed door of their compartment; as two women were just walking past in the corridor. They glanced at her and she smiled graciously, wondering whether they guessed that she and Roberto were newlyweds or if they assumed, from the fact that he was asleep, they were a long-married couple. It occurred to her that they might not think they were married at all, that they were just relations or friends. The thought so disturbed her that she got up and left the compartment to go to the toilet, where she assumed the women were heading, with the idea of washing her hands so that they could see the shiny gold wedding band she was now wearing along with her emerald ring. But the bathroom was empty. Roberto was awake when she returned to her seat,.

"Did Grazia give you all the telegrams before we left?" he asked.

"I'm afraid not."

"I'll call her tomorrow and have her send them along to Venice. It's important to reply to congratulations promptly."

"Yes, I think so, too. Very impolite otherwise. Did you look at many of them?"

"Most. Some from your admirers. You have many of them, you know."

"You included?" she asked, smiling.

"Your greatest fan," he replied seriously.

"My father used to say that even before I came to Italy."

"Perhaps we should have sent him a ticket so that he could have seen his only daughter married," he said thoughtfully.

"That would have been impossible. I mean, to have Papa come to Verona instead of my mother. No, we did the right thing."

"Well, if you feel that way, I'm satisfied." He looked away, out the masked window.

Athena was overwhelmed with a desire to be close to him, so she settled in beside him. He turned toward her and she boldly took his hand. "I will make the sun shine for you," she said, smiling broadly at him. Her eyes glistened and the whiteness of her teeth gleamed between her half-open mouth.

"My God, Athena! You are a lioness, like Norma," he exclaimed. He moved her hand to his crotch; if she was surprised by this, she didn't show it. They sat there silently, the rain beating an even rhythm on the train window. She could feel his warmth and hardness through the fabric of his trousers.

Their suite in Venice was nearly perfect, even if the weather was not. The Piazza San Marco was so covered with water that you couldn't walk across it, and the gondoliers in the canals were having difficulties keeping their boats upright. With night the heavy rains turned into a violent summer storm, and Roberto decided that it would be best to dine at their hotel. They did not linger over coffee and brandy. When they returned to their rooms, a bottle of iced champagne sent by the manager was waiting for them.

"I'll slip into something more comfortable," she said.

He laughed. "You sound like one of those Hollywood movie actresses."

"I didn't know you liked the movies," she called from the other room.

"Oh, yes. Very much."

He popped the champagne and poured two glasses. When he looked up he saw her standing in the bedroom doorway dressed in a flowing white negligee that clearly outlined the fulsome curves of her body. He stared at her in some surprise; it was the first time he had seen her so nearly naked. She resembled a Greek statue, one of their goddesses—the one of plenty or pleasure, he thought, although for the moment he couldn't recall either of their names.

Her breasts were full but firm and high, not pendulous as he imagined Grazia's to be under her starched shirtwaist. Despite her months of dieting, her hips were broad, her thighs heavy. Yet they seemed right for her body, for the soft curve of her buttocks. Though she was too slim to be called Rubenesque, there was something of that grand old painter's brush strokes about the lines of her body and the rich pinkness of her flesh. It was a sensuous figure, very appealing, truly beautiful.

As Roberto stood there staring at her, she advanced slowly toward him, a bit of the vamp in the way she was posing, artfully kittenish, before him. He wondered why a host of men weren't crazy with passion for her. She was, he was certain, a virgin. It was one of her great attractions to him—for he didn't think he could go to bed with a woman who had known other men.

She stopped a few feet from him and he handed her a glass of champagne. "A toast," he said. "To my beautiful bride and the voice that will make her known worldwide as *la Divina*—the greatest of the divas."

"Oh, Roberto," she said, disappointment in her voice, "I don't want to drink to that."

"Of course you do." He came closer to her and brushed her cheek with the back of his hand. "My darling child, you'll have to come to love yourself first if you want the love of others," he said, almost as a caress. "And you'll have to understand that you're not the same as other people. If you were, you wouldn't be my wife. I love all of you, you see? And that means the voice that brings you fame and the fame that brings me such great pleasure."

"You do love me then?"

"Very dearly," he replied, realizing for the first time that, indeed, he did. This caused him a moment of confusion. He had never made love to a woman before and until this moment had not considered the sexual expectations of his young wife. He believed a wife's role in the matter of sex was to pleasure her husband. Athena excited him, the first woman he could recall who did, and now she was absolutely *glowing* with carnal desire.

He took the glass from her hand and placed it beside his on a table, then led her into the bedroom, where he dimmed the lights before helping her onto the bed. He undressed with his back to her; when he turned around, he was cradling his erect penis in his hands. "Come closer to the edge of the bed," he said. "Take it gently in your mouth. That's it. That's it. Be careful of your teeth. Good girl. Sweet girl. Darling girl." A moment later a spasm suffused his entire body.

He climbed into bed with her and she lay in his arms. To his surprise, a tear was coursing down her cheek. "Is something wrong?" he asked.

"I'm not sure." She raised herself up on her elbow and looked down at him. "Was what—I did—all right?"

"Of course," he assured her. "Between husband and wife nothing is wrong." He reached up and wiped the tear from her face. "You made me very happy. And this way you can't get pregnant, which would be a catastrophe considering how important it is that you spend the next few years concentrating on your career." She slipped down beside him again but was silent. "Are you already disappointed in married life, *mia cara?*" he asked, stroking her dark, thick hair back from her face.

The question immediately alarmed Athena. She wanted him to believe she loved him entirely, to win his trust, to fire his ardor for her so much that he would forget the ways of his past—forever. And yes, perhaps then he would sow the seeds that would give them a child. With that thought in mind, she smiled. Through the dimness of the room she turned to him and said: "Oh, no, Roberto, you mustn't think that. It's just all so new to me. I must seem terribly naive to you."

He patted her shoulder comfortingly and turned on his side. "Good night, *mia cara*," he said.

She cupped her body, spoon fashion, around him. He fell asleep moments later, but Athena remained awake for a long while, listening to the steady rain, to her husband's even breathing, to the thumping sounds of a couple making love in the room next door. She clasped Roberto closer to her. The warmth of his body began to meld with her own, which seemed to relieve her—although only sleep, much later, quieted the aching throb between her legs.

Roberto didn't tell her that he was not going to South America with her until they had returned to Rome and their new apartment. She tried to persuade him to come with her; afterward, she proposed, she would travel with him to the places he needed to go. "It's not proper for an artist to be involved in business," he insisted. "And with you there I wouldn't be able to concentrate properly on what is truly important—calling Athena Varos to the attention of the opera world and protecting both our interests."

In the end he won (although, of course, there had never been a contest; he had made the plans and had no intention of changing them). Athena and Vesta went shopping for clothes for the tour. In mid-August, less than ten weeks after she and Roberto had exchanged their wedding vows, Athena and her new entourage departed for South America. Roberto, on his own, went to New York via Paris and London.

Entr'acte

> The Island of
> Zephyrus, 1955

14. "FIRE!" MANO SHOUTED AT HIS OVERSEER, COSTA KOLIARES.

Three evenly spaced shots cracked through the crisp air of the late spring morning. A large black dog, which a moment before had been poised between the bright blue arch of the sky and the white rock upon which he stood, yelped, collapsed, and rolled out of sight down the other side of the escarpment to the sea below.

A pack of wild dogs ranged on Mano's privately owned island; where they had come from was a mystery, since Zephyrus had been an uninhabited paradise before he bought it. Fanciful members of the household staff believed the animals had swum the thirty-four kilometers from Athens during the war, when similar packs terrorized the city. Another theory was that they had been brought by boat and left on the island as a threat to its owner, whose enemies perhaps numbered greater than his friends. Whatever their origin, Mano was determined to rid his private Eden of them—for the safety of his guests, his wife, himself, and his large staff. His reign over this two thousand acres of land could not be absolute as long as the dogs roamed free.

A wilderness of sand, white rock, and cypresses when Mano had bought it seven years before, Zephyrus now boasted a harbor, a heliport, and an inlet made safe and luxurious for swimmers and sun-worshipers. Its smooth, golden sand had been combed of all rock and debris and a sea wall had been built to protect it against unkind east winds (Zephyrus, after all, was the god of the west wind in Greek mythology). During the height of the season when anywhere from twenty to thirty guests could be present, there was also a bar, a canteen, and servants to man them.

Roads to the main points of the island had been laid out, paths cleared for pleasant strolls. Where thistles once proliferated, magnificent olive trees now grew, many brought in fully grown by boat. The main villa, with its Doric columns and statued porticoes, was situated in a clearing on the highest point of Zephyrus, with extraordinary frontal sea views and breathtaking vistas of the island on the other three sides. The gardens were filled with exotic flora, and brilliant purple bougainvilleas trailed over every wall. To the rear of the villa, a sixty-foot swimming pool and poolhouse were set in a marble terrace amid Greek statues and massive containers of flowers and plants. Behind the pool were two tennis courts and a badminton court. There was a stable, but due to the roughness of the land only donkeys were kept in it, as well as the goats used to pull carts over the more inaccessible areas of the island.

Several guest cottages were located on a plateau below the main house; accommodations for those staff members who did not live at the villa were on the far side of the island, near the heliport. Sixty-three people were needed to keep Zephyrus running to Mano's standards. It was his island kingdom, where but for the dogs he reigned supreme.

Mano was now one of the richest men in Europe, although he would have preferred to have held that distinction in America as well. However, certain financial irregularities in his company, which had enabled him to quadruple the size of his shipping empire in a short span of three years, had also caused him to be denied American residency—proving that millions do not always buy a man his most treasured dreams and often, in fact, force him to make decisions that will doom him to great unhappiness.

His marriage to Nikki was a case in point. It had provided him with the ships he needed to significantly increase his fleet. But life with Nikki was proving to be a stiff price to pay for Konstantine Sylvanus's grudging but vital backing.

He turned away from the scene of the wild dog's destruction. Even from this distance its blood could be seen splattered on the chalklike rock, and although he could be ruthless, Mano did not enjoy the sight of violence—a reaction, perhaps, to the vicious massacres of Greeks by Turks he had witnessed as a young boy. Except for the wild dogs, no hunting was permitted on the island. Meat was brought in frozen by boat. Fish was plentiful. There was a chicken coop, goats, and cows for milk and cheese.

"How many of those devils do you think are left?" he asked Costa.

"Hard to say," the overseer replied, the heavy-lidded gray eyes set deep in his sun-leathered face looking quizzical as he thought about it. "The problem is that they all look alike—makes it damned difficult to know if you've seen ten of them or the same dog ten times. But the last brute we got was a bitch. Which accounts for our problems. The black demons are breeding."

"Well, we've got to get them. They're killers. Last year it was that young boy at the hatchery. Poor soul—who deserves to die like that? And every week it's a chicken, a goat, a cow. It's driving Mrs. Zakarias crazy; she's certain they'll kill her poodles. She won't walk around the grounds, swim in the pool, or even go down to the beach."

"They never come near the house or the beach," Costa said in an attempt to reassure him.

"You tell my wife that and she'll say that's where they're going to hit next." His back was to the sun. He lowered his dark glasses down on the bridge of his nose and made his way to a black Land Rover, one of several on the island. "Back to the house," he said when he got in next to the driver. A moment later, Costa climbed into the back and the car made its way with painful slowness over rocks and rough ground until it turned onto the unpaved road that wove around the island like a dark, velvet ribbon. Shifting loudly into a lower gear, the driver headed the car up the incline to the circular drive in front of the villa, which Nikki's friends called the "junior Acropolis."

Nikki's clique said many unkind things behind Mano's back, things he always managed to overhear or was told about by Nikki herself. Her friends said he had no class. They were, however, more than willing to overlook this defect because he was very rich, richer than any of them, and now even richer than Nikki's father. They also said he screwed around and looked at every woman as a potential mistress. He found this kind of talk malicious, and he felt bad for Nikki when he learned of it. There were other women in his life, true, but none of them meant much more to him than a night of amusement. And he was discreet (at least, what he called discreet); he never made love to another woman in his own home. Such encounters were transacted in hotel suites in Paris, Rome, Monte Carlo, Buenos Aires—whenever and wherever he was traveling without Nikki. But this was happening with greater frequency lately, for she had developed a fear of almost everything involving travel—their private plane would crash, the ship would sink, the train would overturn, her car would be ambushed, she would be kidnapped and held for ransom. Her terror of the wild dogs was another addition to her growing list of phobias, and the only one with which he was in full sympathy.

Nikki was a bundle of tension and fears ready to ignite at any moment. The lively, sexy girl he had married had been consumed by drugs and alcohol, which she obtained covertly and took in the same manner. Mano tried to find reasons for her behavior but could not. She had lost the child she had been carrying when they were married, and for some time he thought a baby might be the answer. Now he suspected that she had aborted on purpose. Nikki had loathed the idea of giving birth. She really didn't like children and made it a rule for her friends to leave theirs at home.

"Poor Nikki," they said. "It's because she wants one of her own so badly."

Bullshit! Nikki wanted to be the only child; when she wasn't petted and fawned over, she reached for a drink and her uppers and downers. Mano had tried to make her stop: all prescription drugs coming into the house were carefully screened, her closest servants reported the contents of her medicine chest to him, and her dressing-room drawers were searched daily. Yet Nikki always managed to get pills and hide them someplace—where or how he couldn't imagine.

She was standing in the marble hallway, caught in a dazzling beam of sun, when he came in. Self-abuse had not dimmed her beauty, the glow of her fair skin, the halo of her golden hair, the amber sparks in her eyes. She wore a brightly patterned silk Emilio Pucci pajama suit that molded sensuously to her lithe, slim body.

"How many did you kill?" she asked.

"Costa shot one."

"Only one?"

The maid who had let him in closed the door, and the shaft of sunlight disappeared. Shadows crossed Nikki's delicately carved face and small lines rimmed her full mouth. Even so, she was a beautiful woman. She was still young—only twenty-six. Her pale white hand fluttered mothlike when she raised it to push a loose flaxen strand of hair back from her high forehead.

How long was it since we last made love? Mano thought. At least a month ago, in Athens, after the celebration of their eighth wedding anniversary. Two hundred of their intimate friends, as she liked to say. Nikki greatly enjoyed being a part of the social whirl. She was a consummate hostess, extravagant, a collector of titles, famous people, and those whose greatest talent was simply to amuse. She brought them in droves to Zephyrus. She hated the island, really, and Mano very much knew it. The wild dogs seemed to symbolize to her the malevolence she felt pervaded the place.

"We'll have them all soon. I promise."

"I don't know why you let those beasts terrorize us like they do. Why can't we go back to Athens and while we're gone have an exterminator crew come here and get them all?" She shivered, and her skin rippled beneath the soft silk of her pajama suit.

"That's not a bad idea," he agreed. He started for the arched door that led to the library, but abruptly stopped before he reached it. "Where is everyone?" he asked.

"Fitzy and Martha and the Glendowers have taken the launch to Grattos to do some shopping. They won't be back until cocktails. The Dimetrioses seem to still be asleep. A bit more champagne than they could handle last evening, I would say. Sally Jo, Lexie, and the prince are at the pool with Yorgo watching Mimsy and Biba for me. I can't understand why they don't swim. Dogs are suppose to be naturals at it."

She went over to him, took his arm, and looked at him speculatively. "Except for the staff we're alone in the house," she said. She leaned in close to him. "We can go upstairs. No one even knows you're back." She pulled at his arm. "I need to fuck, Mano. I need to fuck, really bad."

"Nikki, this isn't the time," he said gently.

"Yes it is. It's the right time whenever a bitch is in heat."

"I hate it when you talk like that. You're not a bitch. You're my wife."

"You haven't fucked me in weeks."

"You haven't been sober or off your damned pills in weeks."

"Well, I'm sober now—and I haven't had a pill all day."

He stood there studying her for a moment, wondering when he had lost his lust for her, pondering why and how it was that with other women he could have an instant erection, but with Nikki lovemaking had become a tedious, difficult, humiliating event. "Another time," he said. He turned away, planning to continue on to the library to make some calls.

She reached out and grabbed him by the arm. "Don't you dare ignore me!" she warned. She tightened her grasp, her body hard against his.

"Oops! I'm afraid I've intruded," Lexie von Luenhalter said as she stepped into the hallway from the long gallery that led to the pool area.

Nikki's hold on his arm immediately loosened. Mano stepped

aside, grateful for the tall, striking woman's sudden apparition. Although she liked to think of herself as a princess—for she was married to a member of the deposed royal house of Prussia—Alexandra von Luenhalter was what Mano called an "American Beauty Rose": long-stemmed (with very shapely stems at that), high-breasted, and with a mane of shiny red hair that was now falling loose, in soft waves, over her bare, bronzed shoulders. She wore a brightly flowered sarong and a pair of open high-wedged sandals that revealed her scarlet-lacquered toenails and feet as tanned as her legs and arms.

The older daughter of a Supreme Court judge and a mother with social connections but no family fortune, Lexie had met Prince Rudolph von Luenhalter in Paris; the duke and duchess of Windsor introduced them shortly after the war. She obviously very much liked the idea of becoming a princess, for the prince didn't have a sou to his name; the Von Luenhalters spent much of their time as professional guests in the homes of friends, like Nikki and Mano, who liked to hobnob with royalty. That Luenhalter had become a French citizen years earlier and that even his claim of being a prince of Prussia was questionable (his birth had been illegitimate) seemed inconsequential to her.

"No, of course you haven't," Nikki smiled. "I was just welcoming Mano home from the hunt."

"What hunt?" Lexie inquired. "Don't tell me you've stocked Zephyrus with foxes and hounds now, Mano?"

"It was just a figurative statement," he replied with a warning side-glance to Nikki.

Lexie looked from husband to wife, and Mano saw the glint in her eyes. Nothing escaped Alexandra von Luenhalter's attention, nor his own.

"Well, I came in to look for you, Nikki. Rudi suggested we might have a picnic lunch down on the beach if it wasn't too much trouble. It's such a glorious day. Not too hot. A gorgeous spring breeze. I can't bear the sun in summer. Sweat and freckles and blistered skin. Ugh!"

"I think a picnic lunch is a fine idea," Nikki said. "I'll tell them in the kitchen, but you won't mind if I don't join you, will you?"

"Not another one of those migraine headaches of yours?" Lexie asked solicitously.

"Oh, no. Just letters to write." She turned on her heels and walked away.

Mano stood looking absently after her for a moment.

"Nikki has beautiful legs—and feet," Lexie commented to his surprise.

"I suppose she has," he replied.

"She told me how crazy you were about her feet when you fell in love with her. She said you were obsessed with women's feet."

"Nikki has a tendency to exaggerate." He meant to look away, but he first glanced downward. Lexie was wiggling her bare, red-tipped toes at him. "You're going to get us both into trouble if you don't watch out," he said, grinning.

"We've been in deep water for ages, Mano. The problem is we're both good swimmers."

"And if we weren't?"

"We might try to rescue each other."

"I didn't think you needed rescuing."

"That's curious. I've certainly sent out enough signals."

"I make it a rule not to save bored wives in the presence of their husbands."

"Oh, but I'm not bored. Rudi fascinates me. Always has. He knows so much about everything, and he's accepted everywhere. We were even invited to Sandringham for a weekend, but he refused because he's so loyal to the Windsors. You know, he's a third or fourth cousin—I can't recall which—to the duke and the king. And the wonderful thing about him is he's not a snob—or a pansy."

"Then what's your problem?"

"It's twofold. One—I'm sexually curious about other men. And two—I'm addicted to power, just as you are to feet. It excites me like nothing else in the world. Sends the adrenaline literally streaking through my body. Then there's money. We don't have a helluva lot. It would be nice to be able to say "no thank you" to some of the invitations we receive. But if we did, we would be prisoners of our apartment in Paris, which I loathe, but since it was given to us by a member of the duc de Richelieu's family, also a distant cousin of Rudi's, we are—for the moment at least—stuck with it. He's ill, poor man, and unable to cope right now with the disposal of his former mistress's flat. Still, it's a port in the storm. And the address is good."

She came a little closer to him, and the scent of her musky perfume filled his head.

"It's not Rudi's fault that he lacks the means for power," she continued. "Without money, power is elusive. Wouldn't you agree?" She was several inches taller than Mano; she tilted her head and glanced sideways at him, her mouth slightly open as she waited for his response.

"Money helps. But power is like sex appeal. Some people have it and some don't."

"Interesting theory." She turned to go, took several lilting steps and then, pivoting on her toes, faced him again. "Rudi goes on a tiger hunt to India next month for six whole weeks with the maharaja of Kumar. The idea was that I should use the time to visit my parents and my sister in New York, whom I haven't seen in ages. Six weeks is a long time. I'm sure I'll have a free weekend and hey, the world is growing smaller every day. We could just happen to catch up with one another anywhere you like—Paris, London, Rome, New York."

He said nothing, but his face was creased in a wry smile. He was considering her proposition and Lexie was aware of it. She nodded her head and then continued back toward the long gallery. Again she paused to look over her shoulder at him.

"I've never been to bed with a man with a foot fetish," she said. "But Ali Khan says I'm the best cocksucker on two continents."

"Which two?"

"Europe and North America."

"Funny thing," he grinned. "I'm flying to Buenos Aires in a few weeks. Who knows, perhaps you could make it three."

Her laughter trailed after her like scarlet ribbons as she glided up the gallery on her way out to the pool.

When Nikki came to look for Mano, she found the library door closed. A short while later Yorgo joined him, and the two men spent the afternoon working. They had lunch served to them on a tray. The library, in fact, was more an office than a place to read, although its name and decor—the walls were lined with bookcases and maps of the world—were Mano's concession to Nikki that Zephyrus would not be turned into an extension of his office in Athens. But there were two secretaries in his employ on the island, ready to come up to the villa immediately upon his request, and the vast, two-story room was equipped with ticker-tape machines, several telephone lines and, on the balcony that overlooked the room, desks, typewriters, and numerous antique chests converted into file cabinets.

Early that evening Mano and Nikki and their houseguests gathered, as usual in formal attire, in the lanai for cocktails. What wasn't usual was the service bar that had been equipped for drinks to be mixed on the spot, so to speak. Rudi von Luenhalter had cribbed the idea from the Windsors; the duke took great pleasure in his knowledge of cocktails and their ingredients, and could shake up the most exotic request without having to glance at a recipe.

Rudi, who had the arrogant features of his Hohenzollern ancestors, was tall, slim and elegantly mustachioed. He had never forgiven himself for marrying Lexie at a time when numerous authentic American heiresses were swarming Parisian salons looking for titled husbands. But Lexe had intrigued him as no other woman, and since she flatly refused to become his mistress, he had capitulated. Such were the vagaries of love.

"What will it be?" he called out to his attentive audience. He was standing behind the shiny brass service trolley in his impeccably tailored dinner clothes. "Nothing ordinary like gin and tonic, please.

I mean to show off my encyclopedic knowledge of the subject. The drinks have to be in the *Savoy Cocktail Book,* which the duke and duchess use as their bible. But I want unusual ones, like the Loud-speaker Cocktail—Cointreau, dry gin, brandy, and lemon juice. Shake well, strain. The drink accounts for why radio announcers have such peculiar enunciation. Three of them will produce oscillation, and after five it is possible to reach the osculation stage."

This was met by a modicum of laughter.

"The Golden Slipper Cocktail, prince, honey," Sally Jo Merrivale requested after someone whispered it to her. Sally Jo was from Merrivale, Mississippi, where her great-great-grandfather once owned the largest plantation; her family still owned the town. Sally Jo had attended convent school with Nikki; she had been sent there, it was said, to make sure she remained "untouched" until she was engaged to a suitable young man. In seven years she had managed to be married and divorced three times.

"Remember, if I clink it, you drink it!" the princely Rudi warned.

"What's in it?" Sally Jo asked. Her wide blue eyes looked doubtful.

"Yellow Chartreuse, the yolk of a raw egg, and eau-de-vie," he informed her.

"No, thanks. Anyway, you knew the recipe."

Mano edged to the door, hoping to escape without being noticed, but as he was leaving the room, he heard the sound of a woman's high-heeled shoes on the marble floor.

"Mano," Nikki called out.

He turned. "Yes?"

"You can't just leave a room filled with guests without saying something," she reprimanded.

"I just did."

"Where are you going?"

"To the library. I'm expecting a call from Paris."

"One of your lady-friends, I assume."

"No, Nikki, a business call. But anyway I couldn't stand one more minute of that idiocy in there."

"What do you expect people to do when they're isolated like this on an island?"

"There must be better ways to pass time—or more interesting people to do it with."

"Than your wife, you mean?"

"Nikki, please." He went over to her and took her hand, kissed it, and then kissed her cheek.

"Oh, Mano," she cried, leaning her head on his shoulder. "I'm so sorry."

"It's all right, beautiful child. Now you go back to your guests and I'll join you in a little while."

Reluctantly, she pulled back. He smiled affectionately, kissed her again on the cheek, quickly walked away, entered the library, and closed the door. Yes, what he wanted for friends and guests were not these social climbers and freeloaders but men like Winston Churchill, Lord Mountbatten, American political leaders, celebrities like Garbo or Deitrich, or great men and women of the arts. He enjoyed the idea of having royalty in his home, but wanted the real McCoy, not a synthetic character like von Luenhalter.

He had lied to Nikki. There was no call from Paris. But at least he would now have some time to himself. He poured a straight whisky and sat down in one of a pair of leather chairs that were separated by a globe on a stand. He ticked his fingers on the orb, absently spun it, and stared out the window.

It was a hell of a thing to own every pebble and grain of sand on an island paradise and find so little happiness there. He had thought he could create his own world here on Zephyrus, but he knew now that wasn't really what he wanted. He wished to be a vital part of the world beyond these shores. The scent of power that Alexandra von Luenhalter said obsessed her also consumed him. But to have power meant control over a weaker—or less clever—force. It meant an enemy had been quelled or checkmated or vanquished. On Zephyrus, only the wild dogs could be called the enemy, and they persisted in taunting him. His helicopter had not been able to locate their lairs. This very day Costa and five armed men had failed to find them although they had tramped over most of the island. The dogs chose to appear whenever they wanted; they seemed to materialize out of a great void.

"Perhaps this one today was the last survivor," Costa had told him after he and the men had returned. Something inside him, a nagging apprehension, told Mano this was not true.

No wonder he had no patience for the silly games of Nikki's friends.

The day had not been easy for him. No matter how busily he occupied his mind, the image of the dog's blood splattered on the bone-white rock remained, and with it came the dreaded memories that he never was able to put to rest.

It was midday and the sun was at its height. It shone blindingly on the white walls of his home in Smyrna. The sound of machinegun-fire echoed in his ears, there were screams, and suddenly something exploded into thousands of particles and a spray of red splattered against the wall he was facing.

He was a boy of nine, son of a successful Greek shipowner living in Turkey, happy and proud to follow in his father's footsteps. He was protected, only dimly conscious of the great hatred of the Turks for the Greeks. The sun shone in his eyes and he put his hand up to shield them. He was hot and sweaty and his face was dirty. Moments before, his father had pushed him under the steps of their front porch. Then came the gunshots, his mother's cries. He heard voices—a pair of Turkish soldiers were bending down over two bodies at the foot of the wall. One gave them each a kick with the toe of his boot.

"Dead!" he pronounced.

Mano was suddenly aware that he was not entirely concealed by the overhang of the porch. Slowly, terrified to make a sound that would make the men look his way, he pulled his legs back and squirreled deeper into the loose dirt. The two men turned, stood there poised. Mano was certain they had seen him. Then there were shouts from other soldiers up the street and the men ran in that direction. Mano held his breath and waited until he was sure they were gone. Then he crawled out from underneath the porch, and, on his belly, afraid of being shot if he rose higher, he made his way to his parents' bodies. He knew they were dead. It was just that he had to see them one more time.

They both lay facedown in pools of blood. He used all his strength to turn over his mother's body; he tried to stifle his sobs but was unable to control the tears that streamed down his grimy face. His mother had been hit by so many bullets that she was unrecognizable. He reached over to touch his father and felt the hard butt of his gun, which was partially concealed by his body. Pulling with all his strength, he freed it.

Screams and machinegun-fire filled the air. The acrid smell of smoke burned his nose and eyes. A moment later he heard running footsteps. Recalling what his father had once shown him, he raised the gun, steadied it, and fired. There was one short cry and a man fell to the ground about twenty feet from him. Mano stared across the space. The man wasn't moving. He was also not dressed in a Turkish uniform. Nor did he appear to have been armed. Only then did Mano realize it was one of his neighbors, the father of his best friend.

He crawled on his belly again to the back of the house and hid in a small toolshed. He remained there for days, using the night as cover to forage for food. After a few weeks he gained enough courage to go down to the port, where he stowed away in the hold of a cargo ship. As luck would have it, the ship was Egyptian and was headed for Piraeus. He spent several years on the streets of Athens until he apprenticed himself to a shipbuilder. Often he would wake up terrified in the middle of the night seeing, not his parents, but the face of the man, the friend and neighbor whom he had mistakenly killed.

As he sat in the darkening library, those images took hold of his mind. He could even smell the smoke from the machineguns and feel the heat of that terrible day.

Radzi, his butler, knocked softly to inform him that he was expected for dinner. He rose from his reflections to join Nikki and their guests. As he entered the hallway, Costa greeted him, obviously greatly disturbed—he seldom would dare to interrupt at such an hour.

"Mr. Zakarias, the dogs, we think we have found their den. I thought you might want to come with us."

"No, Mano," Nikki said, appearing on the scene. "You shouldn't even consider such a crazy idea. We have guests. Dinner is ready, and you are the host."

"I'm sure they can entertain themselves. They were doing a noble job earlier." He turned and left her watching him head for the front door with his overseer.

It was a fine evening. There was a cool sea breeze that carried a pungent mix of odors: sweet, intoxicating flora, peppery greenery moist with sea spray. The sky was navy blue, studded with stars and flooded with light from a half-moon. Two Land Rovers were parked outside the front door. Mano got into the first vehicle beside Costa. Three armed men were in the second car.

"I brought an extra gun if you want to use it. It's in the back seat," Costa told him. The Land Rover ground down the steep hill, angled onto the main road, and then turned off to make its way along an ungraded, bumpy stretch that led to the cypress forest on the far side of the island. As they neared the first clump of trees, both cars turned off their headlights. They drove on for a short distance until Costa drew to a stop. The driver behind him followed his lead.

The men got out of the cars, and Costa handed Mano the gun from the backseat. The overseer led the way. Black tree trunks were rising to either side of them; they were walking carefully, in single file, unable to avoid snapping twigs and fern fronds beneath their feet however lightly they stepped. Suddenly Costa stopped and pointed across the narrow, open glade they had reached.

Straight ahead, about two hundred feet away, the glade ended; it fell away into a sudden dip in the land, almost as though a deep hole had been cut across the forest by an earthquake or some other equally powerful force of nature. The uprooted trees there were natural cover.

"That's why we couldn't spot them from the helicopter—trees and brush blocked the view," Costa whispered to Mano. "We only figured it out when we developed the photographs we took today. Two black heads were visible just above the brush."

"How many do you think there are?"

"I wish I could be sure. Could be a whole pack—or just a few of them."

"You have a plan?"

"We have grenades. We'll get as close as we can, throw as many as we can, and then, when the dogs we haven't hit make a break for it, we'll aim to kill and pray we succeed," Costa explained. "Please stay by my side. If I say shoot, by Jesus pull the trigger. If I say run, waste no time. Both cars have keys in the ignition."

They began to edge closer. Mano held the gun poised to shoot. They came to within a hundred feet of the brush-covered chasm before Costa raised his arm. Everyone froze. A moment later the black figure of a dog could be seen on a ledge behind the crevasse.

Costa signaled his men, who rushed forward, hurling the grenades through the air. The explosions were deafening. The dogs that had survived were yelping wildly, and the animal on the ledge howled, leapt to one side, and then bounded straight for them.

"Shoot!" Costa ordered.

Gunfire filled the night. For a moment the large black creature seemed unharmed—it was still coming at them. Then, suddenly, it yelped, dropped to the ground, growled, and then was silent.

The men started forward, stopping every few feet to listen for any animal that might still be alive. Finally they reached the ravine. Costa's flashlight revealed a horrifying scene. Blood and animal parts covered the area. There was a muffled, whimpering noise. Costa and Mano both cocked their guns. A small pup, little more than a few weeks old, stumbled out of the debris.

"No!" Mano shouted.

But it was too late. Costa had already shot it.

They drove back to the house in near-silence. "I'll have the area cleared and the gorge filled in and planted over," Costa said when they reached the villa.

"I'd appreciate it if you would start tomorrow morning," Mano replied. "You did well, Costa," he added, and slapped him on the shoulder.

When he went into the house, he could hear the laughter of his guests. They were still at dinner. He started toward the dining room. Nikki stood up the moment she saw him in the doorway. "What is it, Mano?"

"The dogs are dead," he said. She was framed in the glimmer of the dozens of candles that lighted the room. He stared at her, realizing at that moment that they were no longer really husband and wife. They were two hostile strangers. He felt as if he had no place at this dinner party, that the house and the island could not be really his until Nikki was gone too.

"Thank God it's over," she sighed.

"Yes, thank God," he replied.

Act Three

> Buenos Aires and
> Venice When the Sun
> Shines, 1955–1957

15. ATHENA STOOD, TAKING HER SIXTH SOLO BOW, BEFORE THE curtain of the Teatro Colón. The whole hall was pandemonium—an avalanche of applause, roaring cheers, and aisles full of men elbowing as close to the stage as possible. Bouquets lined the proscenium; red roses fell from the gallery to Athena's feet. President Juan Perón was seated in the presidential box with his newest mistress, but all Athena could see was an ocean of faces and a tangle of arms outstretched toward her. She picked up a rose and tossed it to the maestro. She placed her hand on her heart and then threw a kiss to the audience. It was not a mere gesture; their zealous approval had come close to moving her to tears. And as she stepped back behind the curtain, their shouts and applause still thundering, she allowed herself a brief moment alone before coming out for another bow.

This was her second visit to Buenos Aires, and both she and Argentina had changed greatly in the intervening six years. Eva Perón, the president's fiery, power-driven wife, was dead, and in her absence the flame that had once made the Peróns omnipotent was flickering. Economic reverses and Perón's anti-clerical laws had so badly jeopardized the president's hold on the country that revolution seemed imminent. And although she had experienced as many disasters as triumphs (even, sometimes, both at once), Athena was the most celebrated opera performer in the world—*la Divina*.

By now she knew that her marriage to Roberto would always be marked by long, lonely separations. She could never understand why her great love for him was not able to change his nature. But she accepted his sexual passivity and managed to look the other way when he "strayed," as she liked to put it, and was grateful to him for the discretion he displayed during these sexual wanderings.

Her gratitude extended to Roberto's slavish devotion to her career. She believed with total conviction that he alone was responsible for the great wealth, power, and celebrity she enjoyed. Not that she doubted her talent or felt undeserving of the acclaim. But it was Roberto who fought to get her the best productions, contracts, and billings, who had helped to make her into a charismatic, stunning woman, the quintessential star, her tantrum and triumphs front-page news, her performances gala events, and the happenings in her backstage and social life hot copy in society and gossip columns.

Not everything that was written about her was true. She was not, as often portrayed, a *monstre égocentrique,* but merely determined to be *assoluta,* the best, and this contributed to the scandals and feuds reported so minutely by the press. Now famous enough to refuse to sing opposite a tenor who could weaken her performance, to work under a maestro who was not as tireless a rehearser and perfectionist as she was, or to appear in a production in which the costumes and sets were second-rate, she only fought to protect her reputation.

When she was on tour she missed Roberto's astute judgment, his constant attention. She would often slip into fits of moodiness and suffer painful bouts of loneliness. She had Vesta and Luigi and dear, dear Yanni to confide in, but socially she was on her own. The men who were photographed squiring her to dinners and galas when she was away from Roberto were either business associates or belonged to her large coterie of homosexual admirers. They were sweet and attentive but seldom interested her. Their fawning adulation presented no challenge.

Vesta, as always, was waiting backstage after her final curtain call (number twenty-three), authoritatively telling visitors and fans when to enter and when to leave Athena's dressing room. This was never an easy task because Athena could not be counted on to cooperate. Sometimes she insisted her well-wishers remain, that champagne be poured, that everyone be invited out for a late supper, even though she knew there would be hell to pay for it the next day. Other times she could summarily dismiss important guests—members of the press, dignitaries, and opera impresarios.

"There's never been a Lucia di Lammermoor as you played her tonight," Vesta said, after the room was cleared and she stood watching Athena's dresser help her out of the flowing costume she wore in the madwoman scene. "When you raised your arms, they were like the wings of a great bird, an eagle! Everyone backstage was bewitched. Even that bitch soprano, Peralta, who came back up to wait for her bows, ran back and forth crying—*really* crying, tears flowing like a pipe had burst—and saying, 'She's marvelous, marvelous, marvelous!' "

"She was probably crying because she thought if I was so marvelous she wouldn't get her usual curtain calls," Athena said. She pressed closer to the mirror, smeared her face with cleansing cream, and then carefully wiped off her stage makeup with a soft cloth. Lately her eyesight seemed to be growing poorer and when the stage was badly lighted, as it had been in some of the gloomy scenes of *Lucia,* she had the extra burden of worrying that she might trip over some misplaced prop. "I'll wear the blue dress, Carla," she told the dresser, who was hovering nearby.

"You can't wear that. You're having supper at the presidential palace with Perón and his bosomy blond lady friend," Vesta reminded her.

"I'm going to the hotel," Athena insisted. "Roberto is calling me from Paris."

"He'll call you later. You can't back out of an appointment with the president," Vesta countered.

"He's a fascist. I hate all fascists. In fact, Buenos Aires seems to be filled with Nazis and fascists. Roberto says we must be careful. They're going to overthrow Perón very soon. Maybe even tonight, while he's having supper and I'm snug in my bed at the hotel."

Vesta took the blue dress out of Carla's hand and substituted a brilliant red taffeta gown that was hanging on the clothes rack next to Athena's costumes. "Signora will wear this one," she advised the dresser. "Well, he is still the president and you are a guest in his country."

"And you are most tiresome, Vesta," Athena complained.

"If you find being a prima diva too difficult, you can always return to Italy and raise a houseful of bambini—not Roberto's, of course!"

Athena's face turned almost as red as the gown she was being asked to wear. She swept the cold cream jar up in her hand and was about to heave it at the mirror or—she had suddenly shifted position—at Vesta when there was a knock at the door. Carla glanced from one woman to the other with fear in her small, dark eyes.

"Answer it, Carla," Vesta ordered.

It was a delivery boy with a tremendous basket of magnificent white roses. Athena's anger relaxed into a happy smile. "From Roberto. He always remembers." She said no more about going back to the hotel; when she was dressed, she took one of the roses and tucked it into her neatly coiffed hairdo before examining her reflection in a full-length mirror. What met her glance pleased her.

She had shed over forty pounds in the past two years, mainly by nearly starving herself. But Roberto also maintained that divas in general were sadly lacking in glamour, and that if Athena could add an element of it to her appearance, she would even further glitter what was already her star presence. Vesta was given the task of dressing Athena in a manner that would create this image. She was clever at securing fabulous outfits from designers, who were pleased to give them as gifts—if they were sure that *la Divina* would appear or be photographed in them. The red gown was a Balmain, and its brilliance and simplicity—the high neck, long torso, and sweeping skirt—made Athena look fiercely elegant.

With the loss of weight, the bones on her face became more

pronounced and her dark eyes seemed wider, almost too large for her face. When she focused her eyes and opened them fully, the myopic stigmatism she suffered from made them seem mesmerizing. Although more startling than beautiful in appearance, she possessed something of the stature and passion that graced the image of the new Italian film star, Sophia Loren.

Vesta handed her a crimson lipstick that matched her gown; while Athena was painting her lips with it, Vesta slipped an intricate, jet-black necklace around her neck.

"I don't recall this piece," Athena said.

"A local jeweler thought it might suit you." Vesta stepped back and examined her. "And he was right." She glanced at her watch. "You're expected at the palace in thirty minutes. There's a general waiting outside to escort you. *Très distingué.* A broad, manly chest bristling with medals and ribbons. Thick black hair streaked with grey. You'll make a grand entrance on his arm."

Resigned to the social task she was about to undertake, Athena took a deep breath, which had the effect of instantly narrowing her waist and ballooning her breasts. Taking her evening bag from Vesta, she went out to greet the general.

Strings of incandescent lights shimmered like an endless strand of jewels along the nighttime streets of Buenos Aires. In the rear seat of an enormous limousine, Athena and the general were on their way to the presidential palace.

"Have you seen much of Argentina?" he asked.

"When one's appearing in a country, it's difficult to see much other than rehearsal halls, opera houses, and hotel suites."

"That's unfortunate. My country is a beautiful place. There's a great deal more to it than the nightclubs filled with tango dancers and the quaint flower stalls and shops along the narrow streets of La Boca and Belgrano, where most tourists go." He was making polite conversation, but there was a dark, serious look in his hard, narrow eyes; he was staring straight ahead, his thoughts obviously somewhere else.

231

"My husband is concerned that I might be in danger, being here at this time," she ventured rather daringly.

He turned and looked at her in surprise. "Why should that be?"

"Ah, my dear general, I was hoping you might explain to me."

"There's no reason for you not to be entirely safe in Buenos Aires, Señora."

"That's comforting to know," she smiled. "I heard rumors of revolution. I grew up in Greece and my family suffered painfully during the civil war there."

"That's sad to hear, but Argentina has a great leader who has the love and faith of his country." His tone left no room for contradiction; they rode the rest of the distance in near-silence, the general asking two or three simple questions as to her future plans while she was in Buenos Aires.

"I'll be here three months and do four operas in that time. In mid-September I return to Rome for a short while, then go on to Venice in late October to open the season there in early November. Do you like opera, General?"

"I haven't attended too many performances. But, Señora, if you represent the world of opera, I'm sure I would find it delightful."

"I don't know why that should be the case," she retorted. "I hate armies and war. However charming I might find you, I shall always hate them." It was their last exchange before they reached the presidential palace.

Athena had not been famous enough to have been invited to the president's home on her first tour to Buenos Aires, and although she felt a great distaste for Perón, she was sorry not to have met his late wife, the notorious Evita. The idea of a woman having such power as Eva Duarte Perón had over a man and an entire country fascinated her; there was something operatic about it, and about the woman's early death. It appeared to Athena that the shorter his or her years of glory or infamy, the more mythic a person became.

Some thirty people were gathered in an imposing white-and-gilt sitting room dominated by a massive portrait of the dead Evita, cool in an emerald velvet gown, hair upswept and diamonds aglow. All talk stopped when Athena entered the room with the general. To Athena's surprise, Perón, who was standing beside a chesty blond woman in a glittering white bouffant gown, immediately stepped up to her.

"Señora Varos, I am not a great opera aficionado, but never have I seen a performance that was so spellbinding," he said. "With the overwhelming volume of your great ovation, my *bravas* could not be distinguished. And so now I give them personally to you." He stood slightly away from her, squared his broad shoulders, and, throwing back his large head, shouted: *"Brava! Brava!"* There was immediate applause in the room, and he took her hand and kissed it. When he straightened, he signaled to a photographer.

"Would you honor me with a picture of us together, Señora?" He didn't wait for Athena's reply but turned to face the camera. Athena smiled obligingly.

Mano studied the photograph of Juan Perón and the amazing-looking woman smiling beside him. The newspaper caption in the morning paper read: PRESIDENTE PERÓN Y SEÑORA ATHENA VAROS. The article went on to say that the previous night the president had held a special supper in honor of Señora Varos following her startling performance in *Lucia di Lammermoor*. "The Greek-American soprano held her audience in abject slavery," it continued, "never letting them down and reaching a peak of eloquence in the closing mad scene of the opera."

Something about the woman captured Mano's attention. The statuesque carriage, the huge, penetrating eyes that seemed to stare right out of the photograph at him, the bold, clean-cut features. She wasn't beautiful in the style of most women that he admired. What she had was a commanding presence, which was, judging by the look on his imprudent face, apparent even to that old goat Perón.

Although Mano did not think too highly of Argentina's president, he always respected power, and it impressed him that a man like Perón was honoring an opera singer. She could, of course, be his new mistress. But something in Athena Varos's expression led him to believe this was not the case.

"Mano," Lexie called from the doorway to the bedroom of his suite, "wouldn't you like to come back to bed? I bet we could work up a real appetite for breakfast."

The light from the bedroom windows was shining behind her and making her tousled red hair look like a circle of fire. She wore a sheer aquamarine chiffon negligee that left little to the imagination. But after a week with Lexie in Buenos Aires, Mano was well acquainted with her body, its intoxicating curves, and its musky cavities.

"You like the opera?" he asked suddenly.

"Depends."

"On what?"

"The alternatives."

He laughed, put down the paper, and went over to her. He was pleased that Lexie had joined him on this trip. She was a good companion, great fun, adventurous, uncomplaining and, although damned expensive, with an unerring eye for costly jewels, a woman with—as she claimed—a prodigious talent for fellatio.

He went back into the bedroom with her. She drew the curtains and he stood watching her. No matter what shocking words Lexie pronounced or how raunchy she appeared, she was never able to conceal her excellent breeding. Even naked and engaged in sex, Lexie had class and style. He knew no other woman he could say that about. It was in the way she held her head, moved her hand, breathed; the perfume she chose, the finishing-school nasal twang in her voice, and even in the manner in which she made and took love—languorously, with a touch of amusement, never overeager, and yet with a deliberate reverence that placed her actions on a higher plane than merely satisfying sexual urging.

In the short week they had been together, Mano had developed a great fondness and a respect for Lexie. She was in Buenos Aires by her own choice. He had not sent for her, but had made it clear that if she joined him he would happily take care of all her expenses. He had added that he would be very busy during the day and she would have to find things to occupy her time. He smiled to himself as he glanced over to the bureau top, where a newly purchased diamond-and-emerald bracelet rested.

"Of course, if it's too expensive," she had said, "I can take it back and say you couldn't afford it."

She undid the belt of his silk robe and then dropped her negligee to the floor. As she scooped it up, she drew her hand along the inside of his thigh. Then she led him to the bed, placed the negligee neatly at its foot, and plumped up the pillows. "I do believe that things should be visually attractive," she said, climbing onto the bed and posing artfully.

He felt embarrassed that for the first time that week he couldn't get an erection. "Maybe I'm getting old," he complained.

"Or I'm too greedy."

They were lying side-by-side on the bed. He pushed himself up onto his elbows and studied her. Sunlight striped the room; a band of it came through the curtains and snaked its way up the middle of her golden body. "I'm not in love with you, Lexie," he said honestly.

"Were you in love with Nikki?"

"Maybe I don't know what love is," he replied, avoiding a direct answer.

"Sure you do. You're in love with power. You pursue it like most men pursue women."

"You're a clever lady, Lexie."

"Not nearly clever enough, or I never would have married Rudi. Women like me—that is, women without the talent or desire to achieve on their own—seal their fate in who they marry or who they embrace as lovers. Even if you do find you love me, you wouldn't divorce Nikki to marry me. I've no power to hand over to you. I bet you were dying to marry Nikki. In fact I'm certain of it."

"I was talking about love. How did we get onto the subject of marriage?"

"Reasonable question. Guess it's because of Vicki."

"Who's Vicki?"

"My kid sister. She's getting married just after I return to New York. To Clark Cameron McMaster. Cam, as he's called."

Mano suddenly seemed interested. "Related to Jonas McMaster?"

"His son and heir. Now that's rich and powerful! Hard to believe little Vicki won such a plum."

"You're not close to your sister?"

"I adore her. *Really.* But she was always the shrinking violet, the intellectual. Mother had almost given her up, what with her twenty-fifth birthday fast approaching. And then, what do you know? Wham! The jackpot! Cam McMaster. I'm staying in the States a little longer for the wedding. Quite a do! I'm to be matron of honor, Lordy-ha! Sounds awful, doesn't it?"

The telephone rang. He sat up and swung his legs over the side of the bed to answer it.

Lexie rose, put on her negligee, and headed into the bathroom. By the change in Mano's attitude, the seriousness on his face, and the hardened tone in his voice, she knew he was back to playing the power game. It was not yet 10:00 A.M. She had a long day ahead of her. While she showered she thought about what she would do to occupy herself. She was bored of shopping and she knew no one in Buenos Aires.

Mano stuck his head in the doorway. "I have to be downstairs in fifteen minutes," he announced.

Fly back to New York, Lexie suddenly decided. The best way to keep a man interested was not to be at his beck and call.

Athena woke to the sound of the telephone. It was only when she sleepily lifted the receiver that she heard the curious sounds outside the windows of her hotel suite. At first she thought it might be fireworks. Then she sat up, truly frightened. *Gunfire,* she thought.

"Athena?" the voice on the phone was saying.

"Vesta—what's happening? Where are you?" Athena reached over to turn on a light, and in her nervousness upset a carafe of water. It went crashing to the floor.

"What was that?"

"I just knocked over . . ." She paused in mid-sentence and glanced over at the clock on the bedside table. "It's four in the morning," she said.

"I'm on my way upstairs," Vesta announced. "The shots are coming from the direction of the presidential palace."

Vesta hung up. Athena gathered her robe around herself and went to the door to wait for her. There was noise and confusion in the corridor outside. Athena decided not to open the door until she heard Vesta knock, and even then she did so with some trepidation.

"There's no danger in the hotel," Vesta assured her when she was inside and the door was closed. "I called the manager. He said our street is safe but that we shouldn't leave the room. If he knew what was going on, he managed to sound as unsure as we are."

Vesta was fully dressed in khaki cotton trousers and a polo-neck sweater, but she had no makeup on and her hair was in disarray. "I tried to get Luigi before I woke you up. The outside lines are cut, so I couldn't get through to his hotel."

"You mean I can't call Roberto?"

"Why would you want to even if you could? Honestly, Athena, you drive me mad! Roberto! Roberto! Always Roberto! He's made you believe you can't move without his advice."

"Let's not quarrel. I thought he'd worry if he heard there was trouble here." She sat down in a chair. "I can't believe this is happening. The other night at the presidential palace—everything seemed so pleasant between Perón and General Seruda."

"What would that mean?"

"There must have been bad blood between the army and Perón, but I didn't catch it. You're really a babe in the woods, Vesta, for all your posturing. If the gunfire is coming from the presidential palace, it means a military coup is taking place. That's the way it always is—armies against dictators, all of them fascists fighting for power." She got up and began to pace the room. "I'm singing *Aïda* tonight. What shall we do?"

"I doubt if there'll be a performance. The maestro is at an estancia in the country, watching how they breed cattle. He's to return this afternoon, but I have a feeling they're not going to let anyone in or out of the city. At least that's what I just overheard two men say in the elevator. They were going to the penthouse. To see some big-time shipping tycoon, it seemed."

Athena was standing to one side of the window, her head angled to look down the length of the avenue her suite faced. The streetlights were out, and it was impossible to see anything at all except the erratic flashes of gunfire in the distance that momentarily lighted the sky and then quickly disappeared. There was a knock at the door and Vesta went to answer—it was Yanni, who had come from her room in the service wing to make sure Athena was safe.

The next few hours seemed endless to all three women. They ordered coffee, which took nearly an hour to arrive. The guests milling about the corridors had gone back to their rooms; amid almost unnatural silence, the women strained to hear if the gunfire, which had stopped before dawn, would begin again. The grinding sound of tank-treads was heard at regular ten-minute intervals. In between, there was nothing.

Finally, the radio, which had also been out, came back on at 8:00 A.M. It was announced that there had been a military coup with a minimum of bloodshed. President Perón was alive and on his way out of the country, though no one seemed to know where he was going. General Pedro Arumburu was in charge of the provisional government. To maintain calm in the city, a 10:00 P.M. curfew was in effect.

"That answers our question about tonight's performance," Vesta said, switching off the radio.

"I think we should leave," Athena said.

"You can't break a contract. You're scheduled to sing six performances."

238

"Talk to the hotel manager," Athena continued, as though she hadn't heard Vesta. "See if there is a plane or boat leaving here today. Then try to get a few hours sleep."

"We can't possibly be packed and ready that soon."

"Yanni is a whiz at packing in a hurry. And whatever we don't have time to include can be forwarded. Vesta, I know about coups and revolutions. If we don't get out now, we could be stranded here for months under God knows what kind of circumstances. I'm due to open in Venice on November 6, and here it is the second week in September. More important, I don't intend to be separated from Roberto any longer than necessary."

"I'll see if I can contact the maestro."

"You'll speak to the manager, Señor Vincente, about travel arrangements first—then, you can tell the maestro what we're planning to do." She started toward the bedroom. "And Vesta, if it's leaving behind that tango dancer that has you in such a tizzy, just remember—she doesn't pay your salary. I do."

The moment Vesta had stormed out of the suite Athena was sorry for what she had said, but she was just too tired to go after Vesta and apologize. "Yanni, you go to her room. Tell her I'm truly sorry and see if you can help her with anything. I must see if I can reach Signor Vallobroso."

There were still no outside lines, and the stress of the extraordinary events and her desperate need to leave Buenos Aires was wearing on her nerves. She realized her anxiety was overblown. Not only was she a celebrity, she was traveling on an American passport. If there was any danger in her remaining in Argentina, she could contact the proper authorities as well as all the highly placed officials she knew. It was unlikely that the new government would hold Athena Varos against her will.

Yet, somehow, since the moment of Vesta's early-morning telephone call and that first report of gunfire, Athena had been overcome with a sense of impending personal upheaval. Roberto felt further away from her than ever before. She sensed the threat these long separations were posing to their marriage. They were experiencing too many things independently, and it was creating distances between them that might one day be too difficult to cross.

They had once doted tirelessly on each other when they were together; now those times were limited because of the pressures of her career on them both. Then, too, both of them were changing; each had friends the other did not know, could not even visualize. She was just becoming aware of her power over people, her ability to get what she wanted. She would never admit it to Vesta or to Luigi—she could barely admit it to herself—but she was beginning to have a nagging suspicion that perhaps Roberto was trading on her power, not the other way around.

As soon as this faithless thought came into her head, she worked furiously to rid herself of it. To embrace it could only mean detaching herself yet more from Roberto—and if she did that, what would she have? What would she be? And what would she do?

She mustn't allow herself to languish. Call it a half-filled glass of water, not a half-empty one, Uncle Spiros would have advised her. Don't wish for things you can't cope with, he might as well have added. She had wanted marriage and great acclaim in the opera world, and she had both. What right did she have to be depressed and dissatisfied? Everything in life is a matter of trade-offs; if something's price is too high, then give it up. Ah, but which did one abandon, career or marriage? Neither, of course. It was all foolishness. She would have both.

The telephone interrupted her train of thought. "Athena," Vesta said, exhaustion in her voice, "I've had the hotel try to book us out of here today, but everything is either jammed or grounded—boats, planes, even buses. There's a chance that we can get on the Pan-American flight to New York the day after tomorrow, and transfer for Rome there."

"Did you speak to Vincente personally?"

"Of course I did."

"All right, Vesta. Thank you. And—did Yanni tell you . . ."

"Forgiven," Vesta said quickly. "Luigi just walked over and we're going to put our heads together to see what we come up with. Try to rest."

Athena knew it would be impossible for her to rest—nor did she want to be alone right now. She decided she would speak to Señor Vincente herself about travel arrangements. She dressed quickly, not forgetting that she had to look as good as possible at all times. After being assured that Señor Vincente would be waiting for her in his office, she left her suite for the meeting.

There was a man in the elevator along with the operator when she entered. He immediately removed his fedora hat. He had dark glasses on, but after they had descended a floor and were still alone, he removed them.

"Signora Varos," he said and smiled. "Let me introduce myself. I am Manolis Zakarias."

She nodded her head in acknowledgment. The name rang a bell somewhere in the back of her mind, but she couldn't place it. He was looking at her face with an intense, searching gaze that made her feel uncomfortable, as though he was seeking something specific and that he knew was there.

"You seem troubled," he said.

"Isn't everyone in Buenos Aires today?" she replied.

The elevator stopped and two more people entered the car. The man moved closer to her. His cologne had a lemon-verbena scent and his pin-striped suit was impeccably tailored. They were about the same height, and since he was looking straight at her she could not help but note the curious color of his eyes—like the sea at night.

"The *Peronistas*, of course. Was the president a friend, or merely an admirer like myself?"

The elevator door opened onto the lobby. He stepped back to let her out first, but then followed her and took her gently but surely by the arm.

"Please forgive my forwardness, but you *do* look troubled. And perhaps, there's just a chance, of course, but perhaps I can help."

"I don't think so." She drew back and he released his hold on her arm.

"Try me," he said, grinning.

Something about the impudence of that smile made her laugh. "Military coups seem to play havoc with transportation," she said.

"Ah! You want to leave Buenos Aires."

"Today!" She started toward Señor Vincente's office, but Mr. Zakarias was still right behind her.

"Signora Varos," he called out. She stopped and he came up to her. "I would be happy to put either my private plane or one of my ships at your disposal."

"You can't be serious."

"But I am."

Suddenly his identity came to her. The famous—or infamous, depending on which newspaper you read—Greek shipping magnate. "There will be four of us," she said. "I'd prefer to fly."

"Where to?"

"Rome."

"And so it shall be. I'll ring you later with the time."

He bowed slightly, smiled encouragingly, as though to say that everything would be all right, and then strode out of the hotel.

16. THE LIMOUSINE CARRYING ATHENA AND HER SMALL EN-
tourage snaked its way across Buenos Aires late that afternoon en
route to a private airfield on the outskirts of the city. The sun had
withdrawn, the bright day dulled, and lowering clouds threatened
rain. Athena looked out through the limousine's tinted windows at
the surrealism of anarchy. Tanks, turret guns swiveling, were rumbling down elegant but deserted avenues; squads of soldiers and
policemen were patrolling government buildings in expectation of
riots that did not occur; roadblocks had been set up in what seemed
a haphazard fashion. The journey, which should have taken no
more than thirty minutes, lasted over an hour. But the plane they
were to board was privately owned, and Athena knew it would be
waiting for them.

"This looks like the revolution no one attended," Luigi said over
his shoulder. He was sitting in the front seat next to the chauffeur.

"I'll be a lot happier when we're watching it from the air," Athena
commented.

"How do we know the authorities will allow us to take off?" Vesta
asked.

"Because Mr. Zakarias had no doubts," Athena replied.

Vesta leaned in closer to her so that the driver couldn't hear her words. "Is that drawn from tea-leaf readings, or do you have something upon which to base such trust?"

"Instinct."

Vesta straightened and sighed.

"Also, he's extraordinarily rich and owns an important fleet that transports a lot of Argentinean beef to other countries."

"I like that better."

"Do we know who else will be on this flight?" Luigi asked.

"Do you ask your host who his guests are before you accept an invitation?" Athena snapped.

"It might be a handy bit of knowledge during a military coup," Vesta said. She turned her head to look out the rear window. "Someone could ambush us thinking we have Perón in the car," she muttered—not quite under her breath.

The color drained from Yanni's face. She stiffened, backed away from the window, and pressed herself into the corner of the rear seat.

"Stop it, Vesta," Athena chided. "There's no need to be frightened."

The silence inside the car was almost palpable from that moment on. They were halted at the roadblock (the third they had encountered) set up at the entrance to the small airfield. A sleek twin-engined plane sat on the runway, its silver wings shimmering under the now-falling rain. Written in tall, bright blue letters along one side was the name KONSTANIKA.

"Passports," demanded a tall, rangy soldier who looked like he belonged on a cattle ranch.

The three women handed theirs to Luigi, who passed them through the front window. The soldier took them and walked away to confer with three other uniformed men.

"What if they don't return them to us?" Vesta whispered.

The tall one loped back with the others and, two soldiers standing on each side of the limousine, ordered them to open the front and back doors. After poking their heads inside, staring at the occupants and then the passports, the soldiers shut the doors and handed the documents back to Luigi. The drivers in the two trucks that were blocking their way were signaled to clear a path for the limousine.

"That's as close as I ever want to come to soldiers carrying guns," Vesta said, sighing with relief. The gates to the airfield opened and their driver pulled the car up alongside a frame building. Before the car came to a halt, their benefactor appeared from the entrance and sauntered down the steps to greet them.

It was only the second time Athena had seen Manolis Zakarias, but she was somewhat taken aback at how familiar he seemed to her. In part the feeling could be attributed to the boldness of his features, which made him look so memorable. But intuition, presentiment (however much Vesta might ridicule it), and something deep inside her confirmed the feeling she had experienced at their first meeting. This Greek millionaire, brusque in manner, short in stature, and impulsive in his actions, would come to play an important role in her life.

"I trust the roadblocks didn't frighten you," he said, placing his hand under Athena's arm and leading her up the steps to the building. "We'll have some coffee or a drink if you like while your baggage is being put on board and the plane readied for takeoff."

"Are we to have the pleasure of your company on the flight, Mr. Zakarias?" Vesta asked once they were inside.

"I'm afraid not. I haven't completed the business I'm here for. It seems that I was negotiating with the wrong regime. But I'm hoping you'll have a pleasant journey. The weather reports are good. Your pilot and crew are expert. You'll set down only once in Lisbon to refuel. You're scheduled to arrive in Rome shortly after ten tomorrow morning—Italian time." He glanced at his watch. "You'll be airborne in ten minutes," he promised.

Not until they were being escorted to the plane did he take Athena aside to exchange a few private words. Evening had not quite descended, the nose of the plane and the headlights were pointed toward the horizon, and the half-light threw the area in which they were walking into veiled shadow. A man ran up to Mano and handed him an umbrella that opened to something the size of a small tent. Mano's grip was firm under Athena's elbow as he hustled her across the open field toward the aircraft. They were unable to avoid the many puddles, but neither seemed to care that their shoes were muddy when they reached the ramp to the cabin door. The others were already inside and a uniformed steward stood waiting in the doorway for her to join them. Mano held Athena back.

"This has been a most gracious gesture, Mr. Zakarias," she said before he had a chance to speak.

"Mano," he grinned. "Call me Mano. And you? Shall it continue to be Signora Varos?"

"My married name is Vallobroso," she replied. "But of course, please use Athena."

"Ati," he said slowly.

She stepped back, surprised, and he tilted the umbrella to keep the rain off her.

"Too familiar?" he asked.

"No . . . no. It was a childhood name. I was startled when you said it."

"You object?" He glanced at her and waited for her reply.

"I can hardly find fault with a man who has put a plane and crew at my disposal," she answered.

The plane's motors whirred louder and the propellers shrilled through the rain-splattered evening. She drew away, stepped onto the steps, and turned to him. She had meant to say a simple *good-bye,* but she was caught off-guard by the earnestness of his expression. For the moment she stood frozen, staring at him, aware as though for the first time that his large features formed a full face whose bone structure made it seem grave even when the wide mouth smiled, that the navy-blue eyes were staring at her with an almost insolent, penetrating gaze. He offered her the umbrella for the few steps she had left, but she ignored the courtesy and, with a small wave, turned quickly away, and rushed up the steps into the cabin. Not able to resist one more look at this curious, fascinating man, she wheeled around in the doorway, certain that he would still be watching her from the foot of the steps as they were being pulled away.

Through the scrim of rain and the howl of the propellers, he stood looking up at her. There seemed to be an invisible thread connecting them. She could not make out the expression on his face, but she was convinced he could see hers clearly. She smiled and waved her hand again. The steward, whom she now realized was a young Greek, asked her to step clear of the door. When she did, he closed it and the gossamer strand was severed. Although she could not see out of the cabin windows because of the rain and the darkness, she knew that Mano Zakarias still stood in the rain, watching.

Anxiety gripped her while she allowed herself to be strapped into her seat. She wasn't sure what was happening to her. Something—someone—had come between her and thoughts of anything but Mano Zakarias. She twisted herself around to look out the window next to her. The flashing lights on the steel wing of the plane, the splatter of rain as it hit it, were all that was visible. Inside the cabin the overhead lights flickered; the aircraft rumbled across the runway, accelerated, and then lifted quite suddenly off the ground.

"*Adios,* Buenos Aires!" Luigi yelled from the seat behind her. Vesta and Yanni were seated across the aisle, Yanni with her eyes closed, resting from the day's ordeal, Vesta nervously drumming her fingers on the arms of her chair.

They were now airborne, the lights were on in the cabin, and the steward was closing the blue brocade drapes over the windows on both sides. Athena took a good look around her. The area they were in was set up like a sitting room of a yacht, with club chairs and tables secured to the floor. All the chairs pivoted so that the occupants could turn to talk to one another comfortably. At the front of the cabin was a bar; since she smelled food cooking, she assumed there was a galley beyond it. At the rear center of the cabin was a large retractable movie screen that was now being lowered.

"There's an office and four compartments with beds and private baths behind the screen," Luigi leaned forward to tell her. "I did a thorough walk-through before you came on board." She turned her chair toward him. "The steward's name is Peros and he speaks mostly Greek. But I did learn that there is caviar and roast beef for dinner and that the three movies they have aboard all star Marilyn Monroe. Seems Zakarias is a fan."

He stared at her for a moment or so, stroking his red goatee with thoughtful concern. He had been her private accompanist for over seven years, traveling wherever she went, working with her on her repertoire several hours every day. They were close friends who shared many personal thoughts and experiences, and he not only respected her for the great artist that she was, but loved her for the caring person she could be. His decision to devote his work to her had involved much soul-searching. It meant forfeiting his own ambitions for a concert career. He was never sorry he had made the sacrifice.

Athena Varos was more than a diva. There simply was no other singer like her. She gave so much of her voice and herself. Even in their private sessions, she never held back any part of her glorious voice. She could reach a high B-flat and hold it six, seven, eight beats. When she was Mimi in *La Bohème*, you believed she really *was* dying. Sometimes he wanted to run out onstage and lift her limp body in his arms and breathe life into it. He knew that was how many of the people in the audience also felt, and why they were defensive, *protective*, when the press exploited her propensity for drama. Unlike him, they knew very little about her private life.

Watching her shift nervously in her seat, Luigi fought to hold back his emotions. He interlocked his long fingers and clasped his hands so tightly that the knuckles turned white. She looked pale in the harsh light of the cabin, and there were small, fretting lines at the edges of her mouth. She drove herself too hard and Roberto did little about it. But if she didn't slow down soon she would wear out her glorious equipment—and perhaps her heart as well. "You're all right, aren't you, Athena?" he asked gently and reached over to touch her shoulder.

She managed a wistful smile and patted his hand. "It's been a most unusual day. I didn't realize how exhausted I was until I sat down before takeoff." Peros came by with a tray with champagne and caviar, which he set down beside her. She said a few words to him in Greek and he grinned at her, pleased.

"Oh, God! I'm going to be sick!" Vesta announced. "I don't know whether I loathe boats or planes more!" She jumped up from her seat, Yanni directly behind her to assist, and the two of them disappeared behind the movie screen.

Athena took a sip of the champagne, leaned back against the headrest, and closed her eyes. Not only was she dog-tired but her head was throbbing. Her mind returned to the moment when Mano Zakarias had called her "Ati." How could he have known her family nickname? Perhaps their meeting had not been as accidental as she assumed, she suddenly thought. Perhaps Mano Zakarias had not only planned it but investigated her past to find out what he could about her . . . But that was ludicrous! Why? Unconnected sounds and bits of memories skirled through her head. Over everything were sudden bursts of gunfire, and with them a flashing image of Sofia Galitelli running through thick brush, blood coursing down her face, crying, "Ati! Ati!" But of course Signora had never called her Ati.

It was the story Yanni had told her of how Sofia Galitelli had been ambushed and shot by guerrilla fighters; somehow the day's events brought it to her mind. Nonetheless, despite the ludicrousness of the idea, she couldn't help but wonder if she and her entourage had been used as a cover to smuggle someone out of Argentina.

"All the cabins were empty?" she asked Luigi.

"That's a strange question. Of course they were."

"I just wondered if—maybe—there were other passengers."

"Only us sheep."

"Somehow I wish you hadn't said that." She sighed and rested her head again on the back of the seat, feeling angry now that she allowed herself to entertain such an outlandish notion. The truth was that she did not want to consider the idea that Mano Zakarias was as attracted to her as she was to him. She wasn't sure if this had anything to do with his very generous gesture. Still, that could hardly account for her extreme anxiety, the tightness in her chest, her pounding heartbeat.

No, it wasn't Mano Zakarias that was at the root of her painful confusion. It was her strange ambivalence, now that she was safely on her way to Rome, about a reunion with Roberto. She would never admit it to anyone—especially not Vesta, who had been against it from the very beginning—but something was very definitely wrong with their marriage. It wasn't Roberto's fault, she was certain of that, and it was more than the lack of sex between them, or the fact that when they did make love it was always oral. It would shock a priest or a doctor to learn that she remained "intact" (for she couldn't honestly call herself a virgin). In the past, their sex life had seemed unimportant to her. It was Roberto's devotion that counted, the gratitude she felt for his dedication toward making her an international opera star.

But since she had lost so much weight, not only her physique but her entire personality had undergone a drastic change; at times it seemed that she was another woman entirely. From a buxom wife who looked older than her years she had been transformed into a chic, youthful celebrity—she was, after all, not yet thirty—with the figure of a fashion model (an impression the glamorous clothes Vesta found for her did much to underscore). She had long been accustomed to the overwhelming love extended to her by her male fans. With her new persona she found that other men, too, looked at her with a certain gleam, something she hadn't noticed previously except, perhaps, during the chance encounter with Mark Kaden so long ago. She had become what her former Bronx neighbor saw her as being in Rome before Roberto: a sexually desirable woman. This knowledge aroused her own carnal appetite, but, mercifully, that passion was spent in her music and the hard work involved in always giving her best—and then some—onstage.

She picked up a picture magazine from the table beside her and began to thumb through it in order to distract herself. She was amused to find a photograph of herself taking a bow after the successful opening of *Lucia di Lammermoor* in Buenos Aires. She studied it for a long time. The shot had captured her raising her arms to the gallery; a trace of tears was visible on her face. She could never overcome the tremendous emotion she felt when looking out over the orchestra pit to the hundreds of faces, the waving arms and shouts of *brava*. Given such acclamations, she knew she should never feel insecure. Yet each time she began a performance, the same fears of failure assailed her—which was why, she realized, she was so relentless in her striving for perfection.

She handed the magazine to Luigi and took a short walk aft to see how Vesta was doing. She was sitting up in the bed of the first compartment; Yanni was applying cold compresses to her head. "I think you should come back into the main cabin and stop concentrating on the motion," Athena suggested. "Actually, the flight is quite smooth. It's all in your mind."

"Go away and let me die!" Vesta cried.

"Well, when you're through playing *La Bohème,* come out and join Luigi and me," Athena said, laughing.

Dinner was served by Peros and his assistant, another young Greek, on silver trays, with fine china, crystal, and linen. The food was well-prepared and she ate everything set before her; she was famished, she realized, after having missed lunch in the rush to pack and prepare for the flight. When dinner was over, she, Luigi, and Yanni watched Marilyn Monroe in *Gentlemen Prefer Blondes* and then *How To Marry a Millionaire*. Afterward she retired to the largest sleeping cabin, which took up the whole rear of the aircraft. It belonged to her host, of course. The bed was large enough to sleep two comfortably. Several pair of monogrammed silk pajamas and a paisley robe were folded neatly in the bureau drawer, and in the medicine cabinet in the private bathroom was a bottle of the lemon-verbena cologne he wore. Well, she thought as she slipped into a fitful sleep, if busty blondes with little-girl voices appealed to him, she was entirely safe.

*　　*　　*

The plane was coming down fast, tilting to one side so that the view Athena got of Rome was angled dramatically. She was not yet fully awake. Her few hours' sleep had been interrupted by the landing in Lisbon, and she hadn't been able to doze off again. She opened her purse and took out her compact. Dark circles underlined her eyes. In disgust, she quickly clicked the gold case shut. She glanced over at Vesta, who had slept through most of the flight with the help of a sleeping tablet and now appeared refreshed and full of energy again.

The *Konstanika* (*Whose name was that?* she wondered) straightened, tilted again, and then sank lower and lower until it gently touched the tarmac. Its engines racing, the aircraft shot forward for a short distance before slowing down enough for the pilot to turn it around and guide it toward a hangar. When it came to a complete stop, Athena glanced at her wristwatch. It was five minutes after ten. Precisely on time.

Peros opened the cabin door and lowered the silver steps. The sun was out, but half-hidden by low clouds.

"Italy! Home!" Vesta cried as she stood in the doorway and breathed the cool morning air.

"Did anyone let Roberto know we were coming?" Athena suddenly asked Luigi.

"I don't believe so," he replied, helping her with some of her parcels.

"I've never done that before," she said.

"Well, it wasn't an ordinary journey. I'm sure he'll understand."

"Of course he will," she agreed. She followed Vesta down the steps, with Yanni and Luigi behind her. While they were all walking across the tarmac behind Peros, her anxiety rose again and she swallowed hard in an attempt to calm herself. She felt ashamed, somehow neglectful and disloyal to Roberto, so she was overcome when she walked into the small private terminal and saw him waving frantically to her from behind the customs station. Once she was through, she rushed over to him and wrapped her arms around his neck.

"Roberto! Roberto!" she cried, tears streaming down her face. "I'm so thankful to see you. How did you know I was arriving?"

"There was a call from the office of Manolis Zakarias. You'll have to tell me all about him. They say he's now one of the richest men in Europe. I'm wild with curiosity."

"Later, later," she begged. "Now I just want to hear about you and everything you've been doing since I've been away."

He made a big fuss about the others, who were to be driven back into the city in a limousine Zakarias had provided. Then, once they were alone, he led her to a shiny, red, custom-built sports car parked outside. "What's this?" she asked.

"Our new car," he said proudly and came around to open the door for her.

"It's so low to the ground, Roberto. Hard to get into without ripping my stockings," she complained, sliding uneasily into a bucket seat. He seemed not to have heard her; humming happily to himself, he got in behind the wheel. He turned the key in the ignition, stepped on the gas, and—to his delight and Athena's irritation—the car jolted forward with a loud, grinding noise that drowned out all other sound.

Roberto opened the door to their apartment with an air of smugness. On the way in from the airport he had announced that considerable renovations had been done while she was in South America. He had bought the apartment directly below, incorporated it, via a circular staircase, into theirs, and converted it into a media room with a large-screen television, the finest to be found in high-fidelity equipment. Some of the rooms in their original apartment had been completely redecorated.

When Athena entered the front hallway, everything appeared strange. Black marble had been laid over the floor, and white marble busts of Puccini, Verdi, Donizetti, Rossini, and Bellini, all in Roman togas, with sightless eyeballs and gold nameplates, were perched on black-and-white striated marble columns. (*Where,* she thought, *could he have found them?* She decided they must have come from an old concert hall that had been torn down.) The walls were covered in gold brocade; a crystal chandelier, not the familiar brass one, was hanging from the center of the ceiling. To Athena's amazement, the room had been artificially curved to appear circular.

"Since I had no idea what would happen in Argentina, it's a miracle that the work was completed in time for your homecoming," he said. "Come, you won't believe how wonderful the sitting room looks now."

He took her hand to pull her forward but she refused to move. "How could you redo everything without consulting me?" she asked.

"Why, Athena, you were never interested in such things before." He looked at her with astonishment.

"That was before. This is *my* home, too."

"I thought you'd be pleased. It was a special surprise I was preparing for you. What was right for us when we first married no longer seems appropriate. You're an internationally known diva, one of the greatest in the world. Where you live must reflect your uniqueness. Now, come, follow me."

He darted ahead of her, leading the way into the sitting room, which had taken on a much more formal tone, to the dining room, which had also been reconstructed into a circular shape through glass-fronted vitrines filled with beautiful china she had never seen before. Then he led her back through the hall and down the new staircase to the media room.

"I'm not sure I'll be able to work all this complicated machinery," she said.

"Of course you will. I'll show you."

"I don't know what to say, Roberto. I feel like I'm in another apartment, someone else's. Not mine."

"You'll soon get used to it. I've left your bedroom and your study for you to do with as you wish."

Roberto's eyes were fixed on her, and she realized she had to say something. "It's a bit of a shock and I'm very, very tired. It was a long flight and it's really still the middle of the night for me. And yesterday—well, it was terrifying. I worried so about what you must have been going through, not knowing how I was."

He came over to her and took her hand. *"Mia cara,* I'm a blundering fool. I just wanted to make you happy."

She was immediately engulfed in guilt. Whatever her feelings about the work done on the apartment, he had spent a lot of time and thought on it. It was true she asked little of her surroundings except that they be comfortable, commodious, and well-staffed. And she had always relied upon his judgment and taste. It was grossly unfair of her to be angry at him for something he could not know he was doing wrong.

"All I need is a little sleep, Roberto. Please forgive me if I've hurt your feelings. That's the last thing I want to do."

"Would you like a drink to relax you?"

"No, thank you."

"Of course, you're right, rest is what you need." He helped her back up the circular stairway. "I've left a great stack of mail in your study, but wait until Vesta is here before going through it. There's also the schedule for Venice. You have three weeks before rehearsals, and I want you to enjoy that time. You don't often have such a long stretch between engagements. I don't think you should even go through a score. All the roles are familiar to you, anyway, since you've just sung them in Buenos Aires. In fact, I think I'll lay down a law. No more than two hours a day practice with Luigi until rehearsals begin. That will give you time to pick out new fabrics for your room—though only if you like, of course. But it would take your mind off your work."

They were in the hallway just outside her bedroom. "You've lost more weight—hmm, this is getting serious. Soon you'll melt down to nothing." He chucked her gently under the chin. "I'll send lunch in to you on a tray. Something simple, all right?"

"Fine." She was suddenly aware of the sweet scent of his cologne and the amount of talcum powder he used on his face to cover the persistent shadow of his heavy beard.

He kissed her on the cheek and opened the door for her. The

room was unchanged, and there was a huge bowl of white roses on the bureau. When he was gone she drew the blinds. She wanted darkness, to shut out everything. She undressed clumsily, dropping her clothes on the floor, and crawled into the bed in her slip, not having the energy to put on a nightdress. Her head sank into the pillow, but her body refused to relax. She tried to empty her mind of all thoughts and images, and her head began to throb from the effort. She rolled over and buried her face in the pillow. Impressions continued to flash in her mind.

The expression on Mano Zakarias's face when she boarded the *Konstanika* appeared to her as if in a film close-up. The deep, warm gruffness of his voice echoed in her ears; the scent of lemon verbena seemed to fill the room.

At least twenty sleepless minutes had passed, and she was about to get up, dress, and go find Roberto when the telephone beside her rang. Only a very few people knew her private number.

"Ati?"

"Who . . . who is this?" But she knew.

"Mano."

"Where are you?"

"Buenos Aires. The telephones are working again and my business is almost finished. I leave here tomorrow. Was your flight comfortable?"

"Very."

"Good."

"How did you get this number?"

"Ah! That is one of my little mysteries."

"I should thank you again."

"Are you glad to be back in Rome?"

"Yes, naturally."

"Will you be there long?"

"Three weeks. Then I go to Venice."

"What a splendid coincidence! I'll be in Venice about the same time."

The line developed static and his voice faded in and out.

"Mano . . ." she began.

"Yes?"

"I'm very glad you called."

It was dark in the room, since the drapes were heavily lined, and she fumbled to hang up the receiver once he had said good-bye. She lay looking up into the darkness above her. Her tension had disappeared and she felt suddenly at peace, but very, very tired. She turned on her side, hugged one of the pillows close to her body, and was asleep in a matter of moments.

17. Sun streaked through the piazzetta and across the Piazza San Marco. The city was alight with the glory of a perfect autumn morning. Athena sat alone on the terrace of a café, facing the four golden horses on the façade of the Basilica, sipping from her steaming cup of coffee, and listening to the *marangoni* bells that for centuries had proclaimed the beginning and end of the working day in Venice.

Her first rehearsal was not scheduled until afternoon, but she had awakened early. Rather than disturbing Roberto, she had dressed and gone out for breakfast. The square was not yet crowded, the way it would be by mid-morning, and it was easy for her to imagine Venice in the fifteenth century, when it had been at the height of its splendor. Much of the ancient grandeur had survived.

She turned to look at the façade of the Ducal Palace, with its graceful arcades and porticos of sequential gothic arches, and met the candid, admiring gaze of a good-looking young Italian. She smiled because she thought he might have recognized her, but she immediately realized her mistake. He answered her smile with a beckoning one of his own. She put on the large pair of sunglasses that were resting on her table and swiveled her chair so that her back was to him.

Venice was overrun with Don Giovannis watching out for the

258

sway of buttocks, the small signals of receptivity that meant that a woman, already intoxicated by the romance of Venice, had assessed his wares and found them irresistible. Rich foreign women traveling alone or with a group of other single women were expected to be the most vulnerable and, therefore, were most prey to the lingering looks and love games that unlocked bedroom doors and caused even intelligent females to cast away their caution as well as their clothes.

He was standing beside her table. "Please leave," she said.

"Just for one moment." He pulled back a chair and sat down.

She removed her dark glasses and looked directly at him. "I am Athena Varos. If you don't know the name, it doesn't matter. But I am well-known and so I thought you might be a fan. That was my mistake. But either you go sit someplace else or I shall call the *polizia,* and I assure you they do know who I am." She replaced the glasses and from her large handbag drew out the score of the first opera she was to sing, *Turandot,* which would open the season in Venice. She immediately set down to work notating one of the arias.

Don Giovanni sat watching her for a few moments, then slid his chair back and got up. Out of the corner of her eye she saw him move to another table, where he sat down, legs splayed, leaning back in his chair, face raised to the sun, no doubt alert to the possibility of tempting another lone woman.

She had not been surprised when Roberto insisted on joining her in Venice. It was the city he loved most, where he claimed he felt the greatest pride in being Italian. Also, its proximity to Verona enabled him to see to family affairs and visit Grazia for the day. Still, she suspected there was another reason—his interest in her new friendship with Mano.

Jealousy played no part in his eager curiosity, of that she was certain. Never once in the eight years of their marriage had Roberto displayed mistrust. He proudly bragged to their closest associates that they were so tightly bonded that distance and time apart only drew them closer together. Until recently, Athena had agreed with him. Now, holding her changing emotions in check, she was confident that Roberto did not guess the truth—that she found herself falling in love with another man, a man whom in fact, she had met only twice in her life.

No, Roberto could never entertain the notion that she was on the brink of infidelity. He saw the friendship extended to his wife by Mano as a great social conquest for both of them. The Greek was larger than life, a power figure to equal and perhaps even surpass men like Henry Ford, John D. Rockefeller, and Joseph Kennedy. And his wealth was legendary. The loan of his private plane had been a generous gesture, but for him no more extravagant than someone else lending you his car for a trip to the corner store. Roberto had even encouraged her to accept the Greek's offer to throw a party in her honor on the opening night of *Turandot*. On the other hand, Roberto did not know that Mano called her at least once a day, and that he had been deterred from appearing at her door in Rome only by her threat not to see him in Venice.

Now, in only seven days, he would arrive here on his yacht, the *Atlas*, along with numerous celebrities (Marlene Dietrich, the duchess of Kent, and Noël Coward among them) and his wife, Nikki—the mysterious Konstanika about whom Athena had wondered so much.

The very idea that she was considering having an affair with a married man (and her thoughts were focused on little else, except her music) was shocking to Athena. Yet her one concern was how it could be managed in a discreet way when both their spouses were to be in Venice.

"Athena."

She glanced up into Luigi's broad, smiling face. "Luigi! Sit down. Join me. I thought I was the only one up at such an hour."

He ordered a coffee from the waiter. "Where's Roberto?"

"Still sleeping."

"You seem distracted."

"A bit."

"Want to talk about it?"

"No, I don't think so."

"Nothing to do with *Turandot*?"

"No . . . no."

"Because we could spend some extra time on it if you like."

"If you could, I would appreciate it. I always prefer to be over-prepared than just plain confident."

"It's one of the secrets of your success. The other being genius."

She laughed and studied his kind, clever face. She always felt that Luigi knew more than he said, that hidden behind those clear brown eyes was a depth of knowledge that he could, if called upon, dip into. She knew no one more sensitive to her inner feelings regarding her music. He was, in fact, a consummate musician and she wondered why he remained in a job where his talent could not bring him the acclaim he deserved. He could have succeeded in the concert world as an accompanist or a member of a trio. Yet for all these years he had dedicated himself to assist her in the perfection of her art. And to her chagrin, she knew little about him except the obvious: his musical brilliance, his homosexuality, and his loyal friendship to her.

"What do you think about Roberto and me?" she asked suddenly.

"That's a strange question. How do you mean?"

"Well, I mean—do we appear to be suited to each other?"

"Jesus, Athena! People can't be matched up like accessories. I spent the happiest year of my life in a clandestine relationship with the priest in my village—I was a nonbeliever of sixteen and he claimed he was trying to save my soul! The truth was, I was desperate to believe and he was frantic that if I accepted Jesus I would reject him. The tension made us passionate lovers."

"What changed your feelings?"

"I won a scholarship. Left the village and somehow never looked back." He pressed close to the table, nearer to her. "If you have to question it, the answer is usually no. But that doesn't mean you can't be happy with the status quo. That is, until another force enters your life. At which time—well, life has got to be lived. That's all there is to it."

"You know, don't you?"

He laughed gently. "I was the first person you looked at when you entered the cabin of the *Konstanika* after parting with Mr. Zakarias."

"It's like being out in a storm, Luigi. I'm half-terrified and half-exhilarated. I'm blind from the lightning and soaked to the skin from the deluge. But I don't know what caused the thunder. Worse than that, I don't seem to know enough to get out of the rain."

"Don't worry. A little water never hurt anyone. And when you want to get out of it badly enough you'll find a way."

People were now beginning to fill the square. A tour group was lined up two-deep in front of the Palace of the Doges. A woman at the end of the queue was taking pictures; she had walked some feet away and was focusing her camera when another woman ran up to her. A moment later they were headed in Athena's direction.

"Time to go," Athena said, seeing them approach. But it was too late; she had to smile brightly while Luigi agreed to take a picture of the two women with the famous Athena Varos in—of all places—the Piazza San Marco.

The week was so filled with practice and rehearsals that she had little time left for her growing anxiety about seeing Mano. The gala party he was hosting was to be held at the Palazzo Tiziano, which was owned by an American meat-packing heiress, Jeanne Bernenheim. Mano had leased it for the month while she was off on a world cruise to inaugurate her sixth marriage. There were to be almost two hundred guests, all with select seats at La Fenice, who would enjoy a week of Mano's hospitality either on the *Atlas,* at the Palazzo Tiziano, or at the Hotel Grand.

Giusto Anfossi, the tenor singing the role of Prince Calaf opposite Athena's Turandot, flew into a rage when he learned that she was going to have such a large claque. The day before the first performance, he threatened to leave the cast if she were allowed to make even one solo curtain despite the angry protest this might provoke in the audience. The fact that he had also been invited to the gala did not appease his ego, which he feared was in imminent danger of being severely bruised.

"Giusto, you're a good tenor and a stupid man!" Athena shouted backstage before the final rehearsal. "I don't have a claque. Signor Zakarias has not paid his guests to cheer me. They could boo me for all I know!"

"I refuse to discuss it further," the portly Anfossi snorted. "No solo curtain, or I leave!"

"Fine!" Athena replied. "I make my reputation when the curtain is up, not down!"

Anfossi stormed off but was onstage when the rehearsal began, and singing, as Athena noted, better than she had ever heard him. Roberto was waiting for her in her dressing room when she returned.

"He's here!" he announced.

"Who?"

"Zakarias, of course. I never saw such a sight. It seemed all of Venice was crowded around the port when the *Atlas* pulled in. I went to the hotel roof to get a good view. Guess who I saw?"

"Who?"

"Dietrich, sheathed in something silver, standing on the highest point of the boat, the sun making her seem to shimmer. People were shouting and cheering and throwing confetti and the other boats in the port all blew their whistles."

"How did you know it was Marlene Dietrich?"

"Because everyone in the crowd was calling her name."

Anfossi stuck his head in the doorway. "Remember, my darling, no solo curtain, or there will be no Prince Calaf at the next performance." Then he was gone.

"What was that all about?" Roberto asked.

"We'll discuss it later. I really am tired now, and I want to come back in a little while to walk down that staircase in my costume a few more times. Walking down those steps is really the only acting I do, and it has to be just right. What with the heavy headpiece, the weight of the costume, and my eyesight, I must have every movement memorized." She sighed and removed the elaborate Chinese-style jeweled and feathered crown from her head. "I think I will take *Turandot* out of my repertoire. It's terrible for the voice. All those loud, high passages. It could ruin me if I sang it too often. And although she is commanding, Turandot is not onstage enough." She was removing the long, scarlet artificial nails she wore in the role of the cruel Peking princess who finally succumbs to love. "No. That isn't really the reason. It's not the music or the kind of role I want to sing. The maestro says I should do more *bel canto.*"

"Of course, he may well be right. But *Turandot* is very popular with your audiences."

"I'm not a pop singer who has to please my fans," she said with more than a touch of petulance. "And I'm not a machine you can turn on and off like a record player. If they want to hear me sing *Turandot*, after this engagement let them buy the record."

This last was said with such finality that Roberto decided to drop the subject, at least for the present. "Before I left the hotel we received a note from Signor Zakarias."

"Oh?"

"He asked for us to join him for dinner tonight on the *Atlas*. But if you prefer to come back here . . ."

"Yes, I would," she replied nervously.

"You want me to turn down the invitation?"

"Yes. Right away."

"I think that would be insulting. The man has been most generous to you. We are both indebted to him for getting you safely out of Buenos Aires. And now he has come here to honor you. I understand your need to feel secure in the staircase scene—I never did approve of the length of the costume's train, but you were sure you could manage. What I suggest is that we accept but leave early so that you will be fresh for a morning rehearsal of the scenes you want to review."

"It seems you've left me with no choice of my own."

"Not true. I'll refuse on your behalf if you wish me to do so."

"On my behalf?"

"Well, I can't see how your rehearsing could excuse me from going." As he spoke he was slipping his arms into a stylish overcoat made of the finest broadcloth.

"That's new," she commented.

"Umm." He reached over and kissed her lightly on her cheek. "What shall I say?"

"We'll be pleased to come but we'll have to leave early."

"Good. I'll wait for you in the front office. I can call the boat from there."

Athena sat studying herself in the mirror for a few moments while the dresser, who entered when Robert left, waited to help her out of her costume. Her mind was spinning and she could not believe she had been so deliberately deceitful to Roberto. Not that she had lied to him; it was the impression her words made and the manner in which she had spoken them that was false. Never had she more wanted to be with Mano than tonight, and never had she been more scared of a confrontation than of this one. She would have to give her finest performance if she was to hide her true feelings from her husband—and from Mano's wife. And, perhaps, if she was wrong about Mano, to hide her emotions from him as well.

She and Roberto arrived at the *Atlas* a fashionable fifteen minutes late.

"Hello there!" Mano greeted them from the rail of the boat as they started up the ramp.

Athena's hand was shaking and she steadied it by tightening her hold of the gangplank railing. Glancing up, she smiled, waved, and called back, "Hello!" When she stepped onto the deck, Roberto just behind her, she found herself immediately face-to-face with Mano.

He was wearing a white dinner jacket, a curious choice for an evening in October, but nonetheless it suited him; his skin was bronzed from the sun and the contrast was striking. For the first time she saw the gray that peppered his dark hair. "You, of course, are Signor Vallobroso," he said to Roberto, shaking his hand. Then he turned to Athena. "Signora Vallobroso, we meet again. Under starry skies and better circumstances, I trust." He brushed his lips against the back of her hand and gazed deeply in her eyes, a small smile on his face.

"In Buenos Aires we were Mano and Athena," she replied.

"Christian names, of course!" he beamed. He took Roberto deliberately by the arm. "Do you like boats, Roberto?" he asked.

"Why, yes. Of course."

Mano led them through a door then down some steps to a magnificent lounge, large enough to accommodate many more than the handsome group of twenty-odd people already gathered there, many of them famous enough that Athena had no problem recognizing them. The party was already well under way.

"I slept with that man for two years," Dietrich, wearing a form-fitting white gown, was saying to Noël Coward, "and he serves me caviar. Wouldn't you think he'd remember that I hate fish?"

Despite being the only man in the room in a lounge suit, Coward appeared to be the most elegantly dressed. "Marlene, darling, you just don't recognize when a man is being discreet," he responded.

Having seen the new guests arrive with her husband, Nikki immediately came over to welcome them aboard.

Athena had formed no clear image as to what Mano's wife would be like, but Konstanika Sylvanus Zakarias was still a surprise. She more than held her own in this room of many beautiful women, and she was considerably younger than Athena had anticipated. She wore a chiffon gown that was almost the color of her startling amber eyes, and her long, tawny hair was drawn back from her high forehead by a pearl-and-diamond headband. Only when she took Athena's hand to introduce her to the rest of her guests did Athena notice the small nervous twitch at the corner of her mouth and discern the lines under her eyes, which were partially disguised with heavy makeup.

The boat was more lavish than Athena imagined it would be;

although luxurious, the *Konstanika* had not contained any "decorator" touches. The *Atlas* more than made up for that omission. Along the rear wall of the lounge was a striking mural of a godlike Atlas holding up a brilliant cerulean blue sky on his shoulders. The bar was white marble with a polished gold rim. White leather sofas and chairs dotted the room and were brightened by large pillows whose motif was a smiling yellow sun backed by a blue sky. The rug was thick gold pile. The white lacquered piano top and many of the tables held huge vases of magnificent fresh flowers.

As she glanced around the room, Athena silently gave thanks that she had decided to wear a cerise Schiapparelli, stark in design but sinuous in fit—it was the most sophisticated gown in her wardrobe. The duchess of Kent was surely the loveliest-looking woman in the room, so regal and yet feminine, with cool, classical features in a perfect oval head held high on a straight column of neck. Casting around her melting brown eyes and a slightly crooked smile, she moved through the salon with tremendous panache. Athena briefly wondered about her presence on the *Atlas,* but then, when she heard her distinctively clipped and accented voice as she spoke in English to Noël Coward, she recalled that she was a member of the Greek royal family who had married Prince George, the younger brother of Britain's king. Coward and the duchess were standing close enough to Athena that she could catch some of their conversation.

"The press have been beastly the way they have persecuted poor Princess Margaret," Coward was saying. "I'm sure she'll do the right thing and give up her hero airman. Still, I'm terribly sorry for her."

"Private sorrow is difficult enough," the duchess replied with a sigh, "but public sorrow is unbearable."

Athena thought about the duchess of Kent's words as she absently listened to the exchange between Roberto and a lesbian Hollywood screenwriter (brought by Dietrich, she later discovered) about filming an opera, perhaps *Tosca*—with Athena starring, of course. Mano was on the other side of the salon, and she was having such difficulty keeping her eyes off him that she feared her effort would be noticed and arouse suspicions.

Seeing Mano again had raised her emotional temperature to an unprecedented high. The invisible thread that had bound her to him during their brief moments together at the airport in Buenos Aires was there once more. It was as though she shared some vital part with him, could feel his presence inside her.

The cocktail hour seemed endless, and she was grateful when they filed into the dining salon for dinner. She was seated with Noël Coward on one side and Yorgo Pappas—a tall, affable Greek, obviously a business associate of Mano's—on the other. The table was large enough to comfortably accommodate everyone. Mano was at the head, her hostess at the foot, and Athena was seated halfway between them. She could not help but notice the angry glance that Mano cast down the length of the table to his wife, nor Nikki's scalded expression when she turned away from his dark look. A moment later, to Athena's surprise, he rose from his seat and came around the table to where she was. The eyes of his guests followed him and then quickly and discreetly looked elsewhere.

"I trust you do not feel offended, Signora Vallobroso," he said.

"Offended? For what reason?"

"You are the honored guest. You should be seated on my right. My wife appears to have left the placement of the name cards to someone else."

"I could hardly feel any affront when I have two such charming dinner companions," she smiled.

"Thank you for being so gracious," he said, and returned to his seat.

Coward leaned over to her. "I loathe boorish behavior," he sniffed. "Frankly, I'm grateful to whomever placed you beside me. I heard you sing *Norma* at Covent Garden and was—*am*—completely captivated by you. You are not only a great singer but a superb actress. I could have kicked that fat cow of a mezzo who tried to pinch the show from you, and I cheered privately when she didn't succeed."

"Rosa Measori," Athena laughed. "She always has a large claque in the audience paid to roar and applaud every time she sings an aria."

"Well, in the end you received an ovation the likes of which I've never heard. And rightly. Quality should triumph, although it seldom does. But at least it has where you are concerned."

"Noël, darling," Marlene called from across the table, "you're not going to get pissed tonight, are you? Because I thought we could sing some songs together later."

"If that's what you're planning, I think I *must* get pissed." He turned to Athena with a wry smile. "Don't be fooled by my wicked tongue. I really love Marlene."

Shortly after desert was served, a strawberry meringue tart with a rich cream sauce named "Mont Varos" in the menu in her honor, Yorgo pressed a folded piece of paper in her hand.

"To read later," he whispered, his tone indicating it was a private matter.

For the moment she wasn't sure what she should do with the paper, but finally she slipped it into her evening bag.

"Some day soon I hope you and your husband will come visit me at my house in Jamaica," Coward was saying. "The weather is perfect. Sun every morning, I promise you, and at exactly two-thirty every afternoon a biblical rainstorm. Then sun again. The beach is golden and the Caribbean divine. If you don't want to swim in the sea, I have a perfectly serviceable pool under the same sun and the same spectacularly blue and heavenly sky. Although I have to admit that I am always having to plunge into the pool to rescue various frogs from perishing in the chlorine." He pressed in closer. "Not one of them has as yet had the courtesy to turn into a Prince Charming, I might add."

"Although a few Prince Charmings have been transformed into frogs!" interjected Dietrich, who was listening from across the table.

When everyone rose to go back into the salon for coffee and after-dinner drinks, Athena excused herself and went to the powder room, where she took out the paper Yorgo had passed to her. It read:

Ati: I will come collect you at your hotel, at the side door on the canal, exactly one hour after you depart the Atlas. I must see you. I feel like a boy of twenty. But I assure you that I love you with all the passion of twice those years. Mano.

Instead of leaving early, as she had originally planned, Athena departed at 1:00 A.M., when the party broke up. She was grateful that she and Roberto had a suite with two bedrooms and that they were separated by a sitting room. She said she was exhausted and wanted to go directly to her room, although Roberto was feeling exuberant and seemed anxious to talk about the evening.

"You're right, of course," he agreed. "You must get your rest. I'll have a nightcap and read for a little while." He kissed her on the cheek and she went to her room. Thirty minutes later, the sitting-room light was still shining beneath her door.

As quietly as she could, Athena slipped out of her gown, dressed in a simple blouse and skirt, threw a cape over her shoulders, and then sat down on the edge of the bed nervously to wait for Roberto to retire. After five minutes the thought came to her that he might have done so but left the lights on in the sitting room. She rose, took off the cape, and put her bathrobe over her clothes in case he was there. Slowly she opened the door. To her relief, she had guessed right—the room was empty. Although it was not quite time for her rendezvous, she decided she had better rush out before he returned and made her escape impossible.

Holding her shoes in her hand, she tiptoed hurriedly to the front door of the suite, noting out of the side of her eye that light was shining from under Roberto's door, which meant he had probably taken his drink to bed. But it also suggested that he might return at any time for a refill. Not until she was in the corridor did she remember that she had left her wrap and was still wearing the bathrobe. Smiling nervously to herself, she took it off, rolled it into a ball, lifted the top off a tall cylindrical ashtray near the elevator, stuffed it inside, and put the top back in place.

She was about to ring the bell to call the elevator but decided against it and took the stairs that wound six flights down to the lobby. Filled now with the excitement of the adventure and with the prospect of seeing Mano alone, she raced down them. The moment she stepped outside into the darkness she was sorry she had cast away her bathrobe; the night had turned cold. She rubbed her shoulders for warmth. The sky was clear. No sign of rain. She was ten minutes early. It seemed foolish to remain outside. She was about to go back into the lobby when she heard the sound of oar-churned water in the canal. A moment later a gondola drew up to the embankment out of the murky darkness.

"Ati," Mano called.

He was concealed in the shadows. She descended the stone steps that led down to the water. A gondolier jumped off the boat and offered her his hand, but Mano was by her side before the man could help her into the boat. He took her in his arms and kissed her. They clung to each other, and she could feel the warmth and eagerness of his generous mouth, the strength of his hands as he held her against him. The blood rushed to her head and she found it almost impossible to break away. When she finally did, she began to shiver—perhaps from the chill in the air, or perhaps out of sheer nervousness. He removed his jacket (still the white one, she noted), placed it around her shoulders, then helped her into the boat and onto the seat under its small canopy. When he sat down, he slipped his arm under the jacket and around her waist.

"Where are we going?" she asked.

"To the home of a good friend who is presently in Paris." He drew her closer to him. "It will be all right. Don't be frightened."

The canal narrowed and the boat made a turn. There were houses on either side, but no lights in any of them. Most of Venice was either sleeping or conducting its nocturnal games behind shuttered windows. Athena could not help but wonder if she was living some strange fantasy. An air of unreality enveloped her. It was as though this was an operatic performance, that a curtain would eventually come down on it and reality return. She considered herself a moral person. And yet here she was, a married woman, about to commit adultery with another woman's husband. Most shocking of all, she was eager—*oh, so eager*—for the infidelity to be consummated. Even seeing Nikki face-to-face had not altered her decision. Nor did she feel guilt toward Roberto.

Her passion for Mano and his for her seemed so strong that words like "wrong" or "guilty" did not apply. They were following the dictates of grand passion. They were Tristan and Isolde, Pelléas and Mélisande—partners in a forbidden love that was destined to become historic. The immensity of this idea so overcame her that she suddenly felt faint; afraid she might pass out, she grasped Mano's hand so tightly that he let out a small cry of surprise.

"Ati! Ati," he repeated, enfolding her in his arms and holding her close to him. The boat continued to move with a rocking motion through the canals of Venice, and finally it docked at the side door of a handsome eighteenth-century building.

"This is the Palazzo Carbanio," he explained as he opened the door with a key and they entered. "It belongs to the Princess Alexandra de Markovitz. Sasha is now an elderly woman, past eighty I would say, although I would never be so discourteous as to inquire. Thirty years ago she taught a young man his first lessons in love. We've remained friends. She is a remarkable woman. I would like you to meet her sometime—she is a great fan of yours."

They were obviously not alone, for freshly stirred fires were burning in the various hearths. He led the way through a large entry, up a staircase to a reception room and down a wide corridor, past several open doorways that revealed finely decorated rooms of great size, to another stairway at whose top was a pair of doors. Mano flung them open. They were in a large room dominated by a wide canopied bed and furnished in muted shades of rose and green with delicate, pastel, hand-painted wood pieces made by Venetian artists in the eighteenth century. The pitched-ceilinged chamber was lighted by a roaring fire and a series of candles in graceful silver holders on the mantle above it. The first thing Mano did was to douse the candles and, with a poker, separate the logs in the hearth to bank the flames.

Athena kicked off her shoes and came over to where he stood in the light of the dying fire. Without heels on she was slightly shorter than he. She pressed her body against his and he pulled her even closer. She smiled slyly up at him and he kissed her, a gentle kiss filled with a surprising awe, as if he wanted her to know how beautiful he thought she was, how grateful he was that she was here in this room, in his arms, a kiss that truly came from something deep inside him.

"Ati," he said, "I believe I love you, and this from a man whom I know now has never before truly loved a woman."

She didn't laugh, although he was half-afraid she might. After all, he was a man, nearly fifty, who led a sophisticated life. He no longer knew how many women he had made love to, could not even recall the names of those who had become his mistress for a time. And, of course, he was married to a beautiful woman. Yet in all those years, with all those women, he had never experienced the deep emotion he was feeling for Athena, even though they had yet to know each other in the biblical sense.

He thought about this as he took her hand and led her to the bed, then sat down next to her. If he believed in such things as people having loved each other in past lives, his feelings might have made some kind of cockeyed sense. But he considered the idea impossible and somewhat ridiculous. Still, he could not deny that from the first time he had seen a photograph of her he had become obsessed with her, something that had been difficult for him to rationalize. He kissed her again with the same gentleness as before and loosened the pins in her hair. He watched, fasci-nated, as it cascaded like dark waves over her shoulders. He unbuttoned her blouse and she helped him remove it. In her rush to dress she had not put on a brassiere and her full high breasts, their nipples hard, thrust forward each time she took a deep breath. He traced them with nimble fingers, as though to engrave their shape and curve forever in his head.

He got up to undress; as he did, she removed the rest of her clothes and lay back naked on the velvet bed-cover. She was struck by how solidly he was built. Nothing about the look or feel of his body indicated age. And as she moved her hands tentatively over his barrel chest and taut stomach, she was surprised to find how familiar he seemed to her. He helped her slip beneath the covers. He led the way and she followed, holding none of her passion back, and yet never needing to direct him. He was keenly attuned to her body. She arched to meet him when he finally entered her body. She made a slightly muffled sound, a small but discernible cry. He instantly stopped and raised himself up on his arms to look her in the face.

"I'm not hurting you, am I?" he asked.

"Only for a moment. It's the first time a man has ever . . ." She stopped and then, her eyes wide, trying to see him as clearly as she could in the growing darkness, she added softly, "Roberto is homosexual."

Mano had known that, but had also assumed he was bisexual. *Why . . . why*, he asked himself, *would she have ever agreed to such a marriage?* He filed this in his head to ask another time. For now he was aching with desire. He kissed her; she relaxed, and gently he pushed deeper inside her. "Ati, Ati, darling Ati," he whispered, propelling himself into her with a smooth, rhythmic motion. She moaned and writhed beneath him, clinging tightly to him until they reached an explosive orgasm together.

He kissed her endlessly. "I love you, Ati. You are mine, only mine," he whispered in her ear and kissed the lobe. He kissed her parted lips, her nipples, the soft curve of her belly, the still-quivering flesh of her inner thighs. "Mine alone," he murmured. "Mine alone."

She lay awake in his arms a long time after he had fallen asleep.

She had never felt as close to another human being in her life. It was as though they were one heart, one soul. She watched the fire until it flickered out. He stirred and clasped her to him and drowsily kissed her on her neck. The gesture seemed like a benediction to Athena, and she fell into a warm, secure sleep of her own.

18. ROBERTO WAS AWAKENED BY THE GLARE OF THE SUN streaming through the open shutters in his room. He turned away from the light, his head throbbing and his mouth dry as parchment. Too much champagne and brandy the previous night. The thought came to him that he was expected somewhere this morning. He pushed himself slowly up into a sitting position and through the slits of his barely opened eyes attempted to bring his hotel bedroom into focus. He did not recall having left the shutters open, but either he had done so or the maid or Athena had let in the daylight to awaken him. He glanced at the clock on the bedside table. Ten past eleven. Memory came back: Athena had been due at the theater two hours earlier for rehearsals, and he had promised to accompany her.

He stumbled out of bed, grabbed his robe, tied the belt around his waist, opened the door to the sitting room, and called, "Athena?" He was answered only by the low hum of a vacuum cleaner in the corridor outside. Athena's door was open and so he went in. "Athena?" he repeated. The bed was made and there was no breakfast tray, which led Roberto to believe that she had risen on time and had gone to one of the street cafés she so enjoyed for her morning coffee. He briefly wondered why her cape was slung across the bed, but decided she had realized the day would be warm enough without it.

He went back to his own room to shower, shave and dress. On his way into the bathroom he closed the shutters. *There*—that was much easier on the eyes. The dazzling sun, so unusual for November, when Venice was so often deluged with rain, had turned the white-faced buildings, the bronze and gilded statues, and the water in the canals into glaring mirrors. He would have to get rid of this headache and the soreness in his eyes if he was to conduct his business successfully today.

Athena could concentrate on the one thing that mattered to her—her performance that evening. For him, there was another and much more complicated matter.

Never once since he first saw Athena perform had he doubted her unique talent. But without his vision, his constant supervision and promotion, he had serious doubts that she would have become the famous and much-adored *la Divina.* He felt totally responsible for her transformation from dowdy opera singer to the glamorous woman who had captivated the opera world and won over the critics. She was his Galatea, his design, his creation. *His.*

There were many young women who possessed potentially great voices; few of them, however, had someone to usher them into the spotlight, someone to find the right opera houses for them to perform in, the roles to sing that would best display their talent, someone who understood the importance of directors, conductors, co-performers, the value of new productions, costumes, sets, and publicity campaigns in making their names and their personalities so well known that for opera-goers to miss one performance would be a bitter disappointment.

To transform Athena Varos—that plump, serious, initially insecure young woman—into la Divina had not been an easy task. But, to Roberto's delight, she very soon became what he was creating her to be. Maybe too much so, he speculated as he stripped off his pajamas and stepped into the shower, quickly increasing the force of the cold water to help him clear his head. Her demands for perfection on the part of her colleagues, her indefatigable energy, and her strong opinions had caused scenes, tantrums, and havoc in many of the opera houses in which she appeared. They had also made her numerous enemies and a constant source of press stories. Rumored feuds with other divas. Refusals to appear when the production was not up to her standards. Such stories—most of them true enough—should have made his job difficult. But they didn't, because Athena Varos was recognized as one of the greatest singers alive. Audiences clamored to hear her, and opera houses bowed to Roberto's conditions.

His head clearing, he turned on the hot water tap and began to lather his body. Still youthful, he thought, stomach flat, thighs taut, no problems—unlike some men his age—getting an erection. He raised his face and let the water cascade over him. Today he hoped to secure a new contract for her at the Metropolitan in New York that would leave no doubt as to her power and drawing capacity. He did not like Rudolph Bing, the imperious Austrian who managed the Met. They were always at loggerheads. Bing insisted their negotiations take place in English; Roberto, Italian.

"I don't speak Italian," Bing contended via cable. (Roberto was certain this was a lie.)

"Surely you speak German then," Roberto cabled back.

"English only," came Bing's answer.

"Italian. I can suggest a good interpreter," Roberto replied. He had won the final round, and they were now, via cable and transatlantic telephone, in Italian with Bing using a translator, dickering over Athena's contract for the season eighteen months hence. But Roberto had managed to make it clear that Varos would not appear at the Met unless a new production was mounted tailored for her and over which she would have approval in terms of costumes, sets, and director. He also demanded a higher salary (plus his own expenses) than any other singer at the Met. Such a press release—HIGHEST-PAID SINGER AT THE MET—would greatly enhance Athena's fame while leaving Bing in the awkward position of having to appease the rest of his company. Still, both men knew that Athena Varos sold more tickets than anyone else.

Roberto stepped out of his shower, dried himself briskly with a large towel, prepared to shave, and then changed his mind. He rang downstairs for the barber to come to the suite. Then he ordered a strong pot of coffee. He had drunk too much champagne, perhaps, but it was the finest one could obtain. And then, the brandy—well, it was a hundred years old and quite exceptional.

Everything about the evening aboard the *Atlas* had been distinctive. Never had he been in such stellar company. He had not been able to take his eyes off Marlene or the duchess of Kent. But it was Noël Coward who had fascinated him most. Coward was the epitome of sophistication, a man he truly admired for his wit. He would persuade Athena to accept his gracious invitation for them to visit his house in Jamaica. Coward, he suspected, would have a coterie of handsome young men in attendance.

Roberto had managed to keep his sex life in low profile since his marriage to Athena. Though seldom lonely when she was on tour or he was away on business, he had come to follow one cardinal rule: no entanglements that overlapped her return, no relationship that looked like it might cause complications. Several times his best intentions had gone astray and he had found himself in a delicate position. He sighed as he recalled the young tenor who had played Pinkerton once to Athena's Madama Butterfly; he had threatened to kill himself onstage before Athena sang her famous swan song unless Roberto swore to leave her and declare his love for him. Poor boy! Roberto had slipped him a strong laxative a few hours before the performance and he had to be replaced. That was the last time Roberto was indiscreet with members of his wife's company.

The barber arrived along with a manicurist and Roberto gave himself over to the delicious relaxation of being pampered and groomed. Athena was obviously rehearsing and would refuse (he was certain) to take a break before lunchtime. That gave him a little time to pull himself together.

When he arrived at the theater it was already half past one and all hell had broken loose. Athena wanted to go through an entire second dress rehearsal that afternoon, although it had not been scheduled and several members of the cast, including Giusto Anfossi, had refused.

"What is the matter, *mia cara?*" Roberto asked as he came into her dressing room. He found her still in costume from the morning's run-through.

"It's the lighting engineer. He doesn't know his cues. We shall all be in total darkness at the wrong moments."

"But everything went so smoothly in yesterday's rehearsal," Roberto said with surprise.

"That was when Franco was in charge."

"Where is Franco now?"

"Vanished! Disappeared! No one seems to know. It's a disaster!"

"Has anyone gone looking for him?

"There are search parties out all over Venice!"

"We'll find him. I'll make sure of it."

"And if you don't, we shall stumble all over the set. No! There must be a full rehearsal with this new lighting man."

The director, Vincenzo Ambretti, entered. He came over and took her hands, careful not to stab himself on her false fingernails. A slim man with an angular face and large, soulful, dark eyes, he relied on his ability to calm his diva by proving his love for her. "Athena, I want you to do your best. I adore you. You know that. Remember two seasons ago, before the first night of *Lucia*? It was the baritone then. He was ill and we had to substitute a singer you had never worked with. I said it would be all right. And it was. This will be, too. First, we will find Franco, and I will restrain myself from wringing his neck until after the performance. Meanwhile, *just in case,* I will go over every lighting cue personally with his assistant. He has worked with Franco all along, and the cues are all recorded. But nonetheless, you can count on it—Franco will be behind the lights for this evening's performance."

"I don't know why there is so much resistance to making sure the lighting will be correct by simply doing another rehearsal," she insisted.

"Because none of the cast contracts permit a full dress the afternoon of a performance. And Anfossi, specifically, is afraid it will strain his voice."

"Anfossi!"

"Count on me," Ambretti urged. "Franco was last seen with a beautiful, long-legged creature at a café. That was at midnight last night. He has a weakness for the ladies, but he's a consummate technician. He'll be here. Trust me." He started for the door and she rose to follow him.

"You'll go through the entire opera with the other man, every light cue?"

"I give you my word." He kissed her on the cheek and left.

"There's a cable for you from America," she said to Roberto as she sat back down at her dressing table.

He opened it hurriedly and grimaced. "Bing's Italian translator must have studied with a Greek," he commented, then slowly read through it. "They have agreed to a new production of *Medea,* but they want you to alternate it with *Lucia.* You would only have eight days in between to lighten your voice from *Medea* to *Lucia* and then just four days to bring it down for *Medea* again. I think that's a serious problem. Also, they agree to your fee but refuse to pay my expenses."

"Is it imperative that you be there?" she asked. "I mean, it would be marvelous if you were, of course. But is it really imperative?"

"Of course it's imperative! If it wasn't, Mr. Bing would have gladly paid my expenses. He wants to control you and he knows that I would stand in his way. He is clever—but not as clever as I am, *mia cara.*" He came over to her and placed his hands on her shoulders. His eyes met hers in the dressing-table mirror. "I'm sorry I was sleeping when you left this morning. I was a very bad boy. But you should have awakened me."

"I knew you had a lot to drink on the boat," she said, praying that her flushed cheeks didn't betray her nervousness.

"What a splendid evening!" he crowed. "Such famous, glamorous women, and my wife was the queen! Tonight, I understand, there will be even more celebrities and aristocrats. I've been told they have been arriving all morning. Have you decided what you're going to wear?"

"The red Balmain, I think."

"Perfect choice." Her hand instinctively slid to a large jewelry box beside her makeup.

"What's that? A gift from an admirer?"

She opened the box and handed it to him. It contained a spectacular diamond and aquamarine necklace.

"My God! From Zakarias?"

"How did you know?"

"Who else could afford such extravagance?"

"Perhaps I should return it."

"Not on your life! Wear it tonight. I think it would be an insult not to."

After he had gone to the front office to compose a cable to Rudolph Bing, there was a knock on the dressing-room door. Ambretti stuck his head in. "Franco is back," he grinned. "All is well!"

No one could imagine how well, Athena thought.

She went back to the hotel a short while later to rest before she was to return to the theater for the gala evening performance. When she stepped off the elevator, she waited until the door closed and then opened the top of the tall ashtray stand. Her robe was gone. It made her laugh—she wondered what the cleaning person must have thought about such a curious thing. She wasn't sure who might have seen her leave the previous night, although she recalled that the hall porter in the lobby was at his desk, but hadn't seemed to glance her way. Even if he had, she doubted that he would have recognized her at such a distance.

She let herself into the suite, went straight to her bedroom, and closed the door. She did not want to be disturbed when Roberto returned. She was glad now that Vesta had not come with her to Venice. Nothing would have slipped past Vesta, and for the time being she didn't want to explain her actions to anyone.

She closed the shutters, turned back the covers, undressed, got into a negligee, and fell exhausted into the bed. But sleep eluded her; her mind was overrun with the scenes and sounds of the last fourteen hours. She lay back on the pillow and closed her eyes.

She could see his face above her as they made love, his eyes with a degree of tenderness and longing she had never seen before. He kept repeating, "Ati, Ati," and she could not help but recall that the only two men who she had loved—her father and Uncle Spiros—had also called her that. It sealed her feelings for him, placed him in a triumvirate, a trinity of love at which she was the center. She was not a truly religious person, although she was a believer, but when she and Mano were joined in their passion she felt as though it was a religious experience, that fate—and something even more mystic—had led them to this moment, that her unconventional sex life with Roberto was part of a greater plan to keep her untouched and waiting for Mano to be the first man to possess her.

They had made love again when they woke up, the warmth of the sun stroking their naked bodies as they explored each other, seeing, trying what they had not the previous night. She remembered him laughing when she said to him, "I heard you have a foot fetish."

Then his deep blue eyes grew serious. "Without real love, one has to make up passions to amuse oneself. But with you, Ati, there is an entire, splendid woman to love." His solemn look became a smile and he had kissed her on the lips with fresh emotion.

She opened her eyes and stretched her body against the smooth sheets. *What did the future hold for them?* she wondered. As they nestled together before rising on the first day of their avowed love, neither of them had discussed what might happen next. Their love was still too new. On her way to the theater that morning she had thought that the only thing she wanted was to be with Mano, that her career, the opera was insignificant in comparison. Never had she been happier in her life.

Then, during rehearsal, her old instincts fought their way back and took her over. She was Athena Varos, and tonight she was appearing as *Turandot* before the critical eyes of thousands. Only this night—this very special night—Mano would be in the audience. She had to give her best performance; he had to see how deserving she was of his love.

She rose from the bed, unable to contain the energy that was building in her. This was no time to languish like a lovesick girl. There was so much to do, to plan. She paced the room several times and then went over to the window and opened the shutters to let in the warmth and light of the sun. Outside, Venice stretched itself languorously in the clear brilliance of the day.

She thought she might like to dress and take a walk along the embankment, to wander through some of the city's quaint stores, stop for tea and cakes, watch the parade of lovers strolling hand in hand through the squares and narrow streets and over the omnipresent charming small bridges. But, of course, that was impossible. It was already half past four. She would have to be at the theater by six. And the walk could tire her too much, or the sun might go down and a chill threaten her throat. Also, Mano might call.

She remembered now that the necklace, which had been delivered to the theater only an hour after they had parted that morning, was in her handbag. She took it out and stared at. She held it in the window so that the light sent sparks from it in all directions. It was the most beautiful piece of jewelry she owned. Roberto had given her many lovely objects—broaches, rings, bracelets, necklaces—but nothing to equal the masterly design and beauty of Mano's gift. She reread the enclosed card:

My darling Ati, The diamonds are to remind you of the stars that shone on us last evening, the aquamarines of the lagoon seen from our window this morning. What came in between I will never forget. My love to you in Venice.

"No, not the red dress," she said aloud to herself. She crossed to the wardrobe and, after examining all the clothes hanging there, decided on a deep-blue gown. *Like the night sky,* she thought, *and Mano's eyes.*

Roberto was still at the theater when she returned. "Bing agrees to everything but insists that you tour for them after the season ends. I told him that the conditions on the last tour had been unacceptable; the hotels were inadequate, the trains smelly, the schedule too strenuous, and the cities were not on the international press circuit," he said as soon as they were in her dressing room. "I thought you were wearing the red Balmain," he added as the maid was hanging the blue gown she had brought from the hotel.

"I've been photographed in it before."

"Yes, that's right," he agreed.

"So what was the end of it?"

"A conference call is being arranged for tomorrow, five P.M. our time. I'll have my interpreter on the line and he'll have his."

There was a knock on the door. When Roberto answered it, Giusto Anfossi stormed in. "It is not acceptable!" he shouted.

"What on earth are you talking about?" Roberto asked.

"That man Zakarias has bought an entire block of seats in the center of the orchestra."

"Well, we knew they would have to be somewhere," Roberto replied. "He has invited two hundred guests."

"I cannot sing with Marlene Dietrich and Sophia Loren looking directly into my face!"

"Well, if you bend over they can look up your ass!" Roberto shouted.

"Stop this nonsense right away!" Athena ordered. "And Giusto, leave my dressing room before I really get mad. Such stupidity! An audience wears only one face. They are only individuals before the curtain goes up and after it comes down. During the course of the opera you are singing for yourself and the only person you must look to is the maestro."

Anfossi made no reply but left the room, slamming the door behind him.

"This is the last time I ever let you appear with Anfossi," Roberto said, still fuming.

"He's upset. His wife has run off with a cellist."

"Who told you that?"

"Luigi. He learns everything. Look, please go calm him. Anfossi is a fine Calaf, the best I've sung with. He's a strong performer, a good actor. As soon as we're in performance, all this foolishness will be forgotten." She took his hand. "Go. Please go, Roberto. I need some time to myself."

"Of course," he said, kissed her hand, and was gone.

As the final curtain lowered, Athena knew in her heart that she had never sung better. It was a curious thing, for Turandot was the complete antithesis of most other roles that she had mastered—Norma, Tosca, Lucia, Violetta, Butterfly, Lady Macbeth, Medea. That was because Turandot symbolized power but had no dramatic motivation, no history or great tragedy to explain her nature. But tonight, Athena had endowed Turandot *in her head* with everything that was missing from the libretto. Yet it seemed to her that all the answers were there in Puccini's glorious music, a deep undercurrent in Turandot's arias that revealed the real person, not the cruel, bitter princess but a woman who has never known love until she sees another woman die for it.

Her last aria brought the entire audience to its feet. She stood, unmoving, waiting for the wave of applause and the shouts of *brava!* to subside. Out of the corner of her eye, terrified he might break out of character, she caught a glimpse of Anfossi. But he did not. Fully five minutes passed before they could continue, and he never appeared to relax a muscle in his body. She was right about Anfossi and pleased she had not allowed his tantrums to overcome her reason.

"Take a solo bow," he pressed after they had taken several together and with the rest of the cast. Shouts of "Varos! Varos!" still continued to echo through the theater.

"But you said . . ."

He gave her a small shove and she went through the curtain by herself. She was too shortsighted to see if Mano was in the audience or if he was cheering her, too. Yet, something made her sure that he was. That morning he had confessed to her that he was not fond of the opera and understood very little of what took place onstage during a production. What he recognized was genius and what he admired was the power such genius had over people.

She lost count of the number of curtains she took solo and with the rest of the cast and the maestro, but finally she decided not to return for another bow and made her way back to her dressing room. When she entered she was stunned to find Mano sitting on the edge of her chaise. He rose immediately and took both her hands.

"Careful! These nails are lethal weapons," she laughed as she pulled back her fingers with their false, talon-like tips. "How long have you been here?"

"You had already taken many bows."

"Did I convert you?" she asked a bit coyly.

"Opera still sounds strange to my ears. But you, Ati. There's something mystic about you when you're on stage. There is no way to explain what you do except to attribute it to some god. You are inimitable, something amazing, something quite splendid. No wonder they call you *la Divina.*"

A rush of footsteps could be heard in the outside corridor. There was a knock on the door and then Athena's dresser slipped in and closed the door after her. "How long do you want before I let anyone in?" she asked.

Athena turned a questioning gaze to Mano.

"I'll leave now." He came close to her and kissed her on the forehead. "Come to the palazzo whenever you're ready." He opened the door and left as quickly as he could, pushing his way through the crush of admirers waiting outside and moving past Roberto, who was on his way in to see Athena, without realizing who it was.

The Palazzo Tiziano was on the Grand Canal, the most exclusive address in Venice. Built during the seventeenth century, when affluent Venetians vied for social prestige by playing their own game of keeping-up-with-the-Joneses on the Grand Canal, it must have been a showplace even then. Massive rooms were decorated with marble, statuary, gold leaf, and mosaics. Several of the ceilings had been painted by one of the great Venetian artists of the time. Over the centuries the elements had stripped the exterior of much of its original frescoes and ornamentation, but what remained—the carved friezes, the Tiziano family crest, and the Venetian Gothic design—was still enough to dazzle.

As with all the palazzos on the Grand Canal, the main entrance and most elaborate façade faced the waterway, which was now jammed with decorated gondolas and *gondolieri* in colorful costumes debarking passengers for the gala in Athena's honor. Nikki had wanted a masked ball, but Mano had refused. "It's pretentious nonsense," he argued. "And most costumes waver between absurdity and vulgarity."

"You mean you don't want to dress in a costume."

"That's right, Nikki, and if I don't, then neither will my guests."

The gowns and jewels the women wore were, however, so spectacular that they could not have been outdone by costumes. Venice had not seen such glitter and glamour since the 1920s, when it had been invaded by the international smart set.

With foreign guests, the cast and management of La Fenice, the leading social lions of Venice, and the city's officials, some five hundred people had come to honor Athena and enjoy Mano's extravagant hospitality. There were two orchestras; one that played waltzes only in the romantically lighted courtyard, with its Venetian statues and running fountains, while a famous American dance band kept a lively beat in the ballroom.

Athena arrived about an hour after the curtain had rung down on *Turandot* and was greeted on her entrance in the ballroom by a chorus each of the Greek national anthem and "The Star-Spangled Banner." She looked radiant in her deep blue gown, the jewels at her neck shimmering in the light of the myriad of candles. The huge ballroom, with its painted ceiling, gilt decoration, and massive crystal chandeliers, was also brilliantly lighted by candles. The Tiziano was a magnificent place, but it had never been wholly converted to electricity.

Roberto remained by her side as Nikki moved with them among her guests, introducing them to those who they did not know. From time to time, Mano—grinning with pleasure—seemed to appear from nowhere and then disappear just as quickly.

"Mano, do stop bobbing about," Noël Coward finally exclaimed. "You're making me absolutely seasick."

Athena refused to dance with anyone. "For the moment, for the moment at least," she apologized.

The dancing was interrupted at 2 A.M. and the doors of the large dining room were thrown open. Huge buffet tables, decorated with imaginative flower gondolas, were laden with a marvelous display of food. Champagne was served from magnums, and by this time Roberto was visibly drunk. At about 3:00 A.M. Mano drew Athena aside to tell her that Roberto had passed out and had been taken to one of the unoccupied bedrooms in the palazzo.

"What shall I do?" she asked. "Shall I take him back to the hotel?"

"I suggest we leave him here and I escort you home," he said. "Wait—Yorgo will bring you your wrap."

She was standing just outside the doors to the ballroom and watched Mano reenter and approach a small group. Athena could not make them out too clearly, but she instantly recognized Nikki from the dazzling gold lamé gown she wore.

"Signora Vallobroso," Yorgo said, startling her as he placed her white fox stole around her shoulders. Mano joined them a few moments later, and the two men escorted Athena out of the palazzo and to the berth where dozens of boats were waiting. She was helped into one. Mano stepped in after her.

"*Bon voyage!*" Yorgo called from shore, waved, and disappeared.

Mano put his arm around her waist; as the boat moved through the moonlight, upstream, around the bend, past the palazzo where Wagner had written part of *Tristan and Isolde,* drawing on the melancholy cries of the gondoliers as inspiration for the plaintive prelude to the third act. Venice was a city of beauty and music and Athena felt great happiness in being there. She leaned back against Mano's shoulder, hearing Wagner's great love theme in her head, and let the emotion she was feeling cover her with its warmth.

She paid little attention to where they were going, which bridges they passed beneath, or the waterways they traveled. Neither of them spoke. When the gondola came to a stop, Athena was surprised to find that they were at the house where they had spent the night.

"I thought we were going to the hotel," she said, more in passing than anything else.

"I said 'home.' And since we spent our first night together here, this will always be our home to me."

His sense of poetry moved her now as it had when she read the note that had accompanied his gift of the necklace. A tear tumbled slowly down her cheek; he brushed it away with the tips of his fingers and held her close to him as they entered the house.

Roberto found himself in darkness in a room he could only barely make out but that he knew was totally unfamiliar to him. His head was throbbing once again and he felt a wave of nausea when he tried to sit up. He had no idea of the time, but as he rested back on the bed on which he had found himself stretched out, fully dressed, he recalled the party and the fact that he had consumed a great deal of champagne. He assumed he must have passed out. The humiliation of such a lack of control, if that was the case, made him feel even more sick.

He was not at the hotel, so he must still be at the Palazzo Tiziano. He decided he had to find a bathroom immediately, and so he forced himself up into a sitting position and swung his legs over the side of the bed just as the door creaked slowly open.

"Athena?" he called.

"No. It's Nikki Zakarias."

She stood in the doorway, holding a candle, looking like some unearthly or demented figure. Her hair fell wildly about her face, which was all sharp shadows in the shifting flame of the candle. She came slowly across the room and sat down beside him.

"What's the matter?" he asked.

"Your wife and my husband are having an affair. Right now Athena is in his arms. She's taken him away from me."

Certain now that Nikki was unbalanced, or perhaps drugged (her eyes looked glassy), Roberto attempted to appease her. His only thought was to get out of this room and find a toilet.

"Now, Signora Zakarias, I'm sure your husband loves you very much. I saw the way he looks at you. You're a beautiful woman, and he's very proud you're his wife. I saw that in his eyes. Men know such things." He managed to stand up. The door remained open and the corridor was dimly lighted. There was no sound of music or of guests; the party must have ended. *Perhaps Zakarias has escorted Athena back to the hotel,* he thought to himself, starting toward the doorway.

"I will kill both of them," she said. "I have no qualms about it. I'm especially sorry for you. A cuckolded husband is always such a laughingstock."

He turned back into the room. She was standing now, the candle only inches below her chin, the metallic cloth of her gown seeming like flames about her.

"You are wrong, Signora. My wife is faithful."

"Poor, poor Roberto," she sighed.

Something went *click* in Roberto's head. Buenos Aires. The *Konstanika*. The trip to Venice. The party on the *Atlas*—and that expensive diamond necklace. Zakarias was in pursuit of Athena. And Athena? Roberto turned on his heels and hurried from the room, but only a few feet into the corridor he was no longer able to control his stomach from heaving. *Athena!* he thought. *That dirty Greek bastard is trying to rob me of her!*

He stumbled down the hallway and a steep, wide flight of stairs. A servant was dousing all the candles. When the man saw him, he came over and offered his assistance.

"That dirty Greek bastard!" Roberto shouted.

"Mi scusi, Signore?"

Roberto made his way outside and hailed a boat.

"That dirty Greek bastard is not going to steal my wife!" he said, this time under his breath.

19. ATHENA STRODE BACK AND FORTH ACROSS THE HUGE LIV-
ing room of the apartment in Rome; she loathed it here, and the
place never felt like it was hers. Roberto's stamp was everywhere,
etched indelibly in the cold museum quality of the decor, the white
marble floors, the wall tapestries and massive vitrines that housed
his growing collection of antique Venetian glass. There wasn't a
comfortable chair to sit in, and the room's one redeeming feature—
the panoramic view overlooking the rooftops of the city—was
mostly obscured by the elaborate draperies. She would not miss this
room, the apartment, nor Rome. And she was certain that she
would not miss Roberto.

In fifteen minutes Mano's driver would be downstairs to take her
to the small airport, where the *Konstanika* would be waiting for her.
She was to meet Mano in Paris, where they were to spend a week
together before flying to Athens and from there take the *Atlas* to
Zephyrus. The day after the gala party at the palazzo Tiziano, they
had decided to leave their spouses. Out of respect, they had agreed
not to tell them until Athena was back in Rome with Roberto and
Mano in Athens with Nikki. They were hoping to confess their
plans in a manner that was generous and gentle.

However, Roberto and Nikki acted so strangely in the days that
followed that the plan no longer seemed viable. On the night when

the *Atlas* was to embark for Nice, where Nikki and Mano's guests would go their own ways, Athena returned to the hotel at five in the morning to find Roberto dressed and standing by the sitting-room doorway.

"I hope you know exactly what you're doing, the sin you are committing," he snapped in an icy tone.

"You know that Mano and I are in love," she said quietly.

"Unfortunately, I'm not the only one who's aware of your adulterous behavior. I'm willing to do everything to keep the scandal to a minimum. But you are never to see that bastard Greek again."

"That's not possible. Please understand, Roberto. It was something neither of us could help. Mano and I have been caught up in a twist of fate. Neither of us planned this, and the very last thing we want is to hurt either you or Nikki. But we are truly in love. I sing about deep emotions like those I feel for Mano; I play women who give their lives for the men they love. But until now . . ." She saw the muscles in his face grow taut, his expression harden. Her voice took on a softer, pleading tone. "Please, *please* understand—I'm not blaming you. I'm the guilty one. I went into our marriage with my eyes open. Grazia had made sure I knew the truth about you. And I am grateful for what you have done for me. But try, *try* to appreciate the situation from my point of view."

"What are you trying to say?" he asked through clenched lips.

"Mano and I have decided to spend the rest of our lives together."

"You are a stupid child! Do you think this fornicator will be faithful to you?" He was white with rage; as she moved past him and into her room—she wanted to avoid further discussion until he had calmed down—he grabbed her hard by the arm and pulled her close to him. "You are forgetting that you are my wife, that we were married by a Catholic priest, and that in Italy there is no divorce," he said in a menacing voice. He released his hold on her with such suddenness that she almost lost her footing.

She had promised herself she would try as best she could to keep from hurting Roberto too much, to do and say the right things to appease his pride. But she hadn't anticipated his fierce anger. Her thoughts tumbled one upon the other. Having set their confrontation in motion, she could not now backtrack, nor did she want to. She was more certain than ever that her life with Roberto was over, that she must extricate herself from their marriage, that Mano was at her very soul. *Reason*—she had to use reason. Roberto was a lawyer. She had to present her side to him in a way he would understand.

"I believe a case could be made before the authorities that we're not really man and wife. I would be prepared to swear that we've never consummated our marriage, that you have denied me the right of conceiving a child, that you engaged in unnatural sexual acts," she said coolly, shocked at her ability to speak in such a way to Roberto. But she was immediately sorry to have done so, because he looked as though he had just received a blow of tremendous force. He even stepped back as though from the impact, his face creased with pain.

The telephone rang. Both of them stood there, unmoving. It rang again. Roberto went over to the desk and answered it. "You want to speak to Athena, you come up and speak to her with me!" he shouted into the mouthpiece before slamming it down. "Your lover is on his way up," he announced mockingly.

"Roberto, I beg you to be dignified about this. It's over between us. There's nothing else to be said."

"It will never be over, Athena. You belong to me."

"People can't own one another, not even husbands and wives."

"We've been more than that to each other. I made you into what you are. Remember how dumpy you were, how unsophisticated? It was I who made you a star in opera houses around the world. You had a miraculous voice, but I performed the miracle that turned you into *la Divina*. I, Roberto Vallobroso, your husband in the eyes of God and the laws of this country, created you, and I can destroy you just as easily. You are a whore, an ungrateful wretch, conscienceless, contemptible."

"How can you say such things to me?" she sobbed.

The iciness was still in his voice. "I won't allow you to go off with that man. He has no right to you. You're lucky that I have enough character to conceal your sin from the world. You will tell Zakarias when he arrives that he is never to see you again."

"I will do nothing of the sort!"

In her initial distress, Athena had left the suite door ajar. Mano burst in at this moment, rushed to her side, and wrapped his arm protectively around her.

"Get away from my wife," Roberto shouted.

"Collect yourself," Mano said. "These things happen in life."

"I ought to kill you!" Roberto spat between his teeth. He reached out to grab Athena, to pull her away, but Mano pivoted sideways so that he couldn't reach her.

"Perhaps we should talk alone," Mano said evenly.

"No . . . no . . ." Athena repeated, still sobbing.

"I have nothing to say to slime like you. You invite me on your yacht and then stab me in the back. You know nothing about this woman. When you tire of her you'll cast her aside just as you are doing with your wife. You are a lecher, a whoremonger, a thief!"

"I may be all those things, Roberto, but I also love Athena. As long as she wants to be with me, I will never give her up." He had eased Athena behind him and was motioning for her to step further back.

"Please, no violence," she cried.

"You've made her lose her senses. You're ruthless."

"Whatever I am, Signor Vallobroso, I am not a cocksucker like you," Mano said, drawing closer to Roberto. "Nor have I ever denied my wife a natural life."

Roberto swung wildly at him. Mano caught his arm and held it in a tight lock. "You don't think I know what's going through your mind? You're scared shitless you'll lose your golden goose. Well, all right. I'm a reasonable man. How much do you want for Athena? Five million, ten? Name your figure." He loosened his grasp and pushed Roberto away.

"You turn my stomach," Roberto said, straightening and running his elegant fingers through his rumpled hair.

"I will stay in this room until you pack and leave," Mano ordered.

"You have the audacity to say that to a husband in his own suite, before his own wife? Get the hell out of here or I will call the police!"

"Both of you stop this," Athena intervened. "I'm very tired and I have a performance to give tonight." She went over to Mano and took his hand. "Please, go back to the boat. I'll be all right. Please. We'll talk later." She turned to Roberto. "I think it's a good time for you to go to Verona to see Grazia. I'm going to call Vesta and ask her to join me here. We all need time apart to deal with this situation in a civilized manner." She walked Mano to the door, Roberto's furious gaze following her every step.

"Are you certain you'll be all right?" Mano asked.

"Fine."

"You make sure of that," Mano said to Roberto.

"Get the hell out!" Roberto repeated in a harsh, strained voice. "And may you never have peace for the rest of your life!" he cursed.

"I'm sorry, Roberto," Athena said tearfully when Mano was gone. "Please forgive me. I know I'm breaking a holy vow, but I can't help myself. You have been good to me. I do have much to be grateful to you for. And perhaps I won't have peace. But I will have love. And that I wish for you, too."

She left him standing alone and went to her room, head up, forcing herself to walk evenly, a commanding figure without a trace of defeat in her attitude. Athena Varos was a master at exits. She never once glanced back, even as she closed the door behind herself. Exhausted, she fell asleep fully dressed on top of the bed, only to be woken hours later by the slapping of the rain against the windows. It was early afternoon. The sun seemed to have deserted Venice along with Mano. The day was filled with November gloom. A note under her door in Roberto's small, precise hand informed her that he had taken her suggestion and gone to Verona and that Vesta would arrive the next morning.

She was to sing Lucia that evening and needed to regain the energy the part required. It was so easy for a performance to fail if she didn't direct her day's activities solely toward the few hours she would spend onstage. The wrenching scene with Roberto and Mano had drained her, and she was afraid that all her shouting and crying might have affected her voice. She ordered some tea with honey and rested until it was time to go the theater. She was grateful that it was Luigi who came to collect her.

"Something's wrong," he said immediately.

"No, no," she insisted. "I've just been trying to get into the right mood for poor Lucia."

He said no more about it but made sure she wasn't disturbed when she was dressing and applying her makeup. He stood guard in front of her dressing room for the last fifteen minutes before curtain.

God bless Luigi, Athena thought as she opened her dressing-room door and made her way backstage to the right wing for her entrance.

The rain continued for the rest of her stay in Venice; the Piazza San Marco was covered in water. Mano called several times a day and assured her that Nikki, to his relief, had accepted the situation with fewer histrionics than Roberto.

At the end of her engagement Athena returned to Rome with Vesta and Luigi. Roberto called daily, and at her request—or rather, after her constant pleas—agreed to give her a few days alone before he returned from Verona. Despite her repeated declarations, he still refused to accept the fact that she intended to leave him and join Mano. He gloated over the advantageous deal he had finally struck with the Metropolitan. He talked about a vacation for the month of December, before her appearance at La Scala.

"The island of Mystique," he told her. "It will be warm there, and very private."

"Roberto, I've told you a dozen times, I'll be joining Mano."

"I will hear nothing about that man, Athena. Mystique will do you a world of good. You shall see. It's important that you be well-rested for La Scala."

She decided she would leave Rome to meet Mano in Paris before

Roberto returned; she would simply be gone from the apartment when he got there. That way there would be no ugly scenes, no attempts on his part to stop her, which she felt confident he could not do. Her love for Mano only grew deeper with each passing day. No, nothing could stop her from leaving Roberto for Mano.

But in the last few hours, as she was going through her possessions to make sure she had everything she wanted, she felt uneasy. Her bags were stacked in the entryway, a leopard coat she was fond of thrown over them, and her best jewelry was stored safely in her makeup case. Yanni, who would accompany her to Paris, was downstairs waiting for the car. Mano had called not more than fifteen minutes earlier to assure her of his devotion; his voice had been as light and happy as that of a man about to be reunited with his beloved could be.

Yet somehow there was this heavy feeling in her chest, a sense of anxiety. She had just decided to go downstairs to wait with Yanni when the front door opened.

"Yanni?" she called. There was no reply, and she went out into the entry.

Roberto stood staring at her packed bags.

"You weren't coming back until tomorrow," she said.

"This is still my home."

"Yes, of course."

"And you are my wife."

"Roberto, please, no more fights. Not now." To divert his attention, she asked politely, "How is Grazia?"

"She intuitively sensed everything."

"She'll be a good support for you."

How much like a stranger he seemed! She wondered if she would even recognize him in ten years' time should they meet again.

"Grazia is a clever woman. She suggested I come back here early, without warning. She has been saying all along that you planned to betray me and your vows. At first I refused to listen. I believed you would come to your senses. But yesterday, when you made such a fuss on the telephone about *exactly* when I was returning, I had to acknowledge that Grazia was right. You intend to run off with that lousy Greek."

"Call him what you wish, Roberto. It changes nothing. I've been trying to convince you of that for the past two weeks."

"I think you should know that yesterday I considered going to court and denouncing you. Since you are an American citizen, I realized you could not be criminally charged. But before God's eyes, it is all something quite different. You will suffer for this, Athena, as you have made me suffer. You have disgraced the name of Vallobroso."

"I'm sorry you feel so bitter now. But one day soon, when we're separated and you have a new life . . ."

"I told you, I shall never let you go," he said with fury. "Only death will separate us."

"Not as far as I'm concerned." She turned toward the door, feeling that she had to get away from the ugliness in his voice, the cold rage in his eyes.

"I've worked with the accountant on our business affairs. This apartment is in my name alone, and I remain in control of all your contracts and the income from them. Your life belongs to me," he said.

She paused for a moment but did not look back. "You've gone mad, Roberto."

"You are the one who has lost your senses."

"No," she said, glancing over her shoulder, "I've just come to them—with the help of a man who truly loves me."

"One day, Athena, I'm going to kill him."

The house phone, which hung on the wall beside the entryway, rang. She lifted the receiver with a shaky hand. "Yes, please send the porters up for my bags," she said. She opened the door and stood in the hallway, listening for the elevator to reach their floor.

"You will both be cursed," he shouted at her.

She turned slowly and looked at him with disgust. "I feel sorry for you, Roberto. And sad for me. The Roberto Vallobroso I admired and held in such esteem is apparently dead. You bear no resemblance to the man I married and once loved—yes, *loved*. Because I did, although that was before I knew what real love between a man and woman could be."

The doors to the elevator yawned open. Two liveried porters crossed the hallway and entered the apartment to collect her bags. She turned away from Roberto briefly to give them instructions, and when she glanced back he was gone. A moment later she heard an inner door slam.

She spotted Mano from the window of the *Konstanika* as the silver plane coasted gracefully to a stop. She could not really see him clearly but he was already familiar to her, even at this great distance and in the last few bleary rays of pale winter daylight. Foremost was the shape of him—the black fedora hat held with one hand on the large, leonine head, the broad shoulders and short torso, the solid stance that gave him a pugilistic air. Mano had a way of commanding the space and the light around him. He was a man who held center stage, even against Nature.

By the time the door of the plane was opened, the steps lowered, and she and Yanni were told they could descend, he was standing on the ground below her, grinning, shouting up at her, but the propellers had not yet stopped spinning and she couldn't hear what he was saying. To her surprise, as soon as she started down in front of Yanni, he leapt up several steps to greet her. "*Brava!* You're here!" he said. "My Ati!" He kissed her lightly.

"Ati, Ati!" he repeated. He took her hand and guided her downward to the ground. "Are you all right? Was it very nasty before you left? My poor darling. I could kill that man."

"Please, Mano, don't talk that way."

He kissed her affectionately on the cheek. "What matters is that you are here and will never go back to him."

"Never," she agreed.

They moved across the field together, holding hands. His car was waiting by a side gate. Her baggage, he told her, would go directly to the Hotel Crillon, where he had a permanent suite. He had also reserved a room for Yanni, and while she unpacked he wanted to show Athena "something special." Paris, he claimed, was one of his two favorite cities.

"The other?"

"New York. We shall have homes in both."

He talked vibrantly about what they were going to do in Paris. They would see only a few close friends, people he thought would amuse her and whom he wanted her to meet. They would eat at his favorite restaurants—Le Grand Véfour ("The best in the great tradition of French cuisine. In short, there is no better anywhere"), Lapérouse ("Only for the soufflés, which are a work of art"), and, of course, Maxim's ("Because it's fun and the best-known faces in the world eat there. We will sit at the table reserved for royalty").

The light was fading fast and the trees, shorn of leaves, were casting long shadows across the great boulevards. Winter had driven the big cafés to immure themselves behind great glass cages. Perhaps Paris was more beautiful in other seasons, but even in winter she was a creature of rare moods.

"Ah," he sighed as their enormous car approached the Place de l'Opéra, "the first surprise." The chauffeur pulled up to the façade, a daring move, for nearby gendarmes were blowing their whistles for him to move on. "Out," Mano ordered, and then led her up the steps to a large poster. "There!" he said.

The poster announced upcoming events. Her name appeared in large type over the notice that *Norma* was coming the next April.

"The whole of Paris shall be at your feet on opening night," he exclaimed.

"Feet," she laughed. "That word again."

He gave her a small tap on her rear and they hurried back down the steps, where the driver was having difficulty with a gendarme.

"Cette dame, vous savez, c'est Madame Athena Varos!" Mano explained.

The gendarme waved them on.

"You see, Paris is already at your feet," he said as soon as they were back in the car.

"He had no idea who I was, but he recognized your voice of authority. Frenchmen are like that."

"I see that you're not going to be taken in very easily," he said, smiling.

They had dinner alone in the hotel the first evening, for there was much they had to discuss about their plans for the future: where she would be appearing and when; what time she had between engagements; where she would now consider home.

The hotel restaurant was a magnificent room of old-world elegance. They sat at a quiet table in a far corner and could not help but be aware of the surreptitious side-glances cast their way by other guests. Mano reached across the table and took her hand. "We're not going to be able to avoid the press," he said. "Soon the news of our affair will be known. I'm not the sort of man who can hide his feelings."

"I can cope if you can."

"Yes, of course."

"A home base, you were saying?" she prodded.

"It's not an easy matter. We have to rule out any place in Italy. Nikki will have the house in Athens. London is so stodgy that I don't think I could be happy there, even though it would please me to be in the country that is home to one of my great heroes, Winston Churchill. I have never made my peace with the Germans, so West Berlin is out of the running. And I didn't think either one of us would want to be as far away from Europe as South America. That leaves New York and Paris. Unfortunately, in the United States I still have a situation to work out with the government. So—Paris seems the lone survivor. But if you find the idea unacceptable or have another place in mind, that's fine with me. And, of course, there is Zephyrus. Nikki has no wish to be there."

"I love the idea of Paris. Yes! That's a grand suggestion!"

"Good! Because here's my second surprise."

"Oh?"

"An apartment was brought to my attention. It was once owned by Princess Alice of Monaco. She was born in America and raised

303

in Europe, much like yourself. She was also known for her extraordinary taste and beauty. She was a friend of Edward VII and many great men and women of her day. The apartment is up for sale. I would never buy it without your seeing it. But if you like it, it's yours."

"When can we see it?" she asked eagerly.

"First thing in the morning, if you like."

"I like."

The Luxembourg Gardens are the most popular and beautiful gardens in Paris. Even on the gray December morning when Athena and Mano chose to meet the real estate agent, Madame Blume (a middle-aged woman of aristocratic bearing and background, disdainful of her clients and resentful that the war had robbed her of her inheritance), in the apartment on the Boulevard St. Michel. Across the street in the gardens children crowded the circular pool, sailing toy boats, and the paths were full of energetic walkers, muffled in scarfs to ward off the icy fingers of the wind while leaves swirled around their feet.

Athena fell in love with the grand old apartment. Despite the gloomy day, a wonderful light flowed through the vast rooms, almost each of which led onto a balcony or terrace through wide glass windows and doors, all of them facing the gardens, the view from each entirely unobstructed. At the rear of the apartment, a staircase with a handsomely scrolled wrought-iron banister led up to a second floor, where there was a master bedroom, a sitting room, and a handsome conservatory that enjoyed even more spectacular vistas.

The *grand salon* and the *salle à manger* contained distinctive Creole murals that, Madame Blume informed them, the New Orleans–born princess, a patroness of the arts, had commissioned in the 1880's, before her marriage to the prince of Monaco. The princess was then the young widow of the duc de Richelieu (a distant relative, she had claimed). Proust, Rostand, Fauré, Massenet, Saint-Saëns, and Sarah Bernhardt had frequented her famous *salon*.

The rooms had a lyrical ambiance even if they were devoid of furnishings, the floors bare, the walls unadorned except for the murals. Athena somehow felt a communion with artists of other days who had passed through the apartment.

"You are happy here?" Mano asked

"Very."

"My representative will be in touch with you this afternoon, Madame Blume," he told the agent. "Madame Varos will want to take possession immediately."

"Well, there are, of course, contracts, arrangements . . ."

"He will be authorized to pay in full, in cash—for the premises, the legal work, and, most naturally, your fee. And there will be a bonus if this can be transacted with sufficient haste."

They were driving along the Seine a short while later; she was gazing at the gray swirls in the ageless river and the winter blackbirds that were swooping in graceful yet vaguely menacing arcs above it.

"No second thoughts?" he asked.

She turned and nodded her head. "Oh, no. I just was wondering if the apartment was a place you could also be happy in."

"Yes, I like it very much."

"And the big bedroom upstairs? Will it be single or double occupancy?"

"Double, of course!"

"It will be *our* bedroom, then?"

"Ours," he repeated.

"I only spent the night with Roberto during the first few days of our marriage. After that we always had separate bedrooms. You won't hate waking up and seeing me without makeup, my hair uncombed?"

"Ati, you are a beautiful woman—naturally. As I looked at you still sleeping on the pillow beside me this morning, I thought, 'How wonderful to wake up next to someone so lovely.' "

The car veered away from the river, with its rows of outdoor bookstalls and art dealers, wound its way through the narrow, crooked streets that bordered the river, and finally drove onto a wide, tree-lined avenue of elegant shops and antique stores. The driver drew to a stop before one of the grandest.

"To commemorate this day and our new home, I thought we should make our first purchase for it together," he said.

She was thrilled at the idea, and the two of them disappeared inside the marvelous shop with its antique and new pieces of silver and crystal and unique *objets d'art*. Led by the owner, Monsieur Oberon, a small, dapper, silver-haired man wearing shiny black shoes and a red flower in his lapel, they wandered through the establishment's three floors and selected numerous things—Art Nouveau candlesticks, several small enamel boxes, a Sèvres service for twenty-four, hand-painted with pastoral scenes, and a pair of graceful wrought-iron chairs for one of the balconies. An hour had passed in this pleasant way, and they were surprised and delighted to find how their eyes invariably went to the same item.

Monsieur Oberon escorted them to the door.

"There seems to be some disturbance outside. Perhaps you should wait here until it has been settled," he suggested.

"Nonsense," Mano said, and went to open the door, but as he did so an excited clerk came running over.

"Monsieur! They have recognized you!"

Mano, thinking a group of Athena's fans had seen her enter the shop, brushed the clerk aside. "Madame Varos does not hide from her admirers," he said, and, with his arm linked through hers, opened the door and stepped out into the street.

They were immediately surrounded by shouting newsmen, several dozen of them, cameras flashing, blocking their way to either the waiting car or from returning to the shop. The news that each of them had left their respective mates and that they had eloped to Paris had been leaked to the press.

Mano held up his hand and shouted, "Let us through, you apes!" He held Athena close to him with one arm and swung out at the men nearest to them with the other. One of them stumbled and fell to the ground. There were angry shouts. Mano pulled Athena forward with him toward the car, whose motor was already running. Only once before had Athena seen such crowd madness: the time Serafina had been attacked in front of the St. Demetrios church. As a journalist reached out to grab her arm in the hopes that she would stop to answer his question ("Do you plan to divorce Signor Vallobroso?"), something clicked in her head.

She started to scream and sob hysterically; images of Serafina's shorn head and the fury of her attackers flashed through her mind. The chauffeur had opened the door from the inside and Mano almost lifted her into the rear seat of the limousine, where she fell onto the floor. Once he was inside he helped her on to the seat and took her into his arms.

"Ati, Ati," he soothed, stroking her head, kissing the tears that were streaking down her cheeks. "It's all over. They're gone." But he was aware that this was not going to be the end of it, and he was furious at himself for not having seen the obvious. Athena Varos was not like any other woman in his life. She was the beloved *la Divina,* and if her tantrums made front-page news, then how could he have not realized that their affair would be an international scandal, a top story for the world's leading newspapers?

"We'll go to the Crillon's back entrance," he told the driver. He took out his handkerchief and handed it to her to wipe away the tears. "Ati, it will be all right. I swear to you. We'll prepare a statement. Call a press conference at the hotel. And then, if you don't mind, we'll fly to Greece, to Zephyrus, and wait until the storm ebbs before we return to Paris. Okay?"

"Okay."

She slumped in his arms, her head resting on his shoulder, trusting him yet for some reason apprehensive at the idea of returning to Greece.

20. KURI STARED AT THE NEWSPAPER IN HER HANDS, AT THE picture of Mano and Athena on its front page, and then threw it onto the kitchen table. She looked up at her visiting daughter.

"I should have known that your father's sins would finally be visited upon you," she said.

"That's an absurd thing to say! Papa didn't sin—you deserted him. What did you expect him to do, a man alone for all those years? And my sin wasn't leaving Roberto for Mano, it was marrying Roberto in the first place."

She was spending a few days with Kuri while Mano negotiated a large shipping contract and handled the final arrangements for his divorce. For the moment the paparazzi had not followed their trail to Athens. To outwit them, Mano had sent the *Konstanika*, with Yorgo and Vesta aboard, on to London before he and Athena left Paris. The press was now going mad trying to locate the lovers, who had flown to Greece in another private plane, landed in a small town north of Athens, and driven to the city, where they took separate suites at the Grand Bretagne Hotel—she under the name of Varosoupolos, he as Yorgo Pappas. Mano wore a ludicrous false nose and wig whenever he entered or left the hotel, but she was sure that the clerk recognized both of them and was just being discreet.

This was Tuesday. On Friday morning they would board the

Atlas for Zephyrus and remain there for the Christmas holidays.

Kuri's happiness at seeing Athena—for she was a lonely woman and could not conceal her initial gladness at her daughter's presence—was tempered by her disapproval of her recent actions.

"You're not the first person to marry someone you later find is not compatible. Nor was I. But running off with a man who gets you plastered all over the front pages of newspapers, who lets you become a scandal, is sickening. I'm grateful to God that Spiros was saved from this humiliation and from the shame of seeing how you've treated your mother."

"What are you talking about?"

"You've been a selfish daughter, Athena. You know that without me having to tell you. Look at the terrible financial troubles I have had. And Serafina? The poor woman is now confined to a mental home, but until she was, did you help me with the costs of caring for her—or myself?"

"Mama, how can you say such a thing? I sent what I could, I always have. You think I've made so much money, but you don't understand the expenses of a career like mine—the travel, the staff. I work hard. Do you care? Singers don't have long careers. My future had to be taken care of. I can fault Roberto for many things, but he was as concerned as I am about your welfare. Since my first successful tour, you've never had to worry about your rent, food on the table, or buying a new dress."

"While my daughter lived like a reigning princess."

"Oh, Jesus!" Athena got up.

"And forgot the struggles, the sacrifices I made for her. Why do you think I *really* came back to Greece? For you, *you* Athena. I had no way of knowing that we would get caught in a war. I thought your chances for a good life would be better in Greece. What did you have in New York? Your father was and still is a failure. We were poor immigrants, treated like rubbish. Then during the war, others starved to death—you didn't. Serafina and I saw to that. And now that you are successful, even the pittance your father used to send me has stopped. So what do you give me? Two hundred dollars a month. How much do you pay that perverted secretary of yours? Or Yanni? You come here in furs, jewels on your fingers. You travel in private planes and yachts. And you give your mother two hundred dollars a month."

There was no use in Athena telling Kuri that what she received was a handsome sum in the current economy of Greece, that she was also supporting Serafina's private hospital costs, that she never even knew how much money she made because Roberto spared her these details, and that she had trusted him to do what was right.

Kuri's words hurt her far more than her usual complaints did. Not only was she insensitive to Athena's situation, she was shifting all the blame on the wrong decisions she had made onto her and then using it to intimidate and coerce her into sending more money. If Kuri had just *asked* for more, or even once inquired about her own welfare, she would have rushed to her aid. Not that Kuri was in need, despite her cries to the contrary.

"Mama, I've asked you many times to come visit me or to take a trip wherever you wanted to go. The answer is always that you can't leave Serafina."

"Of course I can't! She's my sister. I have deep feelings and re-spect for blood ties, even if you don't."

Athena dropped back into the chair. "What is it you want, Mama?" she asked.

"Only what is due me in the eyes of God and society."

"Which is?"

Kuri slapped her hand on the newspaper. "Recognition as the mother of Athena Varos, the famous opera star. An apartment fitting that distinction. A wardrobe that is suitable to that station. I've helped you to fulfill your dream. Now, Athena, it's time for you to return that favor to me."

"I can't believe I'm sitting here hearing you say these things!"

"I'll tell you what else I expect—that either you go back to your husband or live without a man, as I have done. How can you be so loose in your morals after all you have seen in our family—your father, Serafina. Am I now to suffer the shame of a sinful daughter?" Kuri lowered her head and began to cry softly.

Athena studied her mother's bowed figure with an element of surprise. She noticed for the first time how Kuri's pink scalp showed through her thinning hair, how the shriveled skin on the back of her hands was blotched with brown liver spots. However cruel her attacks, greedy her demands, or selfish her aims, this was the woman who had given her life, and now she was lonely, old, disappointed, and bitter. It would be of no service to either of them to answer her in kind. So many differences kept them apart: generational, cultural, personal, and perhaps the most important of all, certain differences in their self-identities. Athena was a woman with talent and a career of her own. Kuri was dependent upon the munificence of others.

"It will be all right, Mama," she said gently. "Tomorrow we'll look for an apartment in a better neighborhood and you can hire a housekeeper. I think that would be a good idea, don't you?"

Kuri lifted her head. Her large brown Gypsy eyes were rimmed with dark circles. Tears slipped down the parchment skin. "It will, I suppose, ease your guilt," she said.

Athena sighed deeply. *Too many bridges to cross,* she thought. They were simply too removed to ever find their way back to what had never been much more than a fantasy anyway.

She went into the sitting room and got on the telephone to real estate agents. Guilt had no part of her motivation. Quite simply, she could think of nothing else to do, and she knew in her heart that it would be her last gesture to Kuri. The road ended for both of them right here. She had not told Kuri that the woman she had chosen to be her enemy, Maria Agostino, her husband's mistress, had died after a year's courageous battle against cancer. Kuri no longer had any part in her husband's life—nor in her daughter's.

The next morning Athena went into the country to see Serafina at the St. Ignatius Home for the Mentally Ill. Her aunt was led into the visitor's room for the meeting. She appeared smaller, shrunken. Her hair was gray, although still luxuriant and smoothly brushed.

Serafina had retained an element of pride even in this institutional atmosphere. Dressed in a flowing gray dress that reached her ankles, she moved in ashen swirls. In one hand she tightly grasped a book, which from its black binding Athena assumed had to be a Bible. There was no smile of recognition. Yet her eyes seemed to plead for something—what, Athena could not for the moment discern.

"Hello, Serafina," she said, and reached over and kissed her on the cheek. "It's Athena. Remember?"

Serafina remained mute.

"Well, of course, I was so much younger the last time you saw me." She tried to hand her the box of chocolates she had brought. Serafina pulled back, hiding her hands and the book she held behind her. "Never mind," Athena said, smiling encouragingly, "I'll leave it for you." She put the box down on a nearby table.

"Shall we sit for a while?" she asked, sitting down in a chair and motioning Serafina to take the one opposite hers.

For a moment Serafina stood there, unsure. Then she lowered herself into the chair with a soft billowing of gray fabric. She clutched the book in her lap.

"That's better. Now, let's see. What shall I tell you first? Oh, yes. I sing often in big theaters now. And I've made many records. Before I go I'll ask the sisters if there's a phonograph here, and if so I'll send you some. You always liked music. I remember how you used to sway to the rhythm whenever we played music on Uncle Spiros's old phonograph. Especially waltzes. Yes! I recall that you were very fond of Strauss waltzes."

She hummed a few phrases from a waltz in *Die Fledermaus,* and as she did so she noticed a flicker of interest in Serafina's eyes. Then to her delight, her aunt swayed in her chair to the music.

"That's right, Serafina! You do remember. You know, perhaps you should have studied dancing. Well, I'll send you some waltzes." She reached over to take Serafina's hand in a gesture of affection. Serafina pulled back into the chair, holding the book close to her body. "What do you have there, Serafina? The Bible?" Serafina shook her head. "No? A prayer book?"

Serafina moved the book onto her lap, her hand covering the binding.

"Never mind. I just thought maybe I could also send some books if I knew what you liked to read."

Her aunt grudgingly proffered the book.

"Why thank you, darling."

Athena took the offering and lifted it so that she could read the title: *Naked in Paradise*. To her amazement, the author was Mark Kaden. Serafina leaned forward and opened the book for her and pointed to the dedication: FOR SERAFINA. Underneath was an inscription written in a large, bold hand.

To Serafina—I'm not sure this book will find its way into your hands. But if it does I hope you are pleased with it. This is a novel about the gift of love. Yours to me was the inspiration—Moisha Kadinsky.

Her aunt was smiling broadly, waiting for her comment.

"That's beautiful, Serafina. I remember Moisha very well. He was the butcher's son. He's a famous writer now." She had been greatly moved when she read the inscription. She wiped away the tears in her eyes, closed the book, and pointed to the name in gold on the cover. "Mark Kaden. That's Moisha's name now."

Serafina snatched back the book and held it tightly to her chest. Athena wasn't sure how much she could understand and she knew she could not find out from Serafina how the book had reached her. Well, it didn't matter as long as it had, for it obviously meant a great deal to Serafina. Since the book was in English, she suspected that the sisters of St. Ignatius were not aware of the contents; with the word "paradise" in the title, they probably assumed it had a religious theme. Knowing Kaden, Athena was certain if they could read it they would receive a bit of a shock.

"Mama said to tell you that she will be here tomorrow afternoon to visit. I'll send along some records for you if there is a phonograph at St. Ignatius. If not, I'll send you one. All right?"

Serafina nodded. Athena stood up and she followed suit. "Good-bye, darling," Athena said, and kissed her on the cheek. To her surprise, her aunt placed her head on her shoulder and clung to her with her one free arm. "Oh, Serafina, darling, darling, Serafina," Athena whispered, kissing her again and then quickly, to keep herself from breaking down and crying, tore herself loose and hurried from the room. When she reached the hallway, she turned to take one last look at the frail creature who had so influenced her childhood—and *yes,* her life.

Serafina was standing before a large Christ on the cross, holding the book to her cheek and swaying with it, as though the cloth binding was the scented cheek of a man with whom she was dancing.

When Athena returned to the hotel there was a message simply saying: "Darling, I will be late. Please don't wait for dinner." No signature, but of course that wasn't necessary. She gave little thought to the matter of Mano being detained because she knew his business dealings were complicated. She ordered supper in her suite and went through the mail, mainly fan letters, that Vesta forwarded to her. A large manila envelope on the bottom of the pile was from Roberto's law firm. She set it aside, not wanting to read it without Mano being present. When several hours passed without his return, or even a telephone call from him, she grew edgy.

More to fill the time than anything else, she opened the lawyers' letter. Her eye skimmed the first few paragraphs. She could make little sense of them, so she reread the letter. *Just a lot of legalese,* she thought. Then the meaning of the words began to sink in.

Roberto was asserting that because she was his wife, all her earnings were legally his. And, since her contracts past and present stipulated that all her income be payable to him, he was placing her on notice that he would retain all the fees from her current contracts and the royalties on all the recordings she had made. The Italian word *tutti*—"all of"—leaped out at her from the single-spaced, typewritten text of the document. Roberto was claiming legal entitlement to her total earnings. But there was more.

Attached to this proclamation were copies of her numerous major contracts, with tabs that indicated her signature on each of them.

She did now what she had not done at the time the agreements were made: she read the three or four pages of clauses that preceded her signature. They constituted a diabolical abuse of her personal rights. Each contract was designed to rob her of any income from her career. In essence, if deemed binding, these contracts chatteled her to Roberto; in another contract, a contract between herself and Roberto, she had signed away all her rights as a recording artist and as a performer with any opera company. She was even to be held personally responsible for any loss to him if she did not honor contracts still in force.

What a fool she had been! Trusting Roberto as she had, and not wanting to fill her head with anything but her performances, she had signed whatever document he asked her to. Looking back, she recalled that he had a habit of appearing in her dressing room at the moments of greatest pressure on her. With profound tenderness he would say things like: "My poor, poor darling. I won't let you worry about such things as these contracts. You know, of course, my only concern is for you and your career. So sign—here. You don't have to worry about anything else." He would push the last page toward her, hand her a pen, and—stupidly, she now realized— she would sign, happy not to have to clutter her head with the contents of a boring document.

The impact of the letter so stunned her that for a few terrifying moments she was unable to breathe. When the air returned to her lungs, her heart was beating so rapidly that she was scared she might be having a heart attack. She sat motionless, not daring to move, forcing herself to take slow breaths. She calmed down, and her anger began to overcome her apprehension.

How could she have been so blind to Roberto's Machiavellian behavior? She doubted now that he had ever been in love with her. All he had wanted was to possess her. But why? He was a successful man, comfortably rich before they met. Money could not have been his original purpose; when they were married she was far from commanding top fees. Then again, maybe he knew she could, with the proper guidance, and was greedy for greater riches.

She rose from the chair and, her hand symbolically over her heart (its pounding had ceased), she paced the room. "Mano, Mano!" she sighed. Where was he? She needed him badly, right now—he would know what to do. She went to the telephone and asked the operator to ring his office number. She held on for over a dozen rings.

"Try it again. You must have dialed the wrong number," she insisted.

Still no reply.

Panic seized her. Something might have happened to him. He had told her how dangerous some of his negotiations were, the many countries that wanted to control his fleets, the other shipping tycoons who would be happy if he was out of the way.

She mustn't allow herself to become one of those silly women who were afraid of their own shadows. Mano would lose respect for her, as he had for Nikki—who was, by his description, unable to cope with even ordinary, everyday occurrences. No, nothing had happened to Mano; she would know in her heart if he were truly in danger. He was probably on his way, right this moment, to her side. Yes, of course. Any second the door would open and in he would walk, filling the room with his presence, and her heart with renewed love for him.

Mano impatiently glanced at his watch. This confrontation with Nikki—it certainly was not a normal discussion—was going on far too long and getting nowhere. Nikki was in the clutch of one of her "scenes," and as she talked her agitation increased. Past experiences with Nikki's emotional displays made him aware that she was high on whatever drug she was taking, that reasoning with her would be close to hopeless, and that the only thing to expect was the unexpected. He was sorry now that when she called him at the office, he had, after much persuasion on her part, agreed to see her. But their last meeting had been amicable, Nikki calm and responsive to his requests.

From the moment she opened the door to him, he had seen signs of the drugs—the speed and higher pitch of her speech, the glazed look in her eyes, the rapid movements of her hands—and had been on his guard. Despite her constantly irrational behavior, the great pain and difficulties she had caused in his life, Mano felt guilty about Nikki. He had tricked her into marriage when she had been very young, vulnerable, and obviously blindly in love with him. Her father had turned against her because of him. She was a lonely, childless woman of great beauty and no talents or special interests other than the shallow friends with whom she surrounded herself; he was often away and almost always preoccupied with the pressures of his business. And, certainly, he had not been a faithful husband. For these reasons, he had tried to keep the marriage intact. Yet even before Athena entered his life, he knew he had to sever his relations with Nikki—there was no longer any basis upon which they could continue. There had been too many scenes, too many obscene public displays of her sexual needs, too many highs and lows to deal with; embarrassing episodes like the dinner party at which she had slipped her hand under the table, unzipped the pants of an English bishop, jerked him off, and then announced with great glee what she had done. Afterward she had claimed she couldn't remember any of it, and an equally disturbing, tearful scene of contrition followed.

Though he knew she was in the habit of blaming him, it was difficult for him to erase such memories. Her doctors (and he had taken her to many of the world's top psychiatrists) strongly advised she enter a drug rehabilitation program. And, God knows, he had done his best to convince her to.

There was no use in soft-pedalling the truth. Nikki was a confirmed and inveterate addict. He had done everything humanly possible to help her, but she refused to be rescued. How many aborted arrangements had been made for her to go to a sanatorium, for nurses to take care of her around the clock? Nikki outwitted every attempt to help by using all the charm and dignity she could muster in those less and less frequent periods when she was clean.

He studied her now as she nervously drew on a cigarette and glared at him across the all-white sitting room of what was formerly his home in Athens, an apartment decorated in what Yorgo called "Nikki's drop-dead style." She was wearing a crimson velvet dressing gown with trumpet sleeves. *Ever fashionable, even in moments of crisis,* Mano thought. She was gaunt, her face drawn and pale, much thinner than when he last saw her. The amazing thing was that her fragility only added to her startling beauty.

"You shouldn't have done this, Mano," she said in short breaths between puffs. "Flaunting your affair, bringing in the press, making me look like some old hag to be thrown on the ash heap!"

"Those goddamn drugs make you paranoid. Do you think I would do such a thing? What sense does it make? Someone leaked the story, and I have a damn good instinct that it was one of your suppliers! Whoever has been selling you morphine and amphetamines or whatever the hell you take to push you further over the top."

"It's you who's paranoid, not me. What am I supposed to do when the man who marries me suddenly wants me to be someone else? And don't deny it! Well, I'm who I am. I like sex. I like to be fucked. I'm good at it. It's probably the only thing I am good at!"

He stood up, hands deep in the pockets of his blue gabardine suit jacket. "This is getting us nowhere, Nikki. I don't know what you want. I thought we already came to an agreement. Last week you accepted the plan for an amicable separation and divorce."

"That was last week, before you made a laughingstock of me."

"And this week? What do you want now?"

"Not your money. I have enough of my own."

"Which has been most fortunate for your suppliers."

"I want the world to see what an evil person you really are," she countered, ignoring his words.

"I've committed adultery. That doesn't make me evil."

"And I take something to help me forget how you tricked me into a marriage and then used me, how you fuck every woman who comes within twenty feet of you, but never make love to me."

The glowing tip of the cigarette had burned so low that it

scorched her fingers, yet she appeared unaware of any pain. Mano pulled his hand out of his pocket, flicked the cigarette from her grasp, and ground it with his heel into a charred black stain on the thick-piled white carpet.

"Someday you'll start a fire," he said.

"Not with you." She looked over at him with wide, injured eyes; eyes filled with years of self-inflicted pain.

These emotional scenes had become increasingly common over the last year, and they never failed to grieve him. He recalled the early days of their marriage: her high spirits, her insatiable sexual appetite, her constant, compulsive attention to keeping her weight down. The signals had been there all the time, but he had ignored them. Nikki had been on the verge of self-destruction for years.

He tried a softer approach, his voice warmer, his gaze softer. "Nikki, be true to yourself, not to this madness that's consumed you," he pleaded. "You've already agreed, in what I considered a dignified and admirable manner, that you would let me go. Whatever you want, you can have. The houses, the boat, the plane. I know you love your father and that his rejection has hurt you deeply. I'll go to him and do all I can so that he reconciles himself with you. And even if you say you don't want my money, I'll make sure that you have a fair share of what should be yours as the former wife of Manolis Zakarias. But let me go."

She crossed her hands over her chest in a flutter of red fabric. The lines that etched her full mouth quivered, giving her a bruised look. "Oh, Mano, I'm so afraid," she said in the wispy little-girl voice that had won him over so often in the past.

"No wonder you're afraid. You take forty Dexedrines a day, which is what I was last told you were gulping, so of course you're going to be afraid. That's enough to keep a mule up for ten years! Then comes the morphine to help you sleep. You think I don't know you need a narcotic sledgehammer to get any rest at all? And that your so-called friends help you to acquire it."

She blinked her eyes, wincing from the brightness of a nearby lamp, turned her face away from the glare, then reached up with a shaky hand and flicked it off. "At least they're there if I need them," she said.

"I don't understand you, Nikki. If I failed you, which I suspect I have, there were many answers other than drugs to turn to. You could have left me years ago, found a young, virile man who would be happy to fuck you all day and all night. You're a beautiful woman, and a rich one."

"That wasn't enough for you."

"Maybe I'm just not your average man. Perhaps nothing is ever enough for me."

She took a cigarette from a silver box on the table but had difficulties holding the lighter steady. Mano reached out to help her, but she pulled away and, the flame dangerously close to her face, lit the cigarette and inhaled deeply. "Not that I give a shit, but you're going to ruin her life the way you've wrecked mine," she said.

"We're back to square one, are we? You've wrecked your life, Nikki, not me." He retrieved his coat, which in his tentativeness, in his desire to remain with her as short a time as possible, he had tossed over the arm of a chair, and started for the door.

A wild look in her eyes, Nikki watched him go. Her hand flew to her throat, a wing of red. "Mano! Just a minute," she called in a brittle voice. "I want to give you something before you leave."

He turned on an angle toward her, meaning to say a final goodbye and then leave. But she picked up the glass of ouzo she had been drinking earlier, and before he realized fully what she was doing, took a vial of pills from the pocket of her robe, emptied the contents into her mouth, and swallowed them along with the contents of the glass.

"Oh, my God!" he shouted. He dropped his coat and bolted over to where she was standing, gagging, fighting to keep the pills down. "Are you crazy?" he shouted.

She placed both hands over her mouth and tightly interlocked them.

"Let go! Spit them up!" he yelled, shaking her hard by the shoulders.

With a sudden surge of energy and strength that took him off-guard, she pulled away, ran a few steps toward the door that led to her bedroom, and stumbled. She would have fallen to the rug had he not grabbed her around the waist and flung her over the arm of a chair, wasting no time before starting to pound his hands against her back. "Spit them up, Nikki! Do as I say!" he ordered. She was coughing; he turned her over, planning to stick his hand down her throat if he had to.

"It's too late," she said, raspy-voiced. "They'll say you killed me, that I died for love of you. 'Poor Nikki,' they'll say. 'Ba-aa-d Mano.' " She tried to laugh but the effort was too much for her, and the sound trailed off into a small animal cry. Her eyes brimming with fear, she began to slip to the floor.

Mano pulled her up onto her feet and half-carried her across the room to the house telephone near the door. "Get an ambulance right away," he said to the female servant who picked up in the kitchen. "There's been an accident."

Nikki was limp in his arms, mumbling incoherently. He lifted her, conscious of how light she was, hurried out of the sitting room, down the corridor, into a bathroom, and, without a second thought, stepped into the shower with her and turned on the cold water full-force. Her lips were white and slightly parted, and she gagged on the water he compelled her to swallow.

"Damn you, Nikki! Damn you!" he shouted over the sound of the rushing water, his clothes soaked and clinging to him.

She slumped in his arms and he struggled to hold her up against the white marble wall of the enclosure, which suddenly seemed to resemble a coroner's slab. "Oh, my God. Oh, my God!" he repeated. Pinning her against the wall with one hand, he slapped her hard across the face several times with the other. The red robe stuck to her slender body and her tawny hair fell in wet strips over her shoulders. She was slipping out of his grasp. He grabbed her under the elbows to pull her up, and as he did so one soggy trumpet sleeve fell back to reveal several ugly bruises. So Nikki was not only taking pills, she was mainlining. He had no idea when her last fix had been, but it, combined with the drugs and the alcohol she had taken, accounted for her swift descent into unconsciousness.

He pulled her out of the shower by her armpits. The sopping wet hem of her robe dragged across the glistening white marble floor, looking like a swirling stream of blood. A heavyset uniformed maid he didn't recognize was standing terrified, in the doorway.

"Help me get madam to bed," he ordered, lifting Nikki's slack, drenched body up in his arms. Time had stopped for him. His ears were buzzing. The dread and exertion of his attempt to revive Nikki had almost overcome him. He was wet and cold and the water in his shoes made walking difficult. Still, he made his way with her down the corridor, the maid running ahead to open the door to Nikki's bedroom.

"You called an ambulance?" he asked as he lowered Nikki onto the peach satin cover of her wide tufted bed.

The woman, still speechless with fear, nodded.

Nikki's lips were blue, her eyes glazed and staring. He got onto the bed, raised himself above her, and administered mouth-to-mouth resuscitation, hammering her chest between each deep breath. She moved, choked, coughed. He pushed her up on the pillows and then held her head down while she spewed vomit. By the time the medics arrived, he knew Nikki would live.

He called Athena as soon as Nikki was taken to the hospital and told her what had just happened.

"The *Atlas* is being readied," he told her. "I'll collect you in less than an hour and we'll take the boat directly to Zephyrus. I want you to be out of the reach of the press when they find out about this."

Some of his personal belongings remained in the apartment. He hastened into his former bedroom, which adjoined Nikki's, and after drying himself, he dressed, paying little attention to his selection of clothes. He called Yorgo and asked him to contact his private doctor, accompany him to the hospital, and stay there until Nikki revived. "Then I want you to call her father and tell him she tried to commit suicide—but don't mention that I was with her."

He waited in the car while his driver went into the hotel and rang Athena's room. The man stood by the elevator as she stepped off, took her suitcase from the porter, and herded her through the almost deserted lobby, past the doorman, and into the backseat of the car.

Mano reached over and took her hand. A moment later the car jolted forward through the dark, empty city streets in the direction of the dock where the *Atlas* was berthed.

He drew Athena close to him, his arm around her. "Ati, I saved her this time, but the next time I won't be there—so who knows? The drugs have already ruined her and they will probably kill her."

"She has friends. She's not alone. She'll overcome this illness. You'll see, Mano. You mustn't blame yourself."

"You can't make sense of anyone on drugs," he said, almost to himself. "It's complete, total paranoia. I don't mean that Nikki wasn't conscious of what she was doing. But she had no idea of the consequences."

He leaned back against the seat, still holding Athena in his arms. The car passed under a streetlamp and she watched the tears sluice down his cheek. He sighed deeply and closed his eyes. She wasn't sure if he had fallen off to sleep, but she remained in the same position, careful not to stir in case he had. She would not, she decided, show him the contents of the envelope from Roberto—at least not for several days.

They were soldiers exhausted from battle. The people they once had loved lay strewn on the killing fields of their lives.

Act Four

An Historic Affair

21. As Mano promised Nikki, he called her father, his old enemy Konstantine Sylvanus, and begged him to go see her at the hospital.

"She's no longer my daughter. She's your wife," Sylvanus replied. "She's already dead as far as I'm concerned."

"Look, Sylvanus, I screwed you, I admit it. I made it my business to make me and Helle Maritime more powerful than you and your company. Okay. I went after you and used any means I could. It was war and you damn well knew it, but you took my challenge and you lost. I don't blame you for hating my guts. But, for Chrissakes, Nikki is your only child, your blood. She's in deep, deep shit. She's a drug addict. She's suicidal. She loves you. At night I heard her cry because you refuse to see her."

"She's your wife, you little prick. Why should she cry for me?"

"I don't know, Sylvanus. I wish I did. But I'm not a psychiatrist. You sent her away when she was very young. She wants to have that time back, something like that. And, Sylvanus, she won't be my wife for long. We've agreed to divorce."

"*Pousti gamimenoi!* You think you can throw your rubbish at me and have me pick it up!"

"This is Nikki we're talking about, not some tramp. Your daughter."

"I told you, my daughter is dead." His voice was frosted with resolve.

"He's like a brick wall," Mano said to Athena after he had hung up. "He's held together with cement."

"You tried."

"That's not enough. I get up every morning to *win*."

They had just had supper and were sitting opposite each other in the same room in which Nikki's friends had once gathered to play games. Except for the staff, they were alone in the house and on the island. Outside, a robust wind was blowing, and the December evening was cold. Inside, a comforting fire burned in the hearth, and a week of being together, of sharing memories and making love, had warded off the chill of winter and its discontents.

"You would have thought that old pirate could have found even a single drop of compassion for a daughter who damned near died. The same goes for her hosts of so-called friends. No, only those bloodsucking news-hounds. Whenever there's a profit to be made out of someone's ill fortune, there they are. Yorgo tells me that one of these creeps even managed to get into her hospital room yesterday."

"You mustn't think about Nikki now," Athena said. "You saved her life. There's nothing more you can do."

"It's what I might already have done that troubles me. She said I was evil. I don't know—maybe I could have saved us both from all this pain if I had taken a stand years ago. But I never thought of myself as evil."

"She didn't mean it, Mano. She was sick and didn't know what she was saying." She reached out and took his hand and kissed the palm, in what was a surprisingly maternal gesture, as though she had willed the touch to ease his pain.

To be alone with Mano, the center of his world; to be made love to as a desired woman; to be asked no more of than to be the object of that love—all these had lulled Athena into a paradisiacal state that pushed aside all her own problems and concerns. And whenever a disturbing reminder of Roberto's actions—and with it the fear that her career, at least as she knew it, might be over—flashed into her mind, as it irritatingly had just now, she forced herself to suppress it. She wanted to bring Mano utter happiness. And, perhaps, just perhaps, she was apprehensive that he might not love her quite so much if she added more complications to his already heavy burdens. She saw it as her responsibility—the price for the love she received—to make his life easier.

She was thus caught off guard when he glanced over at her, melting concern in his dark blue eyes, and said with strong emotion in his voice: "Ati, I would have done anything to save you all this unnecessary drama."

"Drama is my special domain," she reassured him with a loving smile. Once again she entertained the idea of bringing up the subject of Roberto but dismissed it, not wanting anything to change, however slightly, between them.

He sat pensively for a few moments. Then a smile spread across his broad face. He called Yorgo in Athens. "Those ten new tankers, I want you to transfer ownership of them to Sylvanus . . . Yes, that's right. Then I want the tankers to be delivered to his dock . . . Well, hell," he laughed, "just say I owe him one and now I'm getting ready to put the shoe on the other foot."

He rubbed his hands, grinned, and said to Athena, "There's nothing two Greeks like better than to bargain." He talked no more about Nikki.

Mano liked the fact that Athena was Greek, and it was what they spoke when they made love. He believed it brought them closer together. He had the chef cook Greek food and lustily showed her how to eat "like a Greek peasant, with your hands." Ouzo and Greek brandy replaced champagne and French wine; the previous night he had played bouzouki music on the phonograph and danced for her, smashing some of his best china plates with shouts of glee.

Now he closed the door to the room, threw sofa pillows on the floor, and pulled her down beside him. He was greedy in the way he made love, as though he wanted to consume every drop of passion she felt for him.

"In Paris, I can be more swank Parisian than the baron de Roth-schild himself. But for now, Ati, I am on Zephyrus, and it pleases me much to be Greek. We Greeks are all traders at heart. We like to bargain, we love to win, and we like to show our women what a real man is."

They were still entangled in each other's arms. She stroked his shoulders and let her hands wander down his back. His skin had an odor, a texture, a warmth and velvet softness that even now, after the explosion of their lovemaking, aroused her desire for him. Sens-ing this, he kissed her throat and traced the full curve of her breast with his lips. Then, he pulled back and stared hard at her.

"You are very beautiful," he said. "Not like any other woman I have known. There is an aura of power that moves and talks and sings when you do. I find that exciting. I think you feel that way about me, and that it excites you, too."

They made love again, and this time he coaxed her into being the aggressor, into mounting him and bring them both to climax. They fell off to sleep afterward. When she awoke a short time later, she was still on top of him and the fire had burned down to embers. She rolled over and sat up.

"Ati?" he called and took her hand. "It's cold in here. Put on my jacket." He reached over, pulled it off a chair, and placed it tenderly over her bare shoulders. "Are you happy? Satisfied? Still in love?"

"All those things."

"Then why do you look so pensive?"

"It's . . . there's . . ." she floundered.

"Yes?"

"The evening before we came to Zephyrus, before Nikki tried to commit suicide, I received an envelope from Roberto. It was a formal letter from him, a legal document, really, saying that he controlled all my recording and appearance contracts and that ev-erything I earn from them will be turned over directly to him. And that, if I don't honor my contracts, I will have to pay him the money he will have lost. Can you imagine! That *he* will have lost!"

"And you kept this to yourself? Oh, Ati. I'm sorry. I've been so involved with my own problems I didn't think to ask if all was well with you and Roberto. But you mustn't worry about it. The man is crazy! Unless you signed such a document, he's whistling in the toilet."

"I did."

"You had an agreement with him?"

"Well, he would bring a contract and ask me to sign it just as I was about to go onstage. He was my husband and my manager, and so of course I did."

"Without reading it or having a lawyer look at it?"

She nodded.

He thought for a moment. "Well, that could be to your advantage. You were denied private counsel. Never mind. I have a team of the best lawyers in the world. I'll have them go over his letter and whatever other documents there are between you. You have copies?"

"He sent them to me with markers to show where I signed."

"Cocksucker!"

He jumped up from the floor with amazing agility. For a man nearing fifty he was surprisingly fit; there didn't seem to be an ounce of excess fat on his muscular body. "Come on," he said, pulling her to her feet, "we have two wars to win and there's no time to lose sleep."

They walked naked through the darkened corridors to their bedroom, not Nikki's but one he called the "Winston Churchill room" because it was waiting for the great man to occupy it—although so far he had not accepted any of Mano's invitations.

"Why must you always win?" she asked when they were under the covers of the oversized bed.

"Like Achilles," he said. "For my own glory."

Before she had a chance to comment, he was asleep on his back and snoring. She gently pushed him and he turned over on his side. The rumbling sounds stopped. She cupped her body to his and held on tightly to him the way she had seen girls in Italy riding on the backseat of their boyfriends' motorcycles. The image was pleasing and she closed her eyes. She was clinging to Mano and they were whooshing through a great void, in a hurry to get somewhere, although she could not think where it might be. One thing she did know: she was not afraid, because Mano was driving and her life was safe in his hands.

When she awoke it was morning, and Mano was standing above her, shaved and casually dressed in a bright sweater and corduroy pants, smiling down at her.

"Costa is going to drive us around the island for you to pick out a Christmas tree," he announced. "Dress warmly. It's cold today." He kissed her on the forehead and started toward the door. "Oh, and Sylvanus has agreed to see Nikki. The old pirate made me turn over two more tankers, but I won," he added, and left the room.

There was a tray with pots of steaming coffee and milk beside the bed, and a plate of warm breakfast cakes that smelled as though they had been freshly made. The shutters were open and a chalky light filled the room. She pushed her arms into her robe and crossed to the window, which looked out over the sea, and was struck at how blue it seemed, since there was a haze over the sun and the sky was a curtain of white mist. They had toured the entire island the previous day, walked on the beach, skirting the foamy edges of the waves as they slid up across the white sand. Then they had had a simple Greek lunch of goat's milk cheese, eggs, and crusty bread served at Costa's house by his dark-haired, saucer-eyed, wide-hipped teenage mistress. The cottage was built on a rock cliff, one room on top the other, like stacked white dice.

She had mentioned that Christmas was only three days off and suggested that perhaps one of the smaller pines that edged the workers' compounds could be cut and brought up to the main house to be decorated for the occasion.

When they visited the workers' compound she sang folk songs with the children, and the men told her about the black dogs that had roamed the island until recently. The women recounted ancient tales of undersea creatures who, it was said, used to mate on the island's shores until a goddess turned some of them into mortals. They had lived on the island-paradise until Turkish sailors, blown off course, came and slew them all.

Zephyrus intrigued her as no other place had in her travels. It was enveloped in beauty. The hill where the main house sat ran straight up to the sky, cypress and olives and pines grew tall and close together, and the white sand and the blue sea and the sky all seemed new, untouched. That Mano was the master of all this was a concept that at first overwhelmed her and then filled her with awe. It was as though this was his empire, where he ruled supreme—as long as he paid Greek taxes, he reminded her. His home, his country, his world. Zephyrus.

They rode in the Jeep with Costa and the young Greek worker who was to cut down the tree she chose. The air was crisp and fresh. The sun was now free of haze, but there was a stiff breeze that brought with it a fine spray of seawater and left the taste of salt on her lips. She insisted on watching, despite the bite in the air, while a splendid tree, about eight feet tall, with branches that extended in perfect symmetry, was felled and loaded onto the back of the Jeep.

She led the men in a round of carols on the way back to the house.

"You sing good," the young worker said to her in Greek.

"And you are a fine woodsman," she rejoined.

"Are you lonely? Shall I send the *Atlas* into Athens to bring back some friends, or perhaps your mother for the holidays?" Mano asked her when the tree was being secured to a stand in the sitting room. She was going through several large boxes of tree ornaments.

"Who ever heard of bringing your mother on your honeymoon?" she laughed. A shadow passed over his face, and she immediately stopped what she was doing and came over to him. "Well, of course, this isn't a real honeymoon. But I don't want or need anyone but you."

They had become close in ways that neither Roberto or Nikki, for both of whom luxury had been familiar since their births, could have understood. They shared experiences that neither of their former mates had. They had survived the severities of war and overcome great obstacles to achieve riches and extraordinary fame. And they were the main performers in their lives, in Mano's case calling the shots, placing the bets, fixing the odds; Athena had created the world she inhabited simply by being who and what she was.

"I won't ever miss people when I'm with you," she told him later, while they were drinking ouzo and trimming the tree together. "But I know from all the calls you make from the library, from the stacks and stacks of papers on your desk, that you won't be around all the time. I recall, too, that I first met you in Buenos Aires, and then in Venice and Rome and Athens. You are a citizen of the world, and I don't think you would like it if I carted around behind you. You'd soon be bored if all I did was talk about what I bought in each city or tossed around the gossip I heard simply because I had nothing else to do with my time."

"You're a clever woman."

"I wish that was true; I wouldn't be in the mess I am with Roberto." After having finally succeeded in securing a silver bell that kept slipping from the tree, she sat down in front of the fire. "Look at this room! Utter havoc," she smiled, glancing around her at the piles of tinsel and paper and boxes that cluttered the floor of the elegant, expensively decorated salon. *All Nikki's,* she thought.

"Don't worry. While we're having dinner the maid will straighten it all up," he assured her. He strode over to her and turned his back to the fire. "Ati, I've spoken to the lawyers. It won't be easy to extricate you from the contracts you've signed with Roberto. It will take time, but it can be accomplished. Meanwhile, I have an idea. None of your arrangements with Roberto includes your appearance in films."

"Films? What could I do in a movie?"

"Act. Sing. Just as you do on the stage."

"Are you suggesting I appear in a Hollywood musical?"

"No, of course not. But you are every bit as beautiful and photogenic as Sophia Loren. I've never seen a bad picture of you. You seem to leap out of any magazine or newspaper photo." The fire was growing too hot, so he moved away and sat on the arm of a sofa facing her.

"I have to be honest with you, Ati. I would really like the idea of your being a movie star." His face cracked open into his wide smile. "You're going to hate this, but I'm not really too keen on opera. Except for seeing you perform, it's always bored me. What I find thrilling is seeing how you weave such a spell over the people in the audience and to hear them shout *"Brava!"* and applaud madly. I confess, when that happened in Venice, I actually basked in your glory. It was like it was happening to me at the same time. But if you ask me what that opera was about, I couldn't tell you."

She looked away from him.

He bounced up, came over, took her hands, and turned her face toward him, leaning in close to her.

"I'm a stupid man. I've hurt you."

"No . . . well, yes, in a way."

"The point is that you're spellbinding. You would be wonderful on screen. I know it." He pulled her up on her feet and held her in his arms. "Hell, I'm a rich man. You want to make a movie, I'll back it. You want to just play for a while, I'll take care of that, too. You prefer to return to the opera—you do it. So, until we get that pansy husband of yours to say uncle, let him collect your fees. You don't need the money. You've got Manolis Zakarias to take care of you like you've never been taken care of before. Which reminds me."

He broke away and hurried out of the room, returning a few minutes later with a square-shaped, gift-wrapped box. "Open it. There'll be more presents later."

Inside was a large velvet jewelry case. She extracted it and slowly lifted the hinged lid. She stared at the glimmering object—a pearl-and-diamond tiara with magnificent stones. She picked it up carefully, still staring at it. "It's dazzling, Mano. Superb," she exclaimed, startled by the extravagance and impracticality of the gift.

"Cartier's guarantees that it belonged to the Empress Alexandra. And you see, my darling, Ati, to be happy, a king must have a queen." He took the tiara from her hand and placed it, as one would a crown, on her head. "To my Ati, my queen," he said.

He insisted she wear it at dinner along with the deep turquoise Dior gown that had arrived by boat that day along with numerous other intriguing boxes.

They slept late Christmas morning and were lazily dressing when one of the servants knocked urgently on the door to report that Yorgo was on the telephone from Athens. He had insisted on speaking with Mano and made it clear that it was an emergency. Since their room did not have an extension of its own, he left Athena to finish dressing while he took the call downstairs. When she joined him ten minutes later in the library, he had just hung up and appeared to be in shock.

"What is it, Mano?" she asked, running to his side.

"It's Nikki. She killed herself." His voice was a hoarse whisper.

"How? When?"

"In the hospital. They withheld all pills. This morning . . . they found her . . . she'd hung herself." He cradled his head despairingly in his hands.

"Oh, my God!" Athena exclaimed.

"Sylvanus went to see her yesterday. Her nurse said they had a terrible fight, that she was sobbing hysterically when he left. She was given a sedative to sleep, and when the nurse went in to wake her this morning . . ." He was ashen-faced and his hand was shaking as he lowered himself into his high-backed brown leather desk chair. "She apparently woke up earlier than the nurse had anticipated. There was an old-fashioned metal light fixture in the ceiling. She stripped the sheets from the bed, tied them together, made a noose, stood on a chair, fastened one end to the base of the fixture, slipped the noose over her head, and kicked over the chair."

He looked suddenly much older. There were tears in his eyes. Athena could find no words to say that might comfort him. Her own eyes brimmed with emotion. The thought of Nikki, so beautiful and golden, dying that way, by her own hand, made her feel quite sick. She could see her moving through the grand ballroom of the Palazzo Tiziano, looking like a sun goddess in her gold lamé gown. She wondered if Nikki had been wearing a hospital gown or her own lingerie when she hung herself. Her head filled with bizarre, horrifying images of Nikki dangling like a bird with a broken neck. She stood up but didn't move—she was unable to—and felt her chest constrict. She watched Mano, aware that he was not wholly conscious of her presence, that his thoughts were in the past, with Nikki.

"I can't help thinking how things might have been," he said without even glancing her way. "She was only a girl when we married. She had been brought up in a convent, was in love with love. And because she thought very little of herself, she was convinced she would be measured in terms of her appeal to men. I happened along. Otherwise she might have married some nice young man Sylvanus could have taken into the business. That's how it should have been—how Sylvanus planned it, I think. She never expected to have to choose between her father and her husband, and when she realized she had lost me, too, it broke her."

He turned to look at Athena. "That was long before us, Ati. None of this is connected with you."

Athena watched, her heart breaking for him, while he rose and went over to the windows, which from this room had a panoramic view of the island. She waited for him to continue. He was staring into the distance. The day was clear, a winter sun casting a full light over everything. The wind had died down. Everything beyond was stilled, an unreal landscape of startling radiance: rocks, treetops, sand, and sea bathed in hues of yellow.

He took a deep, slow breath and walked back to his desk with a quiet, businesslike air. The telephone was ringing and he pushed a button that cut it off. "The vultures are planning their attack," he said. "The best thing is for you to stay here until after the funeral. You'll be out of reach of the press. I'll go back to Athens. There may be problems with the Church because she took her own life." He leaned back in his chair and glanced up at the ceiling. "I don't know what Sylvanus said to her, but I'll have to present a united front with him. That bastard! And after taking my twelve tankers!"

She helped him pack a small suitcase. He showed her the one private telephone in the library on which he would call and gave her a number in his Athens office, through which a message would get immediately to him. The other telephones in the house would ring into a switchboard in Athens. She went down to the dock with him in the Jeep. They embraced emotionally.

"Ati, Ati," he cried softly in her ear, kissed her with mounting intensity, then held her at arm's length. "It's all over for Nikki, but it's just beginning for us," he said.

He took a small launch instead of the *Atlas* so that he might slip into Athens without being recognized—or so he hoped. She stood on the dock until the boat was a speck on the horizon, and then had Costa drive her to the highest point of the island to see if it remained in view.

Sky and sea merged into one blue flow. She returned to the house and tried to keep busy.

She was sitting at the piano in the music room, accompanying herself in her vocalizing exercises, when she heard a strange, mechanical sputtering sound. The late-afternoon light poured in through a western window. Several gulls flew past, as if in formation, and then disappeared. She got up and opened the door to the corridor that led from the music room to the entryway and listened.

Nothing.

Then, when she was closing the door, the sputtering grew louder. It seemed to be coming from outside. There was now some commotion emanating from the kitchen wing, loud voices, running feet, and then the light from the window was darkened by shadow. She pressed back against the wall, thinking she must be losing her mind. A giant, birdlike shape had hovered into view.

My God! A helicopter! she thought.

The engine whined and the machine rose out of sight. She ran to the window and looked out. There was not one but many of the ugly, metallic birds filling the sky, dipping and turning, bobbing up and down. She wasn't sure what was happening. Maybe the island was under attack. She controlled an urge to scream and pulled back into the room when the sun was once again shadowed and the sound of the helicopters reached a crescendo. She ran from the room, heading for the library. All she could think of doing that moment was to call Mano in Athens. She careened right into Costa.

"It's the paparazzi," he said, placing his large hands on her shoulders to steady her. "They're taking pictures from the air." He guided her into a sheltered hallway in which there were no windows.

"What shall I do?" she asked.

"Stay in the house. Pack a suitcase. I'll have some tea brought to you. Eventually they will have to retreat to refuel at Grattos, which is where I figure they came from. When I think it's safe, I'll drive you down to the dock, where you'll board the *Atlas* for Alexandria."

"To Egypt? But why?"

"They'll never figure you've gone there, and it's the opposite direction from Grattos. That means you'll be far away before they return. They're probably trying for a shot of you from above, walking the island alone, something like that. But what I fear they could do is land somewhere along the beach, even though this is private property, and make their way up to the house. I want to get you out of here before then."

"I have to call Mano," she said.

"I already have."

"What did he say?"

" 'Get Madame Varos out of the reach of those vultures.' " He managed a friendly smile. "Perhaps in stronger language. I suggested the plan I've just told you and he agreed. There's a telephone on the *Atlas*. You're to call him as soon as we're under way."

She ran to her room and threw her belongings into a suitcase, removing the tiara from its box so that it would take up less space. The situation was too outlandish to be real, a nightmare from which she was sure she would awaken. She realized the sputtering was fading into the distance and ran to the window. The helicopters were gone. When she turned back into the room with a sigh of relief, Costa was standing in the doorway. He took her bag and hurried her out of the house into a car, which sped down the rocky incline and bounced so much that her insides shook.

The telephone was ringing as she boarded the *Atlas*.

"Ati! Thank god you're safe." Mano's voice was crackling with static and what he said next was impossible to make out.

"What was that?" she asked.

". . . Alexandria . . ."

"Yes, yes. Will I see you there?"

The telephone went dead. She replaced the receiver, sat down on a banquette, and looked around her. She was in the grand lounge where, in Venice, on the night of the party, she had first met Nikki. Athena remembered thinking how vulnerable she looked, how much in love with Mano she was, in an almost pathological way, her great golden cat's eyes seeming to want to devour him. A large portrait of her (painted by the French artist Lenore Fini, she recalled being told) hung on the opposite wall. It was Nikki portrayed as a magnificent, tawny catwoman rising incongruously from the sea.

It was simpler to think of Nikki as predator than victim; somehow it lifted the weight of guilt pressing on Athena. Still, she was feeling uneasy, and the idea that Sylvanus's agreement to see Nikki had been purchased with twelve tankers kept nagging at Athena. Had he been cruel enough to tell her the truth? Athena did not suppose she would ever know the answer to that question.

A steward came in and asked her if she would like a drink or some food.

"Not yet," Athena answered.

Then she was led to a stateroom—very 1920's, the color of pink champagne, with mirrored walls, slithery satin covers, and sleek, white-lacquered built-ins. *Nikki's*, she thought, and immediately went up on deck.

She stood at the rail and looked out to sea. Night had fallen and they were traveling under the white glare of a full moon. She remembered the story about the man without a country. She felt a lot like that. Where was she going? Alexandria. How odd! She was completing a journey she was to have undertaken so many years ago, when the enemy was about to set siege to Athens.

Mano rang again a short time later. The connection was only a little bit better.

"I think we shouldn't see each other for a few weeks," she understood him to say, though his words were fading in and out. "But Ati, I love you, and as soon as this is behind us we'll have all the time together that our love demands."

"We never opened the rest of our presents," she sighed before the reception grew too bad to talk.

"My greatest present is your love," he said.

Then he was gone, and she was on a sea as blue and deep as Mano's eyes.

22. ATHENA HAD NEVER EXPERIENCED STAGE FRIGHT, WHICH she thought might have something to do with her myopia, since she was never able to see past the prompter's box. Audiences, therefore, remained anonymous to her, faceless, and so not to be feared. But from the day of poor Nikki's tragic suicide, with the eyes of the world upon her, she understood how performers might be terrified facing an auditorium of potentially hostile strangers.

The paparazzi were relentless; Mano had underestimated their savage perseverance. They returned in their helicopters and buzzed the *Atlas* during her escape to Alexandria, crowded the dock and flashed their cameras while she disembarked, chased after her limousine in cars that nearly sideswiped hers, and swarmed the lobby of her hotel, making her a virtual prisoner in her suite. Vesta, who had flown from Paris to join her so that she wouldn't be alone, cleverly devised Muslim disguises that covered most of their faces so that they could get past the photographers and to their limousine for a tour of the city, which neither of them had ever seen before.

The day was bitterly cold, but that didn't stop the crowds, most of them wrapped in Arab or Muslim clothes, from milling through the open markets; the stalls, with their ragged bits of awning flapping in the wind, displayed everything from brightly tasseled camel-

342

saddlery to live quail and charms to ward off evil spirits. The two women, with their driver as guide, moved through an alien cacophony of sounds; the imprecations of street Arabs, the high-pitched wails of the hawkers, the clank of copperware dangling from the sides of mules and camels. Despite their disguise, with only their eyes to distinguish them from the monotonous throngs of Muslim women in the market, Athena and Vesta were soon located by reporters who recognized their car and, after sighting the driver, began to close in on them.

Vesta grabbed Athena's hand and the two women tore through the market, their veils flying, holding their black skirts above their ankles so as not to trip on their hems, knocking off wares from the vendors' displays, frightening animals, and causing considerable chaos as they wove precipitously through the jam of people. They came to a jolting stop at the edge of the Arab quarter, where a group of British soldiers were gathered outside a café, their army vehicle close by.

"Please take us to the Alexandria Hotel," Athena begged, tearing the veil from her face.

Whether they believed the predicament in which the two women found themselves or merely fancied the adventure of rescuing two intriguing women, the Englishmen obliged. When they reached the hotel and saw the encampment of paparazzi, who had returned and were waiting to pounce on the women, they formed a military guard and saw them directly to the door of their suite.

Athena would have laughed at the ridiculousness of the incident, but Nikki's death and Mano's and her own notoriety had recast their newfound love into *le scandale* of the decade. To her horror, Roberto gave interviews about how Mano had "stolen his wife" and threatened to bring her to court on charges of adultery (which could be ruled a crime in Italy if the wife committed it). In statements to an Athens paper and to *Paris Match*, Kuri was quoted as saying, "My daughter must be mentally ill to cause all this heartache and tragedy."

Her father was tracked down in New York, where he angrily

warned a reporter from the *Journal-American,* "People in glass houses shouldn't throw stones!"

"What people, sir?" the reporter asked.

"You people. Your readers. How many of you have lived pure lives, eh? And who is to judge another person's actions?"

Dear papa! Athena thought. *He couldn't know he was playing right into the interviewer's greedy, salacious hands.*

"Then you don't think what your daughter has done is wrong?" the reporter asked. "To elope with a married man when she is also married?"

"My daughter is a great singer. What business is it of anyone's what she does in her private life?"

The headline read: LA DIVINA'S FATHER CONDONES ADULTEROUS LOVE TRYST.

Mano called morning and night declaring his love, promising that they would soon be together and all this madness would be behind them. He sent flowers that filled her hotel room and large sums of cash for her to shop and buy anything she wanted (had she been able to go shopping).

"Mano, the only thing I want is to be with you. Anywhere. I don't care," she told him.

"Be patient, Ati. Be patient," he replied from Athens, where he had remained to stand side-by-side with his old enemy Sylvanus at Nikki's funeral. He continued to work from his office there. He was besieged by reporters as well, but his large staff of burly bodyguards enabled him to move about Athens with somewhat more freedom than Athena could manage in Alexandria.

Days and then weeks went by while she waited for word about their reunion, and the strain was beginning to tell on her. She was skittish, looking paler and thinner, and scheduled her days around the likelihood of a telephone call from Mano.

"You haven't sung in weeks," Vesta complained one bright afternoon in late January, when Athena appeared more disconsolate than usual. "Why isn't there a piano in this suite? Where is Luigi?

You are scheduled to appear at La Scala and in Paris this spring. Does Zakarias expect you to give up your career?"

"Why would you ask such a question?"

"Because he's very rich and he's Greek. That's a fatal combination. Greek men like their wives in the kitchen and their mistresses at their disposal—not appearing in the world's great opera houses. So he must provide alternatives."

"Alternatives? What alternatives?"

"Well, he's already bought you the apartment in Paris. Perfect, right? Very private, with a view of the Gardens—and it's on the Left Bank, where social mores are a little bit looser than on the Right Bank. Then he cuts off your income—although Roberto has already helped him with that. What can you do but turn to him for support? So, he gives you a luxurious life that would be difficult for you to maintain without him, especially if your career is in shambles; another apartment in London, maybe a palazzo in Venice. There are private planes, trains, and yachts. You get an allowance—generous, I'm sure. And he pays all your bills. Why not? He's richer than the few kings left in the world."

Athena turned away as though to convey the impression that she wasn't the least bit interested in what Vesta was saying. Used to Athena's tendency to avoid subjects, and intent on convincing her of the danger of her present situation, Vesta pressed on.

"The catch is that one day you'll celebrate your fortieth birthday and he'll need a younger woman to help him hang on to his already disappearing youth. So he puts you out to pasture. That might be okay if you were some sleek filly with little more than good legs and high hopes. But you're Athena Varos, and he's just a Greek prick with a thirst for power and a vulgar lust for money."

They were having lunch in the penthouse suite, which continued to be Athena's refuge in Alexandria since she had refused to venture out after the experience in the market. They were to have joined the American consul and his wife for dinner that evening, along with some other guests, but Athena had just canceled, claiming an indisposition. In fact, she simply could not stand the thought of fighting her way past the pack of press-hounds outside the hotel or of walking into a room where all eyes would be upon her. And Mano wouldn't be at her side.

"I should be furious at you, Vesta, for saying such things. If Mano had simply wanted a mistress, he wouldn't have left Nikki. He's had many women before. But his feelings for me are quite different. Poor Nikki knew that."

Vesta clinked her fork down in anger. "What you have to understand is that the man is a megalomaniac—and that means not only over his business enterprises, but the women who come to his bed!"

"You're wrong, but let's not talk about it anymore. I have a headache. It's been very difficult these past weeks. Nikki's death, the press, Roberto—even Mama. It's just been too much." She pushed her chair back and left Vesta seated at the table beside the room's large picture window, with its view of Alexandria's rooftops and narrow streets, so full of both crushing poverty and exotic beauty. Athena stretched out on a sofa and, leaning back against the pillows, closed her eyes.

Her life was spinning out of control; all her dreams were on hold. Nikki's death had altered everything, changed her reality. She was fighting the thought that what she and Mano had shared was an illusion, that her loneliness now was the actuality. She was terribly confused. To hold on to their love, she somehow had to find a constant in their relationship. She had played so many fictional roles in which she had died for love—but in real life she wanted to *live* for love, for Mano, for what they had created together, to hold that love to her like a child; protect it, nurture it, allow it time to mature. *Some constant, anything,* she thought to herself.

Her profession had made an expatriate of her, although she was not sure from which country. Was she a Greek-American or an American-Greek? Or, perhaps, she was a Greek-American-Italian? The answer seemed vital to her, since each identity came with entirely different cultural and moral baggage. Only one thing was certain—she was the child of Greek parents, and so was Mano, and that was a constant. The way his Aegean eyes looked at her—that was another constant. And the smile that lighted his strong Greek face when she awoke in his arms—that was a constant, too.

"I have to speak up. He's cut you off from everyone else," Vesta was saying, indignation flashing in her flinty eyes.

"He's done nothing of the sort. It's been the press that has made a problem for us."

She studied Vesta for a moment, wondering what *her* life was really like. For all her outspokenness, Vesta was a manifestly secretive person. Oh, it was true, she did nothing to conceal her liaisons or her lesbianism. She now even wore her hair in a close-clipped masculine style and, although she dressed in women's clothes in public (to save Athena from scandal, she claimed), she wore trousers at all other times. Still, Athena knew little of how she felt about the women in her life, the failure of her own career, or even the details of her past. However often Athena probed these questions, Vesta's deftness at sidestepping her left her with nothing. As much as Athena relied upon Vesta, who could always get things done that others could not, she had remained uncomfortable with her even after all these years. Now she wondered if it weren't possible that Vesta envied her "having it all," a career and a great love. She also wondered if, like Luigi, her dedication to Athena was taking a heavy toll on her personal life.

"The point is, Zakarias doesn't realize who and what you are," Vesta continued. "Or maybe he does. Maybe he plans to tame you so that he can say, 'The great Varos, *la Divina,* gave up everything for me.' So that he can pump more air into his already inflated ego!"

Athena sat up, a puzzled expression on her face, a brittle tone to her voice. "Why do you hate him so much, Vesta?" she asked.

"I don't. But he scares the shit out of me."

"Why, in God's name?"

"Because I think he could put out the flame of something quite extraordinary, something beyond his understanding—a voice that could ascend to immortality—and silence it forever." She was interrupted by the telephone. "Big pricks have the biggest ears," she said, after answering it and bringing the telephone over to Athena.

As soon as she heard Mano's voice, all Athena's fears and confusions disappeared. She lovingly cupped the mouthpiece in her hand. "Yes, yes, of course I'll come," she said, so suddenly preoccupied with his much-welcomed and much-awaited plans to finally meet again that she only dimly registered Vesta slamming the door behind her.

The next morning he sent a seaplane for her; they were to rendezvous in the middle of the Mediterranean, where he was cruising on the *Atlas* in the company of twenty or so guests, most of whom were South American business associates. It was twilight when the plane splashed down. He stood on the deck in a purple light, the sun not yet completely set and the moon about to rise, and bent over the rail to help her up the last few steps onto the deck beside him.

"Ati, darling," he cried, and kissed her passionately.

They clung together for a long time. She touched his face; he kissed her again and cradled her head in his wide, strong hands. She couldn't help the tears of happiness in her eyes, nor ignore the music of Wagner's *Tristan and Isolde* that she was hearing in her mind.

"You look radiant," he said when they finally pulled apart.

"It's the rosy spot," she replied. When she realized he hadn't understood the theater term, she added, "The lighting."

She was given Nikki's former cabin, the one she had occupied on her trip to Alexandria. But now the door between it and Mano's more masculine, sea-captain–like adjoining stateroom was unlocked. "We can have the pink room redecorated soon," he promised. "For now you can use it as a dressing room." He pounded lightly on the large mattress on his bed. "Very good springs," he said, grinning.

The first thing she noticed upon joining Mano and his guests in the lounge was that the sea-cat painting of Nikki was gone. The second was that the only other women aboard were secretaries—if their duties were more intimate, everyone managed to be very discreet about it.

Throughout the cruise, she and Mano were seldom alone. He was busy with meetings all day and was constantly surrounded by a retinue of aides. Something important was being transacted, something about offshore oil drilling. Whatever it was, it seemed well out of her province. And while some of the men found time to relax by the pool, Mano did not. Despite having eight different kinds of caviar on board (which was liberally dispensed, as were the finest champagne, old brandy, and food prepared by three French chefs), the *Atlas* was a traveling business conference, and the dining room and lounge were thick with cigar smoke until late at night.

Still, it was enough for her to know that Mano was near and to have him with her at night, holding her in his arms, reassuring her of his love. She needed this desperately; he was the only anchor she had.

"It will be all right," he had said soothingly on the second night, when she had been visibly disturbed by having to spend most of the evening in her cabin waiting for him while he drank and smoked cigars with the group of swarthy South Americans.

His eyes were bleary, and although he was not drunk ("I always make sure I'm more sober than my business associates," he had assured her), he was too exhausted to make love and fell into bed beside her, his breath thick with the smell of brandy and the noxious odor of cigar in his hair.

"We'll soon be together in Paris," he told her. "You'll be happy there. I'll make it so. You just tell me what you want and presto, it's yours." He patted her shoulder, turned over on his side, and was asleep before she could reply.

By the time they settled in Paris she had begun to build her life around him. Once the work on the apartment was finished, there was still the *Atlas* and the house on Zephyrus to redo; then the new plane, the *Athena,* a jet this time, and after that an impressive luxury flat on Grosvenor Square in London, just a few doors down from the new and extremely ugly American embassy, a Stalinist building with a predatory eagle on the top.

Her legal battle with Roberto had not gone well; he had managed to put obstacles in the way by obtaining continuances and delays so that there had been no progress for months and months. Mano was busy and traveled a great deal: Europe, Asia, South America. He trusted no one on his staff except Yorgo and delegated little responsibility to others, although he had representatives in most of the major cities of the Western world.

It still nettled him that he was not allowed to do business in the United States. In what free time he could spare he had been trying, so far unsuccessfully, to overcome the embargo against him through countless meetings with powerful American politicians. With John F. Kennedy, the young new occupant of the White House, his hopes were high. Kennedy was a man with whom Mano believed he could strike a deal; his father was a tough old bandit who had made millions and primed his son for the power of the presidency.

Athena seldom accompanied Mano; she would meet him in various places, a private plane always standing by on the ready to whisk her to and from his side. And, as he had promised, they had some private time together in Paris. She was almost obsessed with the apartment there, doing and redoing rooms, adding extra conveniences—American showers, a built-in sound system, an office for Mano where the upstairs sitting room had been. It was the first time she had created a home, and she wanted it to be as perfect for Mano as it was for her. They went on shopping sprees together, and it was then that she felt more happy than ever.

"Been playing house again today?" Vesta chided whenever she returned from one of these excursions. But Athena felt too content to respond to her sarcastic barbs, and she was now inured to the antipathy between Vesta and Mano. "How can you keep that lesbian bitch around?" he would growl. It was difficult to explain that despite her sharp tongue, Vesta was able to handle all the tasks with which Athena could not cope. Or that she could not so easily dismiss a woman to whom she felt loyal, a woman who had been among the first to encourage her career.

The press had finally backed off, and now only the occasional photographer intruded on her privacy. The press was now more interested in the diva's silence than in *le scandale,* and interviews were on a more respectful basis. Mano had insisted she cancel her current contracts and reimburse Roberto for his losses. This further angered Roberto—but more important, it created great hostility with the managers of the opera houses she was to have appeared at, who were forced to replace her with lesser stars and box-office draws.

Happy in her love for Mano, feeling protected by him, never in want of anything, with Yanni to take care of her personal needs and Vesta to handle business matters—the many letters, invitations, requests for interviews and charity appearances, recording and concert offers—and Luigi working with her almost daily to keep her voice in condition for her far-off and only vaguely discussed comeback, she was lulled into a sense of contentment.

"How can I make a comeback when I never seem to have been away?" she asked Luigi. "I hear myself on the radio every day. And who collects the royalties from those records? Roberto!"

She blamed Roberto for her one great unhappiness: her inability to marry Mano. Since their return to Paris, he seldom broached the subject unless to belittle someone else's marriage. "We have passion, great love, excitement; *they* sleep in separate bedrooms and have teenaged kids on drugs," he was fond of saying. Or, in more dramatic moments, "Remember Ati, ours is an historic affair. We were brought together by the gods. We aren't bound by the conventions of little people."

And so in this way one year and then two managed to pass, and none of Athena's intense feeling for Mano diminished. She would have liked to have had a child, but Mano would not hear of it. "What we do is our business, but to bring an innocent child into this world as a bastard, even one with such an inheritance, would be the first and only immoral act we've committed," he argued sensibly.

Mano had not given up on his fight to regain his shipping license in the United States. ("All Greeks want to go to America," Vesta once chirped.) It was extremely important to him and he invested much time, effort, and money in his attempt. Powerful American businessmen, senators, and labor leaders were frequent guests for extravagant cruises on the *Atlas* which usually included at least two or three glittering names like the duke and duchess of Windsor, Dietrich, Coward, Charlie and Oona Chaplin, Picasso, or Salvador Dali (who had painted a bizarre portrait of Athena that now hung in the boat's salon; she was draped in a fish net, with cockles, periwinkles, and a shrimp or two entangled in her hair and a warped harpoon hoisted high in her finlike hand). To Mano's delight, most of his guests found *la Divina*'s presence the highlight of the cruise.

Athena's absence from the stage had made her even more sought-after, and like the American film star, Grace Kelly, now the princess of Monaco, the press was always running headline stories featuring speculations about her resuming her career.

It was Mano who was finally responsible for Athena's return to the opera, a production of *Macbeth* in which she would play Lady Macbeth—and not on stage, but on film. After several years of negotiation, Mano had made a billion-dollar deal for ships and off-shore oil rigs along the coast of South America. Upon its completion, he leased offices in Buenos Aires and told Athena that he would leave very soon and have to be away for several months.

"I'll come with you," she insisted.

"What will you do?"

"Be there when you need me," she replied simply.

"Ati, that makes no sense. I propose something much better. Why not use the time to reestablish yourself as the great star that you are?"

"You mean work out a new contract with one of the opera companies? Well, of course, that wouldn't be too difficult, except that you're planning to leave in a few months while opera companies schedule their seasons a year or more in advance. I wouldn't be singing until long after you were back."

"I have another idea, and you must hear me out before shouting, 'No!' I've spoken to someone who is very successful in films, someone who knows you. If you agree you could begin work on a project with him very soon."

"A movie? Oh, no, not for me. It may be your fantasy for me, but I'm not and never will be a Gina Lollobrigida. Who is this person?"

"Ugo Gianni, a great fan of yours. And, as you know, an acclaimed film director."

"Ugo! You saw Ugo? He's here in Paris and didn't call me?"

"We spoke by telephone. He's in Rome but he'll fly to Paris if you agree to see him."

"Of course, I'll see Ugo. But that doesn't mean I'll make a film with him. What could I do in a Ugo Gianni movie? He and Fellini and their scatalogical, autobiographical stories. What is it, a cameo? Does he want me to play myself?"

"In fact, I suggested something like that."

"What are you saying, Mano? That you called Ugo and asked him to cast me in his next film?" Her voice rose in her fury. How could Mano degrade her like that? To offer to buy her a role in a movie as though she was some cheap chorus girl. Her dark eyes blazed when she looked up at him. She was seated at the piano in the Paris apartment's music room, where she had been vocalizing before he came in to tell her about Buenos Aires—and to spring this other, unexpected plan upon her.

"I called Ugo Gianni because I know he's the brightest and best of the new filmmakers and because his movies have been both critical and commercial successes," he said flatly, as though talking to a business associate. "I offered to back any film he would like to make, no strings attached, if you were the star. He said that if you were to be involved he would want to film an opera. He said he's always dreamed of seeing you sing one of your great roles on film, where millions could see you. I said go ahead—one million, two million dollars, let me see a budget. He insisted it be *Macbeth* because the Lady Macbeth you did at La Scala was the most electrifying performance he had ever seen, that you were incomparable in the role. " 'Tell her she is Verdi's ideal Lady Macbeth,' he said."

Athena rose from the piano. The music-room walls were hung with photographs of her in her more famous roles. Her La Scala

Lady Macbeth stared down at her; it had been taken during the sleepwalking scene. "It's a bad-luck opera," she said.

"You surely don't believe that? And if you do, then I'm sure Gianni would go with whatever you chose."

"I find it difficult to understand how you could have thought of this and spoken to Ugo without discussing it with me first."

"Because I knew you'd say no unless it was already set in motion." He came over to her and put his hands on her shoulders. "Ati, I only want you to be happy, and I think this will make you happy while I'm away. It will also prove something I've always believed— that you could be a great cinema star. I have already told you that I would like it, like it a lot . . . to sit in a dark theater with pictures of my beautiful Ati filling the screen." He took her in his arms and kissed her tenderly.

"Well, I'll talk to Ugo. But I can't promise anything more," she said when he let her go.

Ugo flew to Paris the next day, and her reservations were swept away when she saw him once again. Success had been good for him. Still a bear of a man, with his perennial trim goatee, he now dressed expensively, his nails were manicured, and he had the air of someone who had taken on the world and won. She was extraordinarily pleased to see him. Much time had passed since she had been able to talk to someone—apart from Luigi and Vesta—who had such a love for and understanding of opera.

It was spring, and the Luxembourg Gardens were in glorious bloom. After lunch with Mano, she and Ugo went for a walk. She wore a scarf on her head and big sunglasses that covered half her face to disguise herself. But if the playing children, strolling lovers, and elderly men and women resting on benches recognized her, the magic of the day diverted their attention.

"The reason I haven't sung for so long is simple, Ugo. I say it's Roberto's fault, but there's more to it. Mano makes me feel like a woman. I mean a *woman*—defenseless, with all her weaknesses. And he protects that woman. I've had this fear that if I went back on stage to become a diva once again—well, you know, it hardens you. It's a constant fight to maintain control, the degree of excellence, the audience loyalty that will keep you on top. You can't allow yourself to be a woman like other women, and your strength attracts needy men who use you for their own purposes. You can't just sit back and be comfortable. You have to look out for yourself. And then they say you're hard, you're trouble on wheels, you're egotistical. I don't think I could cope with that again, Ugo."

A child's ball rolled across the path. He picked it up and tossed it to a rosy-cheeked blond boy who darted away and out of sight without so much as a thank you.

They found an empty bench under the lacy branches of a pale green willow tree. "When I went off with Mano," Athena continued, "I realized there would be consequences to face and a price to pay. For me it was being unfaithful to myself and to my other lover—my singing. Well, I haven't stopped singing altogether, of course. Luigi has been a godsend. Every day he browbeats me into practicing, keeping the scores in my head. But singing without an audience is a lot like swimming in a bathtub."

She smiled dazzlingly at him, the sun lighting her face. "But you want to talk about *Macbeth,* and here I am rattling on about my life."

"A singer's voice is always linked to her state of mind. It's important you say these things. I understand much from things you couldn't know about," he told her.

"Roberto and you? I know about that. I knew about him. Yet somehow I trusted him, thought I could lean on his shoulder."

"First the bait and then he reels you in. That's Roberto's technique. And it's not easy to get off the hook, I tell you!"

"He wasn't that bad in the beginning, but the glory went to his head. It was like wine to him and he got drunk on it. Unfortunately it was my glory, not his. Then there was my mother—she should have been proud of me. Any other mother would have been. But nothing I've ever done has ever pleased her. So when Mano came into my life—well, I couldn't believe such a person could exist. Someone I could lean on, who didn't need my glory, who thought I was just swell."

Her use of such an American word as "swell" amused him and he laughed a big, deep, bearish guffaw.

"So—what about Lady Macbeth?" she asked.

"You'll do it, then?"

"It depends upon when you can go into production."

"Since we have the money and the script doesn't have to be written, as early as ninety days."

"And how long will it take to film?"

"Well, we need only one location—Cawdor Castle. I think something could be found in Scotland or the north of England, or perhaps Denmark, that would do very well. I already spoke to Maestro Capuleti—just in case you did say yes—and he has agreed to act as both musical director and conductor. We wouldn't have to be on location for more than six weeks. The recording and dubbing could be done right here in Paris, since I know you don't want to come back to Italy. The maestro has also agreed to come to Paris when you are ready, to rehearse with you. We won't have to spend much time on location."

"It seems you've thought everything out."

"I've thought about little else for many years now. I'm passionate about films, but I'm addicted to opera. I also like the idea of giving Roberto his comeuppance. He was wrong to have married you, and he compounded it with another sin, avarice, when he refused to let you go. I thank him for one thing. He did get me the job as director for your Verona *Gioconda*. Can I telephone the maestro to tell him you are ready for him to come to Paris?"

Athena lowered her sunglasses and looked Ugo directly in the eyes. "I'll call him myself," she said.

The role of Lady Macbeth is one of Verdi's finest for a singer who is also a good actress, and *Macbeth* is perhaps the most visually dramatic of all operas, so it seemed right to Athena to adapt it for film. She began intense rehearsals with the maestro a week later, and she was overjoyed to see both him and Editta, who had come with him and would also join the cast and crew on location. It was established the film would be shot in a fourteenth-century castle in Denmark, just outside of Copenhagen.

The exceptionally difficult leading role and the expensive production that it demanded prevented *Macbeth* from being performed frequently. But Lady Macbeth had been one of Athena's greatest roles; she had played her both at La Scala and at the Metropolitan. Although the libretto follows Shakespeare, in the opera it is more Lady Macbeth than her husband who is the protagonist.

With each rehearsal Athena began to feel more exhilarated. She had not realized just how much she had missed her work and the stimulation of great talents like the maestro's and Ugo's. The three of them spent several days on the terrifying sleepwalking scene, which, although in the opera it is Lady Macbeth's last scene, was scheduled to be shot early in the production to set the mood for the film.

"Every move must be nothing short of perfection," Ugo instructed. "Your acting must attain Shakespearean stature. The camera will magnify all your facial expressions, every gesture. If you go over the top you will lose it; the same goes if you don't reach a dramatic climax. It will take most of your interpretative and creative powers to hold the perfect balance, both as a singer and an actress. You won't have to worry about your voice while we're shooting the scene—that will be dubbed in later. But you are going to have to know exactly what to do with each aria, the Verdian heights you must reach, so that the action and sound will synchronize completely with your lip movements and emphasis."

She was standing by the curve of the grand piano, listening to Ugo, who was sitting beside the maestro at the keyboard. Luigi looked on from one side. "Will the orchestra be there when I do the scene?" she asked.

"Of course! And in the film it will create a haunting atmosphere," he explained, "while the camera moves through the gloomy, dank halls of the castle. You enter sleepwalking, pause, and rub your hands as if to wash them—'These bloody hands that have been witness to murder,' et cetera. But they won't wash clean. You will study them with growing horror . . ."

"And then you sing *pianissimo,* "the Maestro broke in. He struck the note on Athena's piano, her cue to begin.

"Una macchia è qui tuttora," Athena sang darkly. *Still there is a stain there.*

"As if through clenched teeth, Athena," the Maestro said. "It will give the impression that you are actually talking in your sleep."

She started again and reached the line, *"Uno . . . due . . . gli è questa l'ora."* *One . . . two . . . this is the hour.*

"More unearthly and when you reach the line, *'Chi poteva in quel vegliardo tanto sangue immaginar?"* *Who would have imagined there was so much blood in that old man?* Try to underline the despair by stressing the word *immaginar.* There is a black intensity in *'Arabia inera rimondar sì piccol'mano.'* *All the perfumes of Arabia cannot clean this little hand.* Then I want you to close the scene with the merest trace of a voice. Not easy, of course, because you have to rise to D-flat and then drop an octave on the final note and still be perfectly audible while you somberly sleepwalk away. Your voice, Athena, must be that of the very devil."

He got up from the piano, and Luigi slid onto the bench to accompany her through the aria while the maestro and Ugo walked to the other side of the room. None of them was aware of Mano standing in the doorway while Athena sang; her performance was so dark and heartrending that they felt like spectral guests at the castle of Cawdor. Athena hit the D-flat with magnificent clarity and pitch, and when her voice fell to a hushed whisper and then died out, it was as if a candle had just been snuffed.

"Brava!" Mano shouted, startling everyone else in the room, especially Athena. *"Brava!"* he repeated, clapping loudly.

Athena ran to him laughing and threw her arms around his neck. "Maybe you won't lose your million dollars after all," she said.

"I never believed I would," he replied.

Two weeks later she left for Denmark with the maestro, Editta,

Luigi, Vesta, and Yanni (Ugo was already on location). She was in the highest spirits she had known since before the terrible morning when she and Mano had learned of Nikki's death. On the very day of her departure, Mano flew to Buenos Aires on the *Athena*. It was no accident that Alexandra von Luenhalter, the long-legged Lexie, was waiting for him in his hotel suite when he arrived.

23. Most of Mano's life was doing deals; the rest was waiting. As he grew richer his business transactions became larger, often forcing him to take on whole countries. He was the head of a massive and powerful empire that included, along with his shipping business, vast interests in real estate and air travel—and, now, in the construction of offshore oil rigs and partial rights to everything they pumped. It did not alleviate his gnawing disappointment that he was still not welcome in the United States; he had even received information that J. Edgar Hoover's F.B.I. was investigating him as a spy and a criminal, and was prepared to arrest him on the charge of fraudulently obtaining wartime tankers if he ever tried to reenter the country.

One of the American power figures whom he had been wooing with an eye to quashing this problem was Clark Cameron McMaster, whose father had been old Joe Kennedy's toughest rival, who himself had come close to beating out John Kennedy in the Democratic presidential primaries of 1960, and who had just been killed in a suspicious private-jet crash. Only weeks before that, he, his beautiful wife, Victoria, and Lexie and Rudi had been Mano's guests on a Mediterranean cruise. Athena had not joined them and was not aware that the other two women were aboard. More and more she had come to avoid Mano's business cruises, and in this instance her absence relieved him; because McMaster was known to be a puritanical character whom his sister-in-law, Lexie, labeled as "A righteous lefty . . . the worst kind of bigot."

After McMaster's death, Vicki had inherited one of the largest corporate empires in the United States. She had no brothers. Cam McMaster's father was long since dead. And she had little training in the world of big business and politics. "Poor Vicki," Lexie said to Mano. "Everyone's out there to take a bite out of her. She's a tadpole in a pool of crocodiles."

It was quite accidental that Mano was seeing Lexie again. There was the McMaster connection, of course, but even while playing the good host on the *Atlas* he had remained aloof from her. He had run into her at the America embassy in Paris; she was renewing her passport and he was on his way into the ambassador's office to try one more time to procure a visa for himself.

"How's Athena?" she asked, her voice golden and husky. She was wearing one of those new short skirts, which revealed a tantalizing amount of her shapely thighs.

"She's very busy rehearsing for her film."

"I read about that. *Macbeth*. I heard her sing Lady Macbeth at the Met. It was such a realistic portrayal that I was just as glad she didn't join us on our cruise. A very brilliant and very intimidating woman."

"Who, Ati?" he laughed. "She's a powder puff."

"Mano, I think you get your understanding of women from a Cartier catalogue!"

He grinned, pleased. He liked Lexie, her quick wit, the way she was at home with wealth, the way she took luxury (even other people's) in stride. She was a lightning rod for a man of his background, a man who had fought his way up from nothing to the top. Lexie was born with a taste for money. To Mano there was no higher kind of chic. She was also a very sexy woman.

"How about lunch?" he asked.

"With me on the menu?"

"If you're in season."

"Hot to hump, you mean? Not me, Mano. Not now, anyway. I'm in a very vulnerable stage of my life. Yesterday was my thirty-fifth birthday, and the day before that the bailiffs threw Rudi and me out of the apartment we were gracious enough to occupy for Princess Blodoskaya. Can you believe she had forgotten to tell us that she owed a year's back rent?"

"And where are you now?"

"Tonight I'm at the Ritz, where Cam kept a suite. Tomorrow I'm going to join Vicki on Cape Cod. She's shaken, poor darling. I thought it was about time I did my sisterly duty."

"And Rudi?"

"Gone to hell, for all I care."

"I like your wifely devotion."

"Come on, Mano. This is the real world. We had reached the end of the road. Couldn't take it any further."

At that moment ideas began to spin in Mano's head. "Look, Lexie, forget lunch. Why not meet me in Buenos Aires in a couple of weeks? I have some extended business there. Two, three months perhaps. Athena can't come with me and obviously you're at loose ends. If you want to do it on a just-friends basis, that's okay with me. Plenty of willing señoritas—and señoras—in Buenos Aires. But I would be most grateful for your companionship."

"How grateful?" she asked.

He roared with laughter. "Lexie, you kill me! Are you sure you haven't got Greek blood in you?"

And so after two weeks of tending to her widowed sister on Cape Cod, Lexie—her bank balance now comfortably shifted from overdraft to five-figure credit—flew to Buenos Aires, where she arrived in time to fill Mano's suite with the scent of her expensive perfume and a whole wall of closets with a fashionable new wardrobe. She rose from the sitting-room sofa to greet him when he entered and gave him a formal, decorous kiss. He looked around the room with obvious pleasure. There were magnificent bouquets of flowers everywhere and ice ready in the bar—more of a homelike ambiance than one would expect from a hotel suite.

"I rearranged the furniture," she explained, "and insisted they get rid of some of the most offensive pieces. I even went down to the basement, where they store things. 'Now I know Barbara Hutton once had this suite,' I told them, 'and Babs would never have stood for such tasteless furnishings.' Actually she has appalling taste, but it worked anyway. Lots of Biedermeier, as you can see. Probably brought here by one of Hitler's escaped henchmen."

She watched him pour himself a brandy and then light a cigar, speculating on how to interpret his ironic smile. He was a master at concealing his true feelings. She even found the stories he told her about his past hard to believe. "I think you make it all up," she once told him. "A memory like that would take too much effort."

Why had he brought her here? For old times' sake? For companionship, as he claimed? To fend off mothers with eligible daughters? To resume their once-steamy affair? She decided to force him into playing his hand. "Shall we dress for dinner?" she asked.

"Will you have a drink?" he parried, avoiding the question.

"Sure." She came over to the bar. "Ice in the brandy, please."

"That's sacrilegious."

"Well, hell, from one pagan to another *that* doesn't seem to count for much does it?"

He poured her the drink. "Yes, we'll dress for dinner. A group of important diplomats. They're looking forward to meeting you."

"Me?"

"The bereaved sister-in-law of the late Clark Cameron McMaster. Sure they are—is there a black dress among all those silk creations?"

"Several. I haven't forgot that black is your favorite color." She went to the wardrobe and took out a handsome black jersey gown. "Is this suitably demure?"

His eyes passed over her lithe, curvaceous body. "Demure is not a word that comes quickly to mind when I think of you, no matter what you're wearing."

He downed the rest of his brandy and grinned; the tension in the room—it had been palpable—instantly fell away. He took her by the shoulders, pulled her close to him, and kissed her warmly, then passionately.

"At least I know what we're doing *after* dinner," she laughed.

Things were going exceptionally well for Mano. After years of upheavals, political crises, and military juntas in Argentina, popular elections had been held and a moderate liberal, Dr. Arturo Illía, elected president. At least for a time, Buenos Aires could look forward to peace and prosperity. The country was also ripe for a man of Manolis Zakarias's entrepreneurial skills.

The offshore-drilling project took wings and within five years would be operational. There were great undersea oilfields all over the world, and Mano's research scientists were certain this was particularly true off the coasts of California and Oregon. But that, of course, was another story—a bedtime story.

He had brought Lexie to Buenos Aires for one purpose alone, and it hadn't been sex. In truth, no woman gave him more satisfaction than Athena, and he had never quite understood why. It was beyond him, something over which he had no control. But he suspected it had to do with her unconditional love. Every other woman, including Nikki, had given him passion in the expectation of getting something they valued in return, and for this reason he had always had the upper hand. With Athena, his pleasure was *her* pleasure. And he instinctively knew that if he went bankrupt today her love would not change, except perhaps to become more protective.

Thus with Athena he felt compelled to hold back; if he let his heart rule him, Ati would gain the upper hand, and that was something he simply could not allow to happen. That was why empires fell apart. His desire for power would be extinguished if he gave in to his passion, and Ati understood that only partially. She was a woman with extraordinary spiritual powers. She sensed the true depth of his feelings for her and wanted to play that scenario out. But if he married her, if he allowed her to be in control, it would be the end of all he had lived, profaned, lied, cheated, and fought for.

It was Nikki's suicide that had alerted him to the danger he was facing; were Ati ever to threaten to kill herself, or were she even to become ill like Nikki, he would have to devote all his energy to helping her. A man like himself was not meant for such love, and so he had struggled to walk a middle line. Now, perhaps, he was doing something from which there would be no way back. Ati might never forgive him. He stood to lose her. On the other hand, he might well win the battle that had consumed so much of his life. He could return to the United States a respected man— respected, at least, by those who didn't know how he had arranged such a feat.

"What are you doing?" Lexie asked. She drew herself up on the bed, wrapped her bronzed arms around her legs, and rested her chin on her knees.

"Making some notes," he answered from the writing desk across the room.

"As long as it's not your memoirs." She released her hold on her legs and fell back against the pillows. "It's four A.M. A terrible hour. I hate it. It's nowhere. Neither night nor morning."

"I have an important meeting at seven."

"You don't need notes. You've got the killer instinct. Like an overhead slam—no one can catch, hit, or deflect it."

"Go back to sleep."

She got out of bed, her long-legged, naked body uniformly tanned, and went over to him. Without any finesse, she got down on her knees beside him, slipped her hand into his lap, and unzipped his trousers.

"For Chrissakes, Lexie!" he said, pushing his chair back, jumping to his feet, and doing his pants up. "Stop acting like a barroom slut!"

She dropped onto her calves. Her hair tumbled over her shoulders, resting like splayed fingers on her beautifully pointed breasts. She looked like a centerfold in one of the current cheesecake magazines. "I've tried more classy forms of seduction. Poetic murmurs, tender caresses—no go. It was as though I didn't exist. Then I thought, hmm, at his feet, the slave-girl technique. But no. 'Can't you see I'm busy?' you snapped. So I figured, what do I have to lose trying the barroom-slut approach?"

She shook her head; her breasts swayed and her hair, coppery in the lamplight, covered part of her face. He pulled her to her feet. She slipped her arms around his neck and began slowly to nuzzle him behind the ear, down his neck, blowing gentle wisps of breath that made him shiver. She lifted her face and said, "That feel good?"

He pulled her onto the bed and she hoisted her legs and planted her feet, wide apart, flat on the mattress. *Tamed by Circe to do her bidding,* he thought. Circe, the enchantress, daughter of the sun, who turned men into beasts with the promise of heaven between her golden thighs. But here there were no sounds of soft music or sweet female voices singing. Their lovemaking was energetic, filled with cheerful indecencies and gut-grunting. Five minutes after it began, he fell back exhausted and unrelieved onto the pillows. Failure coming to climax was a more frequent occurrence for him (but never with Ati), and he was greatly disturbed by it.

Lexie was lying on top of him, her breasts against his chest, her hair flung forward and over the lower part of his face so that he had to brush it away in order to breathe. They remained that way in silence for a few moments before she rolled over onto her back. Both of them gazed up at the ceiling, disconnected in mind as well as body.

"Okay, so the magic is gone," she said.

"Blame a tired old man," he replied, trying to make light of it.

She laughed. "You, Mano? You'll die in the saddle, I swear you will!"

"Not a bad way to go."

"But a hell of a problem for your partner."

"If I'm dead I won't have to worry about that."

The idea was so macabre that they both laughed.

"Still friends?" he asked as they pushed themselves up and leaned against the back of the bed.

"Sure."

"Because I have a favor to ask of you."

Her eyes glittered while she gave this some serious thought. "I can't imagine what it would be," she finally decided.

"I want you to be hostess, to make all the arrangements—guest list, ports of call, entertainment—for a special two-week cruise on the *Atlas*. It must take place as soon as possible, and all the guests must have impeccable credentials—the kind of men and women your sister would respect, who would pass government muster. The American government, that is."

"Vicki? You want Vicki along?"

"There will be no cruise without her."

Lexie bolted from the bed and wrapped herself in his robe, which happened to be the nearest one at hand. "You bastard!" she shouted. "You got me here just so I could help you hook Vicki, with her billions and her connections. Son of a bitch! You know, not even Rudi would have asked me to do anything so low."

"My dear Alexandra, I'm not asking you to do anything low. You will be performing an act of great kindness to your sister. She has been through a terrible experience, losing a handsome young husband under tragic and most mysterious circumstances. She is now in control of one of the most powerful business empires in the world, and she knows very little about the barracudas waiting to snap at her as soon as she steps into even the shallowest water. No one could be more helpful in guiding her to safety than me. She is being besieged by the press, even on her estate on Cape Cod, and wherever she goes they will follow. The public is hungry for mysteries. Cam appears to have been murdered. But by whom? The F.B.I.? The mafia? A foreign power? A business enemy? Maybe even a discarded lover? The public and therefore the press will not give up until there's an answer. I can offer her privacy, a refuge, and a chance to feel young and alive again. We do have fun on the *Atlas*, don't we? Ask people you know she will enjoy, others you think she would like to meet. She's more of an intellectual than you."

"Thanks a lot!"

"No offense meant. During our cruise I noticed that she was always on deck, reading. Invite her favorite authors."

"And Athena? Is she to be included?"

"No."

"I get the picture. You're even a worse bastard than I thought!"

"I can't talk to you about Ati. That's another part of my life. But your sister and I—we could control shipping worldwide. She's rich enough not to need my money. But I can teach her how to handle power. And you, Lexie, you can tell people that you came into a sudden inheritance. Whatever you like. You know how generous I can be."

"You are actually planning to lure her into marriage!"

"Let's say that we have a great deal in common. It would seem quite suitable if we married."

"That would be amusing—you as my brother-in-law."

A shadow crossed his face. "Vicki doesn't know about us, does she?"

"Only that you—and Nikki—have been good friends to Rudi and me."

"All right. I'll send you back to Cape Cod tomorrow. The *Atlas* will go to Boston, and we can embark from there."

"And where will Athena be during this wooing-merger?"

"Filming and then recording *Macbeth*. After that I've succeeded in buying her performance contracts from Roberto."

When she went into the bathroom he turned over and glanced at the clock on the bedside table. It was midday in Denmark. He asked the operator to call the number, then sat up and waited for the connection. Athena would not learn anything of this until she was once again deeply involved in her career, and somehow he believed that he could manage it without losing her. Ati was, he realized now, his greatest love, and chances were that he might never be able to truly enjoy another woman after her. Still, it was what he had to do, despite everything.

Love is a kind of madness, he thought. *And no one chooses to be mad.*

The telephone rang. He lifted the receiver and with a lusty lilt in his voice cried into the mouthpiece, "Oh my darling, darling Ati!"

*   *   *

Macbeth was being filmed at Kronborg, Hamlet's ancestral castle in Elsinore. Despite the curious juxtaposition of these two princes, real and Shakespearean, the castle, with its pinnacled towers and thick stone wall, its dank corridors and sinister atmosphere, made a perfect Cawdor. The company arrived in Copenhagen in mid-May expecting spring weather. But there were almost continual storms during the first two weeks of shooting, with dark, thunderous skies, thick, coiling clouds, and tempestuous winds. "A gift from nature," Ugo claimed, for the weather added an even more malevolent mood to the drama being played out inside the castle.

Kronborg was not heated and so everyone shivered and froze. Athena wore several layers of clothes beneath her costume and drank cup after cup of thick, black coffee to keep warm. But she could not wear gloves and her hands felt as though they would never warm up again. Still, she was quite happy in spite of it.

The entire company was staying at the Merienlyst Hotel in Elsinore, only a short car ride from Copenhagen. They were a strongly dedicated, closely-bound unit, more like a large family. Not all of the cast members were singers, since some of the roles were to be dubbed in Paris using vocalists from the Paris Opera, and so local actors were also hired, which kept the project from becoming too inbred.

With the knowledge that they could always reshoot something they didn't like in their performances, Athena and the other singers were, although constantly complaining about the cold, otherwise relaxed. Quite different from the atmosphere that prevailed in an opera house.

Athena heard of her father's death on the day the famous banquet scene was to be shot, in which the ghost of the murdered Banquo is seen only by Macbeth. The room they were using was the spectacular 208-foot-long banqueting hall. The setup was complete, the cameras about to roll. A tangle of thick black wires crisscrossed the stone floor. Athena, looking gaunt and ghostly herself despite her heavy makeup, entered the hall. All eyes turned to her, not knowing what to expect, aware that a cable with the tragic news had been delivered to her only a short time before. She held the crumpled telegram in her hand. Her eyes were haunted and she appeared as if in a trance.

"We can delay shooting until this afternoon," Ugo said, taking her arm and leading her to a bench in a deserted corner of the gargantuan room. He raised his hand to signal his assistant and the others to back off and wait. Then he sat down beside her.

"No, I'd rather hold to the schedule," she insisted.

"Do you want to talk about it?"

"What's to say? I'd like to cry. I can't and I probably won't. It's hard to explain. Do you believe people you love have more than one life, Ugo?"

"I don't quite get your meaning."

"Well, you see, there was the Papa I remember as a child. We were bound together, somehow. Our love and need for each other sustained us both and it had no part of the life we lived with others. I recall distinctly that I could feel pain when he did, humiliation, fear, joy. He wasn't musically talented but there was music in his very being. He was a failed artist. He saw only the failure part. Yet whatever dreams I have were given to me by Papa."

Ugo reached over and took her cold hand in his. "Athena, this isn't an easy scene to do with what you have on your heart. We can shoot around you, do the tight and long shots tomorrow."

"I'll be fine, but maybe you could sit here with me for a few minutes."

"Of course."

"I think that when I can express what it is I'm feeling, I'll be able to carry on."

Ugo raised his hand and lowered it several times as a signal for the gaffers to cut the klieg lights. The set was suddenly cast into shadow. The monstrous hall became a cavern of ancient gloom, but Athena seemed unaware of the change.

"When I think of Papa, I think only of the time when I was a child. I can see him as he was then as clearly as if he were right here before my eyes. I don't believe anyone's childhood was easy. Mine was tolerable only because of Papa. He filled the cracks of loneliness and self-doubt with his ability to share my pain, as I did his. I'm not sure, but I think I lost Papa the day I sailed with my mother and my Aunt Serafina to Greece. One moment he was in the crowd, waving to me. The next he was gone. I never saw Papa again.

"When I went back to New York after the war he was a different man, because I was different, and years of different experiences and struggles and anguishes separated us. Nor had we shared the pleasures and pride that had helped each of us to survive. But that man was also my father, and I loved him even though he often seemed a stranger—as I suppose I did to him, too. I cried sometimes because I wanted to be able to share with him as I once had done. But you can't go back, Ugo. Life is very cruel that way, don't you think?"

He put his arm around her shoulders and squeezed her. "Life is a killer," he said. "You have to work all the time to see that it doesn't get you."

She leaned against him for a few moments and then took a deep breath, let it out, and stood up. "As soon as Helge redoes my makeup I'll be ready," she said. "Could you send her to my dressing room?"

"One question first. Do you want to go to New York for the funeral?"

"For a man who died so very long ago? No."

He watched her walk away. She was rubbing her hands to warm them. The spots wouldn't come off for her any easier than they did for Lady Macbeth. Athena, he knew, felt that she should never have left her father, that her desertion had somehow made her guilty of a kind of murder.

When she returned he was surprised to see her looking even more disturbed than before. She was distracted and somewhat disoriented. At first he was going to tell her that he had decided not to shoot the scene until that afternoon. But then he realized that her emotional distress added just the right element to the scene. He had the camera track in very tight as she spoke the words: "The dark deed is done; the dead cannot return."

"Cut!" he called. He went over to her and took her aside. "We have to do it again," he said. "Your eyes weren't wild enough. You're on the edge of madness, about to fall into the abyss."

It took fifteen minutes to relight the scene. Editta and Vesta came onto the set and remained close by, but neither of them spoke to Athena, who appeared to be preparing herself for the second take. The women, both of whom had been in her dressing room when she had returned there earlier, were worried she might fall into the abyss herself. The makeup woman had been reading one of that morning's English papers, which were delivered daily to the set; when she saw Athena enter, she had folded it and put it down on her dressing table. On the exposed page was a photograph of Mano with, alongside it, one of Victoria McMaster. Above both photos was a two-line boldfaced-headline: WIDOW OF CLARK CAMERON MCMASTER ON ROMANTIC CRUISE WITH BILLIONAIRE SHIPPING MAGNATE MANOLIS ZAKARIAS.

"Did you know about this?" she had asked Vesta.

"No," she had replied honestly.

"Neither did I."

As was his habit, Mano called Athena every morning before she left for the castle. She could set her watch by the punctuality of the calls, and the sound of his voice would always get her through the problems she might face during the day. What she had had no way of knowing was that he was calling her from the *Atlas;* he himself had told her he was still in Buenos Aires.

"Ready, Athena?" Ugo called out.

She got up and took her position by Macbeth at the banquet table. The cameras began to roll. "The dark deed is done; the dead cannot return," she repeated in a chilling voice—which, of course, would later on be replaced by a recording of her singing the end of the aria.

"Take!" Ugo shouted.

The lights were turned off. Athena stood, unmoving. Vesta

stepped over the cables to get to her side. "Are you all right, Athena?" she asked.

She didn't reply. She just turned and made her way back across the ancient banqueting hall where once Hamlet, and now Lady Macbeth, had struggled with death, madness, and the awfulness of betrayal.

24. ATHENA WAS SURPRISED TO FIND YORGO PAPPAS IN THE sitting room of the Paris apartment when she returned from Denmark. Yanni, who had come back several days before, had acquiesced when he had appeared at the door unannounced just before she was due and asked if he could wait for her to arrive.

He stood up when Athena entered the room. He looked awkward, his largeness and lumbering movement at odds with the elegance and grace of his surroundings. It crossed her mind that Yorgo had only been in the apartment a handful of times despite his close and long association with Mano. She knew little more about him than what Mano had chosen to tell her, or what she had perceived: that Yorgo was not only a loyal flunky, but lived vicariously through Mano. She did not know if he had ever been married, but he seemed to have no family. After their first exchange of greetings, she waited tentatively for him to speak, wondering what in the world he was here for.

"I apologize if this is an inconvenient time for you," he said in his gruff voice.

Sudden fear displaced her curiosity. Perhaps Mano had had an accident. "What is it, Yorgo?" she pressed. "Has something happened to Mano?"

"Nothing like that," he said. Avoiding her intense gaze, his eyes roved shiftily over the room before settling on a silver-framed photograph of Athena and Mano displayed on a sofa table. "Mano is concerned that you might not fully understand his present position, and how it does and doesn't affect you," he said, lifting his strong-boned face toward her.

"And he sent *you* because he's too much of a coward himself!" She was wearing a fashionable dark red linen cape over a matching summer suit, and she grabbed one side of it and flung it over her shoulder in a matador's gesture. "You go back to your master and tell him that if he has anything to say to me, let him say it in person and not in this unmanly, sneaky way!"

"That's not quite fair," Yorgo said, looking down briefly at his red, large-knuckled, weathered hands. He clasped them together in front of him and then pulled them apart and stuffed them in the pockets of his beige gabardine jacket before raising his eyes once again to meet her hostile gaze. For a frozen moment he just stood there. He had confronted many of Mano's dangerous, belligerent, and emotionally disturbed foes, lovers, or used-up business associates before. That was his job—to clean up the broken and useless debris of Manolis Zakarias's ruthless ambition. And he did it coldly, clinically, and well. But this was a different assignment, one that required a delicacy he was not sure he possessed. Mano had given him strict instructions not to hurt Athena in any way, to watch what he said, and to leave the door open. He was here not to get rid of Athena, but to placate her, to coerce her into playing a waiting game. And he could see he had already put his foot in it.

"I don't need you to tell me what is or isn't fair," she said.

She swept past him to the wide French windows that opened onto the sitting-room terrace and pulled back the partially drawn silk drapes with a sharp snap like a crack of a whip. The summer morning was exceptionally bright and the sun blazed into the room with such blinding brilliance that Yorgo was forced to shield his eyes with his hand.

Athena was encased in glittering light, her crimson outfit making her look like she was sheathed in flames. Once he was able to focus his eyes, he saw her as one might see something on film—distant, a chimera of reality. Beyond the terrace, the tallest trees in the gardens undulated in a gentle wind and the sky was blue and dazzling.

"You go back to your master and you tell him that Athena Varos does not speak to underlings," she said, her voice projecting operatically.

Yorgo had a wild impulse to turn and walk briskly from the room. It had nothing to do with fear, but self-loathing. He hated the reason he was there. Quite simply, she was right. He had come to do another man's dirty work. It had not disturbed him greatly when he had entered her sitting room or while he was waiting for her to appear. His many years in performing this function had hardened him. But the woman he faced now had such a majestic strength, a power that catapulted across the large, impressive room (which became merely a backdrop once she occupied it), that he instantly doubted if he could carry out his mission. He knew fully well why Mano had sent him instead of coming himself. Even the steel-nerved Manolis Zakarias would have trouble holding his own in a showdown with a spurned and furious Athena Varos.

Opening the drapes and startling him with the blaze of light that immediately flooded the room had been a calculated move on her part. She was using whatever weapon she had at her command to gain control of the situation. Yorgo narrowed his eyes to be able to focus on her. Like all of Mano's women, she was startlingly beautiful, although not in Nikki's slick fashion-magazine manner or the centerfold attractiveness of some of the others. Athena Varos was much more than a face and a body. She was a *force;* there was something about her that reminded him of Mano. They had the same charismatic, imperious personality, an aura of omnipotence that made others feel less sure of themselves in their presence. He saw now why they had been drawn to each other, and why Mano had not married her. To survive, Manolis Zakarias needed to devour; as Yorgo watched Athena—head back like a lioness about to pounce, arms outstretched, hands ready to tear into any opponent

(*God,* he thought, *those hands could do anything she willed them to do*)—he knew that she would never be meat for anyone's table.

He mustered all the inner strength he could. "I've left an envelope on the table in the entry," he said, squaring his shoulders, looking very businesslike. "Mano wants to be sure that you never have to concern yourself with financial matters. It contains the deed for this apartment and the one in Grosvenor Square. The titles have been transferred to you. There is also a letter signed by Mano consigning all of their contents to you as well."

She stood without moving, not one flicker of emotion to reveal what she was really feeling. Yet he did not have the impression that she was cold or impassive. Quite the contrary—she was a silent volcano that could erupt without sound or warning. A fire burned in her deepest recesses.

"There is also the statement for a bank account in your name. One million dollars," he added after a significant pause, wanting the impact of the largesse to take effect. To his surprise, she appeared neither overwhelmed nor pleased, but puzzled.

"Why do you do this, Yorgo?" she asked.

"I'm only a messenger, nothing more," he replied.

Her mood suddenly changed and threw him off balance. She stepped away from the window, moving sideways, nearer to him, a sharp blade of sunlight over one shoulder. He could see her more clearly. She seemed to have become smaller, touchingly vulnerable. There were elegiac tears in her eyes, and when she spoke her voice was choked with emotion.

"No. I mean for Mano. Why do you do his dirty work?"

"That's not my aim, nor his. He loves you, Athena. He would never want to hurt you."

He was instantly sorry that he had said it. Strength and power returned to her immediately. She shook her head and the dark lion's mane flew back from her face; she seemed to grow several inches taller right before his eyes.

"You have no right to speak to me of another man's love or

intentions. What could you know about Mano's true feelings? Does a dummy know what the ventriloquist is thinking?"

He wanted to argue with her but restrained himself. Instead he said, "We go back a long way."

To his surprise, she smiled wryly. "Ah! History. Yes, I understand that," she said. "And how did it all begin between you and Mano?"

He took his time before answering in the hopes that she might lose interest and change the subject. The encounter was beginning to seriously unsettle him. He was sweating under his arms and at the back of his neck. He was unnerved, and that was a great disadvantage when coolness was needed. But she continued to wait for his reply.

"We met in a whorehouse," he finally began. "I was leaving a bedroom just as he was entering. It seemed to bind us, somehow. Later he sought me out—this was in Athens, and we were both hanging around the port—and we became ordinary seaman together on a freighter going to South America."

She remained silent, her eyes steady on his face. "I was the hard-looking tough character," he continued, "but Mano was the one who always saved our necks. He had less conscience and more ambition than I did. He was a hungry bastard then just as he is now," he added with a touch of affection.

"Villains always get the best parts," she commented. Then, "Go on."

"I guess I know about every crime, every sin he has ever committed, every dream he has nurtured." He laughed, a hollow sound. "And why does he keep me around?" he asked.

"Why?"

His mouth tightened and his words were sharp-edged as they slid through the narrow slit between his lips. "To remind himself of what he would have become if he had been less forceful."

She didn't reply but clasped her hands over her arms as though she were hugging herself. Her long, tapered fingers tapped against the fabric of her cape. She was gazing reflectively into space. So many thoughts were chasing one another in her head. Yorgo's presence no longer distressed her. For the moment she was not in this room; she was elsewhere, in another time. Her eyes focused on nothing. All she could see were Mano's eyes, then his mouth, the smiling lips turned upward at the edges.

She walked past Yorgo out of the room, not acknowledging him, and returned a moment later with the envelope. She handed it to Mano's emissary.

"I changed my mind. You can tell Mano something for me after all."

Yorgo waited while she paused for a breath. A slow smile crossed her face as cruelly as if it were a knife.

"Tell him Athena Varos can't be bought."

She went over to the window and drew the curtains. Shadow replaced light. She seemed to be deciding something. She pulled her fingers through her hair and then held it back from her face. Then she stepped forward, a theatrical move, Yorgo thought, a perfect exit. She walked out of the room, leaving him with Mano's offering in his hand.

Only Yanni was witness to Athena's true feelings; she was there in the night and heard her cry. Nothing could comfort or soothe her. She refused to look at the newspapers and had unplugged the television set in the library. Yet however little sleep she had had, each morning she rose and dressed and went to the recording studio to work with the maestro, the orchestra, and the technicians to record the vocal track for *Macbeth*.

The work was demanding, since she had never dubbed voice to picture before. She became obsessed with her performance, insisting that each aria be rerecorded time and time again before she was satisfied, even though everyone else thought she had already sung it to perfection.

"Why do you let her do this?" Ugo asked the maestro. He had just returned from shooting the witches' scenes in the forests of northern Scotland.

"Because Athena has a sixth sense. You don't hear a difference.

Maybe, I do, but even I'm not sure that what I'm hearing will make a difference. But she does. Athena can perform miracles. I knew that the first time I heard her. You cannot understand or explain her or her extraordinary ability. She can switch from nothing to everything, from earth to heaven. And when that miracle happens, she goes from professional genius, which others share, to a magic no other artist possesses."

As soon as the sound was tracked over the film, however, the difference was apparent. *Macbeth* was amazing. Athena's performance as Lady Macbeth was spellbinding and had the power and believability (something operatic characters do not always have) to bridge the chasm between what was normally thought of as a stage form and cinema. Plans were made to enter it in the Venice Film Festival.

Once the work was done on *Macbeth,* Athena became a recluse, refusing to see anyone but Yanni. She had expected Mano to return after Yorgo had delivered her message and the envelope to him. But he had not. Nor had he called. The tomblike silence further alienated her from the living world. When the news finally broke, when the endless stories about the marriage of Victoria McMaster to Manolis Zakarias began to appear in the press, her silence was shattered by paparazzi seeking interviews from the woman they labeled "the spurned lover."

As the date of the wedding approached, she had the telephone removed from her room and seldom ventured downstairs, even to the piano. Nor did she reply to the many pleas from Luigi, Vesta, Ugo, the maestro, or Editta asking to come see her.

It was Vesta who finally took matters into her own hands. One morning she refused to let Yanni discourage her and stormed into the apartment, up the rear staircase, and into Athena's room, where the door had been left open.

"You look ghastly!" she exclaimed, shocked at Athena's appearance as she lay in her bed: the wild uncombed hair, the dark circles beneath the sunken eyes.

"Go away, Vesta. I don't want to see you. I don't want to see anyone."

"Athena, I won't let you do this to yourself. He's not worth it. The man's a despot. We're damned lucky he hasn't turned his thirst for power to politics. You're deluding yourself if you think you mean anything more to him than another disposable *divertissement*."

"You don't understand, Vesta. He loves me. He does. What we share is not like anything he has with that avaricious, money-chomping prig," she said.

"Manolis Zakarias can take care of himself, and don't you ever doubt it. And he isn't going to suffer much guilt if you sacrifice yourself. Remember Nikki? I don't recall him shedding many tears over her. What you're doing here adds up to suicide."

Vesta came over to the bed and sat down on its edge. She took Athena's hand in hers. "Darling girl," she pleaded, "don't let him do this to you. Remember once, long ago, when I told you that you had something special, something immortal that only a great artist can claim? You are more than he is. Believe me. You must let him go."

"It's like watching someone fall out a window and not being able to pull them back, Vesta," she said in a whispery voice. "He's obsessed. I know about obsession. He has to have it all—and that means fighting his way back into the United States. He lost a battle once, and nothing will stop him now until he wins the war. But when he does, it will be the end for him. I know it's the truth. I feel it just as if it had already happened."

She took a pillow and muffled her face in it. Sobs convulsed her body.

Vesta put her arms around her maternally. She held her against her breast and rocked back and forth, trying to soothe her. "Darling, darling girl," she kept repeating until finally Athena's crying subsided. Then she plumped up the pillows and leaned her against them.

"I haven't read any newspapers, but a reporter told me they were getting married on Zephyrus," Athena said. "Is that true?"

"It seems to be."

"When?"

"The day after tomorrow."

"Is it to be a religious ceremony?"

"Greek Orthodox. She's agreed to it after much discussion. The primate himself is going to officiate. God knows what that cost Mano."

Athena paled.

"Look, I'm going to call Pierre's and see if they can send someone over from the salon to do your hair. You'll feel better once you look more like yourself."

Athena glanced up. "No, Vesta. Don't do it. I can't see anyone yet. Yanni will wash my hair."

"You've got to come out of this depression, Athena."

"Please, no more about it," she murmured.

Vesta sighed. "Well, let's talk about some of the better things going on in the real world," she said. "Everyone's been trying to reach you to talk about Venice. Ugo thinks you have a good chance of winning the best-actress award. He'd like you to be there. It gives you two months to pull yourself together. I don't think there is any question—you have to go. The maestro and Editta will be there. So will I, of course. And then there is something else very important. I have had an unusual number of concert requests."

"The answer is no."

"The answer is that you'll consider it," Vesta contradicted her. "The Met would like you to return in *Macbeth* next year. Why wouldn't they? You'll bring them a lot of publicity. Covent Garden has been persistent. Any opera of your choice. If you give them enough time, they'll even mount a new production. But in the meantime you could do a major concert tour. The maestro says he would go with you if you can arrange it for this winter. Luigi is standing by, and you know I'll be right here at your elbow."

"I can't think about a tour right now."

"If you don't want to take Mano's money, you're going to have to go to work. So you'd better think about it."

After Vesta left, Yanni came up and washed and dressed Athena's hair. She still refused to leave her room or reconnect the telephone or the television. She did, however, allow herself the luxury of listening to the phonograph. And so she passed the day and the evening with the piano genius of Rubinstein and Horowitz. She did not want to hear any words, any songs, any arias; her head was too filled with the pressing language of thought.

Vesta hated Mano. Athena wished she could hate him, too. And Victoria McMaster. But her love for Mano was far stronger than her anger at him for his betrayal, and the McMaster widow still seemed unreal to her, a fictional villain. She tried to recall a poem she had once read. Or was it Shakespeare? She couldn't place it, but the words began to form in her memory. Something about there not needing to be a villain, that "passions spin the plot" and that we "are betrayed by what is false within."

At night she lay in bed, pondering it. Did Mano love her, as she believed with all her heart he did? Because if she were mistaken, or had deceived herself into thinking that he felt for her as deeply as she did for him, then there was no betrayal because he had not been false to himself. No, she could not have been wrong. They loved each other with equal passion. Theirs had been an affair of historic, operatic proportions.

Then why had he not made any effort to see or speak to her? She knew what she would never confess to Vesta—that she had disconnected the telephone and refused to see anyone because she could not bear confronting the brutal truth that Mano would not call or come.

The night before Mano's wedding, Athena paced her room restlessly. They had gone to the island on the *Atlas*. Were they sleeping in the bed she and Mano had shared? And which room had they occupied on Zephyrus? Somewhere across the Luxembourg Gardens, in the terrible dark night, a dog howled, and she thought about the wild dogs that had once threatened Mano's paradise. She wondered if maybe the dogs had been sent by some Greek god to frightened Nikki into leaving and, perhaps, that now they would return to rid the island of Mano's new bride.

It was a crazy idea and she struggled to push it from her mind. She had to concentrate on something else, something tangible, real, something that belonged to her. And so she put on the recording of her in *Tosca*.

Vesta had informed her that Mano was to be married at 10:00 A.M. Pacing, crying, her mind filled with disturbing images, she hardly slept that night. Like Tosca's lover, Mano was to be shot at the first sign of morning light. She could see the rifles being raised—or were those the arms of the wedding guests? She played Tosca's final aria over and over, weeping more each time. And as morning approached it was as though the seconds were ticking down to the execution of her beloved, a death that both of them had been tricked into believing would be a sham, that true love would finally conquer.

Her room was cold and Yanni had not brought any logs for the fire. She rubbed her hands, her arms, but warmth evaded her. She wrapped herself in a blanket and put *Tosca* back on the phonograph. From time to time she dozed off, then she would awaken with a start. She wasn't aware when morning came, but at some point she flung the curtains back to see if it was light yet. It was then that the camera exploded in her face and she collapsed. *Was it the crack of the firing squad? Or had she imagined it?*

Several days passed before she recovered from her raging fever and delirium. When she awoke, Vesta and Yanni were standing on one side of her bed and Luigi on the other. She glanced at them one at a time.

"Are they married?" she asked.

"Yes," Vesta replied, "and you are well again."

But in her heart, Athena knew otherwise.

Postlude

ATHENA MADE HER WAY THROUGH THE CROWDS ON THE PI-
azza San Marco to meet Ugo and some film distributors at the
Ristorante Maurizio. The day was supremely beautiful, there was
no other way to describe it. The sky was pure blue, the light lumi-
nous, and the tender touch of the air warm and friendly. This was
an early day in autumn, but summer had not yet relinquished its
grip. Venice was filled with tourists, movie people, and paparazzi
come to view the films and stars featured at the city's yearly film
festival. No one gave Athena more than a cursory glance; her sunglasses covered half her face and a wide-brimmed hat darkly shadowed the rest, rendering her barely recognizable.

She had refused to have Ugo pick her up at the hotel and escort
her to their luncheon meeting. Returning to Venice, where her
odyssey with Mano had truly begun, was a wrenching experience,
and she needed time alone to deal with it. Everywhere she had
looked on the day of her arrival, she had thought she saw Mano
coming toward her, then seem to vanish into nothingness. It had
happened at the airport, in the lobby of the hotel, at the cocktail
reception for the nominees (and Ugo had been right—she was
being considered for best actress), and at the dinner party that
followed.

She thought she might be suffering a relapse into a state of near-dementia, which was surely what had taken hold of her at the time of Mano's marriage. *What can I do? How will I cope?* she kept asking herself when she was back in her hotel room and preparing to face the night alone. And when she rose from the bed in the yawning middle hours, having wrestled and lost her battle with sleep, she could hear, in what seemed to be the witches' voices from *Macbeth,* the words, *He murdered sleep.* She fell asleep toward dawn but was awakened by the insistent ringing of the telephone. When she heard Ugo's reassuring voice, something that was real, at least, she resolved to exorcise Mano from her mind.

"No, Athena, I won't hear of it!" Ugo was saying. "You're a star, and stars do not go to lunch unescorted."

"I promise you I won't run out. I'll be there and on time."

"Well, where do you want to go this morning? I'm only two floors down. I'll come up and get you."

"Trust me and just try to understand. I need an hour or so to myself."

"It's against my better judgment."

"But it's in my best interest."

Finally, grudgingly, he agreed.

"Ugo!" She shouted into the mouthpiece as he was about to hang up.

"Yes?"

"Mano isn't in Venice, is he? I mean, the film was made with his money. You must have talked it over with him."

"I wasn't going to tell you, but I did have a long talk with him, and he agreed that it would not be advisable with all the paparazzi here, that it would disturb you, and that it would take away from the main focus—the quality of the film, not the tabloid exploitability of the star and the film's backer."

"Thanks. I needed to know that."

"Half past one, Maurizio's? You won't forget?"

"My vow."

She dressed quickly, hired a boat, and directed the gondolier first

to the Palazzo Tiziano and then to the Palazzo Carbanio, where she and Mano had first made love. Both were deserted and locked up tight. As the boat moved through the narrow part of the canal on its return to the hotel, the sun reflected in shimmering circles on the water. Bedding was being aired from the windows and balconies of the houses they passed, and the splendor of Venice rose before her, etched sharply against the cloudless sky. In her mind's ear she could hear the sound of the orchestra that had played in the garden of the Tiziano, the comforting hum of the waning fire in the hearth at the Carbanio when she lay in Mano's arms after they had consummated their love. Then the sounds faded away, lost in the activity all around her. The present bore no relationship to the past. In the bright sunshine of day there were no ghosts.

The Ristorante Maurizio was on the second floor of a building at the opposite end of the Piazza San Marco from the cathedral. A narrow staircase led up to it and its long, wide balcony overlooking the square. Alcoves with built-in booths lined the rear wall and in between were a clutter of tables, chairs, waiter's stations, and trollies crowded with appetizers—silvery sardines, glistening roasted peppers, plump black olives, a brilliant array of salads and cold fishes. And with rich desserts—cream heaped in mounds and fruits of effulgent color. When Athena entered the large, noisy room, she was greeted by a blast of warm air and the heady aroma of wine, garlic, and spices. Before the maitre d' had a chance to show her to the table, Ugo appeared.

"Darling," he said, and leaned toward her to kiss her, but with her hat and sunglasses it was an impossibility.

They both laughed. She removed the hat and followed him out to the balcony, where three balding men, one of them Asian, stood up when they reached a corner table. It was shielded from the elements by connecting panes of Plexiglas.

"It won't be too cool out here for you, will it?" Ugo asked.

"No, of course not," she said politely.

"Venice is overrun with small elegant restaurants, and at this point they're all swarming with film and paparazzi types. Being less chic, Maurizio's tends to be avoided. Therefore I thought it might be a good choice," Ugo said, grinning. "It also has the best pasta in Venice."

"You don't remember me," the man seated next to her said in a distinctive cockney accent. "Sam Berenstein. Wardour Street Distributors. We met in London at a fundraising gala. Something like the Gilbert and Sullivan Association." He pondered this for a moment, resting one chin on a stack of others beneath it. "No. It was the English Opera Society."

"Why, yes, of course," she lied sweetly, nothing of the man's appearance stirring even a fragment of memory.

The Asian turned out to be Japanese. "We like very much *Macbeth* in my country," he said.

She managed a gracious smile. The last of the trio was an Italian with thick, shaggy black eyebrows that bobbed up and down when he spoke and seemed rather incongruous on a man with a bald pate. "I told Ugo we have a problem," he explained with dour seriousness. "We also like very much *Macbeth,* but Signora, if you will forgive my directness, I am not sure how well a film will do in Italy that stars a woman who has—very much publicly flaunted church and marriage vows."

"I also walked off the stage of La Scala once when a man in the audience booed. Let's not forget that," she responded caustically.

Ugo directed the conversation elsewhere, but just then the waiter came. They ordered. Much wine was consumed by the men as they waited for their food. Voices rose, laughter sallied across the table, and soon the trio appeared to be in extremely good and harmonious spirits; the Italian was rubbing Athena's leg under the table with his own, an undeniable overture. She was about to speak sharply to him but decided against it. Instead, she smiled and moved back against the Plexiglas so that he couldn't reach her without a good deal of contortions. He straightened up and breathed in deeply, as if offended. She turned her glance away.

She was looking out across the square when she saw the figure of a man walking down its center, where the crowds were the thinnest. She gave a little gasp of surprise. Ugo turned quickly to her and took her hand.

"Is something wrong?" he asked, concerned.

"Oh, no. I'm sorry. I thought I saw someone I know. I was mistaken."

He went back to his conversation.

The man was coming closer, yet her eyesight was not good enough to make out his face. But it hardly mattered. There was the familiar stride, the square of the shoulders, the imperious gesture of the arm that ordered anyone blocking his path out of his way. It was Mano. She jumped up from the table.

"*Scusi! Scusi!*" she said as she collided with a group being seated and then, in her rush to leave the restaurant, brushed past a waiter carrying a tray of pasta and made him spin to keep from dropping it. People were staring at her but she didn't stop, hurrying across the length of the restaurant and then taking the stairs two at a time.

She stood in front of the entrance, frantically searching the faces of people coming in her direction. She had lost him. Mano was nowhere to be seen. She felt suddenly bereft and unsure what to do next.

"Athena!" Ugo called. He came up behind her and grabbed her by the arm.

"I saw him, Ugo! I saw him! He's here!"

"Who, Athena?"

"Mano. He was walking toward this end of the square. I saw him from the restaurant. But by the time I got downstairs he was gone." She glanced furtively about her, making funny little whimpering noises.

Oh God, he thought, *she's going to pieces again.* He put his arm around her waist in a protective gesture, but she shook him off.

"I tell you, I saw him," she insisted.

He took her hand. "Come back upstairs. The food has just arrived."

"No, I can't. Make my excuses. Tell them I suddenly took ill. A stomach cramp. Something harmless."

She pulled out of his grasp and before he could stop her she was running away from him, and then was lost in the crowds.

For the rest of the day she was in a state of fear, although she couldn't figure out why she should be frightened that Mano was in Venice. She did not doubt that it had been him. And why shouldn't he be there if he wanted to? She couldn't expect him to avoid every city to which she might travel. Nor did she understand why she had run to meet him. Was it simply to let him know that she had seen him, or did she want to catch him off guard, perhaps get him to reveal his true feelings toward her, pull her into his arms, gaze at her with tears of love in his eyes?

She pleaded a touch of food poisoning to get out of the large dinner party that she was to have attended that night, though she insisted that everyone else go. "I'll feel better in the morning. I just need some rest," she assured Vesta. Every hour or so Ugo or Vesta would ring her suite to see if she had improved and to ask if she had changed her mind and would like to join them.

"I'm still a bit queasy and I'd rather stay put," she replied.

The telephone rang for the fourth time shortly before midnight.

"Ati," he said.

She dropped the receiver into the cradle.

The telephone rang again, persistently; ten, eleven, twelve times. She lifted the receiver but said nothing.

"Ati, listen to me. Don't hang up. I've got to see you. I'm calling from a telephone directly across the canal from your hotel. I have a boat. Meet me downstairs. We must talk," he implored.

"I have nothing to say to you."

"But I have much to tell you. Please, *please*, Ati."

Her heart was beating so hard that she clutched her hand to her chest as though to still it.

"Mano, leave me alone. I can't stand it anymore."

"That's the point. I want to make things up to you. Ati, come downstairs."

She was aware of Mano's knowledge of her strengths and weaknesses. He knew that once they were face-to-face, once he was able to hold her again in his arms, that she would relent and give in to whatever he wanted of her. It would be so easy to end this pain. Just hang up, get dressed, and go meet him. Yet, something was holding her back; what it was she couldn't define, but she felt as though there were a pair of hands restraining her, another mind controlling her own.

"You are not to call me ever again," she ordered. "Now hang up and go away!"

"I'm coming up to you, then."

"I'll call the manager and have you thrown out!" she shouted, and slammed down the receiver. She knew his pride would not allow him to risk such an eventuality. Not that a hotel manager could keep Manolis Zakarias from breaking down the door to her room if he so intended. But it was beneath Mano's dignity to have to deal with a mere functionary. Nonetheless, she placed the security chain across the door. Then she returned to the bedroom to dress. *This is ridiculous,* she thought. *Why am I doing this? Do I really think he will show up at my door?* She had no answers for herself and continued dressing.

The telephone rang again. It could be Mano, but then again it might be Ugo or Vesta, and if she didn't answer they would come running up to her suite. She felt unable to deal with that. She picked up the receiver.

"Ati, I can't live without you," he said. "You are my blood, the air in my lungs. You must understand that this marriage is business. It has nothing to do with you and me, with love and passion. Victoria accepts that; now you must."

"Go away!" she screamed. Still, she was unable to hang up.

"Be sensible. Be my Ati. Roberto will never divorce you. We both know that. We could never marry. But what is marriage? Just another business contract. What we have is a spiritual link. We were fated for each other. We can't cut our ties like husbands and wives can. Nothing has to change for us, except perhaps that we be a bit more discreet. Please, Ati, I beg of you. If our love ever meant anything at all to you, come down and speak to me in person. Look me in the eyes. Let me put my arms around you, my lips to yours. Then tell me to go away if you can, and I swear I will."

Suddenly she felt curiously calm, as if a drug was now taking effect. The fear had disappeared. The voice, so seductively smooth, had lost its effect on her. It was something she could not understand, like the way pain can be forgotten once it has gone away.

"Ati? Ati? Are you still there?"

"I'm here." She sat down on the edge of the bed and looked at herself in the bureau mirror. "Do you think that life doesn't go on without you?" she said. "You're wrong. I was Athena Varos, *la Divina*, before I met you, and I am still Athena Varos, *la Divina*. In years to come I will be remembered as such, long after you are gone and they say, 'Manolis Zakarias? Oh, you mean that Greek fortune hunter who married the widow of Clark Cameron McMaster. Well, all Greeks want to go to America! Some of them even get there on their own merits!' "

She hung up and continued to stare at her reflection. She rose from the bed and went closer to it, leaning forward, gazing into her own eyes. "I am Athena Varos," she repeated over and over again, until, somehow, she began to feel much better. The rapid beating of her heart had returned to normal. The wave of pain that had gripped her stomach was gone. The heat that had suffused her body had cooled. And instead of nervousness and agitation she felt a great hunger—she could eat a horse. She had not eaten dinner and perhaps should order from room service. She weighed whether or not this was such a good idea so late at night. Probably not. Well, maybe something simple—a chicken sandwich, pasta with a little olive oil.

There was a knock on the door and she froze, a gush of the old anxiety returning. The knock came again, harder.

"Athena? Athena? Are you awake?"

Vesta's voice. She breathed easier. She went to the door, removed the chain, and opened it a crack.

"Hurry up," she urged Vesta, casting a quick look up and down the empty corridor.

"What is it Athena? You're acting strange. I saw the light under the door and wanted to make sure nothing was wrong."

"I'm fine. I think I had a fever. It finally broke."

"Oh, well, that's good."

"Was the dinner successful?"

"A bore. But you were the major topic of conversation. Well, I don't mean that *that* was the boring part. Athena, everyone there felt certain *Macbeth* was going to win the award for best picture and you for best actress. They had the first screening this afternoon, as you know. Everyone in the cinema stood up and shouted *'Brava! Brava!'* for at least ten minutes—I swear! You have reached a new and much larger audience. Oh, Athena! you must go on a concert tour now. And decide in which opera houses you'll perform next."

Vesta was breathless with excitement. She hugged Athena and then began to crisscross the room energetically.

"I think you have to include the sleepwalking scene in the concert tour. And make *Macbeth* your next opera." She paused, studied Athena for a moment, and then began to laugh. "Well, at least Mano did do one thing for you."

"What was that?"

"Sent you back to work."

Athena managed a smile. "Look, would you like to order up some champagne and maybe some pasta with truffles? The most expensive thing on the menu. While you do that, I want to get my diary and start planning a tour. You're not too tired to do that, are you?"

"You can bet I'm not, but I was getting tired of waiting for you to come to your senses."

Athena went into the bedroom. The telephone rang.

"Shall I answer it for you?" Vesta called.

"No. It's just a fan. He'll soon give up."

While it rang she went to the window to close the blinds. She could see down to the landing where the boats were docked and across the stone bridge over the dark waters to the other side of the canal, where lights were on in a tavern that had a blue neon sign. She stood there until the telephone fell silent. A moment later the tavern lights went out across the way and the neon flickered and died. A man was standing under the golden glow of the streetlamp. It was Mano. She would never forget the form and shape of him. But like her father, like Uncle Spiros, the man she knew no longer existed for her.

One has to give up on ghosts, she thought. *Even Lady Macbeth should have known that.*